E.C.H.O.

(Elite Counter Horror Organization)

The Master Gardener

By

David C. James

Copyright Page

Cover Photograph Provided by:
James Kerwin Photography

David C. James

Printed in the United States of America

First Printing: October 2018
Kindle Direct Publishing

Dedication Page

To starting over!!
Also,
While this is for my entire family,
It's especially
For you, "My Boo!"

Richard,
Your wife thought might like my book. I hope you do enjoy it!
David C. James a.k.a. James D Crosby

Table of Contents		
Chapter	Title	Page

Chapter	Title	Page
Prologue		v
Part One	Introductions	ix
Chapter One	Game On!	1
Chapter Two	Pay Back!	7
Chapter Three	Geek-Boy	15
Chapter Four	The Plot Thickens	23
Chapter Five	The Expert	29
Chapter Six	Team Work	37
Chapter Seven	Bethoon The Cannibal	46
Chapter Eight	The Master Gardener	53
Part Two	Set The Table	60
Chapter Nine	Let's Dance	61
Chapter Ten	Acquaintances	72
Chapter Eleven	The Drop	87
Chapter Twelve	In Your Face	113
Chapter Thirteen	The Wild	126
Chapter Fourteen	Homecoming, Sort Of	147
Chapter Fifteen	Ribbon	164
Part Three	The Crossed Line	173
Chapter Sixteen	The Bone Sucker	174
Chapter Seventeen	Damsel in Distress	188
Chapter Eighteen	Battle for St. David	204
Chapter Nineteen	Caves	221
Chapter Twenty	Confrontation	240
Chapter Twenty-One	E.C.H.O.	257
Chapter Twenty-Two	The Master Gardener	278

PROLOGUE

Ghouls love winter!! Seconds after the fall solstice begins, darkness rules; and ghouls flourish in darkness. There are parts of today's world that are dominated by the stench of demons, ghouls, and many other unearthly forms. Therefore, the disastrous effects they have on the humans who live in their realm are immeasurable. Give a demon extra time to maneuver a situation, and they will use it to their advantage.

The number one exploited population in today's modern world is the teenager. Because of a change in our society, teens are no longer afraid of things that go bump in the night. In fact, they encourage those bumps. Enter Erin Hastings, the beautiful, young, sixteen-year-old daughter of the local mayor in St. David, Arizona.

It's 6:30 p.m. on December 23, and instead of being home with her family, wrapping Christmas gifts, she is out laughing, running, and being chased through the local graveyard by her extremely handsome, somewhat older boyfriend, Percy. Slipping on wet grass and tumbling to the ground, Erin continues laughing. As she turns over on her back, her man Percy lightly lands on her abdomen. Then, placing his mouth on hers, he passionately kisses his "woman," as he called her.

"God, I love kissing you, Ms. Hastings," Percy's light British accented voice insisted.

"I love kissing you as well," she sighed.

They kissed and touched one another eagerly, hungrily, for several moments, and then Percy used his countless years of experience to arouse the woman he was with. Erin began to moan, "I want you, Percy. Make me a woman, right here, right now!"

Percy stopped caressing her and raised his body above hers. "Erin, I don't want your purity; not yet. You trust me, don't you?" Percy asked.

"I love you, Percy," she replied.

"But, you don't trust me," he exclaimed, as his smile faded, only to be replaced by a frown.

"Percy, I'm willing to give you my most precious gift. Isn't that enough?" Erin asked.

"I'm a vampire, and you know that!! Your most precious gift to me, especially when your heart is beating so fast, is what flows inside you. I don't want it all, just a taste." Displaying his most loving look, he added, "I have searched for you for hundreds of years; I'm not going to destroy the best thing that has ever happened to me."

Quickly, Erin sat up. Percy thought he had lost his chance until, suddenly, she reached for his face and kissed him, hard. "I'm scared," she softly uttered.

"Erin, baby, I love you. I don't want to scare you," he said softly. His face looked disappointed, hurt, and almost heartbroken.

Erin's only mistake in their entire two-year relationship was about to be made; she trusted his intentions.

"I'm sorry, Percy. You're right. I haven't shown you that I trust you. You have been good to me. You've treated me better than my other boyfriends, better than my friends, and even my parents. Just be gentle and don't take very much of my blood, please!"

As she turned to lie back on the ground, she did not see the sinister smile that oozed across her boyfriend's devilish face.

Gazing up at her beloved Percy, her eyes screamed with fear. She softly pleaded, "You won't hurt me, will you Percy?" She raised her wrist, thinking he would take the blood from there. When he frowned, she knew what he wanted. Slowly, she slanted her head to expose her beautiful young neck.

Percy moved his hands from the young woman's neck and cautiously slid them down to her shoulders. With a sudden jerk, the softness in Percy's touch was gone, replaced by a strength Erin had never felt before. Immediately, she realized she had made a mistake. The creature above her felt her fear. He stopped for a moment and scoffed, "I like it when my prey is afraid; it excites me."

"But, you said you loved me!" she screamed.

"You silly little girl, I'm a vampire; I can't love." And, with that, Percy showed her the face of his internal demon. "By the way, my friends and I are going to drink every ounce of your delicious, pure, untainted blood." He exposed his teeth and rammed his head into her young, tender flesh. Filled with shock and dread, Erin's screams turned to sobs, as Percy was draining her of her life's blood.

After several moments of trying to fight Percy's weight, Erin stopped fighting, and her eyes turned skyward. She felt the beast relax his pressure and lift off of her for a moment, exclaiming, "God, there is nothing like pure virgin blood; join me, brothers and sisters!" She no longer had the strength to fight him off. Instead, she lay there and continued to stare at the night sky.

"Excuse me." Someone with a thick British accent appeared in Erin's vision. "Excuse me, Love." He looked down into the deep pools that were the young woman's eyes. "I think I need to explain that this isn't your fault, dearie. I asked Percy to set you up. Percy really does like you. But, your father is a bit of the git! We are going to use you to send a message, Love." He paused to look about the area for his friends, who were coming from the woods and the crypts where they'd been hiding. "When are you humans going to realize that you are not our friends, our lovers, or anything else? You are our food, our victims, and nothing more." As a final insult, he added, "Rest in peace, Love." He then raised his lips to bare his teeth and was gone from her sight.

Numb to the attack, ignorant of all the bites on her body, Erin had no strength left; not even enough to scream for help. She had no choice but to lay there and wait until she slipped from this world into the next.

E.C.H.O.

(Elite Counter Horror Organization)

The Master Gardener

By

David C. James

E.C.H.O

(Elite Counter-Horror Organization)

The Master Gardener
Part One

Introductions

Chapter One

Game On!

Angela Harrison had her dream job. At 36 years old, Angela was a well-educated young woman from Charleston, West Virginia. She was employed by the Federal Bureau of Investigation and working out of the Washington, D.C. offices. Angela held a Master's Degree is in Abnormal Psychology with an undergraduate degree in Political Science, which helped her gain entry into the FBI. However, nothing prepared the five-foot eight-inch woman in the dark business suit for the assignment she was about to receive.

Michael Cline, her supervisor, was sitting across from Ms. Harrison, looking at her cumulative file. Quickly, he looked up at the young woman, then back down at the data. Clearing his voice, the man whose hair was starting to gray at the temples of his head spoke. "Angela, we are in a fix. While your fitness reports have been outstanding, nothing, and I repeat, nothing could prepare you for what we are facing in St. David, Arizona. Michael lowered his shoulders and then reached down into a drawer in his desk. He pulled out several folders that were wrapped in three large rubber bands. The FBI assistant-director placed the files on his desk. "These," he said, pointing at the stack of records, "are the cases that the FBI still needs answers to before we can close them. I'd like you, with your special gift for interpreting strange and unexplainable phenomenon, to take a look at these files."

As he slid the thick folders across the desk toward Angela, she said, "Excuse me, Mister Cline, but a handful of files doesn't seem so bad."

"There are another 20 boxes of folders just like those that have been Fed-Ex-ed to your office. In fact, we've moved you into a bigger office." As she reached for a folder, he slammed his hand down on the stack of papers and said, "These are the worst of our most urgent cases. To be honest, these are not your everyday criminals. Nor are they common crimes. We chose you because of your expertise in abnormal psychology, and your excellent fieldwork. Before I allow you to look at this case, however, I need your assurances that you will not divulge what you might read here today."

Without hesitation, Angela slid the file out from under his grasp. Before opening it, she stated, "I swear not to say anything. But, if this folder has you so unnerved, there might not be anything I can do." After those words, she opened the file. As she read the first few pages, her eyes became large. After several more pages, her eyes darted from the folder, then back to her boss, then back to the pages. Finally, her stare fixated on the man across from her. She hadn't gotten a third of the way through the folder when the sound of another large file slammed down in front of her.

"What is in that folder?" she asked.

"The solution to this situation," he answered, looking her square in the eyes. As he leaned back in his chair, Angela turned her attention back to the first file in her folder. After several minutes of reading, she looked up at her boss. "Michael, I have just one question. Is this a joke?" He said nothing; therefore, she asked another question. "Have I pissed someone off? Is someone out to get me?"

He shook his head, then leaned forward and suggested, "You were chosen for this because of your work on the Hansen case eight years ago in Missouri. Everyone thought it was the Klan, but not you. You stuck to your convictions. You didn't believe the Klan had burned that man at the stake, and, eventually, everyone here found out that you were right."

The ebony skinned woman quickly responded, "I saved some people, and you think I can handle this?"

"Angela, you see around corners and up the wall. I don't know how you understand some of the things you do, but you are very good at the..." He paused for a moment, as if he were looking for the word, "the weird stuff. Believe me, these cases can definitely be classified as weird. Quite frankly, I don't want to believe this type of thing goes on in the world today. But, I've been ordered to put together a team that will combat this problem. From what I understand, Europe is a whole different kettle of fish, and right now, we are a nation in peril. Believe it or not, you are our stop-gap measure. So what do you think?"

Shifting herself in her seat, she stared down her mentor and friend and asked, "I have a team?"

"Well, I don't know if you can call them a team, yet, but these people are some of the best at dealing with these things. However, you are going to have to recruit each and every one of them. None of the people on that list are FBI. At least, not anymore. I don't even know if they are our type of people. But they are our best hope."

They both sat there for several minutes, and as she ran her hands through her softly textured hair, she asked, "Who do I report to? How much free reign do I have?"

The female agent noticed a change in Michael as he gazed at her. 'Now, he's going to drop the bomb,' she thought. "Angela, this isn't a game. If you are seriously thinking of doing this, you'd better understand the risk before you worry about who to report to or how much freedom you have."

Getting up quickly, she made an effort to stand her ground. "I was fine where I was, Mike. You guys think I'm a whacko. You think I believe in the boogeyman. That's fine. I watch TV and movies, and I have read plenty of our own reports. Whenever there is someone like me put in the position you are trying to put me in, well, to be honest, it's like you're trying to screw me with my pants on."

His sixty-something face tightened as he informed her of what she already knew, "This isn't a movie or TV, Angela. To be perfectly honest, we don't have a clue about Para-Normal activities, ghouls, or things that go bump in the night. However, we have a bean counter, a person who keeps records of these types of cases here in the good old United States of America. Some things are starting to escalate, and the people upstairs want to try, well, they want to make an attempt," she could tell Michael didn't really have the right words for the point he was trying to make.

"Are those what I think they are?" she asked, referring to the second large file by his hands.

"Look, Angel," which was what she allowed Michael Cline and her close friends to call her at times, "when I received this assignment, I thought someone was trying to force me into retirement. I don't know anything about things of this nature. But, I have been fortunate to work with someone who has. You are the best person I know of for this case. When your name was brought up, I jumped at the chance for you. You are not built to be second fiddle to anyone. You and I both know that.

However, if someone, like you said so eloquently, is trying to screw you, it's not me or anyone I work with."

As Michael slid the file half-way across his desk, she reached for the thick folder with the files of the team members in it. As she started to open the file, she spoke, "Let me check out the team you have put together. Give me six months to work a case. If I get positive results, then we'll see what we see."

"You've got three months; we need action on this case now!" Mike insisted, while placing a finger on the top file of the case he had allowed her to look at. "This is your first case. It is a top priority and needs your attention, now!"

Not backing down, and tightening her jaw, which made her look even more attractive than she already did, she answered, "Then I won't take the assignment." She turned to walk out the door.

"Angela!" Michael shouted for the first time at the meeting.

She stomped toward her boss's desk. "I will not take a case that is possibly going to blow up in my face. I will not endanger the lives of the people in these files." She slammed the folder on his desk. "I don't care where they come from, or what they've done to get on your list of sacrificial lambs. For me, this is a suicide mission at best. You're not going to tell anyone of note what we are doing. I don't understand why you chose me. I thought we worked well together. Why would you sacrifice me, Michael? Why?"

Not giving him a chance to explain, she turned to walk out the door again. As she did, his phone rang. "Hold on!" he exclaimed. He answered the phone, and after a half dozen yes sirs, and yes ma'am, Angela realized he was on a conference call. She was polite and stood there waiting while he finished his call.

"They were listening to our conversation the whole time?" Angela asked.

"Yes," he said softly. "Angela, please sit down. I have a lot more to explain. You weren't our first choice. In fact, we tried to tackle this problem without your expertise, and, well, it cost us precious lives. While you may not have been our first choice, you are the best person, I believe, to lead this investigation. Face it, you didn't raise an eye at the reports you read. You didn't flinch. You didn't make any jokes." He paused, and shifted on his feet. "And no, you have not pissed anyone off. You do wonderful work. Angel, we need you to work your magic. We want you to try to help us figure out what's going on. Especially right now, when this is happening here in our own backyard. The things listed in these reports-Werewolves, Vampires, Zombies,-these things are supposed to be..."

"Figments of our imaginations." She had completed her boss's sentence.

"My God," Michael interjected, "they said the same thing, and in the same tone you did." When he finished speaking, he was looking at her similar to a deer caught in the headlights of an oncoming car.

"They? Who are they?" she asked.

With that question, FBI agent Cline grabbed the remote control, which was located by his desk phone, and turned on the seventy-five-inch flat screen monitor, which hung on the wall to his left. "The poor bastard on the left is Jacob Taylor. A great guy, and a wonderful agent. A few years ago, he was bitten." Michael paused for several moments to watch the young man as he sat behind his desk and read his hunting magazine. "Every full moon, he goes nuts and turns into, well, something else. It is challenging to contain him, but Agent Taylor has allowed us to install a tracking device in his neck. The day before a full moon, he drives over into the national forest near Harrisonburg and runs wild for three days. Jacob is not a danger to people, and from what I understand, the man has put quite a dent in the coyote population. He spends the rest of his time trying to track down the thing that bit him. Agent Taylor says if he can find it, and he can kill it, he will be normal again, or so Jacob thinks!"

The female agent noticed her boss take a seat and swallow hard. "This next person is very personal to me, Angela."

She turned to get a better look at the beautiful young woman whose image was being shown on the screen. Michael explained, "Her name is Erin Hastings, and she's my niece. If it weren't for some fast actions by our agents, she'd be lost to us. When they found her, she was drained dry of her blood. We think it was meant to be a message to my brother-in-law, who is the mayor of St. David, Arizona. He's been trying to clean up his mess in this monster town. Apparently, the vampires didn't like what he was trying to accomplish. Therefore, they made an example of my niece, and now, she's a case study."

All went silent as Angela continued to watch both victims on the split-screen television. It seemed as though somehow the girl realized she was being watched and was smiling at the camera. Suddenly, her electric blue eyes went sinister and held nothing but death and destruction inside them. She quickly wrote something down on paper and held it up to the screen. It read, "Angel, come to see me. I dare ya!!"

Michael somberly turned off the screen and sat empty-handed. He looked like a parent who had lost his own child in a tragic event. "Mike," Angela spoke to get his attention. "She may be your niece, but Erin is also a pissed off vampire, and she's looking for some payback!! I tell you what, I'm going to look at these files." She grabbed both stacks and made one neat stack. "But, the first thing I'm going to do is go down to the cage and meet your niece."

"Angela, she's dangerous, and she will kill you if she gets the chance. I know it's not her fault, but she's already incapacitated five agents. Jake's been assigned to her because he's the only one that can go near her. For some reason, she tolerates him, so he takes care of her for the time being. You need to make sure he's there when you talk to her."

"Sure thing, but she just challenged me by inviting me down there, and I have got to get her in the fold, right now. I may have to take her down, hard, so, don't watch. Wait until you think you understand that I know what I am doing. The game's on, Michael. Oh, and yes, I will take the assignment. By the way, I want to talk to the person who was able to bring her around."

Michael looked confused. "Why?"

"Simple, it's never been done before, and I want to make sure this person is on our side." With that, she bolted toward the door, no fear or hesitation in her voice or step. The former Ms. Hastings wanted Angela's attention, and she was about to get it!

Chapter Two

Game On!

Anonymously, Angela Harrison walked onto the third underground floor of the FBI maximum security building. She shed herself of the cumbersome business suit and now had adorned herself with a loose-fitting jumpsuit. This current uniform was for the second visit she would make today. The first meeting had to be with Jacob Taylor. If this new detachment was going to work, it would have to start with Agent Taylor. Walking up to the security desk, Angela demanded to see Jacob Taylor, the man she was about to convince to commit suicide with her. As she walked toward his office/cell, she realized this could go very poorly, and he could say no. However, what Taylor didn't understand was that the word "no" wasn't commonly accepted by Angela Harrison.

She knocked on the outside door of his office. Angela noticed he had a nameplate. His position, the office, everything involved with Mr. Jake Taylor, looked 100% FBI official. "Come in," a soft-spoken voice came from the other side of the door. Walking in, she saw that her quarry sat on the far side of the room.

This space reminded her of a large apartment, much more significant than her own. Several rooms were paneled off, and what materialized inside the area was a well-stocked kitchen, a living room, and a dining room that was currently being used as Jake's office space. What was conspicuously missing was a ceiling. As she scanned the rooms, she raised an eyebrow at the prospect of the cyclone fencing on the ceiling instead of wallboard. "Don't worry, the bedroom and bath both have lower ceilings, with the fencing on the upper side," Jake said, as he stood and walked toward what he presumed would be his new partner. He stood well over six feet tall. Jake had a muscular frame that helped him look more handsome than he was. Understanding that the woman was giving him the once over, he nervously ran his fingers through his hair, embarrassed that she was even there at all. Jake was wearing navy blue Dockers and a powder blue V-neck polo shirt. She started to introduce herself to him, but he interrupted her by saying, "Trust me, Ms. Harrison, I knew you were coming. Missouri was a big deal, and it was assigned reading in training. It's a pleasure to meet you. I'm a fan."

Angela responded, "Don't believe everything you read."

"You mean those things didn't happen?" he questioned.

"Oh, they happened, but I was out of my depth. Kind of like now. Are you really..."

Before she could finish, Jake completed her sentence, "A werewolf? I don't know. What I do know is that for three to four days a month, I'm not myself."

"Neither am I," she said, not flinching.

He smiled at her and started moving back toward the desk in his make-shift office. "Yes, ma'am," he said, allowing his Texas accent to come into play. "But yours is more like an act of nature, not a force of nature. They've run every diagnostic blood test, skin analysis, even some tests I can't explain, and they still haven't told me anything more than I already know."

"Nevertheless, Mr. Taylor, I'm going to need your help if we expect to make a dent in any of these disturbing cases," she said, while throwing the folder that was under her arm onto his desk. "Before we do anything about, well, anything, I need you to look at these files of the people that the Bureau suggests we try to include on our team. None of them are trained as we are. None of them respond to authority at all. Frankly, I don't think we will get anywhere unless we can get them all to work with us as a team." She paused to let him look at the potential team members. She silently moved about the room as she watched him reading the files. He raised his eyebrows, then curled his lips, smiling at the next suggested recruit. His brow furrowed on the following two, but it was when he came to the last person that his soft blue eyes flamed with anger.

"No, no, no!" He stated himself plainly. "I will not work with Erin Hastings. It's not going to happen. Not today, not ever!"

Understanding why he would react this way, Angela moved carefully toward him and said, "It's just this case, Jake. We must have her in this case. She's not even supposed to be here. It was either fate or a miracle that she's here for us to use in this case. There is really no choice here. This is going to happen."

"But, she's a Vampire!" he exclaimed.

"Yes, if there is such a thing. Erin Hastings is a young, immature, inexperienced vampire, and we need to gather as much intelligence from her as we can. As far as I know, we have never had an opportunity like this, and we need to use this for what it is. Besides, if I'm correct in my reading of the case in St. David, there's a nest of these things there, and we need the best information we can get if we are to get a handle on this situation. We already have her in custody. Why not take advantage of it? Trust me when I say, Agent Taylor, this young thing is wanting payback in the worst way."

Agent Jake Taylor walked over and pointed at the picture of Ms. Hastings. He tried to argue, but couldn't. There was something about Erin that caused his blood to boil, something primal, but what could he do? Not many cases were coming his way these days, and the Bureau could have had him put down two years ago, but didn't. He realized that he needed to keep his frayed emotions in check for the moment. "So, what do you want from me?"

"I have to go see her right now," Angela explained. "She wants me to come to her. I know she wants to feed on human blood, not the packaged stuff she's been getting. I need you to hold her off me once she breaks through my defenses. I want to try and talk some sense into her, Jake." Angela walked over and put her hand on his arm and continued, "I believe she is so angry right now, she doesn't know why she's mad. Reading her file has shown me her Modus Operandi. She draws people in with her sixteen-year-old innocence, and then, when she feels the person relax, she pounces. I need you not to relax; not for an instant. Stay on your toes, and if she gets too close, use this." She showed him a syringe that was at least six inches long, and inside was a thick, yellow liquid.

"What is in this?" he asked.

"Enough toxin to kill four rhinos, two elephants, and a dozen lions," she informed him. His eyes widened again. Then she added, "I don't think it will kill her, but it should stun her enough that we might be able to reach her. I know this, it's game time. We can't wait! We must push forward! And we need to move now. I don't know if you are aware, but Michael Cline has called me in on this case because that little demon in there is his niece. We can't save her, but maybe we can give what happened to her some sort of relevance. Can I count on you?"

Taking the syringe from Angela, he stood up and said, "Let's do this." He then picked up the receiver and spoke to someone. He ordered marksmen to come to his office. Once they arrived at his door, he gave each guard a dart gun. If Erin Hastings was going to start something, it wouldn't be very long before she was tranquilized into submission.

As they left his room and headed for their next recruit, Angela suggested, "Bullets won't work on her; you know that, don't you, Jake?"

"Ms. Harrison, we've got weapons you don't know about. For example, we've got weapons that shoot wooden bullets at three rounds per second. Besides, I also told them to bring both lead and silver bullets," he replied confidently.

"Why did you do that, Agent Taylor?" Angela asked.

"Because if the tranquilizers don't work and I get my butt kicked by a sixteen-year-old girl, vampire or not, my friends won't let me live it down," he answered, with sarcasm in his voice. "I figure your friends would do the same. Therefore, we'd be better off dead than alive," he said, chuckling. Surprisingly, Angela, who was always so somber, took a moment to laugh at their predicament.

Before moving another step, Angela offered, "Jake, my friends call me Angel."

"Good to know," he said, while putting on his 'no one's going to mess with me today' face.

Soon they were standing in front of Erin Hastings' cage, and all smiles were gone from their faces. It was time to get back to work.

♦ ♦ ♦

Neither Jake nor Angela were shocked when they first saw Ms. Hastings. She had an agent by the collar. Blood was all around the victim and smeared all over the floor. Erin's fangs were extended, and she looked as if she were draining the victim dry. "You check on the agent," Jake said. "I'm not taking any chances. I'm putting her down, right now!"

"C'mon, wolf-boy," Erin shouted as she let go of the agent's suit and the unconscious agent jerked and fell to the floor. "I need my daily exercise."

There were clicks from above them. Heavily armed agents were putting rounds into the chambers of their weapons. Jake took out his Glock and pointed it right at her beautiful but deadly eyes. Erin started to laugh. As the smile began to disappear, she ordered, "Get up, Tommy. They can't take a joke!" Erin stepped back to allow the man beneath her to rise up. He wiped away the goo that had covered his neck and stood there looking confused.

"She said you would think this was funny," he shyly said.

"What's the matter?" Erin asked, "Can't you take a joke?" Her laugh struck horror into both Angela and Jake. She worked herself back onto her bunk, all the while slithering like a snake. She wedged herself into a corner of the room and set herself as if she were coiling up, getting ready to strike again.

Focusing her attention on the bleeding agent, Angela asked, "Didn't you think she'd kill you? Actually, suck you dry?"

"She wouldn't do that; I saved her life," he responded, as if he were proud of himself.

"You're the guy?" Angela asked as she narrowed her eyes.

The agent, who looked as if he were about twelve years old, placed himself in front of Agent Harrison and said, "My name's Arthur Kensington. My friends call me Tommy."

Feeling left out, Erin shouted, "I thought you were here to see the main attraction," waving her arms up and down the sides of her body, "instead of the hired help!"

"Erin," the other female in the room began, "my name is Angela ..."

"Look, lady, I know who you are." Her dead eyes sparkled with promise as she continued, "What are you going to do for me?"

Sternly, Angela snapped back, "Erin, how about we get you out into the field?"

Before Agent Harrison could react, Erin's hand was around Angela's throat.

Jake was at Angela's side before the vampire could start to squeeze. The syringe was in Erin's neck, just waiting to be pressed shut. "Don't even think about it," Jake insisted. "I will put you down, here and now. Now, let Agent Harrison go."

"What's in the needle? Kool-Aid? Colored water? What?"

"Keep squeezing her throat, and I promise you, you will have about a minute to live, if that!" Jake was in control of the situation. Erin did not have the upper hand.

"Erin, we are only here to help you, and we hope that you will help us," Angela gasped. "Now, let me go before Jake puts your light out for good." Agent Harrison's voice was under control and evenly toned. In a show of trust, and without being told, Agent Taylor slowly removed the syringe and needle from the vampire's neck.

Erin released her grip from Angela's throat and stepped back.

Tommy was the first to speak. "Not everyone is against you, Love. Just relax and hear what they have to say."

Without another second passing, the vampire was on Kensington, fangs exposed, insisting, "What did I tell you about calling me Love again?"

"Sorry, sorry!" His accent was showing to the entire group. "I always slip up when I'm nervous."

"What are you nervous about?" Jake asked the English agent.

"If you guys are here, that means that you are going to take on the St. David case, which means that I will have to go back to that hell hole! I, for one, don't long to return to that place anytime soon."

Interrupting, Angela insisted, "We are not going anywhere until we get this unit together."

All eyes centered on Erin. "What?" she demanded.

"I think," Jake said softly, while attempting to stare into the dark pools Erin now used as eyes, "Agent Harrison is referring to us all working together."

Before Agent Taylor could blink, the vampire had her long slender fingers securely wrapped around his thick, muscled neck. "Do I look like I need you to explain to me what Agent Harrison is saying?"

Everyone in the room stopped moving. Not a sound was made. Then the masculine agent slowly brought his arm up, and without changing his facial expression, he pried Erin's fingers from around his throat. She grunted as she was forced to let go. Jake did not release her hand from his grip. Instead, he dragged the vampire over to a chair to her shouts of, "What are you going to do?" As he sat down, Jacob grabbed her sixteen-year-old body and moved her as if he was going to spank her. "I don't think so," she exclaimed.

Agent Taylor was much stronger than he looked. As he raised his hand to spank Erin's butt, both Angela and Tommy tried to object. However, before he actually made contact, he stood up, quickly, and the young woman fell to the floor with a grunt. Jake chose his words carefully. "I'm from Texas, and I don't care who she is or what tragedy befell her. No sixteen-year-old woman is going to throw herself around, acting like a spoiled brat, threatening everyone, and not expect someone to offer resistance." Jake looked down at her and continued, "I'm not intimidated by you, Sugar. Not in the least. And while I don't want to be a parent in this group. I will discipline you if I have to!" With that, he stormed out of the room.

Jumping to her feet, Erin shifted her clothing and her body to face Angela. "Are you going to let him get away with treating me that way? Talking to me like that?"

Taking all factors into consideration, after several moments, her only answer was, "Yes."

Erin was beside herself as Angela and Tommy both headed to the door, ignoring her shouts of objection and disrespect. Once they reached the door, Angela turned to the vampire. "Erin, we really need your help. We don't know what we are up against in Arizona, but what we do know is whatever can of worms was opened, you're involved. The clan sacrificed you to make a point. Unfortunately, you are here, and no one, living or dead, wants you in their world any longer. Think about that the next time you want to throw a temper tantrum." She turned back to the door, not expecting the silence. When she heard whimpering from behind her, she stopped. "By the way, did you notice, he didn't call you a little girl, which is what I would have done. He likes you. I can tell. Trust me, he's in your corner. I wouldn't blow this if I were you."

Angela left the room with a smile on her face. As the doors slid closed behind her, Jake and Tommy stood alongside the opening of the door. Both were waiting to be chastised by Angela, but it never came. As she walked by them, she merely stated, "Let's get the rest of the team together before I kill her myself!"

Chapter Three
Geek-Boy

"I don't know what I've done," the young man said as he stared out the window, "but, if it gets me out of Bremerton, I am guilty as charged."

He was standing in Seattle, but he hailed from Bremerton, which was a ferryboat ride across the bay. His name was Charles Martin. To his friends, he was known as Charlie-Boy, but he went by the hacker name of Geek-Boy. He was at that awkward stage of his life, tall and lanky, with long arms, legs, and hair, that he used to cover his slightly pimpled face. Charlie was unhappy. As he looked out the window, he had an epiphany. "I'm not under arrest, am I?" He turned to look at the two Federal Bureau of Investigation agents who stood there stoically, not saying anything.

Charlie had made the pilgrimage to the Seattle FBI center. The interrogation room he was standing in with the two-way mirror, the low beam lighting hanging from the high ceiling, in addition to the small table with chairs astride opposite sides, made it appear as if he were in a dire situation. Charles continued to stare at the two agents standing there, not saying a word. "In fact, you want me for something..." While it wasn't phrased as a question, it was more like he was guessing. He was in full analysis mode, for which he made a lot of money in today's world.

Charlie's situation indeed was his own fault. He was one of the most gifted students to ever attend Bremerton Elementary School. Most of his teachers considered him, "a good student with a bad attitude." However, the truth was, while he did have an attitude, he was a self-taught computer genius, with high intellectual ability.

At nine years old, he started having trouble with allergies. Once he hit puberty at 13, his entire body seemed to explode all at the same time. He missed several days of school during the first semester of his seventh-grade year. Therefore, his parents decided to have him homeschooled. "The poor boy was allergic to everything," his father exclaimed. While doctors tried to find the causes of his many ailments, Charlie seemed to be allergic to the very air that he breathed. Eventually, once he finished his high school studies at fifteen, he graduated.

During his downtime, he read everything he could lay his hands on. His favorite topic was anything dealing with computer systems, and he soaked up this information like a sponge absorbs water. "Information and knowledge are tools; I keep them in my abstract toolbox." This was an idea he had heard expressed by the actor Jamie Foxx in a television interview. Charlie hated the fact that some companies wanted to openly share their software ideas, while others kept a tight grip on their assets, no sharing allowed. "Money makes the world go around," he was told once. "No, people make the world go around. Money just makes it spin out of control," was Charlie's response.

Realizing that he could not always get the information he wanted from outside the system, he enrolled at Washington University and majored in computer forensics. He was only one of a handful of people who could perform many of the tasks required to keep the internet viable. This scared the people in the know, a.k.a., the government. So they kept tabs on Mr. Martin. They even asked him to join them once, but his job at the government institution was small and dull, and Charlie-Boy doesn't work well with the small and tedious. Therefore, he had started his own computer forensics service. Presently, he was a computer gunslinger for hire.

Even though he was watched thoroughly, twenty-four hours a day, seven days a week, one thing that could be said about Charlie was that he was a reasonable guy, doing honest work for a fair wage. The problem was, no one in the government believed it. So, they sent in an agent, a beautiful, alluring agent named Carrie-Anne, who had above-average computer skills herself, to keep him under their thumb. However, the agent was so impressed with Charlie and his work, she fell in love with him. The FBI fired her; Charlie married her.

After she was fired, Carrie-Ann finished her law degree. Now, besides helping him in the raising of their two children, she protects the man she loves like a female lion protects her cubs. She was fierce and ruthless when she needed to be.

A smile came to Charlie's narrow eyes as the love of his life walked into the room. "What's going on, Geek-Boy? How in the world did you wind up in an interrogation room at an FBI office? Carrie-Anne asked as she glided across the area, only to be seated next to her husband. Carrie was thirty-five, but looked twenty-five. She softly grazed Charlie's hand, which sent chills through them both. They thrived on challenges, whether it was work-related or in their personal lives. An impromptu meeting at the Seattle FBI office was indeed a challenge. One which the young couple was undoubtedly ready and able to tackle.

"How's it going, Carrie-Anne?" A familiar voice came from the opened door as Jake and Angela stepped through.

Carrie-Anne was speechless as Jake, who was carrying both her and Charlie's files, along with one other folder, immediately sat down at the table. Angela whispered some orders to the two agents in the same area, and they promptly left the room.

"The last person," Carrie-Anne began, "I expected to see come through the door was you." She gave a genuine smile, crossed the room, and gave Jake a warm hug. Jake nodded toward the tall, slender woman who had accompanied him.

"This is Angela Harrison. She's in charge of this case." Angela extended her hand and was polite, but it was time to get down to business. She motioned for everyone to sit down so they could discuss the situation.

With her gaze shifted to Geek-Boy, Angela began to spin her tale. After giving Charles the information about Erin's death and rebirth and the possibility of the extreme dangers located in St. David, she continued, "We don't know what we are going to find there, and what we need from you, Mr. Martin, is your expertise in not only the spec-tech of the area, but we need you to do complete background checks on everyone involved in this case. You can start with me if you like."

Before Charles could say a word, Carrie-Anne interrupted. "What aren't you telling us, Ms. Harrison?"

Angela glanced at Jake, then back to the two people across the table. "You're right, Mrs. Martin. There are quite a few things I want to tell you, but I can't. Not until I know whether he's in or not. Besides, Carrie-Anne, I am only talking to you as a favor to Jake. You are no longer with the Bureau, and, therefore, you are outside the circle of influence in this particular situation."

Carrie-Anne made a move, as if she were ready to take this uptight, high strung, agent on. However, Geek-Boy gently placed a hand on his wife's arm as if to say, "I've got this." He stood and walked over to a window, and the room became extremely quiet. "God, I hate this place. Did you know it rains like 250 days a year here? I was born here and just never thought I should leave because, well, I was born here." He turned back to the people at the table and noticed his wife was smiling at him. He gave a soft smile back. She knew what he was about to do, and as she gently leaned back in her chair to watch the show, she glared at the agent in charge. "You've got a high-risk situation in St. David. While most people won't believe you, you've got some very despicable beasts in that town. You've been tasked with cleaning up this situation. In your own way, I believe you are trying to protect Carrie-Anne and me as much as possible. But, I'm going to be thrust into this situation if I even place my hand on that third file there." He stopped walking toward the table to allow those words to sink in. Once Geek-Boy knew he had Ms. Harrison's attention, the young man continued. "I don't mean to brag, I'm more than likely the smartest guy in this building. And the smartest thing I ever did was marrying this woman right here." He took Carrie-Anne's hand. "While I may be too smart for my own good, she keeps me grounded. I don't make any moves without discussing it with her first. With all due respect, Ms. Harrison, if I do decide to do this for you, I will not do it without her approval, or without her involvement." He relaxed a little at this point because he didn't like being rude. "You brought Jake here because he and Carrie-Anne worked together before and you thought it might make signing me up easier, but the truth is while she was a great agent, Care-Bear here is an even better lawyer. As much as you need me, you will also need her in on this case." He sat back down and began holding his wife's hand. "So, why don't you go ahead and tell us what you are trying so hard to keep secret, and then we will decide not only if, but how, we are going to help you in this situation."

Stunned by his comments, it was Angela's turn to be speechless, so Jake started, "Carrie-Anne, were you still with the agency when I went to Waco?"

"You know I was," she answered. "I was pulled out of Waco right after we raided Hampton Hills." She squeezed Charlie-Boy's hand. "It was bad there, Jake. I thought for sure you died, but here you are."

"I did die there." He paused for effect as he leaned forward to deliver the rest of his story. "I was bitten. Several of us were bitten by the wolves. In fact, my throat was ripped from my body. I was taken to the coroner, and while I was waiting to be looked at to determine the cause of my death, my body started to repair itself. I know it's weird to hear me talk like this, but it's true, I swear. By the time it was my turn to be autopsied, my body was in pristine condition. My heart, and the hearts of several of the others, started working again. However, out of the seven of us, I was the only one who stayed with the Bureau. In the eight years since you left, my sole purpose has been to track down the other six former agents and eliminate them before they could hurt anyone else. Oh, sure, I tried to get them back into the agency. Unfortunately, when I found them, they could not control what they had become. Most of the time, I can't either. However, they lock me up, and on those nights, I howl and carry on. I eat raw meat to satisfy the hunger inside me. Then, it's back to work. I've made it my mission finding the last of my kind, and when I'm done, I'm going to make sure this can't happen to anyone else." He jerked his head once to the right, and when everyone looked down at his left arm, what was once a tanned forearm was now a claw, covered with thick black and brown hair and sharpened nails, at least four inches long. Everyone in the room jumped except for Jake. "I'm what we call a Werewolf, a Wolf Man, or from the Greek, Lycanthrope. I've worked long and hard for the past eight years since working with you, Carrie-Anne. While I wouldn't trust me on a full moon, I am good during the daytime, and for twenty-six to twenty- eight days of the month." He had held their attention with his eyes; therefore, when he looked back down at his arm, all anyone noticed was his tanned appendage once again.

The silent room was interrupted by Angela saying, "This is nothing compared to the dangers you could possibly face if you join with us." She paused, as if pondering her next move. Then she shoved the folder dealing with the St. David information across the table for them both to read. But, before she removed her hand, she insisted, "If either of you divulges what you read in this file, I will have you arrested and locked away forever. Your children will become wards of the state. Just so you understand, I'm not joking around." Her hand slowly slid off of the file, and Agent Harrison sat back, as if giving them permission to read the information inside.

For several moments, both Charlie and Carrie read the file, flipping the pages back and forth as if they could not believe what they were reading. When they were finished, the couple looked at one another. It was finally Carrie who spoke. "While I wouldn't recommend anyone do what you and Jake are about to attempt, I would feel better about your mission's success if Geek – Boy here went with your little group. However," She was quickly interrupted by her husband.

"No! There is always a however with you, and I'm telling you, not this time!" Charles Martin exclaimed.

Carrie-Anne's eyes narrowed in anger as she slowly started again, "However," it sounded more like a growl than a word, "I believe I should come along. I was an excellent agent, and I still do consult work." Her vulnerability was showing through when she continued, "I know you may think I am emotional here, but I believe I could be a valuable asset when you go to St. David."

"No!" Charlie was insistent. "No, no, no, no, no!" The others in the room tried to stifle their smiles, but it was as if he were throwing a temper tantrum. "What about our children? What about the safety of the company? What about..."

"Charlie," Carrie stopped him short. "While I love you with all my heart, you are not up to doing this alone. You are impulsive and reckless, and while by yourself you are a force to reckon with, together, we all just might get out of this alive."

"How did you know she would want to go with us?" Angela asked Jacob Taylor.

"While she was with the Agency, Ms. Carrie – Anne Macklin was on the fast track to a job similar to yours. In fact, Angela, she is a lot like you. If you are looking for a second in command, I believe you should choose her. I don't know what happened to her when she met Charlie here, and I really don't care. I recommend that if you are going to take him, you should consider taking her along as well. Even if it's for nothing more than an observer, to keep us all grounded, and to see to it that we all get through this thing alive."

Angela sat there, considering what Jake had just said, and a slow grin crept onto her face. "What would you do with your two children?" she asked, looking at the other woman.

It was Charlie-Boy who spoke. "You still have to assemble the rest of the team. The team you finally do assemble will need some type of training in working together before we go in there. So," he paused while looking around the room, "give Carrie-Anne and me five days to get everything in order. When we meet you for training at the Bureau in Phoenix, we will be ready to take St. David and all its ghouls head on."

Angela was in director mode now. "OK, Charlie, you've got your five days, but, Carrie-Anne, I need your head in the game. I don't know what the situation is in St. David now, but it isn't make-believe, and it isn't a vacation. If you two go down there with us, you are going to be in real danger. You both, more than likely, will have difficulty coming back alive. Do not take making this decision to get involved with us lightly!"

Yet again, it was Charlie's turn to impress. "Ms. Harrison, do you know what my company or I do for a living? I collect data. I collect, collate, store, analyze, and interpret data. With that data, I strategize and compute probable outcomes. I will tell you something else. You need not threaten my wife or me with information in this file." He tapped the folder Angela had given them to read. "I already knew what was in it. I know what happened in Arizona, and I also know what happened in Waco. But, I guess I should have told you that when we first met. I would go through hell to work with you because I also know all about your escapades in Missouri as well. Most importantly, this nation, the world in general, has mountains of problems which can't be explained. What I don't understand is why it has taken us so long to confront them."

Angela was angered about Charlie bringing up Missouri, and she turned to stare at Jacob, thinking he leaked the information. Her sidekick quietly said, "Don't look at me. I didn't say a word."

"Ms. Harrison, my husband is young, and he sometimes seems to be immature," Carrie-Anne said as she looked at Charlie, "but one of the main reasons why I love him is that when he takes on a task, any task, he is quite exceptional at his job. He will not fail you!"

Angela paused for several moments and then extended her hand. She tried to smile, but it wasn't working very well, because she knew she was headed for hell, and she would be taking these people with her. "Welcome to the group, Mr. and Ms. Martin."

Charlie grinned back at her and offered, "My friends call me Geek-Boy."

Chapter Four

The Plot Thickens

By now, the tears were streaming from the gentle man's eyes. He could not believe what he was witnessing. There she was, his little girl, on his television, being drained of the life-sustaining fluid in her body. Then came the wave of the hand by the beast. He was inviting other monsters to sample his daughter's blood for their enjoyment. "Stop, please, Sir. Stop playing this video."

It had been weeks since the nest of vampires had had their way with the lovely Erin Hastings. Blakely Hoffenpiller, the leader of this group of evil that had infested their town, pressed the pause button on the Digital Video Recording machine, which controlled the media that everyone was viewing. The video presented the mayor's daughter being surrounded by predators who were ogling their prey. The villain had paused the disk just before they made their move on the sixteen-year-old woman's body. "Mr. Mayor, I'm sorry for upsetting you and your lovely family, but this could have all been avoided if you would have just left us alone. Now she's dead and not coming back. But you and the rest of your warm-blooded group can be spared this indignity by cooperating." As the dead man looked around the room at Erin's remaining family, Blakely viewed Dad, Mom, the twelve-year-old twin sisters, and a fourteen-year-old boy.

"I have been cooperating with you since you've come to our community!" Mr. Hastings shouted at the thinly built man in front of him.

The vampire, at these words, reached over and back-handed the Mayor's wife. "Don't lie to me, old man," he hissed. "I know better! It was you who invited the people from Washington to put their noses into our exploits."

"What are you talking about?" the mayor asked with a puzzled look on his face.

The vampire stood up straighter and then questioned, "You mean to sit there and tell me your lies while I continue to take out my angst on your family?"

"Of course I don't want you to take out your frustrations on my family, but I am telling the truth when I say I have no idea what you are talking about!" His voice was louder than his wife, Marilyn, had ever heard it. "We did ask the government to come in and investigate the drug trafficking over the border. But, I had no idea about any of this you are showing me and telling me until this very moment."

Blakely Hoffenpiller quickly turned to find his number one disciple. "Percy, might I speak with you a moment?" The vampires moved outside to the front porch as Hoffenpiller asked, "What's going on here?"

"I don't understand, Master," Percy answered.

"We attacked the girl because you implied that the mayor was making moves against us." The Master was speaking when, suddenly, from out of the darkness, came four sets of Sports Utility Vehicle headlights, and they were all pointed at the two beasts.

"Gentlemen, Gentlemen," a sarcastic sounding voice which oozed confidence was speaking. "I'm sorry to inform you that it is I who has set this entire situation into motion. I hope you are not offended."

"Who are you?" asked Percy, who suddenly screamed in pain as a wooden projectile was shot and now positioned in his upper thigh. As both vampires were watching the wooden stake in Percy's leg, it was starting to smoke.

Percy started to scream from the sting of the wound. The silhouette shouted, "It's the holy water. All of our weapons have been dipped in the stuff. I'll bet that stings like hell. If either of you says another word before I'm done," He paused to make sure he had their attention. "Well, let's just say it would be better for you if you didn't speak."

Percy reached down and pulled the arrow from his leg, but he had no sooner removed it when another was shot into the very same spot. He made a move to shout something, but the Master grabbed his hand and stopped his moving altogether. "Don't do that either," the voice of the man in the shadows suggested.

"They are all well-armed and have thought this out very thoroughly," Hoffenpiller said to Percy. "They know what harms us and are intent on inflicting as much pain as possible to make their point."

Another man, taller than the first, stepped up. "I am giving you fair warning, gentlemen. You have stumbled into something here that is bigger than you. I suggest you gather your clan and leave this town immediately."

The vampire in charge raised his arm as if he wanted permission to speak. "Go ahead," a voice from the shadows ordered.

"Why allow us to settle here at all?" Blakely asked.

"I admit we've let things go a little too far," the first shadowed figure spoke. "However, this is how we are going to rectify it." Two more arrows landed into Percy, one in his right shoulder, and the other in the opposite leg. Just as the vampire opened his mouth to scream, another arrow landed in his mouth. While not destroying him, Percy was in a lot of discomfort. "If we allow you to continue to live after tonight, you are going to want payback for this action. Right now, we have the upper hand, and our employers don't plan on letting go of what is rightfully ours in the first place. So, please, Mr. Hoffenpiller, please leave."

Hoffenpiller raised an eyebrow. 'So, they know who I am,' he thought, as he raised his hand again to speak. "May I at least get the arrows out of my friend here and have the rest of my troops pulled out of the house unharmed?"

There was soft whispering coming from the two silhouetted men. Then the second man, with the thicker accent and the more dominant voice, spoke out. "You and the others in the house may leave, but Percy here, he's going to cease to exist." When the larger gentlemen finished, three arrows were shot at Percy, one into his head, one to his heart, and finally, one to his groin. The large man continued to narrate, "You come into my town, you start corrupting my people, you undermine my plans and my operation, and you think all you're going to get is a stern warning?" As Percy turned to dust, he concluded with, "Not going to happen. Not now, not ever!"

Blakely didn't ask for permission as he spoke this time. "You may think you are in control, Mr. Napier," he said with his fangs were exposed. "However, my clan and I are everywhere. We will find you and your family and friends and destroy you all for this." Six wooden arrows flew through the air with the hopes of entering demon flesh, but they missed and landed in the side of the building where the vampire was standing. Hoffenpiller was nowhere to be seen, and just as suddenly, the monsters inside the Mayor's house were gone.

After several moments, the mayor and his family were freed from their bonds. The two men, dressed all in black, looked first at the paused video on the screen and then at the town's mayor. The older Mr. Napier spoke first. "I came here to kill you tonight, Mr. Mayor, but after witnessing what you have seen, and realizing that you have lost more than we ever intended, I'll say enough is enough in your case." The large man paused, searching for the right words. "Erin was a beautiful young woman." He stopped before saying too much and simply added, "Sorry, man!"

"Digger," the mayor asked, "Did you know about those things? did you know that they were coming after my family and me?"

"Jack, you'd better back off, or," the younger Napier said.

"Or what?" Mayor Hastings asked. "What are you going to do to my family and me that those, those things, haven't already done? When you first came to me and told me about this clan of monsters in this town, my town, and how you were going to take care of it, you were setting me up, weren't you?"

"And what about you, Jack?" The older Napier stepped closer to the Mayor's face. "You brought in the DEA to end us. Do you know how long we have had our hands into everything around here? Why did you lead them to us? We could have worked out any differences."

"I made no such call. You said you would take care of the sickness in this town, and I believed you. Look what it cost me, Digger? Your daughter and my Emily were best friends. Now, I don't have my baby girl." The mayor started to weep, and he was soon joined by the rest of his family.

Digger was uncomfortable and didn't want to deal with the situation. Looking sympathetic, he tried to offer comfort. "I never meant to bring this onto this town, Jack. I was just doing my job, protecting my family and what's mine.

"Oh yeah?" This time it was the fourteen-year-old Mikey who spoke. "What about Elizabeth Ruiz?"

"What about her?" the older Napier asked.

The mayor slowly turned to his son, knelt down in front of him. "What did you do, Mikey?"

Knowing that all eyes were on him, the boy went silent. It was Marilyn, the mayor's wife and Emily's mother, who gave the next bit of information, "Elizabeth was a good friend to him."

Finally, Mikey found his voice. "She fell in with the wrong crowd, and well, now she's dead as well. I thought it was drugs. But, now, after seeing all those," he paused, swallowing hard, "those things, I know I was wrong. I made a mistake. I called the drug people. I called the hotline I saw on tv."

The four adults in the room all stated at the same time, "Oh, Mikey, what have you done?"

♦ ♦ ♦

It was guttural, the sound that came out of Blakely Hoffenpiller's mouth. As he and the others arrived at the enclave, the lead monster in charge started shouting, throwing things, then throwing his fellow vampires around the area. "I hate this place!" he screamed. "I hate the heat; I hate the summers; but I put up with it because in the wintertime, times like now, there is much more darkness, and it's not freezing. It's perfect for harvesting new members of our select group. But now," he sounded as if he were in mourning, "Now they have taken Percy, my oldest living ghoul and friend. If you were impressed with the way Percy seduced that Hastings brat, you should have seen him one-hundred years ago in Florida. By all that is evil, he was tremendous." As he stood there pondering over the events of the last few hours, he ranted, "I will have my revenge! We will start slowly at first. We will operate from here, but we will start recruiting drones from Tombstone, Martin, and Bellville. Then, when we are ready, we will come back and wreak havoc on the Napiers."

A lone voice asked, "How did you know it was the Napiers, Sire?"

Seeing this question as a challenge to his authority and questioning his ability to rule, Blakely found the drone that asked the question and quickly decapitated it. Then he turned and spread his arms as if calling all those he sired or were sired through him. "I am Sir Blakely Hoffenpiller, a member of the Queen's Court of 1539. I have conquered kingdoms for Monarchs who didn't need them conquered. I spilled more blood when I was alive than it would take a vampire two hundred years to spill." At these words, some of the beasts started to howl and growl viscerally. He continued, "I saw the future. I settled in this country at the turn of the seventeenth century. I stayed until the plague of Christianity captured the hearts of the people. I moved to Baton Rouge, but found it inhabited by the Rezae Clan. Finally, I arrived here, fifty human years ago. While the summers were miserable, I endured. Now, the inhabitants believe they can dictate to me? It will not happen. I will dig in like a tick. I will sink my teeth into every single person in the town of St. David." By this time in his speech, the others of the group were frenzied.

"I will suck the marrow from their bones. I will make St. David like the kingdom I gave up to come here. I will rip out their hearts and destroy every single family in this town, in Percy's name. And I will start with the Napiers!" The screams and cries for revenge were uncontrollable by this time, and it aroused two of the female vampires. So much so, that they could not control themselves any longer and attacked their leader, demanding his attention. Sex, like the blood they devoured on any and all occasions, was the driving force right now. Thus, the three melted into each other while the others in the room succumbed to their own desires.

Once Blakely Hoffenpiller finished with his female cohorts, he surveyed the arena in which they all laid and smiled to himself. He realized his new plan had worked. He was taken by surprise back at the mayor's home. Yes, he had lost his beloved Percy, but he needed to regroup his power-base and make a new plan. Most importantly, he needed to distract his troops while he began thinking of a better idea. His project, the plot that Percy had first sought to plan, now had taken a turn. Yes, it was thickening, but to get it to the right consistency, he was going to need help this time. Blakely Hoffenpiller needed a vampire more ruthless than himself. He needed someone as demonic as the Devil himself. He demanded Bethoon, the Cannibal.

Chapter Five

The Expert

Transferring the FBI's assets and equipment to Phoenix did not cause the new team any real difficulty. The Martins met up with Angela and Jacob at the exact time they planned. Once they were all settled in, Angela broke the news to the couple about bringing a vampire back into Arizona, but there was a small problem. They needed an expert in paranormal activity.

Once the subject was broached, Charlie Boy reached into his leather briefcase and pulled out a two-inch file and explained himself. "Because you never mentioned to us that you needed someone in the paranormal field with the expertise to help pull this whole thing off, Carrie and I went to work and built a profile with specific parameters that would be key. Most of the people in this area are theoretical. There is only one person with any substantial experience. His name is Eric von Bruton.

Geek-Boy went on to explain that once the doctor earned his Ph. D. in Abnormal Behavior from Princeton, he began his fieldwork experience at the tender age of twenty-six and married Ms. von Bruton at thirty-five. Eleven years later, while on the hunt of a vampire nest, his wife was killed. The professor quit his fieldwork and returned to the classroom at a small state college in Michigan. In his twenty years of fieldwork, he had tackled the Haitian art of Voo-Doo, Werewolves in South America, Poltergeist all over the world, and finally Vampires. Former colleagues have indicated that Dr. von Bruton ran up against the oldest vampire known to humankind. He almost bested it as well, but once he lost his wife, all passion for fieldwork stopped.

"What was the name of the vampire that escaped Dr. von Bruton that day?" someone asked.

Geek-Boy answered with, "Doesn't say in the report, but if I had to guess, there are whispers of a guy way up in the Arctic by the name of Buffoon, or something like that. We can ask the good doctor when we see him.

"There's no one else available?" Angela asked.

"If you want theorist, there are tons," Carrie-Anne interjected. "It seems von Bruton is the only one working from practical experience, although it's about twenty years old."

"Keep looking," came the order from Angela Harrison. "In the meantime, I guess we need to go check out Dr. von Bruton." Everyone agreed as all four members of the team had a flight scheduled to the Detroit Metropolitan Airport.

♦ ♦ ♦

Adrian College, located in the South-central part of Michigan, has been a part of academia since 1856. It is a consistent member of the top twenty-five best small colleges in the mid-western part of the United States. It is a college that very few people have ever heard of. That said, the best unknown part of Adrian College is that it houses some of the brightest minds in the world. One such soul is Eric von Bruton. While he does have the classic Germanic name, and both his parents were of German descent, he was actually born and raised in the fertile farmland of central Michigan.

Eric is the who's who in the field of Para-Normal Activity, or explaining the unexplainable. The professor's ideas, speculations, fieldwork, and coursework make him an expert in this area. His fieldwork of the 1980s and 1990s was ground-breaking, and was used as the basis of many of today's researchers in the field. However, the Dr. von Bruton of today, even though known as an underground phenomenon, has become a recluse. He appears throughout the week and administers his coursework; however, as far as any new ground-breaking material, such as journal work or rare Para-Normal discoveries, he has recorded nothing. Eric hasn't touched his computer keyboard or typewriter in years.

As the team, which was made up of Angela Harrison, Jacob Taylor, and the newly recruited Carrie-Anne and Charles Martin, walked through the doors of Professor von Bruton's classroom, they tried being inconspicuous. However, it was too late, for the man with the Doctorate degree already had them in his sites. "May I help you?" he asked over the mutterings of his students.

The four agents quickly tried to find seats in this confined classroom. "It can wait," Angela answered quietly.

Without losing a beat, Dr. von Bruton introduced her. "Ladies and gentlemen, I would like you to meet a distinguished agent from the FBI, Ms. Angela Harrison. Her work in the mission district of St. Louis, Missouri is the stuff of legends." The room went deathly quiet as she gave an uncomfortable smile.

"Dr. von Bruton, I apologize for interrupting, but we really need to speak to you," Agent Taylor informed him

"Why, of course, you do. Why else do you think I would allow you to barge into my classroom where we discuss the important issues of the day? I want to offer you my floor to speak your mind about whatever topic it is you want to talk to me about, but I can't imagine why you are here to meet with me." He was in his mid-sixties and his mind was as sharp as it had ever been. There were tufts of grey on the sides of his head, and small hairs were wrapped around his bifocals. As he glared at Angela and the others, she knew this had been a bad idea.

Suddenly, one of the young ladies sitting up front whispered something to the professor that seemed to calm him a bit. After coughing slightly, and clearing his throat, Eric stated, "Class dismissed."

As the class quickly filed out of the classroom, Angela lightly touched the young woman on the arm and asked, "What did you say to him?"

With a worried expression on her face, the nervous young woman answered, "I reminded him that FBI agents are usually armed." The girl threw in a timid smile and exited the room.

Now, Angela, Jake, Geek-Boy, Carrie-Anne, and the professor were alone in his empty classroom. "I don't mean to be disrespectful, Ms. Harrison, but couldn't you have made an appointment? I have very little interaction with my students any more, and I don't like missed opportunities."

"We are very sorry," Charles Martin spoke up, "but we are in dire straits."

"You must be Dr. Martin, from the think tank in Seattle, Washington. You have come a long way, Sir." The professor held out his hand, and immediately, Charles shook it. "This must be your lovely wife." He moved to Carrie-Anne. "How do you do?" When he arrived at Jake, the surprising professor impressed everyone in the room by stating, "There's no real cure for you, young man. You know that, don't you?" It was apparent the professor was a well-informed man.

Politely, Jake shook the professor's hand and said, "I'm not the reason why we are here."

"Really?" The professor seemed genuinely surprised. "Then why did the FBI go to all the trouble of visiting my school?"

Before Angela explained the reason for their arrival, the professor escorted the group to his office, which was actually more significant than his stuffy classroom. As he was being informed as to why they were there, Carrie-Anne walked around the room. She noticed the map with the strangely colored stick pins in it. Without considering the importance of what the professor was being told at the time, she interrupted the group by asking, "Professor, what does this map represent?"

Everyone in the room moved their attention to the map while the professor explained, "The blue pins represent clans of vampires we have been able to identify in various parts of the world. The red are the werewolves, black are zombies, and the white represents fairies, sprites and such."

Then Carrie-Anne reached for a purple pin, which was placed near the North Pole, and asked, "What about this one?"

The professor looked down at the floor and softly muttered, "Don't ask about that one right now. I'll have to get to know you better first."

"Professor, surely your map isn't correct, is it?" one of the four members of the task force asked him.

Becoming annoyed, he finally asked, "What is it you want from me?"

Angela fielded this question. "Dr. von Bruton, we need an expert in unexplainable phenomena. Frankly, Sir, we at the FBI don't have a clue what we are doing."

"Please sit down," he suggested to all of them. "If you were to have asked me even ten years ago, I might have said fine, sign me up. But today, with the way the world is, to be honest, I don't think any of you realize what you have signed yourselves up for." He took a laser pointer, which he had picked up before he sat down, and pointed to the top shelf of books. "You see that up there?" They all recognized the titles of a prevalent line of books dealing with the monsters of the present day. "There has been a changing of the guard. People are no longer afraid of the unknown, the unseen, or the dark. People now go to the movies or choose literature intentionally to be frightened out of their minds. They will tell you that being frightened gives them endorphins, which help them gain their high, in a sense. They actually are enthusiastic and desire any and all news about the immoral, the inappropriate, and especially about monsters. They believe that evil is their friend and often make these creatures part of a romantic fantasy. They think they can fall in love with these monsters and they will have their best interest at heart. You, my friends, are on the wrong side of this, and you can't go public because no one will believe you. It seems to me that evil has gotten better press than religion or the good guys have. Oh, I forgot, you are not allowed to bring Christianity into the conversation. You might offend the common man or woman by trying to express your religious views on someone. It's a well-known secret that various denominational religions have devoted several theologians, priests, ministers, and so on, to battling the harmful elements. Mr. Martin can tell us how well the church has done on this demon issue once he crunches the numbers. Once again, consider what I am saying. Whoever is doing the press releases for the so-called 'Bad Guys,' is doing a much better job than the good guys are."

The truth is that even though the wars in the middle-east have been going on for thousands of years, the battle between good and evil has been going on forever. Presently, sin is on the upswing." Once he finished, his shoulders were slumped over and he didn't look like the energetic, spry man they had first met. He looked frail and elderly.

"But, surely, Sir," Angela began, pointing at the map with all the pins, "the type of evil your map is indicating does not exist, does it?"

Without saying a word, the Para-Normal specialist stood and went to his desk and pulled out a picture frame. He brought it back to the group and handed it to Angela. The picture showed the professor as a much younger version of himself with a beautiful woman, apparently his wife.

Before he sat down, he pulled out another photograph, but this was a framed newspaper clipping. It showed the same beautiful woman on the arm of a hulk of a man. The date of the excerpt was two years ago.

"Oh Lord," Angela stated, before passing the pictures to the others.

"She was never afraid when we researched a town, city, or burial site. That man there is the worst of the worst. They call him the King of the North, and no one has been able to take him on. Anyway, a couple of decades ago, I faced him head-on. He beat me, and he took my wife as his prize. I was supposed to die a hundred miles north of nowhere," he said, as he gazed off into the distance. "I have fought the good fight and lost. I don't know how I could possibly help you today."

"Professor," this time it was Charles Martin who would take his turn at convincing his respected colleague. "You have a map, apparently an extremely accurate map, and while I am one of the best at gathering intelligence data, I don't have anything like that. It's awe-inspiring, if," he paused, looking at the others, "if it's correct."

This comment seemed to snap the professor out of his depression. He stared into Charles's eyes. "They call you Charlie-Boy, don't they?" Charles nodded his head as the professor continued, "And most people perceive you to be a freak of nature, right?" Again, Charles nodded in support. Von Bruton then stated, "I was the original freak. I still have hundreds of followers, and many of them contact me daily. The internet came along just in time to prevent me from falling into the "darkness forever! I'll tell you what, Charlie-Boy," The professor stood up, and walked over to his bookcase, and returned, giving the intelligence gatherer of the group a thick three-ringed binder filled with information he had gathered from the year 2014. The three-ring binder was marked on the spine. "You take a look inside there and tell me if I did a good job."

"Doctor von Bruton, we really need a man of your abilities with our group." Angela's tone was insistent. "We all appear to be in over our heads, except for you."

"My good woman," the Professor was condescending, and his voice was starting to sound annoyed. "Yes, I have knowledge that could help you, but I am not a field agent. While you go after, whatever it is you're going after, I would only slow you down and could cost one of you your life. I've lost enough friends battling things the common person doesn't care about." He noticed that the entire group was now absorbed in what he was saying. Therefore, he concluded, "I'll tell you what, I will consult with you in this case. Let me get my classes in order, and I will join you in Phoenix.

Jake smiled and said, "Already taken care of, Sir."

"How did you know I would agree to help you?" the Professor asked.

"We are good at our jobs too, professor!" Charles Martin exclaimed.

Angela sat for a moment and looked at the other four people in the room. She smiled then, thinking about Tommy and Erin Hastings. She knew that she had completed putting her team together. Now, if they could just get everyone to work together, maybe, just maybe, they might live through this operation.

Just when Angela was ready to get up and assist the good professor in getting his gear together, Charles and Carrie-Anne walked over and asked her, "Did you mention something earlier about working with a vampire?"

The professor stopped packing his materials and waited for her answer. Jake chimed in, "Angela, I do think it's time you explain to everyone about Erin."

The leader of the group motioned for everyone to sit back down. She knew she had some explaining to do. There was no clock timing the group, and since they were using a company jet, they could leave Adrian College anytime they were ready. For the next several hours, Ms. Harrison did her best to explain the use of Erin Hastings in this case. There were "concerns," expressed by everyone in the group. However, it was Jacob who put it all in perspective. "I don't know what it's like to be a creature similar to Erin. However, all of us here know what it's like to be different. We were chosen to be here because we are different. I don't know why they chose to attack Erin, but they did. Frankly, I think they made a mistake. That girl has something to prove. I just don't know what it is yet. I agree with Angela. She wants payback, but I, for one, am willing to put myself into her hands. But, as I say that, I need you all to let me take the brunt of her anger and disdain. I don't think any of you could live through one of her tantrums."

"Jacob!" Angela rolled her eyes. She wasn't buying what he was selling when it came to Ms. Erin Hastings.

"I know what you're thinking," Jacob began, "but it's not sympathy, or attraction to Erin. It's something I can't explain. I'm just asking all of you to take a beat." The FBI agent paused, looked into the eyes of each group member, and finally added, "I don't trust her! But, I do respect her and her abilities. If you don't learn to respect her too, then all of you will wind up dead." He gave the group a solemn gaze when he had finished speaking.

Shortly after that, Dr. Eric von Bruton's satchel was packed. His map was marked correctly and put into a cardboard tube. The marking pins were added to his school bag. The agents left Adrian College with their scientist in tow, and they were now a group that was complete. There were still many questions without answers, but now, at least they had direction. And it pointed them toward St. David, Arizona.

Chapter Six

Team Work

"Ow!! Damn, Jake!" Erin Hastings shouted. "That hurt!" She moaned as she grabbed her arm in protest. She started to move around the room and began rotating her arm around in its socket.

"Ya know, Erin, we've been going at this for weeks now, and you still seem to get hurt. You are the strongest person in this room, and the biggest Girl I have ever met," Jake said.

"Thank you, Jake," Erin said, smiling, not aware her fangs were showing. "I'll take that as a compliment."

"In fact, you hurt me every day, and I don't say a word," he continued abruptly. He was sharing himself with someone. He usually didn't do that. "I find it hard to believe someone like you can even feel pain."

She thought for a moment and then answered him, "I feel pain." She stopped as if she were deep in thought and added, "I still feel the pain from that night."

At that, Jake gave the young vampire a pitiful look, which only served to ignite the flames of anger inside her. They set their stances again, the way Master Quo had taught them, and Jake commanded her, "Attack me again!" She smiled, her eyes narrowed, and she quickly ran at him and jumped in the air. She thrust at her target as swiftly and smoothly as a bullet from a gun. Jake, as resilient and as fast as he was, reacted to the vampire by sidestepping her. Once she landed on the floor, he released his fist with the speed of a Jaguar. To her credit, Erin blocked every punch. Without hesitation, she climbed his muscle-bound frame and wrapped her legs around his head and neck area while leaning back and flipping him. Using her momentum, Erin threw him into the cement wall behind them, causing it to shake. He gave out a grunt and tried to raise himself up. Agent Taylor didn't have the strength. He groaned and collapsed to the ground.

"Jake!" she shouted, while running to him. "Oh, Jake, don't be hurt. I didn't mean to hurt you. Oh, God." Erin bent over and checked to see if he was breathing. While tears were filling her eyes, she softly stated,

"Please don't be hurt. Oh, Jake, I'm sorry, damn-it. I just don't know my own strength."

Suddenly, his left arm came from out of nowhere, and he swept her off of her feet. "You're such a girl," he said, laughing again.

"You were pretending? That's not funny! I thought I hurt you! I can't believe you were trying to trick me into gaining the upper hand." She stood up and walked over to the corner where the half man – half wolf lay and threw herself to the ground. Erin appeared to be breathing heavily, even though she wasn't human anymore. Her body couldn't help her to break its old habits. Neither she nor Jake really minded when their bodies did things that made them appear human. Erin joined him in laughing at herself for being so gullible.

"Erin," Jake said, sounding more like her father than her trainer, "you can't let your guard down for any reason. I know it wasn't fair what happened to you all those months ago. However, if you don't mind me saying so, dropping your guard is what has gotten you into this situation in the first place." He sat there looking at her and then shouted, "Hey, Ben?" He waited for an answer.

"Yeah," a voice that came over the intercom answered.

"Rewind that last bit, and pipe it in here, would you, please?" Jake insisted. Then he commanded Erin, "Watch that screen!" In a few seconds, they both appeared on the flat-screen monitor several feet above them. When the video reached the point where she had climbed his frame and flipped him into the wall, he shouted, "Look at that move, Princess! Now that's a move. That's good stuff." He looked over and saw her smiling, "You know how to take care of yourself."

Ben interrupted with, "That was a good move, Erin."

A smile formed on both of the battling member's faces and they relaxed and lay down on the floor mats.

"Jake, why do you care so much?" she asked.

"That's simple. I don't want you to d..." The FBI agent stopped before he could finish the word.

Erin started to laugh, "I'm already dead. Haven't you seen the videotape? You know what they did to me."

"Erin, if I would have known you before, I would have made sure you could fend for yourself. I want you to get some payback on those guys. You know that old saying, 'If I only knew then what I know now?' When we head back to St. David, I want you to take on Percy and knock him into next week! I know this, Darlin'," he said in his best Texas drawl, "you're ready for anything and everything they can throw your way."

"What do you think will happen to me after St. David?" she asked, with her dreamy voice and sultry eyes.

He thought for several moments and finally said, "I don't know about you, but I was kind of hoping you'd work with us."

"What do you mean?" she cautiously asked.

"According to Dr. von Bruton, there are several nests scattered throughout the world, and should we get lucky enough to survive St. David, well, I would kind of like having you around to watch my back!"

Erin started to chuckle again. "You're such a Boy! I can't believe you work for the FBI!" Then she elbowed him in the midsection.

He stood and offered his hand to help her up. "And you are such a Girly Girl! Now, get up here and kick my butt again!"

Behind the training room wall was a two-way glass. Inside that room stood Tommy, watching the two non-humans and thinking, "They're bonding. This is not good! Not good at all!"

Suddenly, the door to the observation room opened, and Angela walked up to him. "How are they doing?" she asked.

"They're bonding," he stated. "Jake works very well with Erin. Almost too well."

"Why, Tommy, if I didn't know better, I'd swear you were jealous," Angela interjected.

"I saved her life, and I am, intellectually, ten times the man he is."

"You didn't save her life, she's dead. Jake, on the other hand, is trying to preserve the life she has now. Plus, I think he's lonely."

"It could never work," Tommy suggested. "A vampire and a werewolf? Throughout history, it has never worked. At least that's what the fiction that's written out there says."

"Have you been talking to Eric again? Besides, aren't we jumping the gun?" Angela responded.

They both stood there, watching the couple in the next room battle. What Angela couldn't see were the gears working in Tommy's head. If he had anything to say about it, Jake would not make it to St. David. If he did, it would ruin Tommy's chance to carry out his Master's plans, and his Boss would not tolerate that!

♦ ♦ ♦

"St. David has a population of around 17,000 people. That's just the ones that are alive. There are an estimated 1,000 sub-human life forms there that we are aware of at this time. We are not really sure because they could be spread out over a four-county area." Geek-Boy was in charge of reconnaissance and was doing his usual thorough job.

"This information is less than ten hours old. It shines a light on several issues that we have to deal with right now." Charles swallowed hard as he told the group, "Percy, Erin's creator, is dead. He was made an example of by the area's drug lord. I'm not sure how the members of his clan are going to take that."

"That's odd," Professor Von Bruton mentioned. "You would think we would have a reaction from Ms. Hastings by now."

"What's odd?" asked Angela as she, Tommy, and Carrie-Anne stepped through the door of the conference room.

All eyes turned to the expert in the room. "When the dominant creator, or siring vampire, is killed, those vampires which he sired feel it." The Professor paused to see the confusion in the faces of the group. He rolled his eyes and continued. "Good grief, people," he yelled. "Haven't any of you ever seen a vampire movie?"

The wheels continued spinning in Tommy's head as he responded to the professor's explanation. "Maybe that's because he didn't create Erin in his form, I did." The young man had been transformed right in front of them. He now looked like a man very pleased with himself. Once he came back to reality, Tommy realized he was in a conference room with his colleagues, and he needed to explain. There was no time to lose. He had practiced this story so many times, it had become internalized. "She had stopped breathing, and she had little blood left inside her when I found her. I had been doing research in the lab with re-animating someone from the dead, so I borrowed blood from one of the vampires we had brought in for questioning and eventually released. I was acting quickly, not thinking all that clearly about repercussions. I took a vial of vampire blood, shoved it down her throat, added some of my own, and then removed the body from the scene and took it back to my lab. I waited 24 hours to see if there would be a reaction, and there was. When she woke, I had mountains of blood and plasma to use to get her back. I had no idea that it would work. I just knew I didn't want to see her die." He was sweating now, his speech was rapid, and he appeared to be upset because he was baring his soul to the group.

"I, for one," the Professor said, standing and walking over behind Agent Kensington, "am glad you acted so quickly, Thomas. Erin is a valuable member of the group, and we need her if we are going to succeed."

Changing the direction of the conversation, Carrie-Anne interjected, "But, aren't we sort of playing with fire, using both a vampire and a werewolf in our group? Aren't we setting them up for failure?"

"That is an excellent question, my dear," the professor commented. "However, with Jake's added strength, and his other enhanced abilities, if we can call them that, he is an excellent mentor for Erin. It would be foolish not to use all the power we have at our disposal."

"You hear that, Erin? I'm your mentor," Jake said, as he and Erin walked into the room.

"Boys!" was all she said as she took her place at the conference table between Jake and the expert.

Charles, directing his words to the last two arrivals, insisted, "You're late!"

"Sorry," the vampire and werewolf who had just arrived in the room said.

"The professor and I have been going over different approaches we might take heading into St. David; however, none of them seem viable. We were wondering if any of you might have a plan better than what we can come up with?"

"I would be the obvious one to go in first," Tommy interjected, "since I have been there before and know the area pretty well. I have worked on-site for the last twenty months."

No one said anything at first. Finally, Carrie-Anne, drawing from her days with the FBI, said, "And while he gets settled in with the other agents that are already established there, Angela, Charlie-Boy and I will coordinate with local law enforcement and bring them up to speed."

"I will set up an informational base of operations at the University of Tucson, once they have been contacted by the bureau," the Professor added.

"That has already been done," Angela said, sounding very authoritative. Then, looking across the table to her right-hand man, she said, "That leaves you two."

Recognizing that this was his moment to say something from the stare he received from Angela, Jacob spoke, "We are the ones tasked with stirring things up."

"That's not going to be a problem," Erin stated confidently. "Once I get my hands on Percy..."

The room went quiet again. All eyes were still on Erin. She noticed this and said, "Look, guys, I know I'm the most immature person in the room, and I didn't do very well when I first hooked up with you all, but I've adjusted. Yes, I am still angry about being what I am; however, that's not your fault, it's mine. I accept that." Everyone continued to stare at her until she shouted, "What? What is it that is making everyone stare at me?"

"We have found out that there is a drug lord in St. David, and it seems this person has something to do with all the chaos that's going on there," the professor explained. "And it seems that Percy has been slain."

"That's impossible!" both Jake and Erin said at the same time. Erin then stated, "I would have known."

"That's what we thought," Tommy interjected. "Erin, seeing you lying there on the ground, I had to act quickly. So, I gave you a general sample of blood from a vampire we had been holding in our lab. It wasn't Percy's blood." He paused and waited for her to explode.

Surprisingly, it was Jake who spoke, "Well, if that's true, isn't that a good thing?" His eyes were on the Professor. "I mean, doesn't that mean she's independent? That no one in that town has control of her, giving her free reign to fight alongside us?"

"What about my payback?" Erin insisted. "You promised me payback!"

"Yes, I know, but keep it under control, Ms. Hastings," Angela instructed. "You can't go in there like a gunslinger. You have to have a purpose, and most importantly, control. This drug lord, or whatever he is, from the reports we've been getting, is very resourceful. If he can get the drop on this nest of vampires, what else does he have control of in that town?"

"Listen," All eyes went to Jake, who now had the floor. "I know that you 'normal people' think that those of us who are different can be a burden. But, we're your best chance of getting through this situation. While you guys are investigating the vampire issue, Erin and I will check-out Napier's control of this town."

Erin's head snapped around to look into Jake's eyes. "Martin Napier?" she questioned.

"He's the brother to Ethan Napier, the person suspected to be running the drug organization," Tommy informed the group.

"I know them," Erin insisted. "Melissa Napier is my best friend from school." She dropped her head, quickly calculating things in her mind.

"Don't do it," Jake growled. "She, more than likely, has no clue what's going on with her uncle or father for that matter."

"It's not that." Erin swallowed hard, then continued. "She was dating Johnathon. Oh God, I hope she's ok."

"Why should we worry about this Melissa woman?" It was Carrie-Anne and Charlie asking this question, as the stress of the situation shone on their faces.

"Johnathon Silverstone was Percy's best friend, or so they both said on many occasions," Erin's eyes were filled with violence.

"That's our way in!" Angela hated that it came out the way it did, but she was right. If they needed an invitation into this situation, what better way than to save a friend who could be in trouble? They had just found their way into St. David without being noticed or singled out. "We need to get this operation going now!" Angela's suggestion sounded more like an order. "How soon can each of you be ready to move?"

Charlie suggested, "Three hours, because of the equipment." Everyone in the room was good with that, except Jake.

"Erin and I need to get to this Melissa now." He headed toward the door, with Erin close behind. "It might already be too late!" Jake wasn't asking permission as he continued to the exit.

"Stop!" Angela yelled.

"Look, Angela, I know you don't think we're ready, but we are." Jake's eyes were on fire as he spoke. "This is our perfect in. Erin and I try to protect the girl, you guys go after the vamps in St. David, and the Napiers are in the middle. We are the good guys after all."

Ignoring what Jake Taylor had said, Team-Leader Harrison shouted over her agent's objections, "Take this." She threw him a bottle of pills. "I don't know what's in them, but they tell me it will help take the edge off when the full moon comes in five days."

"I thought you were going to stop us," Jake said, with thankfulness in his voice. "I know Erin and I can do this, Boss, I just know it." Both non-humans were smiling at her out of respect. All thoughts of Percy and his death were gone. There was a damsel in distress, and these two were going into the heat of the blaze, fearless, and confident that they could handle the situation.

"Just be careful," Angela ordered. "Keep each other safe. And Erin, take your lead from Jake. He's outstanding at his job." The group director next tossed a sizeable plastic jar at Erin. "I was going to save this for later, but that's supposed to be some sort of super sunblock. I will have more with me when we arrive in the next day or two. Try to do the bulk of your work in the evening hours, but if you have to go out during the day, use it."

"Thanks. I will." Erin was sincere.

"Just watch yourself out there, both of you!" Angela said as Jake and Erin started to leave the room.

Watching them leave, Tommy asked, "Are we going to do this?"

"You scared?" Charlie questioned. His curly red hair sparkled in the fluorescent lighting of the room.

"No," was his quick retort.

"You should be," was the reply. Everyone went about preparing to leave for St. David.

Eric stopped Angela at the door once Tommy left the room. "That boy told you he brought Erin back from the dead with a couple of tubes of blood and some of his own juice as well."

"Yes, Doctor, he did." She paused and looked at Eric. "Is there something wrong, Dr. von Bruton?"

"Do me a favor, Angela, and get Charlie-Boy to run a background check on Mr. Kensington as quickly as possible, would you?"

She nodded, and then they left the room. No one was paying any attention to Geek-Boy and Carrie, who looked at each other, rolling their eyes. Finally, Carrie said to her husband, "What did you get us into, Geek-Boy?"

He simply smiled at his wife as they both cautiously exited the room and went to their respective offices.

Chapter Seven

Bethoon the Cannibal

A vampire's nest is his castle, his domicile, his home. No one is allowed into the vampire's nest unless brought in through harvesting or invitation. Blakely Hoffenpiller, the dictator and sole controller of this nest, began rethinking his decision to ask his guests to come to St. David. Now that monster was standing in the middle of his throne room when it spoke, "What am I doing here in this pit?"

"Hail to the King of the North." The welcoming words were spoken in earnest by members of the Hoffenpiller clan, though the words sounded hollow and insincere.

"Stop your platitudes!" a member of the King of the North's entourage ordered.

As this was said, the members of the St. David clan began to rise up from their seats, or from the places they were lying. The night creatures began to encircle their unwanted guests. Most of the group disagreed with Master Hoffenpiller. "We don't need outsiders to come into our home and upset our delicate balance." Although they were vampires, like any clan or gang, they had their pride. These things from the North were now in their district, and they would not be allowed to stay unless they give tribute in some form.

"Lord Hoffenpiller?" This time, an angelic looking woman at the right of the King took a step forward and quickly knelt. She was Bethoon's queen, and when she stepped forward, her beauty startled most of the beings in the room. She was tall for a female, but it was her inviting stare that was hypnotic and unrelenting. "Forgive our rudeness and inconsideration, my Lord; you have humbled us by your invitation." Her flaxen hair seemed to brighten in the dark, dank cave. At the moment, his anger had been appeased by such a presentation. "Take our offering with the sincerest hope that no offense was meant by any members of this room." Four members of the King of the North's group stepped forward and disrobed, revealing they were wearing just their bras and panties. The way these women moved was meant to distract and arouse. These four perfect creatures were visions to behold. They stood stoically as the light from the flickering candles made their bodies glow, making them even more desirable.

"Good Queen," Master Hoffenpiller spoke. "Tributes will not be required, or necessary, in this situation. I invited you here as a precaution, based on what our soothsayers have informed me of. The events of the last several weeks have everyone on edge. A battle is brewing, and I believe we need to be ready to answer the call."

"Why are we here?" the King asked again. The impatience could no longer be hidden.

"There are things in play that I had not foreseen," Hoffenpiller stated with an unsure nervousness in his voice. "We went after the leaders of the town. We had it planned perfectly, played all the pawns correctly. Then, as I was about to take the mantle of King of the South-West and make it apparent to all who reside here, out of nowhere..."

Just as he was about to give further information, the Queen, now standing, and who had snapped her fingers to have the four members who had disrobed gather themselves together and get back in line, asked, "Where is our beloved Percy?"

The King of the North showed the first signs of movement when Hoffenpiller proclaimed, "He is dead. They gave no warning when they took my beloved Percy. They shot him and bragged about it. They are a formidable adversary. Since that time, I have built my forces and expanded our kingdom. I have also tried to find information about the people who killed him, but there is nothing out there. I have turned over every rock, every stone, and could not get any answers."

"Percy, dead?" the Queen nervously questioned. Her voice was as hollow sounding as the large underground hall they were in. "This will not do. I will not have it." There came a guttural growl from behind the Queen, and she rephrased her words, "We will not have it."

Without warning, the King of the North was in Blakely Hoffenpiller's face with his bared claws wrapped around this Master's throat. To everyone's surprise, the subdued vampire expressed, "Go ahead, destroy me. I would no longer have to bear the embarrassment, or the indignity, of what was done to my clan and me. I would gladly sacrifice my life for Percy. Therefore, do what you will. You will get no objections from me."

The Queen walked over, and saying nothing at first, placed her hand on her King's massive large arm. He slowly released his grip. "Husband," she advised, "explain to these lowly creatures so that they may understand who you are." A soft, barely noticeable smile pursed her lips as the King looked at her. He let go of his grip on the throat of the King of the Southwest as she added, "You know how I love to hear you tell the story of how you became as you are now!"

The King of the North then banged the staff he was holding in his other hand. The ground seemed to tremble under everyone's feet. He moved back to the center of the room and banged the staff once again. The sound seemed to ripple throughout the room, like water when a pebble is dropped into it. Silence overtook the room as he stood thinking of his past, his long-forgotten past. This King stood well above six feet. His age, no one knew because his skin looked untarnished by time. He had muscles upon muscles. He was a rare specimen. He was the King among Kings. He was the Master over of his domain in the North, and now that he was here, he would control the Southwest of America. As he thought back on his story, this outlandish man's face seemed to gain both youth and light. The King banged the staff one last time to make sure that he had everyone's attention. Then, with teeth bare, the vampire master raised his head, and with lightning in his eyes and thunder in his voice, the Cannibal began to speak.

♦ ♦ ♦

"I am the son of a shepherd. I would tend hundreds of sheep in the meadows where the known world began. Even though I was young for my age when I started, my father said that I had a gift for this task. Actually, I had two gifts, Shem and Alou, my dogs. When I found Shem, someone had thrown him out for being too small. Alou had been in my family since I was young. Alou was wondrous in his task as a sheepdog. He had taken a liking to Shem and eventually taught Shem everything he knew about herding sheep.

At seventeen, my human name was Azahd. I was sitting in the meadow and was with both my dogs when, on the horizon stood a line of mounted horses. Alou immediately understood this to be dangerous and tried to encourage Shem and me to run and hide. But, the horses were too fast, and I was much too slow. They were the cavalry from a local warlord, and they took the sheep and killed Alou. Shem, who was smaller and focused on his work of guiding the other sheep so well, was kept alive. I was a prisoner slated for death. However, because I proved my worth by communicating with Shem so well, these men allowed me to live. The warlord killed my father and all of the people I knew. I did what they asked of me and clung to my life. Inside me festered revenge, and I knew that I would one day make them pay dearly for removing my family and my clan from this earth.

It took me ten years to be trusted by the people who captured me. All my time there, I watched those people. They taught me about their customs and their rituals. This tribe was ruthless and spilled blood all over the lands we traveled. They had this practice of slowly drawing sheep's blood, mixing it with goat's milk, and using it as food in the winter months when fresh meat was not available.

The Shamans made a practice of drinking more of the blood than milk. They claimed it would give them visions of the future. Eventually, they were able to sustain themselves on 100 percent sheep blood. I wanted to learn this practice, so when I didn't tend the flock, I worked for the head Shaman of the tribe. It took me most of eight years to complete the complexities of this practice with the sheep's blood.

Also, during this time, I trained with the soldiers of the tribe. I was small in stature then; therefore, I used stealth and cunning to subdue a foe. The clan kept moving east, and somewhere in that period of time, we had crossed the Bering Straits, the ice bridge that led us to the new world. We eventually split up our group. We went south, while some of my dearest friends that I grew to have feelings for, continued to the east. They were the first to see the buffalo and other beasts that inhabited the area called the Plains. My tribe settled here, in what you call Arizona.

Shem was by my side the whole time. We gave the sheep to the Plains tribes, as we became more of a warring tribe. We fought many battles and destroyed many enemies. In peacetime, families and cities were built. But this was never enough for me. I lived for the campaigns.

It was against a tribe that had moved up from Central America that I lost my first battle, and almost lost my life. I was left for dead on the battlefield. If it hadn't been for Shem, I would have never recovered. While the drones of the group were looting the dead for trophies, Shem found me. And though I couldn't move, Shem slowly pulled me to a more sheltered, secluded area. There, Shem would bring me the massive game from that were indigenous to the land. I drank the blood of each animal, whether it was elk, white-tailed deer, or wolves. My strength eventually returned. Therefore, I set out to carve my way through the people that had brutalized my tribe, my home all those years ago. I killed many with my bare hands. Then, instead of sending Shem out to bring me animals, I drank the blood of my victims. Although hard to swallow at first, through the years, I got used to drinking warm human blood. I felt when drinking the blood of a fallen warrior, I was also drinking their spirit, their strength. That is how I grew into the beast you see before you. Shem had kept me alive by providing for me. Therefore, I wanted to repay him. I started feeding him the flesh of my enemies, and as I did, I watched him turn into something I cannot explain. Together, we were fearless. We would march into camps, mainly at night, to catch them by surprise, and we would destroy them before they could react. The trek back to our commune in the Plains took years, but we finally made it. Once there, people would not allow us in. They said that Shem and I were no longer useful, that we were monsters.

That night, the people of my adopted tribe felt the fear of their betrayal when Shem and I attacked and destroyed them all. They never saw us coming. While Shem and I were outnumbered and beaten severely, neither of us was killed. I was pierced with spears and arrows, and my head bashed by tomahawks, but still, I pressed on. Those who were fortunate enough to escape reported my attacks to the other tribal leaders. They named me Bethoon, which in their language meant, "The Devil's Warrior." Because I drank the blood of my victims and fed on their skin and bones, they also referred to me as a cannibal. Thus, I became Bethoon the Cannibal.

Shunned by my own people, Shem and I set out to deliver pain to anyone I could lay my hand upon. My reputation preceded me, which meant I had to change my tactics. I had to infiltrate larger communities. I eliminated people one by one. Then, the worst thing that could happen did happen. I was attacked by one of my victims. I had bitten him and drained his blood, but not enough. Thus, he was reborn, similar to the monster I had become. So, I set out to learn how to create beings just like myself and Shem. Today, you call his kind Werewolves. I tried introducing some of my recruits to the slow drinking process the Shamans had shown me, but instead of gaining strength as I had, people became sick, and many died. Eventually, I became frustrated and would just drain them dry and leave them to Shem. Once, after a gruesome battle with a clan leader, I slit my wrist and made him gorge himself on my blood. He didn't die. Yes, he was sick and in pain, but eventually, he came through it. A few days later, however, I had him killed because I could not stand being around him. Shem and I share a bond that was forged through time, with blood and bone. He ate his fill of the chieftain, and we moved along to the next town.

I built an army. We were devoted to destruction and chaos. After thousands of years, I began to tire of the tediousness of being a conqueror. Should I need someone eliminated, I called upon Shem. He would take care of the undesirables so that I didn't have to bother with them. That's when I became strategic about who I turned. I took great pains to turn desirable young women so that they could be my agents, my angels of death. Today, I remain in the northern regions of North America because of the cold. I am comfortable with the cold, and with death. When my end eventually comes, I am not worried. By that time, it will be the end of life as we know it."

♦ ♦ ♦

When the focus went away from his story, and his mind was in the present once again, the King of the North stood at the center of the cave.

Shem was by his side as he had been for thousands of years. However, Bethoon no longer looked like the master of sheep he had once been. To look into his eyes was to stare death in the face. When Bethoon was finished speaking, he banged his staff once again and declared, "I am Bethoon the Cannibal. I am the oldest of the old, conqueror of conquerors. I will bring down the wrath of all the worst elements of vampires. I have raised vampires from their beginnings to the present, and I will prepare them for their futures. If thou have been offended, Master Blakely Hoffenpiller, I have come to set all wrong things right. We will find the usurpers of your mastery, and we will destroy them. I am Bethoon the Cannibal, and I say it is so."

The dark force in the center of the room stopped speaking, waiting for some reaction, but no one said anything. This did not please Bethoon. He banged the floor once again, repeated the statement, and a few of his group started to shout their leader's name. He slammed his metal staff on the dirt floor. The force was much more significant, and the ground was trembling. Once finished, the area was electric and loud and riotous. The demented beasts started slashing at the air, and people were jumping in each other's faces, while yelling and screaming. Shem was transformed into a massive, monstrous beast, standing beside his master. Realizing that he was holding this large group in the palm of his hand, the Cannibal clutched his Queen's body and drew her close. She in turn, grasped Blakely Hoffenpiller's hand, and they raised them up for all to see. They were united in the battle that was about to come. A lone tear ran down Master Hoffenpiller's cheek. He was amazed at the power that had been released in just a few minutes. "Now," Bethoon the Cannibal shouted to the room while sending his gaze to Blakely, the ruler of these lands, "we are ready!"

Chapter Eight
The Master Gardener

"This will do, Juanita," the elderly gentleman said as the hired nurse positioned him in front of the yellow roses. "Go do something fun," he told the nurse. Then, changing his mind, he said, "Better yet would you get me some of that lemonade you are so famous for? Please?"

She nodded, smiled, and was gone from the massive greenhouse they were in. To this elderly man, this greenhouse was his office, his place of business. It was where the senior member of this family held court and made humongous business decisions. There were things hidden in this room that would make mere human minds explode.

The pruning shears in his hand stopped shaking once the nurse was out of view, and he snipped two of the beautifully stemmed roses and put them in his lap. With little effort, he turned the 1940's styled wheelchair, with the large wicker back and giant wheels, a good ten feet to the next section of roses in his rather large garden. He looked up at the size and depth of this room and softly chuckled to himself, "Only in America." Then he cut two more long-stemmed roses. He was readying himself to move on to the next group of freshly grown roses when he heard the shuffle and waited for whoever it was to come around the corner with whatever information that made this interruption necessary. No one appeared, which prompted the gardener to say, "You can come out; I don't bite." He paused for a moment and thought, 'well, maybe I do, but not you, and not today.' Then he verbally added, "Gentlemen, please. I have more time behind me; than ahead of me. Let's get this over with."

Standing before the gardener were the two men who had paid a visit to Mr. Hastings and his family. They had killed the vampire known as Percy and made threats against the clan leader. "It went as planned, Grandfather. Only one person died, the vampire."

"Digger," the Master Gardener said with a certain amount of satisfaction in his voice, "he wasn't really a person, now was he?"

"No, Sir, I guess not," Austin answered back. He didn't like where this conversation was going.

"You guess not?" questioned the gardener. "Digger, we are trying to build something here. Did we not agree that this was the best course of action to deal with the undead?"

"No, grandfather." It was Ethan speaking this time. "You made all the decisions. You were right; he was not human. But we are playing with forces none of us understand." Ethan took a deep breath and added, "He disintegrated right there on the mansion grounds."

"And the girl? Did you find the girl and kill her as well?" the old gentleman asked.

"There was no girl," Ethan answered. "There were just the two younger daughters of the mayor. We weren't going to kill them."

The chair turned quickly, and the shears slammed to the ground and exploded apart. "What? That cannot be! I had planned this to the tiniest detail. And the girl wasn't there? She was supposed to die in front of him," he said, referring to the Mayor.

"She wasn't there," Digger insisted. "We looked everywhere, but couldn't find her remains anywhere, Sir. The family was acting very squirrelly. They were beside themselves with grief. We questioned them, but all they did was look at the television screen and cry. We watched the tape and saw the girl die at the hands of the man you sent us to kill, but there was no corpse to be found. We scared off the vampires and then checked on the Mayor and his family. Finally, we grabbed the tape to leave, but not before the boy had told us what he had done. Hasting's son admitted to contacting the authorities, and the FBI was sent in to have a look." He reached out to hand the video to his grandfather, but the disc was slapped from his hands.

As if he had not heard anything about the boy or the FBI, the old man growled, "I don't need to see it." The two men had never heard this tone before and stepped back a little, but they didn't leave. Then the grandfather shouted, "Get out, the both of you! And send me my nurse!"

His mind was reeling. How could he have been so incredibly ignorant of what might happen? It was he, the Gardener, who had dropped the video to the vampire clan. He knew precisely where the horde was held up because of his inside source. The source, however, had not been fully compliant. That's why Percy was killed. Mr. Kensington would most assuredly be dealt with upon his return. The tape had been doctored, not showing how Tommy had given her a master vampire's blood and then shuttled her to this garden to hide her in the soil. What had that boy conspired to do?

Now that he was alone again, the Master Gardner went to the next group of roses, white this time. While snipping two more of his beautiful creations, he thought to himself, 'It was not surprising that a government agency would rear its ugly head. The situation would have to be dealt with.' Their drug empire was created to distract local law officials. Every once and a while, there would be a mysterious tip from a not so innocent bystander who would give the police information about where drug deals were going down. This would placate the officers, giving him time to deal with the vampire issue. The Mayor, being in a position of authority, was approached by concerned citizens, stating there was a severe drug problem. This is how he was able to bring Mr. Blakely Hoffenpiller on board. Fortunately for him, Mr. Hoffenpiller had connections to the vampires that were starting to infest his town. It was the Master Gardner who came up with the plan and gave it to Blakely, which, in turn, introduced the idea to dear, sweet, succulent Percy. Get the girl in the clan. She could keep track of both the Mayor and the vampires. All that information would flow back to him, and he would be able to control this entire situation from his wheelchair.

But, not now! Now there is a lone wolf in his organization, and they have taken his pretty little plan and blown it up. He isn't ready to show himself or what he is planning, just yet. The Master Gardener sits and waits for the nurse. As she brings him his requested lemonade, he drinks, he ponders, and he waits.

♦ ♦ ♦

Several months later, the Gardner is sitting in his same wheelchair. However, this time, a different nurse is pushing him about. He suddenly realizes that he is no longer alone, once again. "Dear, I hate to bother you. However, I would like a glass of your wonderful lemonade." He has always told her this to send her on her way. Once she is gone, his two grandsons appear, looking frantic. "What is it now?" the old man asked.

"The FBI is on its way," the oldest of the two grandsons submitted. "They have a team of people, so says our informant. What should we do?"

"No doubt they have heard about Percy and will want revenge," the man in the wheelchair said as he gently cut into the roses. "I don't care how you do it, but bring that traitor here!"

A smile was on the younger man's face. As the giant of a man stood there waiting for the next shoe to drop, the old man asked, "There's more?"

"Bethoon is here as well, Grandfather." Digger took a step back, preparing for some reaction from the man in the wheelchair.

When there was no instant reaction from the old man, the grandson was unsure of himself. "Digger," the gardener asked, "Ethan's daughter, is she still seeing that thing?"

"Yes, Sir, just like you asked her to," Austin "Digger," Napier answered. "Neither Ethan nor Melissa know anything about Erin Hastings, other than she's dead of unnatural causes."

"Keep a close eye on them for me will you, Digger, please? Now, if you wouldn't mind sending in my nurse for me, I'll need her assistance. Also, on your way out, lock the doors."

After Austin was gone, the wheels of the old man's mind started to turn much more as he asked himself, 'Why would Tommy come back here, knowing he would die? What is bothering Hoffenpiller that he would invite Bethoon?' It wasn't the questions that bothered him so much as the answers. He would sit pat for just a little while longer before he would even think of revealing himself.

The nurse was back with his lemonade, and he gratefully traded his scissors for the glass. "Would you please place those on my work table for me, Anastasia?"

"Of course," was all she said as she turned to put the shears on the table before them.

As she passed the old man, the bright sunlight shone through her nurse's gown and revealed an impressive body. He took a sip of the lemonade while watching her walk toward the workbench. He then spit out the drink and poured the rest into the dirt of one of the flower beds without the newly hired nurse noticing. "You know," he said softly, "you should tell Stasher that you were one of the best yet." The words were out before he realized he had said them.

"You said something, Sir?"

"I was just marveling at your beauty, my dear," he said, louder than the last time he spoke.

"Why, thank you, Sir. You are so kind," she said to the old gentleman.

As she walked toward him, he stood up and away from the chair.

"You can stand up," she said, with surprise in her voice. She stopped moving forward, as worry filled her eyes.

"Surely Stasher warned you about me when he went over my file with you." He moved forward as she began to move backward. "You really do make excellent lemonade, but it's not my favorite drink." He kept moving forward, and she could see his facial features began to change. He looked much younger. "You see, Anastasia, things aren't always what they seem. I'm not really ole man Napier, but I did take his place, and I am running the organization that he started." When he was finished changing, he looked to be about thirty-five years old, with coal black hair and streaks of white on each side of his head. He stopped about three feet from the frightened nurse and said, "Don't worry. I know you work for the Federal Bureau of Investigation, but I'm not going to kill you! I'm simply going to glimmer you, wipe your mind. You will never know, understand, or remember what I am about to do to you. First, I am going to enjoy this delicious body of yours for my own pleasure. Then I am going to remove parts of your soul. Oh, not too much. I will nibble at it around the edges like I have done to all the agents that Stasher has sent me. I take just enough to restore the gifts needed to keep up this charade."

She reached behind herself and grabbed the scissors she had laid on the table and threatened him. "Touch me, old man, and you'll die!"

"Anastasia, don't you understand? I've been wiping your mind for months now. The sooner you relax, the more you will enjoy what I'm about to do with you." As he stepped forward once more, the shears pierced his abdomen. He reacted by not reacting. The Gardener grabbed her by the hair, pulling her head to the side to give him a better look at her face. The home care companion could not move. The much younger version of Grandfather Napier looked deep into her eyes until she no longer had a grip on her weapon. He passionately pressed against the woman and kissed her. The resistance that once was present was now gone.

He ripped her nurse's uniform off of her submissive body and had his way with her. He would look back into her eyes every so often until she would respond to him just the way he wanted. He made sure they both enjoyed the pleasures of the flesh, and of one another. After enough time had elapsed, the Master Gardener knew this beautiful interlude had to end. He gazed into her eyes once again and wiped away all that had just happened in the last hour from her mind. However, just before leaving his chosen goddess, and while still digging deep into her body, he found the gift he was looking for, her soul. Old man Napier did as the demon had told her he would do. He nibbled the edges of her soul. This lady was a good woman. Therefore, he didn't need to eat that much. He dressed her back into the ordinary nurse's gown he had all his nurses wear and kissed her lightly on her lips, his way of thanking her for her services to him.

Once he finished with the nurse, he reverted to his old state and planted himself back into the chair. Slowly, deliberately, the old man wheeled himself over to the work table where he had placed the woman's body. He touched her shoulder and said, "Anastasia, are you awake? Anastasia!" She started to stir as he went back into his old facade. "I'm so sorry for working you so hard, dearie. You must have gotten tired and taken a nap."

"Oh, Mister Napier, I am so sorry about this." There was a worried look on her face. She had failed at her job of taking care of him.

"Anastasia, don't worry about a thing. This is my domain. While we are here in my garden, no one can tell me what to do. So, if you sleep, I won't tell anyone." He then winked at her. "It's not the first time I've put women to sleep, you know." He chuckled to lighten the mood. "The late Mrs. Napier, bless her soul, would always be asleep or have a headache at bedtime. Why do you think that was?" he asked, with a deceptive smile.

"Oh, Mister Napier, you are, without a doubt, the best boss I've ever had," she said, as she turned his chair around and headed for the door.

While riding in his chair, the man thought,. ‘Yes, I will bide my time for just a little longer. Then, when the time comes, all hell will break loose. This is my land. St. David is my town to rule. No pack of vampires or agents of the FBI are going to foil my plans. I pity the ones who try.’

E.C.H.O
(Elite Counter-Horror Organization)

The Master Gardener

Part Two
Set the Table

Chapter Nine

Let's Dance

It was mid-February; winter was beginning to dig its claws into St. David, Arizona. On the southern outskirts of town, closer to the fabled city of Tombstone, there was a clandestine meeting about to take place. Once again, the gathering would be between the forces of good and evil. The location was a graveyard where two lovers were running and frolicking in the frigid evening air. The girl was jogging and tripped, ever so lightly, on the grass and fell to the ground, giggling. The young man fell gently on her abdomen. They kissed. They caressed one another and were fumbling for clothing, when the young man, Johnathan Silverstone, asked, "May I have a taste?"

The young woman pushed him away and started to stand, but then he said some more words, and after a few moments, they were kissing and caressing once again. "May I please have a taste, my lovely?" This time she wasn't so put off. This time she threw her hair back, which was an invitation to the young man to indulge himself for the first time with this lovely lady.

"Melissa, I wouldn't do that if I were you," came a voice from a slight distance away.

Immediately, the young woman's hand came up and stopped the young man from moving forward. The young couple looked in the direction of the voice. When there was no other response from that direction, Johnathon said, "Too late," and as he turned back to the beautiful auburn-haired young woman, his smooth face was gone. It was replaced by pure evil.

As he made his move toward the woman's neck, "Melissa, fight him off," came the voice from the same direction as before.

Silverstone started to make another move when he suddenly noticed there was a cross hanging around the young woman's neck. "Gotcha, big boy!" This time the voice sounded very close.

As the vampire turned his face in the direction of the voice, there was contact, and the monster went flying through the graveyard. A hand was extended to help Melissa Napier up, and there, standing above her, was her friend, Erin Hastings. Melissa screamed. Once she was finished with her panic attack, she exclaimed, "Erin, I thought you were dead."

"She is dead," Johnathan shouted. Then he began running toward the woods to get away from the female demon.

"I am," Erin calmly answered Melissa back. "But, right now, I'm here to protect you." Turning in Johnathon's direction, Erin shouted, "I am gonna put you down, forever!!" She threw a wooden arrow at his heart, but her aim was off, and it landed in his upper thigh instead.

"That hurts," the male vampire moaned. Then, he began shouting into the night air, "Brothers and sisters, help me with this." He paused to give his vampiric stare at Erin. While glaring at Melissa he said, "I could have made you immortal like her. You and I could have been together forever and made each other happy until the end of time."

Erin threw her head back and shouted, "I've heard that one before. I'm willing to bet your Master was waiting for you just at the edge of these woods and would have come out after you had incapacitated my friend here. Then you would invite all your friends to come and enjoy a taste."

"How do you know..." he screamed, as Melissa gasped into the night air. There was a sudden whooshing sound, and then, standing right next to the young vampire with the hole in his leg was the Master, Blakely Hoffenpiller.

"Shut up, Johnathon," the Master insisted.

"Hello, Love," Erin said, in a mock English accent.

"What's going on here?" questioned Melissa. She was startled by what had happened in the last two minutes and wanted to know what part she had in this situation.

"Melissa," Erin said in a soft but authoritarian manner, "this is going to get a little dicey. So, when I say run, I want you to turn to your right and run like hell. Whatever you do, don't look back."

"She won't get far," Master Hoffenpiller said with his voice full of sarcasm. "My colleagues will slow her progress. She'll be lucky if she can make it halfway. Go ahead and run if you want to." This Master vampire looked as confident as he sounded.

Suddenly, there were explosions to the far right and to the far left of Blakely Hoffenpiller. Erin shouted, "Go, now!" With a sudden burst of speed, Melissa turned and was sprinting toward the vehicle that was outlined in the glimmer of the night's full moon. Erin went to work. She crossed the expanse between the male vampire and herself in less than a second. Using her right leg, she swept the area where they stood, knocking both monsters onto the ground. Taking the hunk of wood from her back pocket, Erin jammed it into Johnathon's flesh. She missed his heart again, by mere inches.

"Blakely," Johnathan gave a high-pitched scream, "she has stakes. Who the hell is she?"

"A mistake! One which I plan to rectify right now!" the Master said, throwing his fist at the left side of her jaw. Erin blocked his blow, effortlessly.

Backflipping to give herself a bit of distance, she grabbed another two stakes from behind her backside and commented, "I may not be anything like Buffy Summers, but I've got enough going for me that I'm going to kick your a..." Before she had completed her sentence, she heard a scream. She turned to see Melissa being attacked by two lower life forms of the vampire clan. While Melissa fought for her life, two people popped out from behind the tombstones and attacked the henchmen. Erin turned her attention back to the two main troublemakers and said, "You didn't think I was dumb enough to come here alone, did you?" Then she added a sneer and yelled, "OK, ghouls, let's dance."

Realizing they were beyond their depth, both men jumped into the air and transformed themselves into ravens. As they floated away in the windy night sky, Erin looked out at the horizon to see the other ghouls slide back into the darkness and disappear.

She then turned and quickly sidestepped to her left. In seconds, Erin joined Thomas, who had been hiding with Jake, as they jumped out of the darkness to protect Melissa. Together, they subdued the beast to Melissa's right side. Melissa joined Jake, who was unknown to the damsel in distress and vanquished the second vampire with a stake that Erin had thrown to the FBI agent. She shouted, "Jake, here, use this!" Without hesitation, he slammed the stake into the sweet spot of the vampire; consequently, the beast was dust.

Standing in the partial moonlight, Jake said, "Let's get you guys into the car. Once inside, I don't care how many there are, they will not penetrate that car."

Tommy grabbed Miss Napier and herded her into the black Lincoln Continental. Placing her in the backseat, he felt a hand on his shoulder, Erin ordered, "You drive, ok, Tommy?" She slid in beside Melissa as Tommy jumped into the driver's seat. Before anyone inside the vehicle knew what was going on, he was driving 50 miles per hour, trying to get everyone out of the graveyard as safely as possible.

♦ ♦ ♦

It took almost an hour for all the beasts and ghouls to return from the graveyard to their comfortable abode. Johnathon Silverstone, being one of the first to return with Hoffenpiller, locked his gaze on his leader and asked, "What just happened back there?"

"If you know what's good for you, you'll keep your mouth shut so that I can think!" the Master ordered, using a harsh, evil tone. Then, grabbing a large iron goblet, he sent it sailing across the room. As it smashed into the wall, he shouted, "How could this be happening in my town? I own this sewer of a town. That little..." He stopped talking to think about the events of the last ninety minutes as the Warrior-King strutted into the room. "How did she come back?" the Master questioned throughout the cave, not expecting an answer. "We had that Napier witch! Johnathon had her in his grasp. Then, as if it was all in some unwritten plan, she slipped through our clutches like a princess of folklore."

The next voice to be heard was soft and supple. The voice belonged to the queen as she spoke, "Think back, Master Hoffenpiller. Is all as it seems?"

Blakely Hoffenpiller's body stiffened as he stopped spewing anger and started to think back of the night the ravaging of the young woman known as Erin Hastings had occurred. "It went like clockwork. Percy was brilliant. He worked her up, while we waited for the signal. When it came, we drank. We have been in this area for years. We knew what we were doing. That girl should have never left the graveyard alive!"

"And then?" The Queen's voice was hypnotic, nudging him to remember back to that evening all those months ago.

"We drank our fill and left her as a message to her father not to get in our way. Then we were gone into the night," he said into the still air of the room. However, he wasn't actually in the room. In his mind, he was at the graveyard, watching as he and his minions made a meal of the girl. He observed the members of his clan head back into the woods, himself included. He didn't speak as he continued to watch the body lying there. Suddenly there was some shuffling from the opposite side of the site. Out of the shadows of the tombstones, Hoffenpiller saw a tall young man step into the arena and bend over the girl, pouring something into the dead girl's body. She lay there for several moments. Then, her eyes fluttered open, and her arm rose up to brush the young man's face. The boy cut his wrist, and the girl drank from him. The Master screamed in anger. He shouted, "There's another player!"

"Another player?" the queen asked.

"Yes, the whelp, Arthur Kensington." Blakely, still in his semi-trance, continued, "He was working with Percy to get the girl. I think Arthur is with the FBI, but I thought he was on our side." The vampire made a twisted face and growled, "It seems Percy really loved the young woman, and he didn't want her to die after all."

"We can't love. At least, not their kind," the English Master insisted. "We stick to our own."

"Keep thinking," came the Queen's sultry voice once again. "This Erin should have been under Percy's control, which means that she should have been under your control, at least a little. Percy was yours to control, wasn't he?"

"Of course he was," was the Master's hollow reply. "But, she was not! I did not feel her at all," he stated, realizing this was a problem for their clan. A problem Blakely did not need at this time. "There truly is another player in this situation."

"What will you do now?" the Queen questioned.

"Find the whelp!" Then, as Blakely Hoffenpiller's rage filled the room, the leader of the clan turned and focused his gaze on the King and Queen of the North. He screamed his demand, "Bring me Arthur Kensington!"

♦ ♦ ♦

The door of the interrogation room flew open as Miss Melissa Napier sat inside, looking scared and confused. Her clothes were stained and wrinkled from head to toe. "Ms. Napier, my name is Angela Harrison. I'm with the Federal Bureau of Investigation." She flipped her credentials quickly at the girl so that Melissa could see her picture. Then she left the credentials lying on the table, as if she were trying to make a statement. This was the Agent Harrison show, and Melissa had a front row seat. "You were lucky tonight, young lady. Why in the world would you allow yourself to get in with a group like this?"

"Where is Erin Hastings?" Melissa asked.

"She's safe," Angela replied. "Now answer my question."

"No. I want to speak with my friend, Erin Hastings," the auburn-haired woman demanded. Her hazel eyes indicated she wasn't in the mood to be played with.

"Young lady, I don't think you understand what is going on here. Erin, along with my team, helped you out of a pretty tough spot tonight. Don't you think you could show us some gratitude by answering my questions?" Angela insisted.

Melissa swallowed hard, as if she were low on confidence but had large amounts of gall. She was a Napier, and 'we Napier's always get our way,' she thought. The stored up tension was going to unleash itself on everyone in the room if Melissa didn't get her way. "I am appreciative of what you all have done for me, ma'am. I know you know who I am, and who my family is. However, if you don't let me see my best friend, right now, I..." By this time, she was screaming.

The door burst open and in ran Erin. "Hey," she said, as she moved to hug her friend.

"Erin," Angela commanded, "I thought we had an agreement."

Backing away from Melissa, Erin turned to her boss and said, "Look at that face. Does she look scared or intimidated by you? Do you think you are going to get blood from a stone? Angela, give us a few minutes to be friends again. I know she will answer your questions once you let us talk first." Both Erin and Angela looked at Melissa, and then back at each other. "Won't you?" Erin asked, as she looked at her best friend again.

"Yes," was Melissa's calm and controlled answer. "I just want to know my friend's alright."

Jake stepped over and whispered something to Angela. She shook her head and then stepped out of the room. Erin asked him, "What'd you say?"

"I know you heard me," he said, smiling at the teenaged vampire. Then Jake and the other agents stepped outside the door, and he shut it.

"What did he mean by that?" Melissa asked.

"I have terrific hearing now." She paused, and then added, "Now that I'm dead."

The room went still. Finally, Melissa said, "I thought you were joking."

"I wish I were." Erin sat down at the table, thinking deeply about the words she just said.

Realizing what was happening, Melissa asked again, "So what did he say?"

Smiling, Erin said, "First, his name is Jake. He suggested to my boss that they give us some time together and maybe then you would cooperate. By the way, they are watching us. "They can see and hear everything we say."

"Erin," Melissa's tone was that of a best friend, "how are you?"

"Dead," was the first word out of her mouth. Seeing that these words stung Melissa, Erin then said, "But, I've been training and working hard to help my friends stop what is going on here in St. David."

These words seemed to relax Melissa as Ms. Hasting's grabbed a chair and moved as closer to her friend. Then she asked, "So what did happen to you, Erin?"

"Jake," Erin said in a firm voice. "show the tape."

The flat screen in the far upper corner of the room came to life and showed the requested video. Both young women watched Erin's death. Not only was there shock on the auburn-haired teenager's face, but the shouts of disgust and rage were those of a best friend who couldn't believe what she was seeing. After the tape was stopped, Erin explained, "Melissa, I'm sorry to have you watch this, but Angela believes there is an entire clan of these things in our town, and to be honest, I agree with her. I explained to my new friends that you needed to see this action uncensored so that you could understand what I went through. I am not going to let this happen to any more of my friends.

"What do you need from me?" was Melissa's question.

"Well, that's Angela's gig. She's brilliant. She's the one who suggested we watch the graveyards. In a way, I was glad it was you being attacked because that gave me a chance to help my best friend. I can't do anything about what Percy did to me. However, I found out that someone killed him. Your friend, Johnathon's boss, is the same man that controlled Percy. I want him."

Staring off into space, as if she were pondering the universe, Melissa uttered the words, "Well, then, get your boss back in here. I'll tell her everything she wants to know. But, I need you to stay in here with me, if that's ok?" She gave her long lost friend a shy smile that worked on almost everyone, then added, "Erin?"

"What?" came the vampire's reply.

"Thank you for saving my life. By the way, who's the hunky guy you're working with?"

"Hey, what are best friends for?" Erin quickly responded. Then, pointing to the people behind the mirror, she added, "Melissa, I know we're best friends and all, but when it comes to my team members, believe me when I say, we're not that close. Besides, he's way out of our league."

The door opened once again, and Angela, who now looked relieved, anxiously entered with her folders. Let the interrogations begin.

♦ ♦ ♦

The questions were non-stop for two hours. Finally, Erin said, "Ms. Harrison, I think that's enough for tonight, don't you?"

Angela's "glare-stare" meant that she was apparently not done yet. But, looking at the clock behind Melissa's head, which indicated it was 10:00 pm, Agent Harrison finally admitted, "Very well, that's enough for tonight. However, Ms. Napier, we will need to talk to you again, soon. Any information you give us, no matter how unimportant you may think it is, could really help us in this investigation."

"Of course, she will come back and help us," Erin said for the both of them. Melissa shook her head in agreement.

"We will escort you back to your car to make sure there's no one out there looking for some sort of revenge," Angela insisted. "We will then follow you home."

"Can that really good looking guy take me?" Melissa asked, looking at both Erin and Angela. "Hey, I can't help it. I've always liked older boys," she added.

"He can hear you!" Erin warned.

"I know." Melissa used her sexiest smile and a silky voice.

Erin, acting as if her best friend was stepping on her toes, looked at Jake through the mirror and said, "Can you say Jail Bait?"

While turning away so no one could see her smile at the juvenile adoration, Angela said, "He'll be glad to escort you." Then, turning her head to make sure Jake could hear her, she used her authoritarian voice to say, "Won't you, Jake?"

Someone threw the keys into the air and Jake grabbed them, signifying that he would follow orders. "I'm going along," Erin insisted, as if marking her territory.

"I'm going too," Tommy snorted out of jealousy.

Watching the four of them head to the outside door, Angela was worried this could prove to be a problem. However, she also knew that Jake was a professional and was sure all four of them would be safe. Once they were gone, she walked back to the office, which was full of equipment. Carrie-Anne, Charles, and the professor were deep into conversation.

"I don't know, Doc," Charles was saying, "I think you're wrong. The girl is not just an average teenager. I think she was giving information freely in there just to get out of that room. She's hiding something."

"Professor, I have to agree with my husband. I think she was just telling us what we wanted to hear to get out of the room," Carrie-Anne insisted. "She knows a whole lot more than she's suggesting."

"That may be so." All eyes turned toward Angela Harrison as she continued, "After Erin showed her the video, there was something in her voice, a type of recognition as to the situation. Besides that, she never once repelled from Erin, even after she was aware of the fact her best friend was now undead. I don't care who you are, if your best friend tells you she's dead, you don't just sit there like nothing is wrong."

"What should we do with the lovely Ms. Napier?" the professor asked, feeling as if he didn't get out enough to make decisions about people anymore.

"We keep our eyes on her. Don't let her out of our sight," Charlie - Boy insisted. "She is in the middle of this, I am sure of it. How do we know she didn't set up tonight's meeting?"

"How would she know anyone would be there to save her?" the professor questioned.

"We can't know if she did or didn't," Angela submitted. "Whatever the situation with Melissa, we know one thing," Angela stated. The other people in the room asked at the same time, "What's that?"

"We know there is a vampire problem in this town, and there are several players here, not just one master vampire. There are also drug lords, politicians, and Lord knows what else."

"So, what's our next move?" Charlie asked.

"I'm not sure," Angela said, moving toward the young techno-geek. "That could be up to you, Charlie-boy. You are the techno-wizard here. Can't you get us some information that would point us in the right direction?"

"I'm not sure I understand what you mean, Ma'am?" Charlie questioned as he looked for support from his wife and the good professor.

"If I wanted to talk to the people who planted Tommy here, the people who helped him bring Erin back to life," she watched his eyes as he seemed to be searching for an answer, the correct one to give her, "I might want to talk to the FBI agent in charge here."

His body language seemed to relax, giving the signal of relief. He now had direction from which to search for the answers he needed. He started pressing keys on his laptop at lightning speed. He started mumbling to himself as he continued to do his cryptic movements, and shouting words the other members never heard of. Carrie-Anne raised her shoulder, giving everyone the Italian salute, which meant, 'I got nothin.' He finally hit the keys with a flair that indicated he had an answer. "Angela, that person would be Agent James Stasher!"

An expletive escaped her mouth as she repeated the name. "Stasher?" Then her mind seemed to go somewhere else. When she realized that everyone in the room was watching her, she snapped back with, "Carrie - Anne, get Stasher on the phone and set up a meeting. He's smooth and slimy, Carrie, but don't take any guff from him. You make him come to us, here. Don't take no for an answer, and never take any crap from that agent." When she finished speaking, the muscles in her face were as taut as a twenty pound fish on a ten-pound line. As she stormed out of the room, the other members of the group heard her say, "I hate that man!"

Carrie smiled as she watched Agent Harrison walking down the hall. She looked up at Charles and suggested, "Geek - Boy, this just got a lot more interesting."

Chapter Ten

Acquaintances

As Angela stepped through the doors of the Tucson based FBI field office, she felt as if she had been punched in her stomach and all the breath was knocked out of her. She knew that James Stasher had no intention of coming to St. David to meet with her team. He would want her to crawl to him. The entire fifty-five-minute car ride north of St. David, she had fumed about Stasher. Jacob, who was driving, wondered if he had made a mistake and maybe should have let her come by herself. However, he also thought it was wise that he accompanied Angela, to keep her calm. The fact that they didn't say two words the entire car ride made him rethink that decision. She paused for a moment, stared straight ahead to steady herself, and then continued toward the reception desk, "Angela Harrison to see Mr. James Stasher," she announced. The woman behind the counter politely smiled a contentious smile while she spoke into the microphone of her headset. "He will be with you in a moment, Ms. Harrison, if you would like to have a seat in our waiting area," the woman suggested.

Angela turned her head to the left where Jake was standing and said, "I told you. Give me my five bucks. I'm leaving."

Ignoring her statement while placing the five dollars in her hand, Jake looked directly at the receptionist, and in his warmest, most sincere voice, he said, "I'm afraid you don't understand, Miss. We called and made an appointment, and, to be honest, we don't have time to waste."

The receptionist, who had been in this situation before, turned toward Jake and took a good long look at him. She appeared to be attracted to this new player in the welcoming drama, and her facial features began to relax. The receptionist gave agent Taylor her friendliest smile and informed him, "He's in a departmental meeting. As soon as he's..." She paused, as if someone was speaking to her on the headset, then continued, "He's ready to see you now. I would love to take you back if you would like?" The comment wasn't meant for Angela's benefit, and she knew it.

Angela, not buying the woman's instant change over, and said, "No, thanks. We can find it." Jake gave the receptionist an 'I'm sorry, I don't understand what's going on here either,' glance, then followed behind his boss.

"You like her," Angela suggested. "Can't you control yourself? It's not even a full moon yet."

"I am controlling myself. I was just flirting with the receptionist to get us back here more quickly," Jake explained. "You were acting a bit like George Patton."

"I'm not going to stand here and explain my actions, or why I'm feeling the way I am right now. Suffice it to say, I do not like this man, and you will find out very quickly why." She glared at Jake and commanded, "You will not be helpful to these people, especially James Stasher, you got that?" Her voice was firm, straightforward, and full of angst.

All semblance of trying to understand this situation was gone at this point, so he simply replied, "Yes, ma'am!"

Both agents turned to continue their journey to Stasher's office. Angela paused a moment, took a deep breath, and muttered, "Here we go." She knocked on the door. When it opened, there were several people inside the vast expanse of an office. All good manners were immediately thrown out the window as soon as Angela caught sight of James Stasher.

Angela completely surprised Jake by suggesting, "Jesus, Jimmy, are you that afraid of me? You have to be surrounded by your minions before you can face me?"

"Angela, long time no see," James answered back. James was taller than Jake, but somewhat portly. He was wearing a smart-looking pinstriped suit with a buttoned-down collar shirt. His face was slightly pitted on the right side; however, his left side revealed a more tense individual with wide-stretching worry lines. He appeared to be extremely nervous being in the same room with Angela Harrison.

"Enough of the pleasantries. And you can get rid of your protection detail." Angela's voice was venomous, as if she were a snake getting ready to strike!

"Angela, I'm the one in charge here. I know we don't have the best track record, but you will respect me in my office."

"See, Jimmy," the tone of her voice did not change as she continued, "that's where you are wrong. I will never respect you again. I can't believe they gave you this position. You left me in Missouri to die. You bastard! I will never forgive you for that. You cost several good men and women their lives. I can't forget that either! Jake here thought you might want to show me some consideration because of what happened in Missouri. Instead, you decided to pull another power play. He doesn't know you like I do. I expected nothing less from you. I will never forgive or trust you, ever again!"

Stasher stood there, taking it all in, and realized he was in way over his head with this woman. One of the other men in the room cleared his throat, stepped forward, and suggested, "Missouri is over, Ms. Harrison. I'm sure you are here to discuss St. David," the man said nervously.

Giving him very little notice, Angela ordered, "Shut up!"

The room was silent while Angela glared at the group of agents. It was Jake who finally tried to break the ice in the place. He whispered, "Angela, I can clearly see there are issues here, but this is getting us nowhere."

Jake softly touched her arm to get her back into the present. "This is not Missouri," he said, "and if you want to verbally tear this guy a new orifice in front of his peers, I'm in. However, we won't be helping our situation in St. David by doing that."

For the first time, common sense returned, and Angela took a deep cleansing breath. Then, she spoke, "Jake's right. We have other issues to discuss." She moved closer to Stasher and spoke softly so no one could hear her except for the man in front of her. "You should not be here, and we both know it. If you ever try to put me in my place again, I will destroy you. Do you understand me?"

"Uh-huh," was all he said.

As if a breath of fresh air had entered the room, Jake suggested, "Gentlemen, what's say we get down to business?"

♦ ♦ ♦

"Grandpa?" Melissa's Napier's silky voice rang out in the greenhouse. "Daddy said you were in here." She walked toward the area where she always found him, tending to his roses.

"Melissa," the Master Gardener answered, "what brings you to my neck of the woods?"

"It happened, just the way you said it would," she said, first looking at him and then at his nurse. She was choosing her words wisely, like her grandfather always suggested for her to do.

"Honey," the man said, "do you like lemonade?"

"You know I do," the young woman sighed. "Anastasia, would you please bring us some of your wonderful lemonade?" she asked.

"Of course," the nurse responded, and then was gone.

Watching her leave, Melissa said, "She's a good nurse, for an FBI agent. Are you going to keep her around much longer?"

When she turned toward her grandfather, he had already transformed into the slightly graying person that Melissa was very familiar with. She strutted over to him, sat on his lap, and gave him a kiss. "She has outlived her usefulness, but she is so very good at other things," the old man answered.

"Tell me about your adventures," he said in a soft, gentle voice.

"You were right," she said, standing and facing him. "Johnathon was making his move. and I was all ready to welcome him to the family when, out of nowhere, Erin showed up, kicking the crap out of Silverstone and his friends."

"Was the Vampire Master there?" he asked, excitedly. His eyes were about to pop from his head. "Was Blakely there?"

"Yes, he was there, but Erin handled him with ease. She's not like the brain-dead girl I used to know. In the past, I could get her to do anything. That's how we were able to convince Percy to turn her. She was so open to suggestions. Now, I'm not sure. It's like she matured or something."

"Don't worry about her, my dear," the Master Gardener said. "We will take care of her in due time. Was the traitorous Tommy with her?"

"Yes, Master, he was. But, he was relegated to wheelman and gopher." Melissa suddenly started to pout. "Why did you have to kill

Percy, Grandfather? He was my favorite toy to play with, and now he's gone. Now I have no one."

"Get Tommy here," the man ordered. "Then you'll have a new toy to pester and play with." The Gardener did not want to go any further with Melissa, so he ordered, "Now, you go get some rest. When you wake up, you need to find Mr. Arthur "Tommy" Kensington, and I don't care what it takes, you get him here."

A somber look came over Melissa's face. "No matter what it takes?" she asked.

The Gardener quickly reverted to his loving grandfather persona as the nurse returned with their drinks. Politely, Melissa took her lemonade. Then, she planted a light kiss on her Master's cheek and whispered, "Your will be done, Sire."

"Thanks for the cold drink, Anastasia. Have a wonderful day," Melissa exclaimed as she bounced out of their line of sight.

The Gardener's thoughts were solely on the revenge he was going to bring down on Tommy Kensington once he was brought to the greenhouse. That boy would soon be joining all the other bodies buried within his garden. "Humans make such great fertilizer," he mused.

"Did you say something, Sir?" Anastasia asked.

Once he looked up, he saw her pure, wholesome silhouette. The monster in his loins started to churn, and he could not help himself. He was on her in seconds. She tried to scream, but it was too late. One of his fingernails, which had grown long and sharp as a razor's edge, sliced through her throat, and she was silent. "Don't worry, darling," he said. "You're not ready for my garden yet. I will mend you when I'm through with you. I can't be killing FBI agents, or they might find me out sooner, rather than later. But, as long as I keep you alive and beautiful, and you continue and giving them the information that I feed you, all will be well."

She looked into the deep pools of his eyes, and she was gone, for now.

He licked the edges of the cut he had made. The taste of Anastasia's blood made his entire body tremble. As he kissed and touched the wound, the skin fused together, never revealing there had ever been a cut there. Eventually, he brought her spirit back long enough to achieve his sexual satisfaction. Once finished with her, he wiped her mind, as he had done many, many times before, and gently placed her on the table to sleep off the effects of his attack.

He was back tending to the flowers when she woke. She quietly rose and went back to work, never the wiser to what had happened to her. Being an agent in deep cover, she had told her handlers about the blank periods of time, but they could not conclude anything about the episodes. Therefore, they kept sending her back into the fray. As she started to leave with the beverage tray, she asked the old man, "Can I get you anything else from the kitchen, Sir?"

"No, thank you," he used a weak voice. "You have been wonderfully attentive, Anastasia." Because his back was to her, she never noticed the tentacles that were leaving his body and plunging into the earth below to find the life-giving nutrients in the bodies lying there. He felt the energy flowing back into his body. He started to sit up taller, and his skin tightened. The old man was feeling the youth flow back into his body that he had lost when he ravished the nurse. He was finally ready to take his vengeance on that little whelp Tommy, once he arrived.

♦ ♦ ♦

After the dust had settled from their first meeting in years, Angela and Jake sat across the conference table from the seven senior FBI agents, awaiting their next move. Not wanting to wait any longer, Angela said, in the most professional sounding voice she could muster at the time, "Explain to us what in the world is going on in St. David!"

One of the junior agents from the far-left side said, "Whatever we tell you, you're not going to believe us!" A variety of stares came from the agents across from Angela and Jake, making them uneasy.

"Try us," Jake snapped back.

"From the intel we have gathered, there are at least three, maybe four, special interest groups. There may be more; we just aren't sure yet." The agent's voice was nervous and full of speculation.

"Wait a minute," Jake instructed. "Everyone try to relax, take a deep breath, and start from the beginning."

The same agent started to speak. However, before he could get very far, Angela interrupted. "Jim, you're the agent in charge. You tell us what's going on."

Looking somewhat nervous, James answered, "I can't, Angela. I wasn't in charge here back then. I was given this position three months ago."

"Oh," both Jake and Angela said in surprise. "O.K. then, Agent..."

"Keller," the man filled in the blank.

"O.K. then," Jake continued the conversation, "Agent Keller, please give us any information you can."

"We received our first call a little over seven months ago. A boy," he said, sifting through the papers in front of him, then finding the name, "a Michael Hastings, called a drug hotline to report the name of Elizabeth Ruiz. She died while using drugs."

"What?" Angela asked.

"Yes, Ma'am. The reason it was sent to us was that the boy in question was the mayor's son," the man reported.

"We sent two agents to investigate this claim with the mayor. We wondered why the son had called and not the father."

"Where are those two agents?" Jake asked.

"They never returned," was the answer given by a man at the other end of the table. "We were sure the mayor was in on the whole drug issue in St. David."

"What did you do next?" Angela questioned.

"Very little, because we received this message." Someone pressed a button, and a voice that gnawed at both Jake and Angela stated, "We have killed your agents. Don't send anyone else here, or they will die."

"Is that the mayor's voice?" Angela asked them to play it again, then made an accusation. "So, because of this threat, you didn't investigate further?" Angela asked.

Stasher stepped in. "Angela, to make a very long and detailed story short, this situation has deteriorated into a firestorm of activity. Since I've come on board, things have turned from bad to worse. That's why I put in a call to your boss, Cline. I know you won't believe me, but I specifically asked for you. I told him not to let you come alone, and that while I have some insights through our intelligence, this case reminds me of," He paused for several moments, as if he didn't want to say the words, "Missouri, all over again."

"No way, Jim. We put that situation to bed." She spat the words at him as if his thoughts were some repulsive dream.

"Clear the room!" Stasher commanded to the other agents. "Jake, you stay." Stasher looked across the table at the young man and added, "Send in Agent Knight."

There was a flurry of activity, and six of the seven agents couldn't exit the room fast enough. After several moments, there was a constant tap, tap, tap of high heeled shoes, coming toward them. Suddenly standing in front of Angela and Jake was FBI Agent Kira Knight. "Kira!" Jake shouted with sheer delight. "It's you! But, I thought..."

The beautiful dark-haired woman stood five feet eight inches tall, with hard brown eyes. She was thin in stature, and every inch of her was pure business. It was apparent Asian blood ran through her veins. "Hello, Jake. I see you survived your wounds, as did I." Jake merely smiled.

"I've been told you're hunting our kind. Thing is, Jake, I like what I've become, and if I think you are even considering killing me, I will silver-slay you myself." She quickly sat down next to Stasher.

"What are you trying to do, Jim, square off against me?" Angela asked, with contempt in her voice. "Pit yours against mine?"

Stasher smiled at the comment. "Angela, that's your problem. You see this as a pissing contest, and it's not. Kira here did our best intelligence work. She got us all the good stuff." He pressed the button at his fingertips. A screen opened up, and a light hit the screen. Then, the first picture came up on display. "This is Mayor Bruce Hastings, of St. David, and this used to be his town. Now it's overrun," he pressed the button, and the next picture was of the ruling vampire, "by this guy. His name is Blakely Hoffenpiller. He is in charge of the nest that infests the area. It's a mix of undead, vampires, and things we have never seen before." He flipped through several pictures of the creatures that were growing into uncontrollable numbers in St. David. The next photo was of an elderly man. "This is Alden Napier, patriarch of the Napier clan. Don't let his looks fool you. He is the richest man in seven states, and extremely dangerous. About six years ago, this 'man for all seasons' changed. We're not sure why. It was noticeable because his enemies, or should I say assumed enemies, simply disappeared. He became a recluse. The man spends most of his time in his massive greenhouse. We have sent agents in there for several months now, and it seemed fruitless until two months ago. We were able to get one of our deep cover operatives in there, completely by accident. Anastasia." He flipped to a plain-looking woman's photo. He hit the switch again, and it was the same woman, but she looked as if she had a complete make-over. "We know, more or less, that she's been compromised. We just don't know how. She keeps giving us false information. We researched every word, but we kept coming up empty, until," he suddenly paused, "she mentioned Hornersville, Missouri." He stopped for a moment, waiting for some sort of reaction.

All eyes were on Angela. Jake asked, "What about Hornersville?"

"I'm not going there now!" Angela exclaimed. "Stasher, this is low, even for you." The anger on her face was unmistakable. Angela's eyes narrowed as she glared down at the man across the table from her.

"Look, Angela," Stasher continued to address her, "I didn't want to bring this up. I know you've always thought I screwed the pooch in Missouri, but I followed protocol in that situation. I am a lot of things, Angela, but I've never lied to you."

Silence took control of the room. Stasher's hand nervously hit the computer, and Jake looked for a change in the picture. Suddenly, with surprise in his voice, he said, "Hey, look, it's Tommy!"

Now, it was Ms. Knight's turn to react. "Sure is, but look in the background."

As Jake did so, he slowly moved his hand to touch Angela's arm. "Oh God, Angela, look! Look at the sign."

As she slowly tore herself away from glaring at James Stasher, her ebony skin went pale when she saw the sign that read, "Welcome to Hornersville." The date stamp on the photo read eight years earlier. He hadn't aged a day, or so it seemed.

The picture changed again. This time it was a picture of a man that Angela had also seen before. He wore long, dark hair with silver streaks starting at the temples. He was slight of stature, and he looked one thousand percent dangerous. This picture was also dated eight years ago. As another picture popped up, Angela became startled, and she suddenly fell back into her chair. Tears began flowing from her eyes. Everyone stopped and waited for her emotional response to subside. She couldn't stop crying for several minutes. Once she did, somebody from the group gasped when they noticed the date on the picture was three weeks ago.

♦ ♦ ♦

"Your usefulness has run its course, young one," Bethoon growled. "It will do you no good in this place." Arthur Kensington's feet were dangling just above the ground, and it didn't appear he would be touching the ground any time soon.

Tommy, who had been dragged away from a clandestine meeting with the beautiful Ms. Melissa Napier, now stood in front of the clan council. While others in the room were on edge, one person that wasn't intimidated was Arthur "Tommy" Kensington. "I don't see it," Kensington said with guile oozing from every pore. "If you're here, then Blakely has panicked," he added.

In less than a blink of an eye, Hoffenpiller joined Bethoon, and both monsters were in Tommy's face, glaring and sneering at the dog that was in their presence. Oddly, Tommy was smiling; he looked overjoyed at the fact that he was the center of attention. He started to educate them, "I am not working alone, you know. In fact, the late Percy Kensington was working with me, and my real boss." Everyone in the room stopped cold at the mention of Percy. "What?" Tommy looked surprised at their reaction. "I know he's dead. My boss had him killed."

All at once, a noise arose from behind the group in the cave. It was coming from the tunnel entrance. Everyone abruptly stopped moving when they heard a man's voice commanding: "Stop talking, Mr. Kensington!" All eyes were on the entrance as a young nurse appeared, pushing an old man in a wheelchair down the slope of the cave. The nurse stopped pushing at the request of the old gentleman in the chair. Anastasia was void of expression and movement once they stopped moving. The demons in the cave watched as the old man raised himself out of the chair. As he walked toward the group, he began evolving into a younger version of himself. "That's so cool," Tommy said, with a smile etched itself on his face. It took several minutes for the Master Gardener to reach the center of the cave. With no warning, as he knocked Tommy across the entire length of the cave. Everyone watched as Tommy crashed and landed on the dirt floor with a loud "Thump."

"Forgive him," the Master Gardener said. "He isn't housebroken yet, but I'm working on it."

The Gardener, also known as Alden Napier, began to laugh. "Alden Benjamin Franklin Napier at your service. You, my friends," He shifted his head so that he was looking at both entities, "you are messing up my whole business operation here. When I first was made aware of your presence, I thought you would be only a minor distraction. Now, things are getting out of control."

On the outer edge of the cave, Tommy struggled to his feet. While fighting to stand, he managed to make his way back to the three men in the middle of the cave. Napier continued to speak. "This klutz mucked things up," he said, nodding toward Tommy. "But we are not so far off course that we cannot put ourselves back on track to achieve the results that I desire."

Bethoon stepped toward the Master Gardener. Tommy instructed, "I wouldn't do that..." It was too late. The giant warrior, a self-made demon, grasped the old man by the throat and lifted him into the air.

Not saying a word, Napier began rising even further in the air, taking Bethoon with him. Shem started to bark and howl. Bethoon loosened his grip, and slowly, the Master Gardener brought them both back to the earth. Brushing himself off, the Gardener said, "I don't really know what drew all of you to this place, and frankly, I don't care. I was here before any of you, and I will be here after you. I don't know what your interest is with the mayor or his family; however, I have a clandestine meeting with a certain FBI agent, and you all are getting in the way. So,

I'm going to have to ask you all to back off. As for Percy," At the mere mention of his name, Hoffenpiller, Bethoon, and the queen reacted with blazing eyes and flaring nostrils. "Percy was working for me. Bethoon, if I were you, I would head back up north. I do not want to deal with you right now, but I will if I am forced to. I fear all this activity might distract me from my real purpose."

Bethoon stepped forward. Every inch of him displayed anger. As he took another step, his queen started to gasp. "I can't move," she told her king. It felt as if some invisible person had taken hold of her and was draining her of her life force. She struggled to gain relief from the thing that had hold of her. Bethoon stopped moving, and the queen relaxed.

"What are you?" Blakely Hoffenpiller asked.

"Something none of you can comprehend," Napier explained. The nature of his voice indicated he was getting bored. Searching his lapdog, he ordered, "Mr. Kensington, come! You have much explaining to do." Once Tommy moved near the Master Gardener, they started toward the mouth of the cave. Napier reverted back to the form of the old man. As they reached the wheelchair, he was still issuing orders. "You people stay down here and out of my affairs, and we will have no problems."

"This is our town," the leader of the vampires exclaimed. "We can't just stay down here. We need to feed."

"You can, and you will," the old man responded. "As a peace offering, I am leaving my nurse, Anastasia. I am done with her," Napier informed them. As Tommy started to wheel the old man out of the cave entrance, he continued to explain, "Once I leave, I don't know how she might react. Oh, and one last thing, she is an FBI plant. I don't think I would let her leave here." With that, they were gone from sight.

As the fog lifted from her head, Anastasia looked around the immediate area and saw nothing she recognized. She heard a small noise just beyond the scope of her early evening vision. There was a slight noise downward and just to the left of where the nurse was standing. In reaction to the noise below, the frightened young woman started to move backward. There was something about the dark void below her that made her want to leave, immediately. Suddenly, a beautiful vision of a woman stood before her. However, in an instant, the beauty of the woman was gone. Before

Anastasia could react, the woman's head was buried deep in her neck. "Relax, Anastasia," the female voice said. "You are with us now. We will care for you, and I'm sure, soon, you will want to take care of us as well."

"Ms. Harrison, I know of your accomplishments," Kira said. "But, I have done most of the recon in St. David in the last month, for obvious reasons." Her eyes were on Jake as she continued to speak. "I believe I could be of great help to you in St. David."

"Kira," Stasher interrupted, "we have not discussed this. Besides, Angela has her own team to assist her."

Kira's eyes seemed to glow blue in anger. "I'm a team player," she pleaded. "You've kept me under lock and key since I've been here." She then turned to look back at the two agents across the table. "He knows that werewolves and vampires don't mix," she said, pleading her case. "That's why they sent me in there. Let me work with you guys. Jake, let me work with you!"

In a low tone, Jake asked, "You realize what we are working with?" He paused, swallowed hard, then continued, "I'm working very closely with Ms. Hastings, and I can't allow you to hurt her or the relationship I have built up through time."

Interrupting Jake, Angela suggested, "Why not? The more help we have, the better."

Jake turned to his boss and cautiously said, "I don't know if that's wise right now. There is a full moon, and I am going to be gone at night. If she is what she says she is, neither of us will be good for anything for the next three days."

"I'll go with you," Kira said, cautiously. Suddenly, she stood, and without warning, she changed into an exact replica of Jacob Taylor. Next, Agent Knight became a werewolf, then Angela, and finally, James Stasher. As she switched back to herself, she explained, "I am what is called a Morphling. I can turn into both animate and inanimate objects. I have been like this ever since Waco."

Jake got up and was walking toward the back of the room, away from everyone. He turned and looked at Kira. "You weren't actually at Waco, Texas, were you? They pulled you out before it all went down, didn't they? In fact, if memory serves, I was the one who sent you out of there."

"Yes," Kira said with a twinkle in her eye. "But, I went back in for clean-up. You, if I remember correctly, were recovering in D.C., and frightening the snot out of everyone. We destroyed all the dead bodies and found several people like yourself. However, the beast in one of those other bitten casualties woke up before we were ready for him to. I was in the way. That beast was different, and now, so am I. I wish I hadn't killed him so quickly, so I could know who sired him. So, here I am, ready and willing to work with you, and for you, Jake." Her voice was soft and distinctively persuasive.

Her eyes looked eager, but it was Stasher's reaction to the situation that surprised Jake. Nodding in his direction, Taylor asked Jim, "You didn't know she could do this, did you?"

"No," was his reflexive answer. Then his eyes shifted toward Angela. "Kira would be good for this op. She is confident, hardworking, and I will be kept apprised on all phases in this operation, right?"

"Right," Angela responded. Suddenly, Jake realized that it was a done deal.

Jake looked at Angela and interjected, "I want some time for explanations."

"Sure, Jake." Angela was on her way out the door. Suddenly, she stopped, and turned on her heels, walked up to James Stasher and hissed, "I'm not done with you, Stasher. And, now that I know where you are, you had better be watching your back!" Then, turning to the new agent in the group, she commanded, "I want you out to our base of operations by 4:00 p.m. tomorrow. Is that a problem?" Angela didn't wait for an answer. "That will give you time to get acclimated to the change." She looked at her second in command and then added, "This is work, Kira. It is not a conquest or vendetta. Do you understand?" She turned back to face the slim, oriental statured woman with the narrow eyes and waited for a response.

"I understand," the newest team member answered.

"Angela," Stasher commanded, "She reports to me."

"Only after I am finished with her." Angela smiled as she said the words. Jake saw the smile; James never did.

James Stasher reached inside his pocket and pulled out his cell phone. He pressed the speed dial number and said into the phone, "Sire, they are on their way back, with the plant in place."

"Very good," the voice on the other end of the phone said, and then Jim's phone went dead.

Chapter Eleven

The Drop

The black Buick sedan rolled steadily down Interstate Highway 10, at the obligatory seventy miles per hour. Inside the vehicle, the two FBI agents who had been working together for the past several months said nothing to one another. Jake sat behind the wheel, driving, rotating between looking at the rearview mirror, the side mirrors, and staring straight ahead, just as he had been taught in Driver's Education all those years ago. Angela was also staring out at the highway, but her mind was actively searching for answers to questions. She was sure she hadn't found any answers yet. She looked over at her partner as he sat there stoically, not saying a word.

Softly, she said, "You alright there, Wolf-boy?"

Smiling, he answered with, "That's something Stasher might say, isn't it?"

"Not since Kira started working for him, I'd bet," Angela said, laughingly.

"She won't bite," he said, chuckling under his breath.

"I wouldn't be so sure of that," Angela responded, looking out the side window again. "She was saying all the right things, and you, my friend, are right in her crosshairs."

Jake surprised her when he asked, "Angela, are we friends?" His vibrant smile was gone. He looked anxious. Like a kid at Christmas.

"Yes," she said, without hesitation. "Why do you ask?"

"Tell me about Hornersville, Missouri," he requested.

A nervous laugh escaped her as she asked, "What?"

"Hornersville," he said, almost in a whisper, for fear of scaring her off. "Tell me what happened there. I don't really want to pry, but here we are, driving down the road with nothing to talk about, so..." He paused, glanced at her as if urging her on, then added, "And no one talks about it other than to bring up Missouri. I would just like to know what happened. You know my story, and how I arrived here at this point. But, I don't know anything about you."

She could tell he was nervous even bringing up Missouri, so, to calm him, she said, "I'll tell you mine, if you tell me yours." She started to nervously giggle.

"You already know all about me," he answered.

"I know what the reports say, that's it. I want to know what really happened to you in Waco." Angela looked straight at Jacob Taylor, waiting for a response.

"I'll tell you what," Jake replied, "I'm driving right now, so why don't you tell me what happened to you, and I'll tell you, as Paul Harvey was famous for saying, 'The rest of the story.' You can take over the driving while I tell my side of things. How does that sound?"

Angela turned her head and was silent for several minutes. She took a deep breath and let it out slowly. Finally, she started to speak. "This really isn't my story to tell. This story actually belongs to a guy by the name of Stark Hansen. In reality, it's his story, even though he's no longer with us. Ever hear of him?" she questioned. Jake didn't give an answer, so she continued, "He probably would have called his story 'The Drop,' but the name the government gave it was Hornersville, Missouri."

♦ ♦ ♦

The phone rang at 3:30 a.m. It was promptly answered with, "Hansen here." He listened for a few minutes, then said, "I can be there in 30 minutes, sir." He laid his cell phone down, jumped out of bed, and was in and out of the shower in less than five minutes. He dressed in fatigues, ate, and was out the door.

He made it to the base ten minutes later. Over the years, he had turned his Navy Seal body into a weapon, of which he was very proud. He knew the brass only called him when they had an exceptional operation that only a man with his particular skill set could do. He had no family to speak of. Stark had no time for relationships. Therefore, he was always available at a moment's notice. Hansen went through the entrance gates and was standing in the Commander's office door in a matter of seconds. Once inside he realized whatever the situation was, there were far too many high-ranking officials in one room for this to be an average operation.

"At ease, Stark," his Commander said. Then, a different man stood up.

"Son, my name is Admiral Constantine Mortenson." He walked around Stark as he stared straight ahead. "We have a situation in Hornersville, Missouri. When we ran all the scenarios on the computer, yours was the only name that came up." The Admiral stepped back, as if he were awaiting an answer.

Stark snapped to attention and asked, "Permission to speak freely, Sir?"

The Admiral said, "Son, You don't need to be so formal here. We are in a firestorm, and it is we who need you and your skills. So relax."

Stark relaxed his stance, and holding his voice steady, he asked, "What happened in Hornersville, Admiral?"

"It's the damnedest thing I've ever heard of, Lieutenant. Zero one-thirty, two days ago, on the rails outside of the town, not one, but two, trains derailed. One train was going north, the other going south. The chemicals that leaked out of the two trains combined to make a cloud that enveloped the entire town. From the reports we've gotten, only three people originally were infected because they were outdoors. They died immediately. Protocols were in place, and the town was evacuated and quarantined quickly. We went in and cleaned everything up. Finally, we asked the FBI to place agents in town to make sure everything was safe." His shoulders sagged, and he looked as if he were going to break down. Acting and sounding as if he were on his last breath, the Admiral continued, "At 11:30 p.m. the previous evening, some kind of 'thing' walked into Wright's Righteous Bar and devoured one of the town's citizens. Since that time, we have no idea who's alive and who's dead. All communications have been cut off. We need you to go in and be our eyes and ears." His voice wavered, as if he didn't want to say the words he was about to say. The strain on his 60 something veteran's body was evident. "We need someone to go in there, armed to the teeth, and report to us on what's going on." The Admiral looked into Stark's eyes as he said, "We sent several FBI agents in there, but we lost contact at 2:00 a.m. At 2:05, you were suggested. We all thought the town was safe or we would not have sent the people back to their homes and businesses. Whatever this 'thing' is, it came at us from out of the blue."

"At best," Hansen's commander, who continued the briefing, said, "if you drop in from above, try to find a tall building, an overlook, then make your move. If you find anyone alive, get them out, unless they've been," Stark's commander seemed to be struggling to find the right words, "turned. In that case, destroy them at your discretion. From the intelligence we've been given, these things are aggressive and chew through flesh as if it were Cool Whip."

"Your transportation is fueled and on the tarmac," added a third person, a female captain. Her voice was hard and raspy. "Get in, and get out, as quickly as you can, Lieutenant. If you or your position are compromised and you need to get out, you will have to make it to the outskirts. We have set up a seven-mile circumference. From the east side of town to the west is seven miles. If you are at the center, then the city is about three miles out. The FBI and Homeland Security will be awaiting your arrival. They have been ordered to kill on sight anything that doesn't look human. They have your photo and pictures of all the FBI agents, police, and county sheriffs in Hornersville, and will allow you all to pass."

"Sir," Stark Hansen addressed his commander, "you're sending me on a suicide mission."

"No, Son," answered the admiral, "we are sending you on a rescue mission. You are the only person alive who can make it out of whatever hell has taken over that town."

After several moments of silence, Stark was given as much Intel as there was available. After ten minutes of briefing, he was put on the delivery system that would take him to Hornersville. It looked like the military version of the old Sky-vans he used to jump from when he was learning the process while he was still in high school. An hour and thirty minutes later, he was given the sign to drop, and he did. While slowly gliding toward Hornersville, he looked for the tallest building. Then he noticed something that looked as if the street were moving.

He watched the mass of those things below, reminding him of a snake slithering up the street. They were trying to force themselves into a building. Straining his eyes to look for a proper place to set down, he noticed a light flashing from a window. That meant that someone was still alive. They must have seen him floating through the early morning sky. Eyeing a five-story building to the right of the flashing light, Stark pulled his parachute guidelines taunt, which allowed for a soft landing on the hard roof of the building. He quickly unhooked himself, then rolled his chute and tucked it away. It was an hour or so before dawn. Stark set to the task of getting himself prepared for what would come next. He found the neck strap and arm and leg guards the officials had given him and put them in their proper places. Stark needed to be invincible, with these straps and guards were just the right equipment to assure him of that. He then cautiously looked for the front of the building and ambled toward the edge. Peering down, he saw what he didn't want to be seeing.

Stark saw an uncontrollable horde. They were stabbing, slapping, and tearing at the building they wanted to attack. Suddenly, shards of glass exploded outward from the structure, leaving a hole in the mass of fallen bodies, and of the walking zombie-like creatures. Nine people burst through the opening and started toward another building. People at the rear of the group had handguns, and one person had a shotgun. They were firing into the mass of zombie-like people. From the building where Stark saw the light, there were also shots being fired, dropping a few of the walking dead. Stark was aware of his orders, "Get as many people out as you can." The Navy Seal pulled out his silencer and quietly twisted it on to his modified military-issued forty-five caliber Glock pistol. Once in place and ready, he waited for the people in the other building to shoot. Then he aimed right into the midst of the undead. In four seconds, six zombie-type things fell. The people from the other building stopped shooting. They had to realize by now that it was him firing into the crowd. He watched for the curtain to move, and it did. This time when they shot, four of the things fell to the ground. He was grateful for the help, whoever it was. He fired the rest of his clip, and more victims fell.

Stark rolled back from the edge of the building and began to stand up, when he heard a voice. "Who is the filth that is killing my children?" Lieutenant Hansen duck-walked back and cautiously looked down. In the middle of the zombie-like group stood a man with piercing eyes and long black hair. As the sun was starting to rise, Hansen spotted silver streaks of hair at the man's temples.

Stark Hansen took careful aim at his next victim. "Dude," he thought, "your time is done," and he took his shot. As if the demon knew where the weapon's discharge was coming from, the Dark Man grasped the bullet out of thin air.

The man turned his head and was looking straight at Stark. "Bring that defiler to me!" the man bellowed. Stark, who had a full clip, emptied it at the man.

The Dark Man grabbed one of the undead as a shield. Four of the rounds entered the drone's head. Stark Hansen, who was standing on the roof, realized the monsters were headed toward him. The Dark Man had thrown the bullet-riddled corpse down and was glaring in Stark's direction. In an instant, Stark fired three shots and hit the mysterious leader in the forehead. He watched as the man fell. Stark Hansen let out the first full breath he'd taken since he had landed. However, his moment of relief ended when his target stood back up. The naval expert reloaded and shot again. This time, the drones were in front of their master. The bullets managed to bring down seven of the undead creatures. The Dark Man let out a howling scream, and the ground seemed to tremble, as all the undead around him seemed to shrivel up, like prunes, and fall to the ground. It was as if the man had absorbed their energy. The Dark Man stood there, and as Stark watched him, the monster was making the bullets twist backward out of his forehead. The holes in his head were closing. "You are in way over your head, Soldier. You will be mine very shortly," the man shouted.

Stark knew he was up against someone he couldn't beat, but that thing wasn't going to stop this soldier's mission. There had been about thirty dead zombies that were used to revive this Dark Man. Stark knew the evil man could be hurt. Maybe, with a little luck, he could kill him. Hansen needed to get off the roof and make it over to that other building where he had seen the lights. As he turned, he saw several of the zombies had made it up to him, coming from through the building. He shot several of them in the head, and they fell. Hansen moved through their line, searching for a way to get to the next five-story building to his right. He threw his duffle bag to the next building over. After holstering his firearm and putting on his backpack, Stark launched himself into the air. He saw he had plenty of room to land, so he tucked and rolled. When Hansen stopped moving, the Navy Seal grabbed his gun. He was ready for anything, but nothing happened. He looked for an opening in the roof, but nothing seemed promising. Hansen grabbed his duffle bag and started toward the door of this new building. The door suddenly burst open. Stark took one look and started shooting. While slowly moving backward one small step at a time, the Navy Seal continued to drop the mind-controlled beasts. He had to reload several times, but he shot them all with point-blank accuracy. Hansen was very frugal with his ammunition. One bullet for each thing, no more, no less. He looked around and thought, "What a waste!"

Stark cautiously opened the door and took three steps down. He looked around, then took five more steps downward. While making the minimal amount of sound, Hansen continued down the stairs until he made it all the way to the ground level. He found an entrance to the basement, but it was bolted shut. He jerked on the door and then whispered, "My name's Stark Hansen. I've been sent in by Admiral Mortensen to get as many of you out alive as possible. If you can understand me, open this door." He waited, but there was no movement or sound. "Once I leave, I can't come back. Too many people depend on me," he added. He waited again and then started to move away when he heard something. He turned just in time to see the door handle move. As he started toward the door, he heard something from behind him. The undead were waiting in the shadows for the door to open. "Lock it back up!" Stark shouted, then started shooting. Within moments, his attackers were down and out. He had armored himself with a Kevlar mesh material, so they couldn't bite, scratch, or do anything else to hurt him. He was also wearing specially designed clip belts, and he now understood that he would be using much more ammunition until all the clips ran out. The canvas straps crossed his chest and back, making him look like Poncho Villa. He went back to the door. He could hear sobbing now. " They are all gone now," he said. "When you have calmed down, let me in." The door lock clicked, the handle turned, and he slipped inside.

He glanced around. "They were waiting for you, or rather, for me to get you to open the door. They're smart and well organized," he said, talking to the adults in the room.

"No, they're not," a girl of about fifteen years old said. "They're dumb. Some guy out in the street is controlling them."

"Yeah, who is that guy?" Hansen questioned.

"Don't know," one of the older adults said. "It used to be a guy by the name of Harry Trent. He was really well liked, but I watched for myself as Harry shifted into that," He paused and swallowed as if in disbelief, "that thing."

Stark set his duffle bag down, and then lowered his backpack as well. He dug through one of the pouches and pulled out a radio. "This here's to keep in contact with me." He looked around the room and then handed it to the young girl who had spoken before. "There are a lot more of them than me, but if you can be patient, I am going to attempt to get as many of you out of here alive as I can. That's what I've been sent here to do."

"You got any food in that bag, Mister?" one of the young boys asked.

He reached down into the bag and pulled out four pouches of beef jerky and threw the pouches to four different people. "Share," was all he said. Then he added, "I don't have extra water, and I wouldn't drink the tap water. It could be contaminated."

"We've got six cases of bottled water over there," the girl's mother said, while pointing to a stack of bottles.

"I gotta go," Stark said breathlessly. "But, you listen to that radio. I promise I will return for you!" They could read the sincerity in his eyes. "Keep that door locked at all times!" Then he asked, "Is there an outside entrance into this basement?"

"Yes, Sir!" one of the smaller boys said. He led the soldier to the back of the room as the others followed him. There were two metal doors installed there with windows on either side. Someone had taped paper over the windows so no one could see out or in. "That was my idea," the little boy informed him. "Our teachers do that at school to protect us from unwelcome visitors."

"Smart teachers," Stark remarked as he removed the bar from the door. "I don't know what's going to happen once we open that door, but..."

"You got any more weapons in that bag, Mister?" one of the middle-aged men in bib overalls asked.

Stark slowed his movements for a moment and looked at all of them. "I wish I could share them, but I can't. However, I am going to leave that duffle bag here. What's in there can only be used as a last resort, and we are not there yet. I'm truly sorry you are all in this fix. If I'm not back in twenty minutes, or haven't radioed you in that same amount of time, then none of us are leaving here alive." He studied them for another moment and added, "I see several of you have clubs. If they should break through, aim for their heads. Don't hold back, you got me?"

The group all nodded. The soldier managed a sad smile. "I can't leave any weapons right now, but if I come back, I should have some extra then. Hang in there, folks. Now," He started to psych himself up by taking deep breaths then suddenly he said, in a raised voice, "Once I'm out, you shut and bar that door and leave it that way. No excuses. No excuses, no matter what you see or hear!"

A hand was upon him. He turned to see a woman in her late twenties. She kissed Stark on the mouth and said, "You take care now, ya hear?" Then, the men who were operating the door, opened it, and he was gone. The group of abandoned people quickly barred the door shut behind him.

♦ ♦ ♦

"I don't know how he did it, Jake, but Stark Hansen made it to us in about an hour after he was dropped in Hornersville. He came up through the cellar doors of our building, dropping anything and everything that got in his path. We were the light that he saw when he first dropped in. There were three of us left. When we saw him moving toward our building, Harkenson, Stasher, and I decided to make a break for it. We were holding our own, but when he broke through the line of dead corpses downstairs to meet us, we thought we were safe. He escorted us back to the basement. As we moved down to the room, we must have passed thirty or more bodies, all shot in the head. We took a moment to introduce ourselves. He did the same and then said, "I need to take you back with me to another building. Are there any others left in this structure that you know of? Have you got any extra weapons?"

"No, and no," Stasher nervously shouted. "Let's go."

Stark looked at Stasher and ordered, "Calm down. I think I've bought myself some time, but I don't know how much at this moment. Are you sure there's no one else in the building?"

I stepped forward. "Truth is, we are not sure." My voice was hoarse from all we had been through. "We barricaded ourselves in one of the rooms up there and have been fighting that mob ever since. It was when we saw you, and you continued shooting them in the head, that I realized we might have a chance of getting out of here alive."

"I need to search the rest of this building," Stark insisted. "I wouldn't feel right..." You could see the guilt all over his face. He wasn't going to leave any human being behind. "Will you help me?" He looked right through me. He knew I was scared, but there was something about him. I just felt I would be safe.

"I'll go with you," I said. "But, there's a problem. I have no..." Stark reached into his bag and pulled out four clips and a pistol for each of us. It was standard issue FBI arms and ammunition. We all locked and loaded.

Stark gave James one of his own radios and ordered Harkenson and Stasher to close the door and lock it behind us. He also told them if we weren't back in 20 minutes, to get to the fifth building down and pull those people out of there. We were in the hallway in a matter of moments. As we turned the first corner, Stark dropped two of the Dark Man's drones before I could blink. He was good at his job.

He turned, smiled, and informed me, "I knew they were there. This Master guy has some link to them. If they were here, that means there are most likely more people upstairs. Harrison, you got my back?" He smiled as he asked the question.

I reflexively said, "Um – huh." We both chuckled.

We heard a sound from above, and we paused. Then, he whispered, "I'm the one with the silencer, so let me shoot first. You shoot only if you have to." He then started to move toward the stairs.

We scampered up the stairs and discovered that the noise was only a cat. I shushed it away, and we started knocking on doors. There was no response until we were at the end of the first-floor hallway. The door opened, and there stood an elderly couple. They had two of their grandchildren with them. We took them all with us. Hansen's patience was spectacular. He told me to wait with the grandparents and children while he went to check the upstairs. He was back in ten minutes, and we all headed back down. That was when we heard the helicopter. Stark cursed, and we all ran back to the basement. There, we discovered Harkenson had been knocked out. "Stay here," Stark told us as he ran down the steps and outside. Standing there, Hansen watched as Stasher had taken off in the helicopter. He had used the radio to override Stark's authority and get himself out of the danger zone.

As Hansen stood there, he knew he was out in the open and that he would be seen. He ran in the opposite direction, taking all of those monsters and their master with him. Once the undead had passed by the building, I helped Harkenson to his feet. Then Stan and I led the people to the fifth building down, the exact place the former Navy Seal had told us to go. We pounded on the door, and the humans inside let us in, no argument. We were safe for now. Stark, on the other hand, had about fifty or so of those drones, those monsters, trailing after him.

♦ ♦ ♦

Being the good soldier, Stark Hansen looked for cover and began picking the monsters off two at a time. Then he would run up ahead to another spot and pick off a few more. Eventually, he was far enough ahead of his pursuers, and he found a point where he could climb a tree. Using it for camouflage by hugging the large tree branches, Stark had gained the high ground on them. As they moved past where he was, he got behind them. Stark then headed back to the people in the building. What he wasn't expecting was the Dark Man. The evil man had lagged far behind his minions, to insert himself between Stark and his way out. With the Dark-Man to his front, and the zombies to his back, Hansen leaped out of the tree and started running straight toward the villain, putting five rounds right into his forehead. Next, he pulled out a machete, which had been sheathed under his backpack. As the Dark Man tried to recover from the shooting, Stark lopped his head clean off of his shoulders. Picking up the man's head, he turned and faced the mass of zombie followers. They stopped immediately. "I've killed your Master. Now back the hell up!"

Hansen felt something grab his foot. It was the Dark Man's hand, attached to his fallen body. Outraged by what was going on, Stark flung the head to the far right, kicked his way free, and ran back to the building to get the old couple, Harkenson, and Harrison. But, when he got there, they were all gone.

Stark knew that Angela Harrison was a leader, and he also knew that once she realized what he had done, she would get the others to safety. So, he decided to backtrack just far enough to discover that all the zombies were shriveled up, much like the scene he saw earlier on Main Street. The Master was gone; the strange man had healed himself again. Quickly, he ran back to the building where he had left the first group of people. Hansen banged on the metal door, and to his surprise, there stood Harrison, Harkenson, and the others. Sarcastically, he asked, "Did you miss me?" while walking through the door. The boy behind him set the bar in place again. Turning to Harkenson, he asked, "What happened with Stasher?"

Harrison threw Hansen a bottle of water while Harkenson explained, "You guys were still in the hallway when he turned on me and knocked me out," Stanley said. "He even tied me up like I was to be sacrificed. I can't wait to run into him again."

"Harkenson," Hansen said, "I need your help. I need to get over to another building across the way. I know of at least nine people who are in that building. They got away from that thing out there in the streets. But, I don't think I can take on the Dark Man alone. Will you help me?"

"What about me?" Angela Harrison asked. The female FBI agent looked disappointed that he had not asked her to go with him this time.

Looking at everyone in the room, Stark said, "I need to talk to Harrison alone." Staring at the bloody bruise on Harkenson's head, Stark ordered, "Can someone patch Harkenson's head and then get everyone ready to leave this place?" He quickly surveyed the room and then asked, "Have you got any newspapers or magazines down here?"

One of the older men took Stark back through the expanse of the basement and showed him a giant pile of newspapers and magazines. Stark Hansen dug down into his duffle bag and pulled out four rolls of duct tape. He demonstrated what he wanted to be done to one of the younger boys by wrapping the magazine around the boy's arm and then taping it in place. Then Stark moved to the legs. Finally, he carefully placed the more flexible newspaper around the young boy's neck. Once he finished with the boy, he ordered the other adults to do the same for every child and adult in the room.

As the adults went to work on one another, Stark grabbed Angela Harrison. Moving her over to the side of the room, he told her everything about what had happened to him since the drop. Once he was finished with his explanation, she asked him, "Why are you telling me all this? You have to make it out alive!"

"Angela," he said, "did you not hear me? I cut the man's head clean off, and he is still alive. Besides, if you could have seen Admiral Mortensen's face, you'd realize that this thing has to be stopped. We can't let that thing live, no matter the cost."

"He can't have many more things left to kill. You are killing them as you find them. The Master is killing his worker-zombies for his survival, so there can't be that many of the zombies left." Angela replied.

As if he had seen the light, he answered with, "You're right! However, as a precaution, get this letter to my Commander, would you?"

"I'll take this letter, but I'll give it back to you when we are done," she said.

For the first time, Stark Hansen stopped talking and just stared at the woman across from him. Finally, he began, "Angel, is it ok if I call you Angel?" He stood there waiting for an answer that never came. "I'm pretty much a loner, most of the time. The government sends me on these missions, I complete them, and then I wait for the next one. However, this time things are different, because you're here. We are fighting for our lives, and yet, all I want to do is stop and be with you. I spend most of my time running away from people, but when I'm near you, I want to get even closer. I can't explain it, but it's like God dropped you off here to be with me. I know it sounds crazy, but it's the way I feel. But," He paused, as if he was having difficulty finding the right words. Then, slowly, continued with his thought, "The guy that's running this show is searching for something, and I get the weirdest feeling it's you. I won't let him have you. Do you understand?"

Angela took Stark's hand and kissed it. "I know how you are feeling," she stated. "It was so electric when I saw you in the hallway. At that moment I just wanted to run away with you. Hansen, thank you for telling me how you feel. I, too, think we are meant to be together too. So you go do what you do, and we'll meet up after. I'll make us a home cooked meal, and what happens, happens. How's that sound?"

He gave her an all American smile. "You cook?"

"Can I cook? You just go do what you gotta do, and I'll show you how good I can cook."

He nodded and said, "That sounds good to me." When they walked back to the others, they were all wrapped up and ready for what came next. "You little ones stay by Angela," Stark instructed. Then he looked at the other FBI agent in the room. "Stanley, are you up for this?"

Nervously, Stanley said, "Ready as I'll ever be."

Next, Stark Hansen started addressing the group. "I was told that the military, homeland security, and the FBI were going to be waiting for us about two and a half miles from the town. First, though, I've got to grab the people I saw when I first dropped in. Stanley and I are going to do that, but I could use one more volunteer to go with us." The old man who was holding the shotgun stepped forward. "Leave the shotgun, and use this," Stark said. He reached under his vest and gave the older man a gun just like his, but with no silencer. Then he grabbed four more clips from his belt and ordered him, "Chamber a round. Should you need more ammo, you and Stanley can take it from the back of my belts. I'll use the front." Both men nodded, and then fell in line behind Hansen. Stark then commanded Angela, "Ms. Harrison, you choose a direction. I don't care which way you go, just go. If you run into any problems, use the radio I gave you. We're going to try and keep the attention on us. When you make it to the outside, you tell the powers that be to send in everything they've got because whatever is out there waiting for us knows that we are in here looking for a way out."

Harrison nodded at Stark. Next, he focused on the children and teenagers. "I can't guarantee your safety, but what I can promise you is that this woman will get you out, or die trying. You listen to her, and you will be fine. Now go!" His voice was loud and powerful. He knew the risk. He knew the problems of the plan. But they had to go, and go now. The boy who barred the back door before, unbarred it. They were out the door and on the blacktop in moments. "Ms. Harrison?" Hansen called to her softly, causing her to hang back. Stark walked up to her, lightly touched her, and kissed her soft, awaiting lips. "In case I can't do that later," he said with a smile. Then Stark, Harkenson, and the old man walked over to the door that led to the inside of the building. He instructed the old man and Stanley to stand back about fifteen feet from the door. Hansen released the deadbolt lock and turned the handle to allow the door to open. After a few seconds, the door burst open, and the beasts roared in. Each man's aim was deadly, and the zombie-like creatures fell to the floor as if in slow motion. Once the flow of monsters ended, Stark withdrew his machete and sliced at one of the undead's legs. He needed one alive, but it was too late. He had not told his other two partners what he wanted. Once the last beast fell to the ground, both the old man and Harkenson made sure the victim would not get up again. The three men stood there for several moments, getting their bearings. "This is not good," Hansen declared, as the three-man crew stepped over the bodies and into the entranceway of the building. Hansen motioned for the other two men to follow him, though they hung back to give him cover. Suddenly, Stark ran across the street to the building he had seen the nine people go into when he had first arrived. The soldier motioned the other two men across the street. They were there in an instant. "We're going in." He tapped the older man, "You go left. Harkenson, you've got the right. I'll take the middle. Shoot anything you don't recognize as human. One more thing, fellas," he paused to swallow hard, as if the words were sour to his taste, then he continued, "if either of you gets taken, or something bites you, I will take care of you. I expect the same consideration."

"Name's Pouch," the old man said.

"That's good to know, Mr. Pouch. Let's move."

Both men nodded in agreement. Hansen kicked the door open, and the things attacked on all sides. All three men shot their attackers in the head, and they fell like stunned animals and did not get up again. Once they were all down, the two men beside him relaxed. "Don't relax," Stark cautioned. "Keep your eyes open and stay frosty. There are probably more of these things waiting for us. I think we need to follow the bodies," he added. All three men were back to back to back. They moved as one single unit, inching toward the stairs on their far left.

Once inside the stairwell, Stark took the lead. They were up to the second floor in two turns as he said, "Stan, grab that door. When I tell you to, open it." Hansen had moved Pouch to a spot above them in the stairwell. He waited a moment and said, "Go!" Stanley grabbed the handle and ripped open the door. Stark stepped through the doorway. Nothing was there. He stepped back into the stairwell. "It's must be the next floor," Stark said.

They moved on to the third floor. Again, Stanley Harkenson grabbed the door handle and opened it. Stark stepped through the door and found three dead zombies. Once the three men were inside, they spread evenly across the full hallway and moved through it. At the same time the door behind them settled shut with a loud thud. Four zombies, who heard the noise, came around the corner and moved straight toward the three men. None of the men missed their targets. When no more zombies came to greet them, Hansen yelled, "Those of you from the street this morning, my name is Stark Hansen, and I've come to get you out." Everything went quiet. While the three men stood there, they scanned the hallways, high and low, for any sign of life. Suddenly, there came a small squeak, and the sound of a door opening. All nine-people poured into the hallway, along with six others who were with them. They all appeared to be composed and healthy.

Someone from the back of the group said, "Hey, is that Mr. Pouch? Hey, Mr. Pouch, is that you?" The old man at Stark's side never said a word, but there were smiles all around.

♦ ♦ ♦

"So, once you two separated, what did you do?" Jake asked Angela as he continued to drive toward St. David.

"I had to get those people out of Hornersville," Angela fired back at her partner. Then she continued on with her story. "What I hadn't realized at the time was that I had seen too much. There was no way that whoever was running this show could let me, or the other people, leave Hornersville alive. Stark Hansen knew that. That's why we split up. There was no way this Master of evil, could let anyone know what was going on in the town. I followed the instructions that Stark gave me. According to the map I had, there was a side road that led to the outskirts of the town, and it wasn't very far from where we were then. I took a position in the front, but kept my people within arm's reach. We made it to the blacktop road with no incidents. We turned left and headed straight out of town, with little resistance. Stark had given me the rest of the clips that were in his duffle bag. Plus, we had salvaged clips from the other agents who had come with us and didn't make it out alive. We passed a significant portion of the buildings and headed toward the edge of town. The sun was finally up, and we had visibility for at least seven miles. We could see the military vehicles approximately two miles from where we were.

Slowly, cautiously, we moved toward the edge of the town, but we were suddenly caught off guard. Standing in front of us were several FBI agents. We were so excited to see the emblems on their jackets that we didn't realize that all of these agents were made up of the walking dead. They were the remains of the people who had come with us that didn't make it. Some of those agents used to be my friends, and now I, along with the men, women, and children with me, would have to battle the undead FBI so we could escape this town. One thing I have never understood was when the National Guard members and bureau investigators saw us, and saw the zombies, why didn't they come in, guns a blazing, to help us?

Of course, that's when the Dark Man came from behind the dead agents to take control of the situation." He smiled. "Angela, it's so nice to finally meet you. I have heard so many wonderful things about you from my friends here," he said.

"Let us pass," I ordered, raising my weapon to aim right between his eyes.

"You misunderstand me, Sweetie." His face was smug and full of confidence. He had a Fu Manchu styled mustache that was getting longer while we spoke. "All these people here with you, they can leave, as long as you stay."

"You're just going to let everyone go as long as I stay?" she asked.

"Yep, you got it," he said with a smirk.

"Who are you anyway?" I asked, stalling for time.

"Who I am, doesn't matter, does it?" He answered my question with one of his own. "You've been here for two days. You've seen the devastation. This is your chance to get your new friends out. All you have to do is agree to stay with me. This is a one-time offer. I will need your answer relatively quickly."

"Why is that?" I inquired.

"Because I understand what you are doing," he said, brimming with satisfaction. "You are stalling. You are waiting for that young Navy Seal friend of yours to come and save you. But, that's not going to happen." With a quick snap of his fingers, a building behind us collapsed to the ground.

I turned and watched as the cloud of dust and destruction enveloped us, My heart sank to the pit of my stomach. I turned, and when I did, the Dark Man was ten feet away from me, and the group I was sworn to protect. "Who are you?" I asked again, demanding he tell me his name.

"Angela, I told you, it doesn't really matter," His voice was amusing and lyrical

He reached out, and as I turned to the people who were depending on me. "Go," I told them. Then came their cries of "No," and, "We can beat this guy." I shook my head. They were in denial. "I want your word you won't harm anyone in this group, and you will let them go to safety," I finally said to the Dark Man. Regardless of what happened to me, my priority was getting these people out.

"You have my word..." Suddenly, from behind him, where so many undead were standing, the ground erupted with explosive violence. I thought it was from the National Guard, but it wasn't.

One of the children from the group yelled, "Hey, look!" As I turned, I couldn't believe what I saw. It was Stanley Harkenson, carrying a grenade launcher. He fired one round. He was every bit the hero I knew he could be.

"Get down," Stanley ordered. To his left was Stark, who now had his duffle bag on his shoulder. Opposite him, was Mr. Pouch. Behind the three men stood the people those men had saved. Those in my group fell to the ground as the monsters approached us. Stan launched another round of grenades, which landed just behind the monsters. Once the smoke cleared, the entire FBI undead squad was dismembered and scattered all around the area.

While the crowd of people gawked at all the victims of the grenade attack, the Dark Man stretched out his arm, and a bolt of lightning shot out of his hand and hit Stanley, knocking him back about ten feet. Stark ran back to his new friend and checked for a pulse. Nothing. Then, in one smooth movement, Stark pulled out his pistol and emptied his clip into the smiling buffoon less than ten feet from me. The Dark Man fell to his knees again, but this wasn't over. Five feet away from the demon, a vortex opened, and the picture of fear that had been frozen on the face of the Dark Man was unmistakable. He was afraid! When I looked back at Stark Hansen, he had reloaded and was walking straight toward me. While Mr. Pouch had joined him, and they continued to move toward my group and the Dark Man. And you know what Jake?"

"What?" Jake asked.

"They looked pissed!"

♦ ♦ ♦

As the two heroes and the people they saved approached Angela's group, it was Mr. Pouch who ordered, "Everyone lay down until we finish this!" Everyone obeyed and lay flat on the ground as Pouch and Stark Hansen approached the Dark Man. Stark put five more rounds into the Dark Man and holstered his pistol.

Mr. Pouch kept shooting. He emptied his clip into the body of the Dark Man, who was kneeling on the ground. He should have been dead. Instead, a significant growling sound came from the corpse, and the earth beneath our feet seemed to rumble all the way back to town. Just before the Dark Man could reach the apex of his roar, there was a swishing sound. As she looked up, Angela saw Stark with a machete in his hand. He had made a clean cut, and as the head rolled to within three feet of her, she noticed the head had continued to grin even though it was decapitated. "You're done, Jerk," were the final words Stark said at that moment. After several seconds passed, Stark Hansen told everyone on the ground, "Shut your eyes."

All that the crowd of people heard were swishing sounds as Stark continued to work on the body that had been the Dark Man. Then all was quiet and still. Footfalls were heard, then silence again. Finally, it was Mr. Pouch who softly spoke. "You can get up now. You kids might not want to look at what we have done here." The vortex had disappeared from whatever place it had come from.

We all stood up and watched as Stark, who had pulled out a container of fluid from his duffle bag, was spraying the corpses that had been laid in a pile. He then took a lighter from his pocket, lit it, and while looking at the crowd of people he had rescued, he flung the lighter onto the pile of undead bodies. Included in the heap were the remains of the Dark Man, who was lying on top of the collection of his body parts.

The flame launched into the sky, and Stark walked up to Angela and planted an intense kiss on her. The group started to move around the bonfire of dismembered bodies. When they had moved three hundred or so yards toward the military who were awaiting them, Stark, who was happily walking arm and arm with Angela, stopped.

He turned, and looking through the flames to the other side of the burning pile, he saw the impossible. It was the body of Stanley Harkenson.

It was up and moving toward the fire. "Shit!" was the only word the Navy Seal could say. He opened his duffle and took out two M-72 LAWS rockets and sat them on the ground.

"Stark," Angela said, staring into his baby blue eyes, "don't go. You don't have to go back there. You've done your mission; you've gotten us all out."

He stared down at the beautiful woman before him and asked, "Why couldn't I have met you a few years before now?" He then looked away from her and toward the flames. Once his eyes came back to hers, they were loaded with terror. Then he said, "Look over there, Angela. Look at what Stanley Harkenson has become. Somehow, that 'thing' that was the Dark Man is now in the body of your fellow FBI agent." He gave Angela a look of frustration. "That thing just won't die. In a few years, when it is strong enough, it will return and finish what it started here. I can't have that on my conscience, can you? We have to end this, here and now."

As she looked over at the flames, Angela started to tremble and screamed, "Oh, my God!" Stanley had changed. He was now the Dark Man, complete with the mustache, and, at that moment, he was walking through the flames, coming straight toward them.

The female FBI agent felt her body jerk. Then her head was forced to turn and look into Stark's blue eyes once again, "Angela, I have killed him three times, and, still, he keeps coming back! I don't know what is causing this, but it's not normal. He's not normal. I have to go back in there and try to at least challenge him," Stark said.

"I realize that, now," she answered, her voice steady. She understood that the man she had been looking for all her life had to go and fight an impossible battle. "What do you need from me?"

"I should let you know, I've been wired since I've gotten here, so don't say anything you might regret hearing later." He smiled at her; he knew they had made a connection. "I've got to go back there and give him a chance to tell me more about himself, for intelligence purposes. If he's been able to stay alive through all this, he's most likely going to swat me like a fly. I need you to shoot me dead so that he can't transfer whatever he is into me. You must promise to kill me. You have got to kill me!" His voice cracked slightly as he said the words. He called Mr. Pouch over and said the same thing to him. "We can't let this thing survive. Do you understand?" He then extended his hand in friendship to Mr. Pouch.

Angela kept shaking her head no. She surely could not be expected to do this. She had just found the man of her dreams. He couldn't be asking her to complete such a request. Stark kissed the brave, sweet woman he wished he could have spent the rest of his life with. Angela noticed he was smiling and asked, "What are you smiling about?"

"I was just thinking," he replied. "I wish I could spend the rest of my life with you. As his eyes watered, he added, "In a way, we are doing just that! Ironic, isn't it?"

Stark Hansen turned and started to walk toward the Dark Man. Angela realized she needed to say something. "Hey," the woman shouted. When he turned toward her, she said, "That's some duffle bag you got there, Mister. Is there anything you didn't think to bring with you to this fight?"

"Yep," he said, turning back toward his target, "the courage to get this done." At that, Angela's eyes filled with tears. He concluded the conversation by saying, "But then again, that's what I've got you for!"

As he continued to walk toward the body he knew as FBI agent Stanley Harkenson, he quickly raised his first LAW's Rocket, pressed the button to extend its housing, and then fired it at the Dark Man. He grazed Stanley, and the Dark One stopped walking. The projectile landed in the mass of dead body parts, disintegrating them even further. As Stark closed the distance between the two of them, he shouted, "I don't know who or what you are, Mister, but I've killed you three times, and you keep coming back like the energizer bunny. What are you?"

"Nothing you could ever understand, Stark. That's right. I know who you are! You want to find out who I am for your superiors. Am I correct?" His voice was intoxicating, and Stark could feel the pull that was developing between the two men.

What the Dark One had not counted on was Hansen's adrenaline. It was working full time, and he was resisting the thing before him. "So, what are you?" he asked again.

"I am the oldest of my kind. I was here before man, and will be here long after man has devoured everything it can from this planet. I am pure evil, my good man." He started to chuckle, then added, "I like you, Stark. Come join my little club why don't you?"

"Are you the devil?" Hansen asked.

"Stark, my friend," the entity began, "I am like nothing you have ever seen. I take what I want. I do what I want, when I want. I don't have links to any deities. I just am. I will tell you that I set the whole train wreck thing up. I was waiting for just the right opportunity to bring my devastation and deadly drones forward, while constantly adding new converts to the cause. I succeeded somewhat, but it would be a real coup to have you join my team."

"Do you have a name, Sir?"

The entity liked that Stark was showing respect. Perhaps he would give him a morsel of information. It wouldn't help him anyway. "I am called by many names, but the one I prefer is Falstaff. It has a nice ring to it, don't you think?"

While the entity now known as Falstaff continued to revel in his greatness, he never noticed that Stark Hansen had raised the second LAW's Rocket and extended it, until Stark said, "Thanks, Asshole. That's all I need to know to finish my part in this." He fired the rocket right at the midsection of the beast. The explosion knocked Stark back about 15 feet. Suddenly, a vortex opened next to the Dark Man's remains. Stark took this as a sign and understood what he had to do.

He quickly rose up from where he fell as the dirt started to rumble beneath his feet. He pulled his Glock and emptied another clip into the man, just to stop him from growling. He heard the familiar roar coming from the flames. Stark Hansen finally realized that this was how Falstaff was able to transfer his existence from one body to another. He shouted into the air as loudly as he could, "Shoot me, now! Somebody must take the shot!" Stark began to run straight toward the flames. He would burn himself alive to keep Falstaff from taking control of his body, and that monster would have nowhere to go. Stark was running right at Falstaff with his arms open wide to tackle the body of Stanley Harkenson to throw him into the target. But, he just missed the swirling vortex and landed on the ground next to it.

Just as he, the bravest man Angela had ever met, started to feel the searing pain of the fire burning his flesh, the last thing he heard in his invisible earpiece that Angela had given him were the words, "Stark, I love you." The front of his face exploded as the shot ripped through the back of his skull and entered the front skull of FBI agent Stanley Harkenson. Both bodies went limp, fell into the flames, and were gone. The vortex closed. There was no yelling or screaming. The ground no longer trembled on command. There were just the crackling flames, devouring the flesh of Stark Hanson and former FBI associate Stanley Harkenson.

♦ ♦ ♦

Angela finished her story by saying, "It was the bravest, most gallant thing I have ever seen." Then she started to uncontrollably hemorrhage tears. Jake had pulled the car to the side of the interstate and was now turned and listening intently. "I really did fall in love with him in our few moments together," Angela confessed. "He was everything I ever wanted in a man. The sad thing is," she paused long enough to wipe her eyes, "as quickly as he entered my life, he was gone."

The two sat in the car for what seemed like hours, but was actually only about twenty minutes. "Anyways," she began again, "Stark is dead, and I'm branded a hero, all because I was in the right place at the wrong time."

"I don't think so, Angela," Jake said, trying to reassure her. "I think you're the hero because you had the courage to take the shot. You had to do what you did. There's no way Mr. Pouch could have made that shot. You had to take it."

Her head turned to Jake as she said, "Truth is, we both took the shot, but Pouch missed." Her eyes watered up again and she began to sob and could not stop. Whimpering, she gave a few last details. "We never did find out who Falstaff really was, or what he was after. I thought we were done with him eight years ago. Now the same man, or whatever he is, shows up in St. David. As if we didn't have enough issues with vampires and drug lords. Stark was right. He said Falstaff would return if he had the chance, and he did."

"Angela?" Jake spoke her name softly, and when she dismissed it, he repeated her name. "There's more to this than you know." She turned her head to look into the eyes of her partner. "I've got to tell you something," Jake said, "but remain calm, please, until I finish."

She sat there, not knowing what Jacob Taylor could possibly say that would make this situation more intense. He began to explain, "If you hadn't come to me to help you with this case, I would have sought you out. I have been watching you for some time. I read all the reports from Missouri, but I could never figure out why Stark had to die there. Nowhere in the reports did it say half the things about Falstaff that you have told me here. I needed to find some answers for myself, because Stark Hansen was my half-brother!" Jake let the words sink in, then added, "I always thought it was fate that brought you and me together, but now I understand it was faith. Stark wasn't one to throw out respect and love to just anyone. He must have seen something special in you. Something that I felt the first time we met, an attraction. Not sexual, but two like minds on the same mission. I believe Stark brought us together to solve this case."

Angela stared at the handsome agent for quite some time, then asked, "Is that why you wanted to know about Missouri, so you could make your own mind up as to whether you trusted me or not?"

"No," he promptly answered. "No, I needed to know if you were the same person that went to war with my brother, and if you'd be prepared to go to war with me? I am going to face this Falstaff guy, and I'm gonna bring him down. I have always felt that there is a reason for what happened to me in Waco. Now I know what it is. It's to face Falstaff."

The two FBI agents stayed in that spot for another fifteen minutes. They planned different scenarios of dealing with the Dark Man, none that either of them was pleased with. One thing they agreed on, they wouldn't share with the others on the team the true Stark Hansen story. Finally, Jake started the car and they headed toward St. David, Arizona, which, at the present time, could pass for Hell. The two FBI agents weren't quite sure which name fit in this situation, but they were about to find out.

Chapter Twelve

In Your Face

After Angela completed her explanation of Hornersville, Missouri, Jake finished the drive back to St. David. As they entered their building, "Angela, what the hell is going on?" Erin Hastings shouted.

Not one for a confrontation with a demon, Angela took a stance and stared back at the young vampire, who had exposed her fangs and looked eager for a fight. Jake broke the tension by saying, "Erin, we are returning from a terrible meeting. Is there any way you could at least give us a minute to get a drink and relax for a moment."

Erin was in Jacob's face and saying, "Oh, sure, man. Of course, you like this, but we don't need to add someone new to the team. You've got us!"

At that moment, everyone on the team was awaiting a response from the person who was, for the moment, their leader. She now understood Erin's comments. "You mean Kira?" Angela questioned.

Jake Taylor started to shift where he stood. He seemed nervous as he looked at his watch and then interjected, "I better go get ready for tonight."

Erin snapped, "No, Sir!" She stared down her FBI agent friend and ally. "I want," then she paused and looked at the other members of the team before she continued, "we all deserve an explanation! Don't we?"

"Actually, Erin, you don't," Angela explained. "But, I'll tell you what I can. All the information..." Just as she started to explain, she was interrupted.

"All the intelligence that you've gotten about St. David, the drugs, the undead creatures, have come to be because of my expertise," Kira Knight said as she slithered into the room. Her slim body seemed as graceful as a swan as she walked between the professor, Carrie-Anne, and Charles Martin. It was as if she were plotting a course as she floated through the room and stood between Angela and Jake. "Adding to the mix is the fact that Jake and I go way back to a time when he wasn't, well, let us say, the way he is now." The words were sultry and used to provoke a response. Nothing was said by anyone until she moved toward Jake and put her hand on his arm, as if she were claiming him. She looked up into his face and smiled. Still, nothing was said. All eyes were on Erin, but she stood her ground. Then, Kira said, "Besides, having me here also serves to calm Jake. When he goes off into 'the wild' tonight, I'm going to be with him."

Jake quickly took a step away from their little two-some. Once he did that, it was Erin who made the next move. "I go out with Jake. I keep him calm." Ms. Hastings took a strained look into Kira's eyes. She thought she knew what the new agent was, but she saw something different in the woman's eyes now. She needed more time to study the latest member of the group.

Surprised that there wasn't an all-out brawl, Angela said, "Not tonight, Erin. Kira's going with Jake. That would be best for now. She knows Jake, she knows the area, and she can keep him safe until morning."

Not wanting to show her immaturity to the new girl, Erin surprised everyone by stepping back. Jake said, "Well, I'm going to go prepare. It's an hour before dusk, and I want to be far away from here when I change." The way he spoke let everyone in the room, except for Kira, realize he was not happy with the situation. No one knew why, but when he left, Kira followed without question.

Professor Von Bruton spoke first. "She is his mate then?" he questioned.

"No." Surprisingly, it wasn't Erin speaking. Everyone could tell her heart, if she had one, was breaking. It was Carrie-Anne who spoke. "I don't think so, or Jake would be more responsive." She moved closer and then spoke softly, "Something else is going on here, isn't it, Angela?"

In the time it took Carrie-Anne to speak, Angela had moved and was on the other side of the two women. "Erin, honey," Angela said, "she's a plant. For what reason, I don't know yet. Yes, she's like Jake, but she's different too. Jake knows that, and he will be careful. Kira won't get out of this situation what she wants." When there was no reaction from the teenager, both women stepped back.

A sly smile came upon Erin's face. "I know. I've wanted to tell you for some time that Jake and I, well, we have made this connection." As she said the words, looks of horror came over everyone's face, including the professor and Geek-Boy. She looked at all of their reactions and then said, "Ooh, gross! Not that connection!" She paused, made a face as if she had tasted something sour, then composed herself and educated the group. "I can hear him. I hear his thoughts, and it helps us when he goes on his wild nights, as he calls it. I follow him from a safe distance, and I know he'll be OK. He wanted me to get up in Kira's face. So, how'd I do?"

Angela spoke up, "You had me fooled, and I don't fool easily."

"Mr. Martin," Erin wasn't on a first name basis with him yet. He knew more about her and her family than she did, and that made her uneasy. "Can you comb through the internet and see if there is anything like, I don't know, a special kind of ..."

"A hybrid? That's good thinking, Erin." He then turned to Eric Von Bruton and said, "What do you think, professor? Are you up for some research?"

Eric smiled at the younger gentlemen and then said as politely as he could without sounding rude, "You did good, kid. You're still gonna follow him, aren't you?"

"Oh Yeah," Erin smiled back at the professor.

"Do you think that's wise?" Angela asked.

"I could say most anything, and I know you won't believe me. I haven't earned your trust. But, I have earned Jake's. I can read it in his eyes. He doesn't trust Kira any more than the rest of us do. Believe me when I say, I do like Jake, a lot. However, I also know I cannot do what I want to, because, well, I'm not ready. I thought I was ready when I was alive, and look what it got me. I just want to make sure he's safe, that's all."

She was looking at both women while speaking. Finally, Carrie-Ann said, "Boss, let her do this." Then she went to join her husband and the Professor, who had already left the room.

"When did you get so mature?" Angela asked once Carrie-Anne had exited.

"Dying will do that to you. So, any special instructions?" She looked at her leader.

"You say you have a connection with Jake. If you do, you might want to disconnect for a while." Angela was trying to watch the language she used.

"Hey, I'll be ok. Jake's going to be wolf-boy pretty soon, and sexually, he's a wolf as well. I figure she's going to be all over him, trying to be the dominant wolf of the two, in her efforts to form a clan and become his 'Bitch.' Not trying to call her names or anything," Erin answered. "It happens all the time when he goes to the Appalachians. I just don't say anything to him. By the way, there are several packs around here, so she might get her butt kicked." The vampire had a broad smile on her face while she said those words.

"Just be safe and take a radio with you. If there's something you can't handle, I'll come running," the FBI officer, and Erin's protector, pointed out to the young vampire.

"Angela," Erin moved close enough to whisper. "There's something about her. I can't put my finger on it, but, she's different. I saw it in her eyes.

"Good to know," Angela said, deep in thought. Erin turned to leave, but before she went through the door, the FBI agent, her boss, and slowly becoming her friend said, "Don't be a hero out there. I lost one of those once, and it's not pleasant."

Not understanding everything her boss was saying, she gave a nervous, "OK. I'll be back by first light."

'This is all too tidy,' Angela thought. As she walked toward the workroom and confronted the other three members of her team, she ordered, "I want everybody's radio on tonight. I've got a bad feeling."

♦ ♦ ♦

"You little whelp," the Master Gardener said as he was busy choking the life out of Tommy.

"I did as you requested." There was a blank look in his eyes as the Master Gardener choked the words out of Arthur "Tommy" Kensington's mouth. "I gave her the blood as you instructed." He tried to struggle against the pressure that was being pressed upon his larynx.

"Then tell me why you didn't bring her back to me." the Master Gardener questioned.

"It's simple really. There were other people present, and I couldn't get Erin moved without someone asking questions. What did you want me to do, kill everyone to stay with the plan?" Tommy asked. He paused as his master let up on the pressure that was on his throat. Tommy rose up from the dirt and slime he'd been lying in and finally stood. Brushing himself off, he continued, "I did want her to myself, I can't lie. When I brought her back, she was grateful. Really grateful." A smile glowed across Tommy's face. "I like her." He started moving parallel with the Master as he continued explaining, "We are both the same, you and I, and even though you threaten me, you cannot destroy me. I've got these people thinking that I am weak, that I can be walked on anytime they want. You and I know otherwise."

The wheelchair stopped rolling as Tommy's form suddenly changed into the image of the dearly departed Navy Seal, Stark Hansen. The Gardner strongly objected. "Tommy, I wish you wouldn't take that form. You know how it upsets me to see it."

"Is that because you failed to make him one of your followers, or because he nearly destroyed you?" Tommy said gleefully.

"Both," the Master Gardener said. "He was nothing but a muscle-bound freak who did not fear me. In fact, in his last moments, he found love, which I found revolting. Now that woman who was with him," the words flowed out of his mouth like water, "I could have done some serious damage with her. But with him, it was as if he knew every move I was going to make. He worked through the maze of that town and cut me down before I really had a chance to..."

Suddenly, Tommy had changed his form again. This time it was old man Pouch, from Missouri. His gray hair sparkled in the bright light of the greenhouse. "Is this better?" he asked the gardener.

"Yes," the elder Napier agreed, "it is." All anger and disappointment were gone. There was now a kind of gratefulness in his voice. "Hornersville was supposed to be my domain, but if you hadn't thought fast there, I would not be here now."

"That's all over now, father," Tommy said.

"I did not father you!" the older looking gentleman said. "I raised you, but I did not sire you."

"But, you did teach me, and that is what a father does, is it not?" Tommy implied.

From out of nowhere, a smile eased itself onto the Gardener's face. Then, as if it pained him, the smile was gone again. He instructed Tommy, "So, explain to me about the girl."

"It's simple. I was attracted to her, but, also, I found it easier to access one Ms. Angela Harrison." He stood back to see the old man's reaction.

The Master Gardener was up and no longer looking old. He now had his raven colored hair with the trademark silver streaks, the Fu-Man-Chu mustache, and his black eyes sparkled with anticipation. "The one that got away. You have found her?" He anxiously waited for an answer to his question.

"Trust me, Father, it's her. You forget, I was less than two feet away from her. She's here now, and it was I who got her to come." He paused for a moment, then stood taller and stated, "But, you almost ruined everything I had planned by killing my new best friend at the time. I loved Percy, and for a time, he loved me, but you killed him for your own foolish pleasure." When he finished speaking, Tommy was now in the Master Gardener's face and had firmly grasped him by the throat.

Suddenly, they both started to laugh. Percy was a pawn, nothing more. They both knew it. As their laughter grew, they heard the door on the far end of the greenhouse open. Both men quickly turned back into their original forms. The Gardener climbed back into his wheelchair. Tommy promptly went behind the chair and was pushing it when Melissa Napier rounded the corner. As she approached the two men, she said, "Good evening, you two." As she strode up to them, she continued to speak, "Knight is taking the wolf out. Everything's in play."

"Thank you, my dear," the Master Gardener said, gratefully.

"Good to see you, Tommy," Melissa said, sexily, while she checked out the family's gopher.

"Nice to see you as well, Ms. Napier, and thank you for the information," Tommy said politely.

He continued to watch her as she turned. She knew exactly how to walk away and provoke a response from those observing her. "Don't even think about it. She is mine to ravage," the older man said.

Tommy responded, "Yes, but you must idle her brain to get what you want; all I have to do is be in the same room. That woman responds to power, and while we both have it, I believe she senses which one of us is the more powerful."

"Don't challenge me, Tommy. You would lose!" the Master Gardener insisted.

Tommy thought to himself, 'For now, old one. For now!'

♦ ♦ ♦

"Something isn't right here," Blakely Hoffenpiller said with a questioning tone.

"It used to be," the Queen said, "a few of our clan would send fear into the souls of man. Now," she turned to stare at her husband from the north, "people gladly embrace the shroud of terror we bring to their town. They invite us in. They want to mate with us. They want to befriend us. That is not...," She paused, searching for the right word.

"Human?" Blakely completed her sentence. He continued on with his own train of thought. "The more significant issue is all the players we have in this particular game. That 'thing' walked in here and basically insulted us all. He knew Percy. Evidently, he worked with my second in command, and I had no clue. The girl, Erin, came back and rescued our next victim and brought a whole task force with her of who knows what. There is also the mayor and his role in this."

"Enough!" Bethoon the Cannibal said as he slammed down his staff. Its impact made the walls of the cave shudder. "You cry in disappointment. You whine about Percy. You are disappointed about this girl you thought you had sired. You complain about the forces that are surrounding you. The time for crying is finished. It is now time for action!" Bethoon demanded. He moved close enough to Blakely's face that he could see the fear in the vampire's eyes.

"I don't know..." Hoffenpiller began, but was cut off.

"Where is the Blakely Hoffenpiller I have heard about all these decades?" Bethoon asked.

Understanding that Bethoon had given her an opening, the Queen stepped forward and started to whisper into the ear of the local vampire leader. "How many continents have you traveled, Old One?" she asked the shell of a man known as Blakely Hoffenpiller. Suddenly, a gleam came to the ancient vampire's face. "How many lives have you sucked away from the human world? What are you waiting for? You don't take orders, you give them!"

Bethoon took over the conversation as he said in a low tone, which sounded like the droning of a million bees buzzing just over the horizon, "Yes, you must take control of the situation. You must pick a target and confront it. You must devour this place like you have done so many times before." Bethoon moved closer to Hoffenpiller and insisted, "You must prove why they call you the Master. You must set into motion an attack of such proportions that the human element will never again mention the town of St. David. The Master that does that, the leader that devours this town and all the inhabitants in it, I will follow."

Hoffenpiller's eyes were now ablaze with confidence. "You are right. I will take over this town! I will rule as my ancestors have in places like Transylvania, Augusta, and in the mountains of every continent."

"You have a plan in place then?" the Queen asked.

"I do," Hoffenpiller insisted. "I will start with the mayor and his family. Then I will go after Melissa Napier and her family," he said, as he walked away from the two deadly foes who had falsely built up his confidence. He continued to give orders to his minions and was unaware Bethoon and his Queen were making their own plans.

"He is such a fool," the Queen stated. "It's a wonder he has gotten this far!"

Bethoon grabbed his lover's chin, turning her face toward his. "Don't underestimate the old fool. We will continue to support him like good little minions, and then we will run this area. But, first," They both turned away from the conqueror of St. David and saw their next target, the nurse, who was a gift from the Master Gardener. Anastasia, continued to lie on the ground, still in the trance she was placed in. The two rulers of the North could again hear her faint heartbeat. Anastasia was moving in and out of the human world and into the demon realm. The vampires had drained close to the limit of her lifeblood. Her mind was a blur. She was in and out of consciousness. The Queen sat down on the surface of the cave and placed the young woman's head on her lap. "It is time to wake, young one. We need answers to question concerning the people you worked for."

As Anastasia looked up, her eyes glistened. "You want me to tell you about the old man? There isn't much I can say. I was never allowed access to him when he was conducting business," Anastasia confessed.

Bethoon knelt down and inquired, "Not about Napier. We want to know about the FBI and what they are doing investigating this sleepy little town."

♦ ♦ ♦

Scanning the top of his bed, Jake found the extra-large T-shirt he was looking for and threw it on his naked body. The shirt said, "I love (with a picture of a heart) Monsters." Erin had gotten it for him one time when they were out on the town after a hard-fought day of training. Sliding the spandex shorts up to his torso, he was covered when his bedroom door quietly opened. He could smell the scent of the woman he didn't want in the room with him right now. "You're not going to succeed, you know?" he rendered.

"I already have," Kira insisted. "I am driving a wedge between you and your team. I have them, and you, right where I want."

He turned on Kira's nearly nude form and offered, "I have gone this long without you, without a keeper. I'll be fine."

"They are afraid of you!" Her voice was intense and confident.

"They have the right to be," he insisted. Then he grabbed Kira and jerked her near him so that his inner Werewolf could pick up her sent. She wanted him. Jacob knew that. But, he was not about to give her the satisfaction. "You should be afraid as well. Your boss is using you, putting you in harm's way. And for what? To what end? So that you can keep an eye on me?"

"Is that so bad, Jake?" she asked as she seductively wrapped herself in his body. "You always enjoyed the perks before when we used to work together."

He threw her off of him and reached into his closet to grab a clean shirt. "Put this on!" he ordered. Frustrated, she grabbed the garment and put it on with her eyes ablaze. Kira was fueled by anger and rage. Jake thought about the situation as he moved toward the chair on the far end of his room. "I can't help but get the feeling that both you and I are being manipulated into something we have no control over. The team came here to save the girl, who may or may not have needed saving. Then we are ordered to Tucson, and what's waiting for us there but the one woman I could never quite get over being out of my life."

Kira stood and oozed her way to him, giving him a seductive look. "You never got over me?" she purred. She curled herself into his lap and kissed his lips. He did not resist.

Realizing what was happing, he suddenly stood up, causing Kira to fall onto his bedroom floor. "Can't you see?" he said. "We are all being set up, manipulated. And to what purpose?"

Frustrated that she was getting nowhere with Jake, Kira insisted, "I'm not a wolf. I'm a changeling."

As if he hadn't heard her correctly, he asked, "You're a what?"

"You heard me! I don't know how I became this way, but I can change into whatever, or whoever, I want. It's a family trait, as far as I know." She actually looked sad as she sat there on his bed and wrapped her arms around herself.

"So, why did you come on so strong here? That's not the Kira I remember," Jake said, moving closer to her.

"I was ordered by Stasher to get close to both you and Angela. I was told to use any means possible. Sorry about that, by the way."

He took in all she had to say and then demanded, "Prove it," and stepped back away from her. When she said and did nothing, he commanded, "Prove to me you can do what you say you can. Change into someone right here and now!"

She looked into his eyes and said, "Will this do?" Suddenly sitting on his bed was Angela Harrison. As she continued to stare into his eyes, Kira said, "Or, how about this?" In a blink of an eye, she had become a sultry version of Erin. She then stepped toward him and wrapped her now sixteen-year-old arms around him. For once in his life, Jake Taylor became very uncomfortable. Then the woman giggled and became her version of a werewolf.

Jacob stared at Kira for a moment, as if he had been shot. He suddenly asked, "But, are you really a wolf? Aren't you afraid you'll be hurt or killed?"

"When I was first reassigned to Stasher, he tested me by sending me into the wild. I passed with flying colors," Kira told him. She crossed her legs and smiled up at him. Ms. Knight approved of the idea that he was concerned about her welfare. Besides, she knew he had always loved her silky smooth thighs, and she was using every opportunity to lure him into her arms.

"So why the act?" he asked.

"I'm not acting. We were together for almost three years before your accident. If you remember I begged you to let me stay in your world. I could have helped you, but," Kira paused as if the words pained the young FBI agent to say, "you pushed me away. Now, I see you with this new group of people. You can't tell me there isn't something going on between you and that vampire girl, Erin."

"In the months I've been with this group, I have found myself. I have worked hard to learn how to control myself. The Professor has not only shown me what happens to me when I turn, but also how I turn. It's a chemical reaction. He isn't working on a cure, but he is trying to find something that might offer me less violent transformations that will allow me to be me instead of turning into a beast every time there is a full moon. The Martin's are helping me track the packs of Werewolves from ground zero, the place where I was bitten. Angela, well, she is the best leader, administrator, and friend I have ever had. She is very astute. Sometimes I can't believe they waited until now to give her own task force." Jake went silent then and sat down beside his former friend and lover. He was done talking.

Kira asked him, "What about the girl? You haven't mentioned Erin. What about her?"

For several moments he sat next to Kira and said nothing. Twice, he tried to make sense of his relationship with Erin but couldn't quite find the words. Finally, he said, "I have this feeling she's headed for the big Downer. There's no doubt that she got a bad deal. She made some bad choices, but haven't we all done that? I understand how she sometimes feels, ya know? I mean, she was swept into this because she trusted someone she shouldn't have trusted." He took Kira's hand and added, "I'm just trying to protect her, for now," He then gave her his great Jacob Taylor smile.

Not being able to control the disappointment she felt, Kira gave herself away by the anger in her eyes. But, before she could express herself, Jake suddenly doubled over and convulsed with pain. "It's starting," he said, once the pain subsided. "I've got to get going. One last thing, Kira. Once you join me out there, if you notice anything out of the ordinary, please just back away and get out of there." He paused, as if feeling uncomfortable, then added, "Wherever we wind up tonight, I want to apologize right now for anything I might do, because, most of the time I can't remember what I've done the night before." He looked ashamed, and stared down at the floor.

"Don't sweat the small stuff, old man. I've got your back tonight," Kira answered him.

"That's what I'm afraid of," he said, jokingly.

"Go on, get out of here!" she ordered. "I'll lock up."

He briefly convulsed. It was less stressful this time because he knew what to expect. Once he stood up, he smiled at his new teammate and was out the door.

Once he was gone, Kira locked the door and then pulled out her cell phone. She punched in the number and waited for the person on the other end to pick up. "Head's up, guys, he's on his way."

Going back and lying on the bed, she stared into thin air. "You don't know what you missed, Wolf-boy. This could have been the best night of your life. Now, you just might have to die." The body on the bed transformed into Melissa Napier. She thought about all the information the dim-witted Agent Taylor had just given her. Now, she could formulate a plan to destroy each member of the team. By slipping into the body of the lovely Ms. Knight, no one will ever see what's coming.

There was a soft knock on the door. "Jake, it's Kira. Are you ready to go?"

"Not quite yet," Melissa said, using Jake's voice. "You go ahead, and I'll find you." She waited several moments and then opened the door, just a crack, to find she was gone.

Everything was going just the way she and the Master Gardener wanted. "I have them all right where I want them. It's showtime!" Then Melissa said to herself as she chose the form of Professor von Bruton and casually walked out of Jacob Taylor's room.

Chapter Thirteen
The Wild

Making sure her earpiece was in, along with the microphone that the Martin's had given her, Erin Hastings started to speak into the night air. Ms. Hastings knew that her people would be listening to this evening's events. "This is Agent Erin Hastings on the air," she said, with a bit of whimsy in her voice.

"Cut the chatter." It was Angela, taking charge, as usual. "You be careful out there tonight. A lot of strange things have been going on since we arrived in St. David. I don't want to lose anyone on this op."

"OK, Mom," Erin said, sarcasm filling her voice, "I'll be careful. But, this isn't really an op, is it? This is just 'The Wild,' right? You know, one of the three nights Jake goes out and gets his wolf on?"

Angela said nothing in response. Erin began climbing high in the tree that she had chosen to watch tonight's activity. She finally found a branch to perch on when, as if on cue, in bounded Jake, her burley-haired friend, reacting with violent rage The sky was clear, sprinkled with stars, and there was a bulbous full moon. It allowed Erin's view to be more vivid.

Suddenly, there was a cracking sound, and out of a grove of scrubby looking pine trees bounded another wolf. This was apparently Kira. She was smaller in stature and pretty for a wolf girl, Erin thought. Kira moved toward Jake and leaped into the air. The agent brought her girth down on the unsuspecting male wolf. Jake quickly rolled away from her. He stood on his hind legs, and while stretching out the full length of his torso, let out a guttural growl and started to stomp away. Once his back was turned, the she-wolf charged at him again.

Above them, Erin quietly described into the microphone, as best she could, the scene that unfolded before her. After fifteen minutes of watching from a distance, she decided to move to another tree to get a better vantage point of the two werewolves. Erin continued observing, when she noticed something she wasn't ready for. A pack of twelve wolves emerged from out of the brushy area. The wolves began to form a semi-circle around Jake and Kira. Then, another large group of sixteen more wolves entered the clearing from the opposite side. Both groups combined to complete the ring. The two animals in the middle of the circle were now aware that they were surrounded. Erin was relaying the information to the people back at the office when she suddenly went speechless. From the left edge of the circle she saw a human form appear. The human gently caressed two of the wolves on top of their heads as it broke the ring. It was a man, Erin could tell that much. He was tall, dressed in a suit, and was somewhat portly. All Erin could say was, "I've never seen this guy before." Then she stopped describing the man because someone else came out from the grove of trees. "It's Tommy," she said, with shock and surprise in her voice. Quietly, she moved to within hearing distance so that she might learn something that could help explain what was happening.

Behind the two men, all the wolves had lain down except the two in the middle of the ring. The stranger spoke first. "Kira, you did a great job of getting Jake to this spot. You can leave now."

To Erin's surprise, Kira morphed back into her human form. She was wearing a black bodysuit and her hair was up in a bun. "I'm not your errand girl, Stasher. I'll go when I'm ready."

"Ms. Knight, is it?" Tommy took center stage now.

"Yes, Sir," she returned, bothered by the boy's intervention.

Tommy raised his hand, and without making a sound, the woman was drawn toward him. "Stasher, what's going on here?" Kira demanded, as fear filled the woman's eyes.

"You see, Kira," Tommy's voice was smug and confident, "you have done your job here. You brought me the man who is ruining my operation, and you encouraged Erin to come along as well. I want to thank you for that little bonus."

"I did no such thing! Erin was supposed to stay back at headquarters." Kira used her powers of observation to quickly scan the area. Nothing.

Suddenly, Erin bounded from the tree she was hiding in and was within the wolf-lined circle in seconds. "Tommy, what's going on here?" she questioned. "Don't hurt Agent Knight, Tommy, please," Erin begged.

"Why do you care? You don't even like her." He turned his face toward Erin and continued, "It was me who planned this whole thing, you know. I wanted you here, watching him, that freak wolf-boy over there."

Then he added, "You might as well take the earpiece off, honey. No one can hear you now."

Erin removed the hidden earpiece and watched as it burned when she threw it to the ground. "I'm here, so if that's what you want, let them go! I'll go with you if you like. Just don't hurt them."

None of them counted on what happened next. Jake, in his wolf form, jumped in front of Kira, and right into the face of Arthur "Tommy" Kensington. Without hesitation, he ripped through Tommy's throat and then went to sit beside his friend, Erin.

Out of nowhere, a shot rang out. The bullet passed through Erin's body and wound up in the wolf. Jake howled in pain as Stasher shouted, "Get him back to Angela! She'll know what to do. I'll take care of the vampire."

Kira ran to the wolf. Amazingly, she grew more substantial in her arms and upper torso as she raised Jake up into her arms without effort. Jake was starting to transform back into his human form as they were leaving the circle. She stopped and looked back at her boss. She wanted to ask him what was going on when she heard the limp corpse in her arms begin to moan. Carrying Jake's lifeless body, she ran as fast as she could toward the edge of the woods and to the car that was waiting for her. Then it was onward to the sanctuary of the FBI's team office.

Erin, who was down on one knee, stood and commented, "I can't be killed by bullets, you dick! You most likely know that, so why did you bother to shoot me?" She glared at Stasher.

"You were the real prize here, little lady," Stasher said as he pulled another pistol from under his coat. "I needed you immobilized while I did this." Then, pulling the trigger several times, he sent no less than six tranquilizer darts into Erin. She was knocked out in seconds. Stasher was taking no chances. While he could tolerate werewolves, he hated vampires. They were too unpredictable.

Across the way, the body on the ground continued to move. It moaned, sat upright, and moaned again. Stasher watched as Tommy's muscles and tendons weaved together until his throat was back in its original condition. After several moments, Tommy finally spoke his first words, "Why the hell did you let them leave, Stasher?"

"The girl was the target, Tommy. You know that. The Gardener wants her, not anyone else. We are done here."

Tommy stood up and walked over to the taller, well-dressed agent. "If you had let me have my fun, the Gardener would have gotten Erin, and I would have gotten rid of my rival. I don't like Jake. Everyone is aware of that. I was going to destroy him, along with the woman. Now you've set them both free. I didn't want any witnesses. The Master wants no witnesses. Besides that, I hate werewolves. We don't work well with them. The Master Gardener and I wanted them both dead."

"I have no love for Jake either, but I am fond of Agent Knight. She is not expendable. Besides, I was told Erin Hastings was the target, and we have her now. We can take her back to the Master and complete the mission," Stasher explained.

Tommy walked over to the still kneeling Erin. When he saw the blood, he then turned on Stasher. "You shot her? Why did you do that?"

"I thought you were dead. I knew the Gardener wanted her alive, but the wolf would have never let me take her, so I improvised." Stasher walked over to Tommy to get a better look at him and to make sure he was in good enough shape to continue with the operation. "I don't understand why you were trying to take Kira out. All the information I've gotten, she's gotten for me. She's an asset. I could never explain why I stood by and let you kill her."

"I see," Tommy said. "I should have never let you live in Missouri. When the lovely Ms. Knight gets back to Angela and the others and tells them that I am not what I seem to be, what do you think will happen then?" He thought for several moments. Finally, a smile came to his face as he raised up his right hand and snapped his fingers. Stasher stood and watched as Tommy morphed into a duplicate of him. "I have a new plan now!" Tommy said. He then leaned down and took the unconscious Erin in his arms and lifted her up. He started walking toward the car, while carrying her.

Agent James Stasher nervously watched as the circle of wolves began to close in on him. "What are you doing?" the agent questioned. "I helped you carry out this whole plan. What is the Master Gardener going to say?" He tried to quickly draw his weapon, but it was too late. One of the wolves jumped onto Agent Stasher and slammed him into the ground. The man's high pitched screams filled the night air with terror. His shouts of outrage continued while Arthur Kensington placed the vampire girl in the back seat of the car. The pack started sinking their ravenous teeth deeper into Stasher's body. The wolves planned to devour Stasher's flesh and leave nothing but bone.

"I'll just be you," Tommy said, while positioning himself behind the steering wheel. Then he turned the engine over and headed back to reality, away from the screams coming from the agent that he used to know as James Stasher.

♦ ♦ ♦

Kira was into FBI "protect your partner at all cost" mode. As she frantically drove the car, she tried to press the gas pedal through the floorboard and was flying down the back roads of St. David to get Jake to the nearest medical facility. There was a small clinic known to the town as Express-Care. That would have to do. At the same time, she contacted Angela and the team back at the office and informed them of what had happened. Kira explained to them where the clinic was so that when she finally reached it, everyone would be there.

She looked down at Jake and realized the poison of the silver bullet was already taking its toll on him. He had turned fully human again, and his pale skin was an indication that he was at death's door. She brought the car to a screeching halt. They were at the clinic. The female agent shoved open her door and was on the other side of the automobile in moments. Clinic personnel from inside the building were looking out the window, trying to find out who or what had made the loud screeching noise on such a quiet evening. Kira frantically waved for the people to come outside; she had an emergency. Suddenly, the parking lot was flooded with medical personnel and a gurney. No sooner were the medical personnel begun caring for the wounded FBI agent, when another vehicle roared into the parking lot, carrying the rest of the members of the team.

Angela reeled on Agent Knight, demanding answers. "What the hell happened?" Kira's new boss asked. "Jake always goes out during the full moon and has never once gotten shot, let alone by a silver bullet."

"I'm not sure what happened, but it was a setup for Jake, and, I believe, for Erin as well," Kira informed her.

"Speaking of Erin, where is she?" Carrie-Anne asked.

"I don't know," Kira quipped. "But, Stasher was there, and so was Tommy."

"Boy, that guy's everywhere," Charles insisted.

"Ya think?" Angela gave an odd look. Everyone from the team watched as Angela Harrison's anger pulsed through her slim body. She looked as if she were about to lose control of the situation. Then, the unexplainable happened. She snapped to attention and simply said, "We can't worry about spilled milk right now. We will deal with this later."

Just then, they all heard the professor insist, "Doctor, this guy's a special case and that bullet has to come out, right now."

Suddenly, the machine that was keeping track of Jake's heartbeat flatlined, and everyone held their breath. The doctor worked frantically to save his patient, but was not getting anywhere. It was at that point the professor put his hand on the young doctor's shoulder and commented, "He's not lost yet, but he will be if you don't remove the bullet that's lodged in his heart."

The extremely young doctor, who looked as if he was about twelve years old and fresh out of medical school, stared at the professor for half a heartbeat and suddenly commanded, "Scalpel!" He cut just enough skin to give him a little more room to see down into the wound. "Suction!" he ordered. Once the suctioning was finished, he yelled, "Clamp!" Cautiously, the doctor used his fingers to spread the area around the wound out, and then took the clamp and placed it inside. The time it took for the doctor to grab hold of the bullet felt like three lifetimes to the onlookers who were standing in the parking lot. The young doctor gave a sudden jerk of his arm and with a smile of satisfaction, he raised the silver compacted glob of metal into the air so all could see it. "We are not out of the woods yet, Folks. We've got to stop any bleeding and..."

The professor stepped in and said, "If I were you, Doctor, I would step back and let nature takes its course."

The doctor ignored the old man, and when given a new probing tool, he started to re-enter the wound. Suddenly, the flatline was replaced by a healthy, steady heartbeat. Stepping back from the patient's body, the doctor noticed that the man on the table had started to move. The young doctor looked at the professor. "What is going on here?" he demanded.

"Doctor, trust me," Professor von Bruton said, "you did the hard part. Now, let Jake take it from here. In fact, if what I think is gonna happen, happens, we all might wanna take a few steps back." He turned in the direction of Kira and added, "You, my dear, had better be ready to follow him. But, be careful. He's going to be really, really pissed."

Kira turned to look at Angela. She appeared to be lost and needing guidance. "You go ahead," her new boss insisted. "Just be careful, and watch out for each other." Then, giving the woman a look of despair, she added, "As best you can!"

"Yes, Ma'am," Kira said, as she changed into her wolf form, right in front of everyone. She walked around the car and started pushing the gurney away. Kira was 200 feet away, waiting to see what happened next.

The doctor realized that the restraining straps had been put on the patient, and he jumped into action to remove them. Too late! In front of everyone in the parking lot, Jake was making the painful transformation from human into a wolf. His actions weren't as quick as Kira's had been.

The sound of bones cracking and becoming disjointed was the first indication that something strange was going on in the Express-Care parking lot. Then, in front of the medical staff, Jacob Taylor's arms and legs elongated, and his face quickly transformed into an animal's snout. Everyone backed up and watched as his ever-bulging physique seemed as though it would never stop growing. The beast howled and growled with pain at first. However, Jake's pain soon turned into rage until, at last, his body had broken through the straps on the gurney. The FBI agent was now standing next to the demolished hospital bed, screaming into the night air. The monster was a sizeable half-crazed beast, ready to take his anger out on anyone and everyone.

He howled again while the FBI agents unholstered their weapons and took aim at their friend. It was the professor who stepped forward, holding a pistol, and instructed, "Jake, I know you don't really understand what's going on here, but on my late wife's life, I will shoot you where you stand. Then we will have to go through this whole ordeal again. Nobody wants that." Eric looked down at his thirty – eight caliber pistol and added, "And these bullets are made of pure silver, Son."

The wolf acted as if he didn't care. From behind him, the other wolf howled and bared her teeth. She moved around the gurney so that she was directly in the path of the professor, the doctor, and his assistants.

Somehow understanding that whatever he wanted wasn't going to happen here, Jake, now consumed with his anger and rage, turned and ran into the night, followed by the ever protecting Kira.

The crowd was still rattled when, after several minutes, the doctor put the evening's events into perspective. "It must be the full moon!" he said, jokingly.

Angela retorted with, "You don't understand how right you are."

♦ ♦ ♦

Instead of knocking on the front door of Mayor Bruce Hastings' home, Blakely crashed through the door with his foot. Springing to the front of the house to protect his family from the intruders at this hour, Mayor Hastings' throat became entangled in the long, bony fingers of Bethoon the Cannibal. "This is not a cordial visit, Mr. Mayor," Hoffenpiller insisted.

Gurgling sounds came from the mouth of the mayor, who had no idea how all this chaos could be coming full circle in his little town. He tried to speak, but the words that choked out of his throat didn't make any sense.

That was when young Mikey stepped forward, and words started flying from his mouth. "This is all my fault. You ghouls leave him out of this. Isn't my sister not enough for you?" All eyes turned on him as he continued, "Don't you remember, Blakely? You brought us the tape. You killed her, thinking it was my dad who was killing all your people. That was when the Napier brothers stepped in."

The Vampire Queen stepped forward, and oozing her way toward young Mikey, she said, "Thank you, young man!! We needed the names of the people who killed our beloved Percy, and now we have them." As she said those final words, she was very close to the boy's face. Her fangs extended just enough to show her arousal at the hot blood of a young boy.

Just then, a shotgun blast bellowed from the back hallway of the Mayor's house, followed by a sudden cocking sound as someone pumped another shell into the chamber. "Apparently," Mrs. Hastings said as she stepped into the lighted area of the hallway, "information is not good enough for you. You were not invited into this house, so get the hell out of our home! I have had this house and my shotgun shells blessed by our local priest to guard against your form of evil. My gun is filled with special shells, loaded with garlic and rock salt. It might not kill you, but it will sting you right down to your bones, giving us enough time to drive a stake through the heart of every last one of you." She drew the shotgun up to her shoulder and added, "Therefore, you better leave right now, before I forget that I am the mayor's wife and I blow you all to Hell where you belong. I promise you, I will kill anything in this house that moves before I will let any of you monsters touch one of my children again."

Without hesitation, Bethoon threw the Mayor across the room in a show of force and stepped toward her. In retaliation, Abigail Hastings sent three rounds into the hulking vampire. One hit the right side of his face, tearing it off clean to the bone. One went into his heart. The last one left a large circular hole in his belly. Quickly, she reloaded, as the vampires stood frozen in their tracks. Without warning, the Mayor, pulled out another shotgun, cocked it, and shouted, "You are not welcome here." He then looked down at the Vampire Queen and said, "Especially you! Get away from my boy, or I'll shoot you right where you stand!"

Slowly, the five vampires who had forced their way into the Hastings' house backed themselves out onto the porch. There, they were suddenly hit by strobe lights, similar to the ones the Napiers used the first time they had visited the Hastings. This time, however, it was Angela Harrison of the FBI manning the lights. They were surrounded by agents who were holding shotguns on all of them. Blakely was stunned. They had been set up, either by the people of St. David, or by the FBI. "If I survive this..." he spoke into the night air.

"Thing is," Angela said as she stepped forward, "you aren't going to make it. You are all going to die here, if I have anything to say about it."

"You're FBI. You won't kill us," Blakely responded confidently.

"Why not?" Professor von Bruton asked, not giving them any time to answer. "You're already dead, and we don't see you serving any purpose, other than tormenting young girls and scaring the townspeople. We plan to stop you, one way or another." Then, turning his glare to the face of the vampire whose face was half gone, on Blakely's left, and said, "Ah, Bethoon! I'm so glad you decided to join the party. I've waited over 30 years to deal with you." As the professor chuckled, he added, "I've seen you looking better."

A voice from behind Bethoon and Blakely seeped out from the background. "Eric?" The voice paused and then spoke again, a little more loudly. "Eric, is that you?"

The crowd of FBI agents, vampires, and onlookers that had gathered at the front of the Mayor's rather large estate was silenced, as stepping from behind the wall of monsters came the most beautiful undead woman any of them had ever seen. "Eric, it is you. I can't believe it," she said, looking overjoyed at seeing the old scientist.

The professor started to move toward the woman. Charles stuck out his arm to slow the scientist's movement, but the man would not be stopped. "Agnes?" He said the name as if he were in love with the word. Angela, not taking any chances, drew her gun and joined her group member as he headed toward his destiny.

With her gun raised to eye level, Angela nudged the older gentleman and softly asked, "Professor Von Bruton, who is she?"

The answer stunned everyone as he proudly announced, "My wife!"

♦ ♦ ♦

The two wolves dashed around the corner of a large rock, bounded into the clearing, and suddenly recognized the smell of where they had been earlier in the evening. The male wolf immediately found his own blood, sniffed it, and then stood on his hindquarters and howled as loudly and as long as was possible for him. The female wolf moved closer to her male counterpart and was on his inside flank when the pack arrived once again. They formed their circle and moved inwardly, toward them. This time there was no overbearing human pack master, just these two wolves whose aroma gave them away. The entire pack bore down on them, fangs present, eyes ablaze with the lust of the hunt. Suddenly, Jake grabbed what he assumed was the leader. Using his massive vice-like jaws, he effortlessly tossed the biggest wolf in the pack out of the circle and into the surrounding pine trees. There was a yelp, then a crack from the tree, and finally, the snapping of the wolf's spine as he fell lifeless to the ground. Another animal from the large pack tried to attack from Jake's blind side, but Kira, the female wolf, was there to clone the actions of her dominant male partner. There was shock in the eyes of the pack. They couldn't decide who of their group would be next to test the newcomers.

Jake stepped forward toward the middle of the circle as Kira followed, but not too close. She needed the rest of the pack to realize who was in charge at that moment. Jake pawed the ground, then let loose another long howl into the night air. He needed to know where the people who were here earlier went, and this was the only way he knew to get the information he needed. The pack stood there, not understanding what was required to save them from another attack.

Suddenly, from behind an of scrub pines, appeared a white wolf. She glided through the group and stopped in front of Kira. She bowed, showing respect. Then a shaft of bright light from the heavens enveloped the white wolf as she transformed into a beautiful tanned-skinned woman with long flowing black hair. She was wearing buckskin garments that were adorned with Native American tribal symbols. The other wolves seemed to shy away from the glowing light she radiated, except for Kira. Kira stepped into the safe glow of the light, and immediately transformed into her human form. "Hello," she said. But the other woman's eyes didn't leave Jake. Kira turned toward Jake and waved for him to come into the light.

Without hesitation, the werewolf stepped into the bright light. As he did so, his front paws turned to hands, and his head reverted back to his original form. Jake stepped the rest of the way into the light and was human once more.

"Hello, Jacob Taylor," the beautiful glowing woman spoke to him.

"Hello," Jake responded, his voice full of angst. "How can you have the ability to do all this?"

"It would take a lifetime to explain," she answered. "Suffice it to say, when it comes to you and Angela, you have good friends in high places." She offered him a warm smile.

"I don't understand," Jake said, as a confused look consumed his face.

"I am the Watcher of these woods and lands, but that is not important. What is pivotal is that you continue your work in St. David. Things are about to go from bad to worse. Angela and your team are our only hope." Her hair began to glide around her form, covering her natural beauty.

"Why?" Jake asked.

"I can't tell you that. We have to remain as balanced as possible." The Indian maiden closed her eyes, as if she didn't like the words she was using. "Even in cases such as this, we have to play by the rules. I do know this, you and your entire group are about to be tested within this case. Do not be deceived. Stay the course, and you will find the answers you need." The glowing woman continued to gaze at the surrounding area until she found the lone wolf she needed. "I will instruct one of these wolves where to take you to find the present set of answers. However, don't be bold and reckless. Things are not as they seem."

With renewed vigor, Jacob said, "Alright, I'm ready." Then, he started to exit.

"Jake," the watcher said, getting his attention, "your brother says hello, and he would like you to deliver the same message to Angela." With that said, the glowing form was gone, replaced by the white wolf, which stood staring at Jake.

"What's going on here?" Kira asked him.

"I'm not sure, but I think we are getting help from the good guys." His face still looked puzzled as he spoke the words.

"How do you know that?" she asked.

"My brother's been dead for about eight years, yet he sent a message through the white wolf. Kira, you aren't to mention anything you've heard or seen here to anyone." He gave her a stern stare and added, "I mean it!"

A lone wolf showed up at the edge of the circle, and Jake assumed it was their guide. Jake nodded to it and then looked at Kira and said, "Time to suit up!" As he left the light, he was instantly transformed into his alter-ego, and was on the run. Kira jumped out of the glow and she was into her full gait as a wolf before her paws even hit the ground.

Once they were gone, the white wolf turned to face someone who had entered the area from the scrub pines. He walked up to the animal and laid his glowing hand upon her head, saying, "You did good, Watcher."

♦ ♦ ♦

The enormous greenhouse was exceedingly warm, and while it didn't bother the Master Gardener, it did seem to bother the newly constituted vampire. She stopped in her tracks, causing the inattentive apprentice to stumble into his captive. "I don't want to be here, Tommy. This place gives me the creeps."

Tommy, perturbed by his bumping into the stubborn vampire, grabbed her by the arm and pushed her through the various rows of plants, coming to a final stop in the middle of the green-house. They were standing, facing the back of a 1920's style wheelchair. When they made their final scuffling sounds, the man in the wheel-chair quickly turned it around. Seeing his apprentice, he said, "Arthur, you've brought me a present."

"Present?" both Tommy and Erin asked.

"Yes." The Master Gardener shifted in his chair. As he did so, the old image before them started to turn dramatically younger. The black hair with the white streaks, and the Fu Manchu mustache, glistened in the evening moonlight. The Gardner stood and moved toward Erin. He took a lock of her hair into his hand and smelled it, acting as if it were intoxicating. "You may be dead my dear, but the youth in your corpse is exhilarating!"

Showing him no respect, Erin glared at him and asked, "What am I doing here, Perv?"

Tommy jerked her arm and shoulder again, this time harder. "Show some respect, Erin. You have no idea what the Master can do to you!"

She remained silent as the Master walked around them both. He never took his eyes off her sixteen-year-old body. "How old do you think I am?" the Master asked.

"When I walked in, I'd have said 100. Now, I can't say," Erin said, not really caring if he received the answer he wanted.

Gleefully, he laughed at her answer and started jumping and skipping around the area. "No, no, no," he excitedly stated. "Guess again. Go ahead, guess again!

"Look, old man," Erin was acting overconfident, "let's get this over with. Kill me already, if that's what you are going to do. But, trust me when I say, that's the only pleasure you are going to get out of this meeting."

The Master Gardner immediately moved closer to her and said, "Don't underestimate me, Missy. I made you, and I can take you out." Something he said made her snap to attention. "That's right, I'm your sire, and you will obey me," he said confidently.

It started as a small pain, like a toothache, but the longer she stood there, the stronger the feeling became. She was being pulled toward him, as if she couldn't resist herself. Erin pushed back, but soon learned she couldn't help herself. The next thing she knew, her arms were wrapped around him, and she was kissing him on the mouth. Inside her dead brain, the vampire was screaming. Yet, outwardly, Erin couldn't control herself. Then, she felt the urge inside her subside and quickly pulled away. She tried to move back beside Tommy, but something made her stop mid-distance from the both of them.

"Don't make me do that again," Erin pleaded with disgust.

Behind her, she heard footsteps, a light tapping sound, and then the familiar voice of her former best friend. "Erin, I see Tommy was able to bring you to the Master. It's about time."

"Melissa," Erin inquired, "what's going on here?"

"I have no idea what you are talking about," Melissa answered as she walked over to the Master Gardner and planted a single kiss on his lips, to both Tommy and Erin's dismay.

Tommy walked over to the couple while they were still engaged in their dramatic act and whispered, "Does this mean I can have Erin? She's what I have wanted all along."

The Gardner's arm extended outward toward his apprentice. Tommy went flying across the room, landing in a large mound of green goo. Protruding from the goo were no less than six vines that acted as controlled tentacles. The vines shot straight up and paused high above the people in the greenhouse. Suddenly, the plant extensions reversed course and plummeted directly toward Tommy. The first vine quickly wrapped itself around his throat. Four more moved toward each appendage, clutching Tommy's arms and legs in their deadly grasp. The last one still lingered high in the air, as if awaiting final orders. The Master looked over at Erin and winked as the last vine quickly plummeted downward and landed right in the center of Tommy's heart. Tommy coughed up a large pool of blood, and then was suddenly still.

Erin looked at the Gardener and spat words at him that she had never used before. After the sudden rush of anger was gone, she fell silent. "So you loved him then?" Melissa asked Erin.

"I can't love. You both know that. But I was fond of Tommy," Erin stated cautiously.

"Enough games!" the Gardner ordered. "He got what he deserved. I told him to acquire you, and to not let anyone else be with you. What does he do? He lets the FBI tinker with you, they make you stronger, and turn you into a vampire soldier. I did not want that!" The Master Gardener walked toward Erin, his face red with anger, and grabbed her shoulders so she couldn't move. "Open your mouth!" He angrily ordered. Erin looked down at the floor in defiance. "You cannot reject me, Woman! Now, open your mouth!"

Erin, at first, fought with every ounce of resistance that she had. In the end, slowly and steadily, her eyes met his. Using his stare, he forced the vampire's jaws apart. Her eyes widened when she noticed the contorted facial features of the Gardner. Something that looked like a billion flies began pouring out of his mouth and into hers. Each insect was bloated with the evil that had grown in him through the years. His grip lessened as her body succumbed to the entity that passed from his body into hers. Inside her mind, Erin ran to the most profound, darkest corner available, and hid. She did not know what was happening. By some quirk of fate, she was still alive, but now, someone or something had taken over control of her body. Erin no longer existed as before.

Melissa, in shock at the sight of what was happening, shouted, "Why in the hell did you do that ?"

Erin's form walked over to Melissa and planted a wet kiss on her lips. "It's still me, My Love." the Master said from inside Erin's body. Running his hands over the body he now controlled, he boasted, "This is perfect. This body will do nicely." Looking down at the floor, the form that was once old man Napier lay dormant. Erin's body turned back to Melissa. However, it was the Master she saw. "This body is just a vessel, my dear; I am still me. I can shift back and forth like before, but without expending so much energy."

"What have you done?" The voice of Tommy rose from the pile of dead weeds and goo. "She was mine. She was going to serve me."

The Master wheeled on him. "You whelp, I took what was mine for the taking. She would have never been yours. She was meant to be mine. You knew that from the beginning. We both know that I can't kill you, but you can't kill me. I can make you feel the pain of a thousand deaths. I suggest you remember that and learn to follow along."

Arthur "Tommy" Kensington had recovered from his wounds and rose from the pile of compost. He walked directly up to the mustached master he had always known and offered his loyalty. The Master Gardner smiled, then stepped back and looked around the room, asking, "Where's Mr. Stasher?"

Tommy stood silent for a moment before answering, "I'm Stasher now. He knew too much and was making decisions on his own. I thought it prudent to put him in his place. I can still move in and out of FBI headquarters, and no one will be the wiser."

The Master shifted back into Erin's form and said to both Melissa and Tommy, "Take me back to FBI headquarters. We have to re-establish Erin and put Mr. Stasher into play."

"And then what?" Melissa asked.

"I am going to settle an old debt," the Master answered.

♦ ♦ ♦

The professor stopped ten feet away from the vampire queen and said, "Our resident werewolf calls this night 'The Wild.' Can you believe it?"

Time stood still for a moment as all eyes were on the professor and his beautiful young wife, the vampire queen. "Eric?" the vampire pronounced his name with seductive accuracy. "The years have worn you down, haven't they?"

"I thought you were dead, Agnes," he replied.

"She is dead, Professor," Angela interjected, as she continued to aim her gun at the Queen.

"She is correct, my beloved." It seemed as if she were turning younger right in front of everyone. "However, Bethoon and I have come here to straighten out the situation in this town."

"That is why we are here as well," the professor said. "Hoffenpiller and his clan of vampires killed an innocent."

A strange look came over the Queen as she said, "Erin? Honestly, Eric, was she so innocent?"

"Enough of this, Eric," Angela said. "I need you to step back away from her, slowly. It will allow us to better control the situation."

Before anyone could blink, the Queen had knocked Angela down and had the professor in her grasp. Baring her fangs, she ordered, "I want everyone to drop their weapons and back away just long enough..." She suddenly went limp and crumpled to the ground.

All guns turned on the rest of the vampires as Bethoon shouted, "What has happened to my beloved Queen?"

"She's been stunned, Bethoon," the professor said calmly and rationally. "I've always wondered what could have happened to my Agnes. I guess I know now!" Turning toward Bethoon, the professor quipped, "You always were a sore loser, weren't you? I killed your mate, so you took mine. And here I thought you were honorable."

Bethoon responded, "I am a vampire. I am a cannibal. I have no honor, only power."

"What's our next move, Angela?" came a shout from Agent Carrie-Anne Martin.

"I say, kill 'em all!" came a yell from the Mayor.

Angela stood and addressed the vampires. "You have five minutes to vanish while we clean up here. I warn you, don't come back here, ever, or you will die!" The army of agents behind her held their weapons on the vampires as she moved closer to the professor to assist him. "Pardon me, Eric, but how did you know she would be here and that this would work?"

The vampires were fleeing from the front of the house as the professor took something from his glove and showed it to Angela. "First, I did not know she would be here. However, as a researcher, I knew I had to get close to one of them to use this. It's something I've been working on for quite some time. In short, Ms. Harrison, I caused her to short out. Everything living, or in this case dead, operates on some sort of electrical current. So I simply turned her off." He tried to offer a weak grin as he continued, "I quit chasing Bethoon after my wife disappeared. I always feared that he reconstituted her. Now, I know my fears were true."

Angela asked, "What's our next move, professor?"

He stood up and looked her straight in the eyes. She had never given him so much as a glimpse at authority before; therefore, he was cautious when he answered, "Let's get her back to my lab and restrain her. I will wring the information out of her if I have to!"

"And what about the rest of us, professor? What do you want us to do?" asked Charles, who was coming up from behind them.

Angela stepped in with orders. "You and Carrie-Anne stay here and talk to this family. Glean whatever information out of them you can. In particular, find out why Erin seems to be a pivoting point in this case." Charles motioned for his wife to come to the group. Once she arrived, Angela continued, "Either the mayor doesn't have a clue, or there's more to him and his family than any of us know."

"On it!" Carrie-Anne answered. Then, she asked, "Do you think the vampires will come back?"

"Not if they know what's good for them," the professor informed them as he opened his sophisticated toolbox. The professor, pulling out two pistols and shoving them into Carrie-Anne's and Charles Martin's hands, explained, "These are wooden bullet guns. You must aim for the heart or the head." He then handed them three clips of twelve shots each. He then gave them one of the small tools like the one he used on the vampire queen. "You have to be really close to a vampire when using one of these. As you have witnessed, they work. So, if all else fails, use them. I will get you more once I create them in the lab. The others will need them as well. They are only good for one use, I am going to have to create a less expensive, multiple-use device in the future."

Everyone just stared at him. Only Charles was brave enough to ask, "When did you..."

Before Charles could finish his question, the professor answered, "Haven't you noticed I don't sleep well?"

There was a commotion coming from the road, and surprisingly, getting out of a car, was FBI commander, James Stasher. By his side was Erin. They both smiled at their small group of comrades and started moving toward them. Dawn was on the horizon, and the vampires were gone, fleeing from the morning light. Suddenly, from out of the shadows, jumped three wolves, stopping everyone in their tracks. What no one seemed to notice, other than Charles, was that the horizon was beginning to change colors. Charles suggested, "The sun's going to be up in about an hour or so. It's been a long night. I suggest you agents get everyone back into their homes. Carrie - Anne and I will stay here and brief the mayor. Erin, you can stay with us if you want." She nodded in agreement. "Stasher, you and your men can head back to Tucson. Jake," At the mention of his name, the wolf turned and growled at him. Then he went silent as his body started to change before them once again this day.

Charles continued giving the orders. "You and Kira can do what you want. You should rest; you've earned it."

Angela stared at Stasher as he moved toward her. "We need to talk. You want to do it here, or at the office?" he asked.

"At our office," she suggested. She watched both Kira and Jake finish returning to human form. Angela walked up to the two agents said, "One of you comes with me, and one of you stays here."

"I'll stay here," Jake growled. He looked at Stasher and said, "He shot me, Angela." Everyone in the group froze. "If I go with you, I might kill him. Besides, something's not right here. I can't put my finger on it, but something feels..." he paused and sniffed the air, "weird."

"That's fine with me," Kira answered. "I need a shower anyway."

"I thought he was going to attack me, or Erin," Stasher interjected.

"Sure, you did," Jake spat back. "Since when do FBI agents carry silver bullets anyway?"

"Let's just have everybody do their job for now. We will settle this situation later," Angela proposed.

"How did you guys wind up here in the first place?" The question came from Stasher.

Angela explained, "We are here because the professor and Charles thought that if the vampires were to come out again, they would attack the weakest point of our case, the Hastings. It was luck, really. They met with the Hastings earlier in the day and tried to explain what was going on. Charles had the idea to arm them in case the vampires came back and tried to get revenge for Percy, or whatever else they've been hassling this distraught family about. We would have been here sooner but someone shot one of my agents. It took me hours to explain the situation to the doctor who extracted the silver bullet from Jake. How could you be so careless, James?"

"Hey, look," James nervously licked his lips, "I don't like wolves, period. How was I supposed to know that Jacob Taylor was a wolf?"

Angela thought for a moment, then suggested, "What do you say we let them finish up here, and you and I go back and hash this over with a bottle of Scotch, Agent Stasher?" Not waiting for an answer, Angela walked away and joined the other members of her team.

As everyone went their separate ways, no one seemed to notice the odd grins on the faces of Agent Stasher and Erin Hastings as they whispered the words that no one but they could hear, "Revenge is going to be so sweet!"

Chapter Fourteen

Homecoming, Sort Of

A hallowed joy filled the room. Erin's mother had not let go of her daughter's hand since the vampire was invited back into the house she had called home for sixteen years. "Mom," she stated, acting a little shy, "you're embarrassing me! I'm fine, really."

"Enjoy it while you can," Jake insisted. "We have a lot to cover before we reach the end of the line with this case. There are so many twists and turns that I believe we have a long, long way to go before we sleep."

"Why's that?" the Mayor instinctively asked.

Carrie - Anne and Charles had just returned from the kitchen where they had made tea for everyone who wished for it. As they sat down, it was Charles who continued the flow of the conversation. "Statistics have revealed that in cases such as these, seldom has the vampire returned to their home and had a family reunion after a fact-finding expedition. Normally, most of them return home only to destroy their families and any true reminder of what they once were. Of course, this data comes from movies and TV. There is no true-life, real-world, information available."

Suddenly realizing what he was saying and who he was saying it to, Charles blushed in embarrassment. "You'll have to excuse my husband, he doesn't get out much," Carrie-Anne said as she elbowed Charles in the stomach. Then she gave a soft giggle to defuse the tension in the room.

"It is so good to see you, Pooh," the Mayor said to his daughter. "You look well." He paused as he tried to think of the right words to use, then added, "Well, you look as well as can be expected anyway."

"Tea?" Carrie - Anne was asking, then accommodating anyone who wanted a serving.

"I'm sorry to interrupt," Jake said from his seat on the far side of the room, "but, Mr. Hastings, what is going on in your sleepy little town that we don't know about?"

"Frankly, I don't know what you are talking about," the mayor insisted, answering Jacob Taylor's question. "I wasn't even going to run for Mayor this term. I had made a deal with my wife that I would not run for another term, when in walks the Napier clan, offering me tremendous financial backing. They said they believed in me, though it's hard for me to accept that now."

While everyone was sipping on their tea, Jake asked another question. "Who are you talking about when you say the Napier clan?"

"Well," the Mayor thought for a moment then added, "It's Ethan and Martin Napier who are the real business people in that family. But, when we met, the sons told me that it was Alden Napier who really wanted to show his support. I got the impression that Ethan didn't really want their business to grow too massive for fear they wouldn't be able to control it. However, Martin is the real muscle in the family, and he likes power. He supported Alden one-hundred-percent. They also knew that Melissa and Erin were good friends, so they decided to throw their support behind my campaign."

"You didn't know about the drugs, the gambling, or the extortion they were involved in throughout the south-west region of Arizona?" Jake's tone was hard and unforgiving.

Mr. Hastings stood, and looking straight at Jake, he insisted, "The police had not informed me of the Napier's involvement in those things until after..." He paused and looked down at his daughter. His eyes filled with tears as he continued, "I know the events of the past few months have been strange, but I knew nothing of the things you bring up now. We were trying to be good parents to our children when we allowed Erin to bring that creature into our home."

"By creature, you mean Percy Kensington?" Jacob questioned.

"Yes, Sir." The Mayor answered quickly.

"Dad," Erin tried to interject, to stop the conversation from going where she knew it was going.

"Erin," Jake said, "we need to get all the information we can so we can figure out what steps to take next. Did you like Percy, Mister Mayor?" Jake asked.

"No, I did not," the Mayor answered. "Well, not exactly. Truthfully, at first, we all were drawn to him. He was good to our Erin, and to our other children as well. I've never understood why he preyed on my little girl that night. We didn't know what he was. If I had known..." He paused. His thoughts were coming haphazardly. He seemed to be searching for the solution to his problems while answering the investigator's questions. He thought for several moments and said, "He kept pestering me about the Napiers and some land they wanted the city to annex. I just didn't think it was feasible for the city to invest the time, capital, and energy into the southwest corner of the county limits. I've never understood why they wanted that corner of our county to be connected to St. David."

"What's out there?" Jake asked, with a sense of urgency in his voice.

"Nothing really," the Mayor said nonchalantly. "There are some caves that tourists used to explore, but, other than that, there's nothing to speak of. Arizona State did some excavating out there several years ago and found some skeletal remains. The head excavator said they actually saw Indian burial grounds and shut the whole area down. They made it a sanctuary of sorts. You have to get all kinds of permission slips and licenses to go exploring out there, even today."

Erin seemed nervous. She sipped her tea and started to nibble on some shortbread cookies that were just within her arm's reach. Jake noticed her nervousness, but said nothing, as he continued to verbally probe the Mayor. "Are there minerals or something out there that you are aware of?"

"No, not that I know of." The Mayor paused, as if collecting his thoughts, and then continued, "But, come to think of it, there have been several missing person reports from that area made to our chief of police, who reports directly to me. However, he later recanted his statement and told me he was mistaken; he said everything was fine. I know, Mr. Taylor, maybe as Mayor I should have taken a closer look out there, but Alden Napier bought the land eight years ago, and I just figured he thought he could recoup some of his losses if we annexed it under our dome of responsibility. Possibly create a museum commemorating the earliest settlers to the region."

Jake stood for several moments, thinking. Then he looked at the Mayor, Erin, and the Mayor's wife and asked, "I'm sorry to bother you, but do you still have your copy of the tape from the night of your daughter's death that Hoffenpiller gave you?"

Carrie – Anne quickly stepped in to stop what was going on. "Jake, we have a copy back at the office. Don't make them, or Erin, watch that monstrous video again."

Jake turned toward the family sitting on the couch and said, "I'm not trying to put you through the ordeal of watching your daughter die again. However, I think it may hold answers as to why this neighborhood is being stalked by the underworld of St. David." He developed a questioning look on his face. "Our version may be edited. I don't think the family copy would be. They would want to shock your family into submission. Why did they choose Erin? It just doesn't add up. We have a little tidbit of information on Alden Napier and the sons, but it doesn't explain what happened to Erin. Also, why does it seem to fit that the land is coming into play? This is bigger than any of us could have thought. I'm hoping to see something in your copy of the drew his pistol and aimed it directly at Erin's head. "I don't know who you are, young lady," Jake proclaimed, "but you are not Erin!"

♦ ♦ ♦

The first thing Angela and Eric viewed once they returned to their compound was the Vampire Queen. Two members of the team were seeing to her comfort. The professor made sure she was strapped in. There had to be no room for error on that. Everyone knew if the Queen were to get loose, no one would be left alive. Eric stood there, staring at his former wife, lover, and best friend. There was no way that he could be left alone with her for very long. Therefore, once she was strapped in on the cushioned table, the door to her room was locked. The room next to the vampire's cell was being used as a buffer zone. It had windows on both outside walls. There were no shades; therefore, if she tried to escape, the sun would burn her to death. That would make it very hard for the vampire to leave the room during daylight hours. The sunlight was another deterrent to her not leaving the building.

Once Agnes was dealt with, everyone took a huge sigh of relief and relaxed. All, that is, except for the professor. He stood looking through the window at his wife, who lay on the other side. Once the lights were turned off, no one could see the Queen in her cell because of the limited brightness in the room. But Eric could still see her. Her eyes were open and glaring at him. She was angry that he had anticipated her every move and had taken her prisoner. Agnes could also see the sunlight reflecting on his face. It was his protection for now. But, sooner or later, he would let his guard down. Then he would be hers, to be her slave forever, if Agnes commanded it. She slowly turned her head away from the man she used to call her husband.

"Professor?" It was Agent Harrison. "You going to be alright?"

He shifted his head to look into Angela's eyes. "Yes, Dear, I will be fine. The mistakes I made with Agnes I made because I was very young and gullible back then. I thought I had put her disappearance behind me, but seeing her again does bring it all back." His shoulders slumped a little after he said the words.

"I don't usually do this, Eric," Angela said, as she walked over and wrapped her arms around the older man's shoulders. "Don't tell any of the others I did this. Don't forget, I carry a gun, and I'm good with it," she said, jokingly. She leaned back and gazed into the older man's eyes.

"Your secret is safe with me," he answered. Then, disconnecting himself from the embrace, Eric continued staring into the darkness.

"Professor," Angela became the woman in charge once again, "do not open that door, or go in there, without one of our people in there with you. Do you understand?"

"Absolutely," he said, looking directly into her eyes.

"You do realize that as long as she's here, everyone is in danger of an attack?" Angela asked.

"I'm counting on it," Eric answered. "None of us can drop our guard. If we do, we are all dead."

There was some scuffling outside the room in which they were standing. The door opened briskly, and in walked Agent James Stasher. "Do you want my report or not, Harrison?" he demanded.

She gave the professor one more look of warning, and then, before heading back to her office, she said, "Professor, could you check on Agent Knight for me? Send her to my office as soon as she's done cleaning up."

"I would like to join her, if you don't mind?" Eric said.

"I don't mind at all. Your insights will be greatly appreciated," Angela said as she and Stasher headed to her office.

She threw the door open and, quickly and quietly, she rounded on Stasher and threw a right cross that caught the agent square on his jawline. "What the hell was that for?" he asked, as his anger tempered his voice.

"You shot Jake. And from what I understand, you put the same round into Erin as well. I should have called Washington about you a long time ago."

"Don't forget to tell them I shot through the vampire and hit the wolf," Stasher admitted. Before he could finish his sentence, Angela balled up her fist again to take another swing at him. However, just before she could make contact, he said, "Never forget, Agent Harrison, I am your superior, and I can, and will, pull you off this case."

Her fist relaxed. As Stasher stepped back away from her, rubbing his jaw, he said, "Could I have handled things differently? Yes, I could have. However, Kira's safe, and so are Agent Taylor and his booty call."

Angela said, "It's when you say crap like that I just want to knock you into next week." She walked around her desk and reached down to her bottom drawer and pulled out a bottle of Old Taylor bourbon whiskey. She also pulled two shot glasses and placed them on the desk. She poured some of the whiskey into each glass. Angela handed James one and said, "Sorry about the punch. Jake's a good man. I don't like any of my people in harm's way."

"I'm the same way about Knight. But, truthfully, when our agents are working on a case, they are always in danger," he said, downing the shot in one gulp.

"So, what do you or your people know?" she asked, pouring Stasher another shot.

"Not much," he said, as he slammed down the second shot glass full of whiskey.

"Erin said that Tommy was out there with you. Do you have an update on him?"

"Agent Kensington was killed in action by Wolf-Boy. Tore his throat clean out," Agent Stasher insisted. "A gruesome attack. Of course, he hated wolves, while I, on the other hand, find them irresistible. I already called a cleanup crew. They should be finished by now. I'll file a report with Washington when I get back to Tucson."

The two federal agents sat in Angela's office and discussed life in general for several minutes until they were interrupted. Kira and the Professor entered their leader's office. Both were carrying their assigned weapons, and they were pointed right at the head of Agent James Stasher. "Kira told me, on the way back from the mayor's house, that there was something off about you. Personally, I know you're not James Stasher, but I just can't put my finger on who or what you are," Angela said.

The man disguised as Stasher carefully placed the shot glass on her desk. When he looked up at Angela, there was a Cheshire Cat grin on his face. "What gave me away?"

"Stasher didn't drink, ever." It was Kira who answered. "He said it would kill him."

"You'll be happy to know that drink did not kill the esteemed Mr. Stasher." The voice of the creature in front of them was changing. It sounded younger and had an English accent.

"Tommy! I should have known," Angela said. "What in the wide world of sports is going on? Who are you working for?" That appeared to be the more pertinent question at the moment.

The man before them decided to answer Angela's question with one of his own. "You should have known, but you didn't, did you?" His tone was smug as his form began morphing into that of his alter ego.

"Did you have to kill Stasher? He had kids and a wife," Kira asked him.

"I understand, Angela, that you thought of James as a traitor and a coward. Are you disappointed because I killed him, and you didn't get a chance to finish him off yourself? You might as well lower your weapons. You can't kill me." He was now wholly in the form of FBI agent Arthur "Tommy" Kensington.

"Tommy, are you admitting that you killed one FBI agent, shot another, and did who knows what to Erin?" Angela asked.

"Erin's fine," he stated, without hesitation. "James Stasher had it coming to him ever since Missouri, and you know it. Jake, on the other hand, has been a thorn in my side ever since we met. I wanted him out of the way. Too bad it didn't work; but, our little game's not over with yet."

Angela knew she was working in the dark here. There was something about Tommy and his role in this situation she needed to figure out. She wanted to keep him talking. "Lower your weapons," she ordered. "Tommy, can we sit for a moment and have another drink?"

"Oh, Angela, no matter what I tell you, you will never be able to figure out what's going on here. You, dear woman, have a destiny. It's been building for over eight years. I guess you have a right to know."

"You keep bringing up Missouri. Is this all about Missouri?" Angela asked. "I did what I had to do there. You're not going to make me feel sorry for any decision I made."

"You made a terrible enemy there," Tommy answered, as an evil grin grew on his face.

"How did I make an enemy there?" she asked, afraid of what she might find out. "I was forced to kill an exceptional man there. Are you telling me something different?"

"No, you're right. You killed Stark Hansen." Suddenly, Tommy's form changed into that of Stark. His angelic face pierced the veil of Angela's suspicion.

Angela's hand started to tremble as she reached for her glass of bourbon and drank it straight down. "What are you, Tommy? How are you able to do this?"

Tommy, now a seemingly concerned Stark Hansen, stood before the FBI agent. "It's not me you should worry about, Angela. You've always treated me just fine. My Master, on the other hand, wants you dead. And he always gets what he wants."

Angela stared at the form of the only man she had ever opened her heart to. In their brief moments together, Angela had always felt Stark Hansen was the one that got away. It all rushed back to her; getting the people out, the shot. Then, in the center of her mind's eye, she saw him, the man with the black hair with the white streaks and the Fu Man Chu, and he was smiling at her.

Angela, with her face frozen in fear, could only say, "But, we killed him. Stark told me to shoot him, and that would destroy the Master."

"If wishing would only make it so," Tommy said, changing back into original form. "There is no stopping him. There is no stopping me either. We are the same, the Master Gardener and me. You might know him better by his real name, the name you were given in Missouri - Falstaff. Leave this place, Angela and take everyone with you. Otherwise, you and your team, and all other human life in the area, will die, needlessly."

"But, I thought you said this was between her and the Master," the professor said.

"If she stays here, it will be. Falstaff is too powerful. You and Hansen slowed him down in Missouri, but now he's stronger, better prepared. You can't stop him." After the words of his last statement, Tommy changed back into himself. The master of disguise was now in the official agent shirt and tie. He stood up, walked through the door, and then through the walls, and was gone. His work here was done

Kira flew to Angela's side and placed her hand on top of her boss's hand. Nothing. The leader of the group was visibly shaken. Kira, not giving up, turned the swivel chair that Angela sat in so that the two agents faced one another. She shouted, "Angela, Angela, C'mon, snap out of it." Angela just sat there, her eyes frozen with fear. A lone tear ran down the side of her face. She was locked in the terror of her own thoughts. Turning to the professor, Kira asked, "What do we do now, Eric?"

"First, I'm going to my room and get a recording device, in case I need to replay it for evidence," he answered. "Then we wait on Angela to think this out. Meanwhile, you and I are going to interrogate my wife before it gets dark."

♦ ♦ ♦

Erin started laughing while she tightened her grip on her mother's hand, making her cry out in pain. "Erin," Jake Taylor said in a firm, disciplined voice, "let go of your mother, now."

"But you just said I wasn't Erin. You can't have it both ways, Jake," the vampire implied. "Which is it? Am I Erin, or am I a fake Erin? You should be sure if you're going to shoot me. By the way, what did I do to make you wary?"

"Let Mrs. Hastings go, and I'll tell you," Jake answered, his voice calm, but to the point.

Erin released her mother, who quickly removed herself from the sofa. Erin's father then joined Jake. He grabbed his shotgun and pointed it at the imposter, pretending to be his daughter.

"Daddy?" Erin whined, as she pleaded for forgiveness with her eyes. Then, looking at Jake, she asked, "How did you know?"

"Simple. Erin doesn't drink or eat anything but blood. Every day, every night, blood. She said all food or drink tasted like ash or dirt to her, and she would always vomit it out of her system. You should have done your homework." With that, Jake put a bullet in her head and in her heart.

Both the Mayor and his wife shouted with shock and disbelief as they glared at Jacob Taylor, not knowing whether to thank him or shoot him. Erin sat there, slumped over, eyes shut, not moving. But in a short breath, her eyes opened and she began to laugh. As she droned on with laughter, Jake asked, "What are you?"

"I'll admit," the body that was posing as Erin said, "you are good, Jake. Tommy said you were, but I didn't believe him. Still, you should be smart enough to know bullets don't kill vampires, so how did you think you could kill me? Not saying I am one, of course." Her body began shifting into a form that Jake didn't recognize, but, the Mayor did."

"Alden Napier? How can this be?" the Mayor asked.

As everyone sat there, startled, the Master reversed the bullets out of his head and chest and placed them on the table. "This body is in perfect condition? Please don't muck it up again," he sneered.

The form then shifted into Percy. Both men aimed their guns at the figure in front of them as it changed shapes, again and again. Finally, the shifting stopped, and the Master returned. "I don't get it," Jake said. "What is it you want from us? From this town?"

"Everything," the Master responded without hesitation. "But, what I will take, for now, is a meeting with Ms. Angela Harrison. If you get me a meeting with her, I will stop all of this chaos. What do you say? Do we have a deal?" The Master extended his hand.

Something inside of Jake's head clicked. He remembered how Angela told her story about a man in a Fu Man Chu mustache with a horrible attitude. Angela thought she had killed him, but, here he stood, in St. David, very much alive. "Why Angela?" Jake questioned.

"Ah, Mr. Taylor, you must understand why it has to be Angela. I have planned a Homecoming, of sorts, and all the players are here, in this town. You are invited as well, Agent Taylor, and, by all means, bring all your FBI friends."

Jake swallowed hard and asked, "Let me get this straight, I let you talk to Angela, and you will leave everyone in this town alone?"

"Absolutely," the Master said, "you have my word on it! I have worked for the past eight years to get this area in shape. Missouri was a better place, and it was all ready to go until the government stepped in and ruined everything. Now it's time for a little payback. All I want is Agent Angela Harrison, also known as the Angel." He then smiled an enormous, demonic smile, which chilled everyone in the room to the bone, and morphed into Erin again.

"Don't worry, Jake, Erin is still in here; I have not hurt her. Not yet, anyway. I simply needed this shell. My old meat sack was worn out. However, I will need a different body soon because I cannot live inside a body without a soul for very long." Looking around the room, he asked, "Are there any volunteers?"

"Uh-ump," it was Mrs. Hastings, wanting everyone's attention. "May I ask a question of Erin, or whoever she is?" Jake nodded, indicating yes. "Can you tell me why you chose my daughter, and my family, to vent out your hostilities? What did we ever do to you?"

Suddenly, Percy appeared on the woman's couch. "It wasn't Erin's fault, Mrs. Hastings, nor mine. No, it was actually my fault," the form said, changing into Tommy and smiling that toothy, evil smile. "I was smitten with romance for your little girl. However, I couldn't use my own form. Who could fall in love with a skinny bag of bones like me when you could have this guy?" He changed back into Percy.

Jake shouted, "I've seen enough of this!" He aimed his gun at the entity on the couch. "Pick a form and stick with it. I will take you to Angela." He turned to his two team members and told them to escort Erin back to the office. He would be there shortly. Then, turning to the Mayor, he asked, "Mr. Mayor, could I see the tape one more time? I can watch it back at headquarters." Jacob Taylor watched as Carrie – Anne and Charles led Erin toward the door. "Hurt them, and I will hunt you down and destroy you!" were Jake's final words for the thing in Erin's form. She mockingly looked at him and blew him a kiss.

Once they were gone, the Mayor brought the tape to Jake and put it in their DVD player. "If you are going to look at it again, perhaps I can watch it with you and tell you who all the players are," the Mayor suggested.

"Give me some time to watch it alone first. Then, if I need your help, I'll call for you? Is that acceptable to you?" The Mayor and Mrs. Hastings both nodded in agreement and left him to his own devices. Jake sat on a stool and watched Erin's death over and over again. He would rewind the DVD, then fast forward it, watching the same scene again and again, hoping to find a clue. "Finally!" he shouted to an empty room. "I knew it! I knew it," he said as the Mayor and his wife re-entered the room.

"What did you find out? What did you see?" Mrs. Hastings asked.

"Sit, sit," he said excitedly. "Watch." In his excitement, Jake had forgotten for a moment who the young victim was to these people. He paused the tape and apologized. His embarrassment was undeniable.

"Mr. Taylor, if you can bring closure to our daughter's death, then we will do our best to get through it, no matter how many times we have to watch this damned thing," Mrs. Hastings said.

"Keep in mind," Jake instructed, "that you have an unedited disk; ours was tampered with." He pressed play on the remote as the entire family, including the children, had surrounded the agent. The camera followed Percy as he stepped back and let the other demons have their way with Erin's corpse. The camera angle drew back and moved slightly to the right, as if it were bumped. However brief the shift was, it caught Percy's form as it suddenly changed into Arthur "Tommy" Kensington, meaning Percy had nothing to do with Erin's death. As the camera started moving back toward Erin's body, Jake paused the disk and shouted, "There! Right there!" On the video, two people could be seen standing next to Tommy Kensington.

"Oh my God!" it was Mrs. Hastings and the Mayor said at the same time.

Standing next to the smiling Tommy was the Master Alden Napier. The second image was blurry, but standing there, holding tightly onto the Master Gardener's arm, was a young woman. "That's Melissa Napier," the Mayor stated. Jake pressed the play button again, and everyone in the room noticed the Master say something to Tommy. "What did he say?" the Mayor asked.

Swallowing stiffly, as if he had a lump of clay in his throat, Jake repeated the words. "I think he's saying, 'Tommy, let's get this show on the road.' I need to get this DVD back to the office. There is so much more on here than on the one we have. We have better equipment back at the office, and maybe we can see things more clearly."

"Who gave you your tape, Mr. Taylor, the one you have at the office?" questioned the Mayor.

Jake thought for a moment and then raised his eyebrows when he answered, "Arthur Tommy Kensington." His voice was as soft as a whisper the stern FBI agent, turned to the Hastings and said, "I can't say for sure, but I think Melissa Napier set your daughter up."

♦ ♦ ♦

The lock on the door clicked open, and in walked Professor Eric von Bruton and Kira, with uncomfortable looks on their faces. "Kira," the professor began, "this is my ex-wife, and Queen of the Vampires, Ms. Agnes." He paused, trying to find the right words, and then he added, "The Cannibal."

Kira smiled; Agnes did not.

"It hurts you to think that I lay with him, doesn't it, old man?" Agnes asked.

"Yes," he answered.

"Good," she fired back.

"Alright, children, play nice," a voice came from behind them. Enter the five-foot-eight lead investigator in charge, Angela Harrison. After several long moments alone in her office, Angela had sorted out her demons and told her colleagues she was ready to face new terrors. "Agnes, we need some questions answered, and you are the only one who can help us," Eric said.

"What do you want from me?" the vampire queen asked, never once taking her eyes off of her ex-husband.

"Why are you here?" Eric asked.

"We were requested by that fool, Blakely Hoffenpiller. He sent for our clan to come here to help him deal with you humans." She spat the bitter words. "Bethoon couldn't wait to get here. However, there is no love lost between Hoffenpiller and my husband."

"Technically, I'm still your husband," Eric sniped at the vampire.

"Clan?" Kira asked.

The Queen chuckled. "You humans are so stupid. You think that most of the world is good, and you are at the top of the food chain. There are clans like mine all over the world. We lay back and let you come to us."

"But, not this time," Angela interrupted the vampire's speech. "Why are you here, in the sleepy little town of St. David?"

"I already told you. Hoffenpiller!" The vampire was becoming unsettled and started to thrash about.

"What do you know about the Master Gardner?" Angela asked.

"Nothing," the Queen insisted, looking away from them.

The professor motioned for the others to step back. He took his ex-wife's hand and spoke, "Agnes, I'll tell you what, if you answer all of Angela's questions, you have my word, I will let you go as soon as it gets dark." He paused for a moment as tears filled his eyes. "I did not expect to find you here. I came with them because since you disappeared, I have done nothing with my life. I'm still teaching at the same small college where we met all those years ago. I have missed you so much. Seeing you with Bethoon cut me to the quick. I am sorry for the jab at you earlier." Once he was done with his declaration, Agnes turned her head and noticed that everyone in the room was showing emotion, either with their eyes or their facial expressions.

"That is one thing I do miss by being inhuman," she said, looking at all three of them, "the tears." She paused for several moments, then said, "Look at me, Eric. I promise, no tricks." Slowly, the professor's eyes met hers. "When we battled Bethoon all those years ago, it was I who messed up. You told me to ignite the explosives, but you were still battling with him, and I couldn't take the chance of losing you. He had knocked you out and was about to drain you of your life's blood. I couldn't bear to lose you. I yelled at him to encourage him toward me and to save you. He threw your lifeless body into the wall, and I thought you were dead. Once he got close enough, I pushed the plunger that was connected to the explosives, and the ceiling fell upon him. The blast knocked me back into the vestibule wall of that broken-down old church. I could not move after that. My back was broken. Bethoon was stunned, but, obviously, the blast didn't kill him. People rushed in through a hole in the wall and found you. I heard them say you were alive, but that was at the same time Bethoon found me. I didn't want to alert anyone because he would have turned on the small group of people and killed them all, including you! He knelt down and bit me before I could react. He then picked me up and took me to his lair, which was the basement of a cabin in the woods. Once I turned, I convinced Bethoon to move north to save the people of the village."

Everyone in the room stood quietly looking down at the woman for several moments, and then, with Eric still holding her hand, both Angela and Kira unstrapped the Vampire Queen. "I don't know if I'd do that if I were you," Agnes said. "I still get the bloodlust."

Angela left the room and was back in a few moments with two bags of blood. "This should hold you until you get back to your own kind. Just tell them you broke out, or whatever you think will work."

"I don't know of any Master," Agnes said, "other than this guy who paid us a visit while we were in the caves in the southwest of town. He told us to back off and said he was the one responsible for killing Percy. Other than that, he left some FBI agent for us as payment for what we had done up to that point. She was very nice, very friendly. Bethoon turned her for his desires. I believe her name was Anastasia."

"Eric," Agnes said, "I am very proud of you. In your own way, you did everything you could to stop Bethoon. He is very jealous of you. He hates it when I talk about you."

At this statement, Eric von Bruton was drawn to his wife. He couldn't stop himself. "You talk about me?" A smile of pride spread across the elderly man's face.

"Only, all the time," she said, as she ran her fingers through his hair.

"What made you change your mind and talk to us?" he asked.

"I knew you would let your guard down, and then I could do this." Suddenly, without warning, she grabbed her ex-husband by the neck and twisted it until it snapped. The Vampire Queen threw his body off her and jumped off the gurney. She was on Angela before she knew what hit her. "You humans are so gullible. You actually think we care what happens to you?" She grabbed Angela and lifted her into mid-air.

"So, you lied to us? All that stuff you told us was a fabrication?" Angela choked the words out.

"No, it was all true. Eric was a brave man. But, my soul is gone, and I only know one thing: kill, destroy, and feed." She opened her lips to expose the teeth she used to draw blood.

"Hey, Vampire Bitch!" Kira shouted from behind them both. BLAM!! BLAM!! BLAM!! Three wood bullets went through the Queen's back and settled into her torso. The vampire convulsed in pain. "Eric knew you might pull something like this," Kira said. "He armed us all with these wooden bullet pistols." Kira stopped speaking when she saw that the pain from the bullets had caused the Vampire Queen to release Angela. "This is for Eric!" she shouted as she unloaded the entire clip into the woman's head and heart. Kira Knight, an excellent agent, let the Vampire Queen writhe in pain. She had one shot left. She had saved it for the Queen's head. The vampire stopped moving and started to dissolve into ash. To her clan, she was the Queen. To the FBI, she was merely Agnes von Bruton, wife of the Professor. Now, in both worlds in which Eric's wife existed, she was dead.

Angela, who had collapsed to the floor, was holding her throat and was working to avoid the pain that came from inhaling. "Thanks for that," she said, looking at Kira.

"That wasn't for you." Kira looked angry. "That was for Eric. You knew this could happen, didn't you?"

"I knew," Angela admitted, holding nothing back. "I also knew Eric was the only man that could help us deal with whatever creatures we came up against. He knew the risk and the rewards. Believe it or not, I have thought for some time that he was looking for a way to end his existence, and now he has it."

"Angela, you are a cold..." Kira's words ended with the sound of footsteps, walking toward the room where the professor's corpse now lay dormant.

Erin, in cuffs, Carrie – Anne, and Charles stopped as soon as they saw the ash and the professor's body lying on the floor. Charles immediately ran toward Eric's lifeless corpse, only to be slowed by Agent Harrison, who looked worse than she was. "What's going on here?" Charles asked as he assisted Angela to her feet.

"We found ourselves in a mess. Hopefully, you fared better," Angela replied.

Charles looked around the room until he had everyone's attention. He ordered, "We need to clean this up. Carrie-Anne, stay here with the others. I will go do my research, and we will meet in Angela's office in one hour."

"For what?" they all asked

"I don't know if you've noticed during the last twenty-four hours," Charles said, "but, the demons are definitely winning the war in St. David. And, she's got all the answers," he added, pointing at Erin. All eyes settled on Erin, who was wearing a smug smile of satisfaction. Once Angela turned and focused her gaze on their team member, she did not see Erin like everyone else did. She saw the man in black, the one that Angela knew as Falstaff. The case leader suddenly collapsed to the floor. The pressure had finally gotten to her. Her mind was playing tricks on her.

Just then, the door opened, and in walked Professor Eric von Bruton, looking very much alive!

Chapter Fifteen

Ribbon

When Charles returned to his makeshift lab that he and the professor had thrown together at a moment's notice, his eyes became focused on one of the computers. There was a large piece of paper taped to it that read "Press Enter!" Charles followed the instructions and watched the video that appeared on the screen. When he had finished, he quickly dashed over to the intercom button and pressed it, and ordered, "Everyone to the lab. Now!!"

Within minutes, everyone involved in the case, including Professor von Bruton, walked into the lab, questioning why they were summoned by "Geek Boy."

"Where's Jake?" Charles asked.

The door opened quickly, and Jake, who had brought along Erin, answered, "I'm right here, and I have something you all have to see."

"That's got to wait," Charles said. Then, using his iciest stare toward Erin, he asked, "Can we lock her away for now?"

"Whatever you have to say, just say it. I will eventually find out anyway," proclaimed the Master Gardeners' voice, coming from Erin's body. "You might as well spill the..."

"Shut up!" Angela snapped, interrupting the entity that was Erin. She could not stop seeing the notorious Falstaff standing in front of her.

Charles pressed the enter button of the computer, and the screen came alive once more. "Hello, everyone," the voice on the monitor said. The voice was unfamiliar to everyone in the room except for Angela and Jake. The face was that of the professor, but, as he spoke the words, they were clearly not his. "I hope you don't mind, Angela, but I have borrowed the professor's body for a moment." Erin tried to interrupt, but the voice on the screen interjected, "Sleep, Demon!" A bolt of electricity shot out from the screen, and Erin fell to the floor. This drew everyone's attention.

"I know you all must be reeling from the events of the last twenty-four hours. We are here to help, but you will need to trust in us, and in each other, if you expect to succeed in this situation. You have the skills to defeat what has befallen St. David, but you cannot do it individually. You must stick together. The first thing you all should know is that the professor is not dead. He is sound asleep in his room."

"Actually, he's standing right over there!" Kira pointed toward the man and asked, "So, who was it that Agnes destroyed?"

"The professor's face on the screen seemed perturbed as he responded, "I don't have time for a lot of questions. Suffice it to say, we are going to help you if you let us. You all are in ultimate evil up to your necks. Angela, you stepped in a bad situation when you were sent to quell the uprising in Hornersville. I tried to help you then, but they were much too smart for me in my human form."

"Stark?" both Angela and Jake said.

"Yes," The face on the screen smiled. The smile was so bright it was blinding. As the glow subsided, there stood Stark Hansen. "Listen, this thing you are up against is one of the oldest evils in the known universe. Somehow, it established a life here on earth, and it has spawned children. You are battling one of the original evils and two of its children. I was able to surprise it and put it into a deep sleep, but I don't know for how long. What you must do is band together as a unit and work to stop whatever evil you can. The less help I give you, the better it will be for all of you."

"Why is that?" asked Charles.

"This is not a question of good versus evil, Charles. It is a question of faith. If you believe in the concept of good and evil, then you must develop the conviction to do the right thing when times are difficult.

Angela, I believed at the time, that you were sent to Missouri by God to help me battle whatever demon this is. I had faith in you. I knew when the time came, you would do the right thing. You've got to have that same conviction now. I was not afraid of him eight years ago, and that's why I almost defeated him back then. Somehow, you've got to summon your faith and face the demon."

Tears were streaming down her face. The lead agent wasn't worried about zombies, vampires, or the Master Gardener. This was the only man she had ever loved. She wanted more time with him. All she could see right now was Stark Hansen, looking as he did eight years ago.

As she brushed her tears away, she asked, "Stark, will I ever see you again?"

"I don't know, Angel," was his answer. "There isn't much time. Hell is coming, and you must get ready for it. Survive the storm, then regroup and go to the caves. You got it? Go to the caves."

Erin's body started to stir as the screen went black. Everyone was staring at Angela when a crashing sound came from outside the room. Angela looked through the window shade and saw that the sun had set and realized they had undead visitors.

Jake, becoming aware that the full moon was coming, shouted, "The Wild is coming, I gotta go!"

"Kira, you go with him," Angela ordered.

"Hold it right there," Erin shouted. "No one's going anywhere until I find out what's going on."

The urge for Jake to change was gone. The noise from outside was gone. All that remained in the small room was silence.

Erin walked over to Angela and asked, "What did you see on the screen?"

"Aqualax." Angela spat the word at the demon before her.

Erin recoiled, as if in pain. "That witch is nothing but one of God's lesser minions."

"She feels the same way about you," Jake interjected.

By this time, the Master Gardner had turned into his original form. "You have no idea who you are dealing with. I am Falstaff, the Great." The demon was starting to get engrossed in himself. Everyone in the room realized at that moment that they were in trouble. "I was here in the beginnings of man, and I will be here at your end. I am the darkness of human life. Some say I am the ultimate evil, but I am more, so much more. All the wars that first began were caused by me. I urged Cain to kill his brother. Whenever a conflict needed tilting toward evil, I could be counted on. I have served my lord, my master, with the weapons of control, conquest, lust, and ambition. The fuel I use is loss, fear, disdain, sexual desire, disgust, bigotry, prejudice, and hate. Hate is one of the most reliable tools I have."

Angela, who was not afraid, asked, "So, why Hornersville?"

Falstaff turned his pulsating form toward Angela and spittle flew from his mouth as he shouted into her face, "Hornersville?" The demon thought for several moments, then, slowly, deliberately, turned out his answer. "If I could know love, I would have loved living in Hornersville. But, you Federal people couldn't leave well enough alone. I had that town ripe for harvesting until you came in and ruined everything. Buried deep in the ground there, are the energy reserves I needed to survive."

"There's nothing there," Charles interrupted. "We looked."

"Charles, I'm not talking minerals or gems. I'm talking about the mounds that the Indians scattered all over this nation. I can survive for thousands of years on the skeletal remains of the people of this earth. Now that the marrow in their bones has fossilized, it is truly a banquet fit for a king."

"But, you were killing the inhabitants of Hornersville. You were turning them into your servants, zombies, or whatever, Charles said. "

"Yes, I am royalty, and I need servants. The more mindless, the better!" Falstaff responded.

"But, you were stopped," Angela exclaimed.

"Weakened, not stopped," the evil entity insisted.

"Stark Hansen found a weakness in you, and everyone who serves you. He forced you to leave Missouri. You were barely alive," Jake spoke up.

"Enough of this!" the Master Gardner shouted. "I will not stand here and dodge your arrows of despair. You have lost; you are done. If you don't leave this town now, I will destroy you all!"

There came another violent explosion outside the office. The exterior wall of the building collapsed, and in strode Blakely and Bethoon. "Where is my woman, my Queen?" Bethoon bellowed.

"She no longer exists, my friend," Falstaff said.

Both vampires stopped in their tracks. "Who took the life of my mate?" Bethoon asked.

"I did," answered Kira. "She killed my friend, Eric, or so I thought, so I took her out."

"She killed Von Bruton?" A smile grew across the demon's face, but it soon disappeared when he noticed Eric standing in the back.

Bethoon shouted as he stepped toward Agent Knight, "You dare lie to me?" Kira saw him look toward where the professor was standing. She began preparing herself for an attack by the Cannibal. "You shall take her place!" he said.

"Not in this lifetime," Angela commanded, as she and the other agents pulled out their weapons. "If you want to tangle, let's get to it. We are not afraid to dance with the likes of you." The lead agent was testing the massive strength of the one known as Bethoon the Cannibal.

The Master Gardner stepped in. He held out his arms to stop the ensuing battle. "There will be no fighting today. This is my party, and you," he turned toward Hoffenpiller and The Cannibal, "you will not do this now. Once I am finished with them, you may have them."

Blakely Hoffenpiller was an excellent vampire leader. He had come to St. David over two hundred years ago when there was nothing but huts and pueblos. He had started his colony here. Blakely, very subtlety, took a life here and there, and no one was the wiser. Those under his command revered him, as if he were a god. However, on this day, he made one terrible mistake. "Once you are finished with them?" Hoffenpiller was livid. "I am the Master here! I am in charge. I take orders from no one!" He stepped over and grabbed Falstaff by the throat and lifted him into the air.

The Master Gardner started to laugh as he looked down at Hoffenpiller. Blood started flowing from the vampire's eyes and ears. "You fool!" Falstaff said. "Why do you think I am called the Master Gardner?" No answer came as Hoffenpiller was forced, from weakness, having lost so much blood, to set his prey down. "I cultivate lives, people, demons, and yes, vampires into doing my will," the Gardener explained. "You, sir, are in my way. Bethoon, kill this fool!" he ordered.

Without hesitation, Bethoon grabbed the unsuspecting vampire and put him on his knees. "I sent for Bethoon, you idiot," Falstaff informed Blakely. "I have been running this operation for years now. You will not come and take what I have grown for myself. I even visited you and gave you gifts to keep you away from this situation. Say goodbye to this world, demon, for now, you die!" With a nod from the Master Gardner, Bethoon pulled off the head of the vampire known as the Hoffenpiller. As he disintegrated into ash, the room grew eerily silent.

Falstaff then turned to Angela and said, "I've won and you've..." He was interrupted by the sound of another explosion and screams from the outside.

Suddenly, gunshots were fired, and a couple more vampires from the building disintegrated into dust. The ten or so monsters left inside started for the exits. "Take your clan and go," Falstaff ordered to Bethoon.

"But what about you?" Bethoon asked the Master.

"I can leave anytime I want," the Gardener insisted.

The Master Gardner turned to the others and said, "Our time together has been too short, but I am sure we will see each other again soon." Then, he evaporated into thin air and could no longer be seen.

Once the smoke cleared from all the chaos that had gone on outside, a lone person strode up to the hole in the wall. It was Agent Murphy, a subordinate of James Stasher, who came bouncing in the room. He looked like an old Spanish revolutionary with belts of explosives wrapped around his torso and holding his wooden bullet pistols in each hand. "Is everyone ok?" he asked. "I had the weirdest dream, and when I woke up, all these weapons were lying beside me on the bed. I figured one of you had put them there."

Everyone just stood there. The women cried while the men laughed. Through it all, Angela could only think of two things, Falstaff and her beloved Stark Hansen.

♦ ♦ ♦

While Jake and Kira went for another run during "The Wild" side of the night, the others stayed behind to clean up the mess in their office building. The building stood exposed by the gaping hole in the outside wall. It was quickly boarded up and made secure, but it bothered Angela how easily the demons had gained access to them. She quickly did what good leaders do. She instructed the heroic FBI agent known as Murphy to go to the local hardware store and get materials to temporarily patch up the building. Before he left, however, she asked, "How did you know to come here? You really saved our asses tonight, Murphy".

Respectfully, Murphy stated, "Ma'am, it wasn't me. It was James Stasher. I work the late shift at the Bureau, and there was this pounding on my door that woke me up. He told me to gather as many men as I could and get to St. David to help you guys out. Said something about owing you."

"Agent Murphy, I don't mean to rattle you, but James Stasher died last night." Angela put her hand on his shoulder. "A lot of strange stuff has been happening around here. It might be better if you forget about how you got here."

The agent looked unsure of himself, but nodded his head in agreement, and left to get the supplies. Before the young man had gone too far, Angela shouted, "Murphy?" He turned to face her. "Thank you! I don't say that enough, but thank you. However you came to be here, you arrived in the nick of time. I appreciate that, and so do the others."

Angela was standing inside the building, pondering what could happen next, when suddenly a warm feeling came from behind her. "Hello, Stark. You can't stay away, can you?" Angela said.

As she turned around, she was stunned to discover it wasn't Stark Hansen standing behind her. It was an Indian goddess. "Aqualax, I presume?" Angela commented.

"Humbly, I serve you, Angel." Aqualax spoke with a voice that sounded as sweet as honey.

Angela was drawn toward the divine light that was radiating from the goddess. Angela continued to stare at her until she finally asked, "Why are you here? What is it you want from me, or from us?"

"You have struck a chord with the ancient evil one," Aqualax answered.

"I, or should I say, Stark and I, almost defeated him in Missouri. But, as it turns out, we only hurt him, we did not destroy him," Angela humbly explained.

"You did more than you know, Angel. Would you expect that demon to tell you the truth in all things? Demons are not designed that way. You are positive; demons are negative. This evil has no rules that they follow, no structure. Goodness, on the other hand, was designed with the rules in mind. You like to follow the rules, don't you?"

"Did you send those agents from Tucson?" Angela asked.

Aqualax smiled, but said nothing. She was awaiting Angela's answer to her rules question.

Angela pondered the entity's question, but instead of answering, she asked another question of her own. "Why can't I see Stark? Face to face, I mean. You could make that happen. I just need to look at him as himself, not as some different form. Please, can't you make that happen?"

"Angela, you are almost to the end of the road in this mission. Once this task is finished, your assignment will be completed. Those are the rules. You are a rule follower; you should be able to comprehend," Aqualax explained.

"Why must everything in this case be so damned hard?" Angela questioned.

"Angela, you need to maintain focus. You need to keep your head about you. What good would it serve to give someone the prize before the race is won? Stay focused; stay on target. You will see Stark Hansen when you are finished."

"Are you trying to tell me my life must end before I can see him? If that is so, then take me now. I want to see him now!" Tears fell from the far corners of her eyes, expressing the emotional state she had been in since losing Stark in Missouri.

"I cannot say if you are meant to leave this place with your life, but I know that you must face the coming tide of events. You and your team need to remain focused and trust one another in order to complete this mission. Have faith, and you will see your Stark Hansen again," the goddess calmly told her.

"That is exactly what we are doing. But, this all feels kind of suicidal to me. From what I understand, this guy has almost infinite powers. How do we fight that?" Angela asked.

Suddenly, from behind Angela, Charles and Carrie – Anne approached. As her two team members arrived, Aqualax and her protective glow vanished. Angela was staring at the vast emptiness when Charles asked, "You OK?"

"Yes," she said, wiping the tears off her face.

"They've gotten the front wall back in place," Carrie – Anne reported. The side wall is going to take a little more time. What's our next move, Boss?"

"We wait for Jake and Kira to show up in the morning, and then we get to work preparing."

"Angela," said Charles, "It is morning! Jake and Kira are resting. It took all night to get the front secured. Are you sure you're okay?"

The tightly wound agent let out a giggle as she realized what Aqualax had done. She had kept her busy so the others could do their job and complete the repairs on the building without some pencil neck breathing down their throats. She needed to focus on how to get her team out of this mess.

Angela felt that this Gardener guy wanted to tie everything into place with a beautiful red ribbon and a bow on top. Why else would he mention the mound builder Indians? The Master Gardener spoke of Indian remains out in the south-west corner of Wabasha County. Angela now knew that's where he would try to take over. She just had to figure out a way to stop him. She intended to serve him up with a giant can of whoop-ass and see how well he swallowed what was about to happen to him.

The table was set, the lines had been drawn, and it was time to face the ultimate evil. Angela Harrison and her team must win for the good of all mankind. No one person, not her boss in Washington, nor the mayor, nor the righteous citizens of St. David, knew what she knew. It was time they did.

E.C.H.O

(Elite Counter-Horror Organization)

The Master Gardener

Part Three
The Crossed Line!!

Chapter Sixteen
The Bone Sucker

There is darkness. Then there is the darkness that dwells downward in the depths of hate, anger, and despair. That is the place where Falstaff lives. He was no longer sitting in the wheel-chair that was owned and operated by old man Napier. That husk was gone. It was sent to Bel-Zog. A place where this monster placed things that had offended him. He hated Alden Napier. Before Falstaff took over the old man's body, Napier had been a beloved member of society in Arizona. A shrewd businessman by all accounts, he was also considered fair and honest. All the things a demon like Falstaff hated. The chair he was presently sitting in was the chair that had followed him since the beginning of his rise to infamy. From conquest to conquest, kingdom to kingdom, throne room to throne room, the chair went with him. Falstaff no longer resided in Erin Hastings' body. A body without a soul was not worth spending much time in. He should have realized that much earlier, but didn't. He had morphed from the female form to that of his nearest associate, Ethan Allen Napier, the son of Alden. He had Erin's vampiric body thrown into the pit of Bel-Zog. There it would stay for hundreds of years until the Bel-Zog had sucked every single ounce of energy from the succulent morsel.

Now that Falstaff had retaken human form, he could deal with the many things in this world he was about to control. While he dwelled in the realm of the occult, he was so much more. At the beginning of his existence, he had begun as a wisp of smoke that was inhaled by the first beast who ever destroyed another creature for survival. With each death of an enemy that followed, he became stronger, with even greater attributes at his command. Emotions such as anger, fear, retribution, lust, and hatred were all at his fingertips to control. Not knowing precisely how he came to be, Falstaff made contact with the hellish leaders of the evil hoard he had bonded to. Those members saw the strength in Falstaff and relished in the idea of his growing stronger, because this demon would allow them to inhale his essence. It was like a drug to the other monsters, and they welcomed him enthusiastically. The more his abilities grew, the more respected he became, the more feared he became, and the more control of situations he held. This was also how he rose in the ranks of evil until, eventually, realizing that nothing commanded him, he was the ultimate evil.

Other demons who were similar to him did not possess identical traits to Falstaff'. Some developed the one thing Falstaff lacked and had never cared to create, compassion. Falstaff never had it, never wanted it, and when he saw it in others, he saw it as a weakness. Tommy, who claimed to be the Gardener's son, but actually spliced off from him, boiled over with compassion. Once Falstaff realized this defect in his son, the great one shunned him for quite some time. Eventually, Falstaff realized he could reach greater heights of control through the others. That's when he began to absorb their souls. He would gain strength from the evil inside his victims and merely chose to ignore any love and compassion he found.

Still sitting on his throne, his mind turned to the inventory of those who served him. Tommy was the first. Then there was Bethoon and his mountains of followers. He still had the good citizens of St. David, whom he planned on putting to work for his cause. Plus, he had his secret weapon that no one was aware of. He hoped to keep it that way until he needed it. It had been Bethoon, the Cannibal, who had named him the "Bone Sucker." It was a name he detested, but it was true. Falstaff devoured the marrow in the bones of the dead. He waited until the marrow crystalized. That was when he received the most energy from his meals. That was why he was drawn to the town of St. David. The caves of the inhabitants who settled in this region over 1500 years ago, were full of the food source he desired. No one knew this of course, not even those closest to him. Once he unearthed those bones, he could survive this earth well into the next five millennia, or more.

The monster suddenly sensed he was not alone. His newest body acquisition, Ethan Napier, shifted in his chair as he heard someone enter the room. Melissa Napier approached with caution and respectfully asked, "Master, could I ask a favor?"

"Anything, dearest," came his warmest response.

"I am not comfortable approaching you when you are in that form..." Before she could finish the request, Falstaff had changed into the form that everyone recognized him in, the Master Gardener. In this form, the young woman immediately embraced him and offered her body to him without hesitation. He gladly devoured her, but then he wanted to make clear who was in control of their relationship. Once he had finished with her, Falstaff stared into the dark pools of her eyes and said, "You are mine, no matter what form I am in. Get used to it." The demon withdrew himself from her embrace and mumbled to himself, 'Soon, I will no longer need your gifts, little girl. Perhaps I will give you, as a gift to Thomas!'

As he left the room, Melissa wiped the tears from her eyes while a large smile appeared on her face. She was delighted with their meeting. The more control he thought he had over her, the better. The truth was, the Master Gardener had no idea what was going on right under his nose.

♦ ♦ ♦

Charles Martin sat staring at his computer monitor as Carrie – Anne came into the room and asked, "What do you know, Geek – Boy?"

"I know Bethoon will be here soon, and we are not ready." His frown was unmistakable. "But, that's not the real problem. The Problem is Erin, or, actually, Falstaff in Erin's form. How do we battle that?"

"What have you found out about him?" Carrie – Anne asked. Both Professor von Bruton and Angela quietly entered Charles' domain.

"Not much." He exhaled as he stated his facts. "I found some reference to the Prince of Evil in a Babylonian text and some references to Falstaff in the books of Candor, but it's nothing that could lead me to any concrete reference material."

The professor broke in by stating, "When I was younger and was working on my Doctoral Thesis, I had the same difficulty finding any reference of Bethoon. Then I came across a text based on the Incan, or wait, was it Mayan society?" Von Bruton scratched his head. "It was the Aztecs. Yep, that's right, Aztec. Bethoon was mentioned in Aztec records. He had an associate who was a conquistador warrior. But it was he, not the vampire, who was leading the assault on the ancient civilization." The professor walked over to a stack of books, pulled one out, and slammed it on the table. He peeled the pages back and pointed at a hand-drawn picture, that was a likeness of Bethoon. "See, there he is." Bethoon had bloated eyes, like the old dragon drawings. Then, slowly, Angela's eyes moved from Bethoon to the person next to him. The man was adorned in conquistador armor, with his sword raised, and his weapon engulfed in flame.

"Oh, my God, there he is." She spat the words out as if she hated saying them. "There's Falstaff!"

As Jake and Kira walked into the room, refreshed from their nightly romp, the others stared down into the text. There they saw a tall man with long, dark hair with silver streaks on either side of his face. "Oh, my God," the others exclaimed.

"Professor, help Charles stay on top of this," Angela ordered. "The rest of us have to get ready for tonight." Then, glaring at Jake and Kira, "I know you two may be tired, but, right now, it's all-hands-on-deck. Can you help?"

"Absolutely," both FBI agents answered, and quickly got to work.

As if controlled by some invisible force, Angela staggered back to what was left of her office and fell into her chair. Several moments passed as she sat thinking of Erin, Tommy, Falstaff, Bethoon, and the man she once loved, Stark Hansen. There was a connection between all those people, and it couldn't just be a matter of good against evil. There had to be something more. When Carrie - Anne appeared at the door, Angela's eyes were filled with tears.

"We're not getting out of this, are we?" Angela asked. She grabbed what was left of her bottle of courage, poured three fingers of the whiskey, and drank it down. "Alive, I mean."

Carrie - Anne stepped into the room, picked up a chair that was overturned, and sat down. "It depends," she said softly.

"On what?" Angela fired back.

Carrie - Anne's eyes narrowed as she answered, "You!"

Angela slammed her glass on the desk and demanded, "What are you trying to say?"

The thin, attractive, blonde lawyer leaned forward in her chair and began, "I am good at my job, Angela. I can assess a situation and give advice on what steps the FBI should take next. I was just starting out as an agent when you were sent to Missouri. You were a legend, even back then. Only you could go there and get those people out. I could never have taken the shot that you took." She paused, making sure the woman across from her was listening. As Angela's brown eyes burned with anger, Carrie – Anne continued, "But, I'm waiting for that kick-butt side of you to show up. That woman would have a plan. She would take on the Cannibal first, and if she survived that, she would go after that bastard, Falstaff, and bury him where he stands. That Angela would take action, not sit here wasting time with self-doubt."

Angela's stare softened. She knew her partner was right, though the senior agent did not respond. When Angela made no comment, Carrie – Anne continued. "You see my husband out there?" Charles is racking his brain trying to help you and everyone else here. So, I suggest you tighten your panties and get out there and lead us as only you can. You are not going to find what you need at the bottom of that bottle."

Angela was speechless. She couldn't believe Carrie – Anne would speak to her that way. "I think you forget one significant factor," Carrie – Anne added. "God is on our side. Is this situation dark? Is it relatively hopeless? Yes. But God, or someone working through God, sent Stark to us at our darkest hour. He saved Jake and the professor and is now waiting for us to make the next move. So, Angela, what's it gonna be? Are you going to sit here, drink, and give up? Or, are you going to get out there, join us, and help us develop a plan to save the citizens of St. David?"

Angela sat there for several moments saying nothing, but analyzing every word Carrie – Anne had spoken. Finally, Angela Harrison gave her most penetrating smile to her new friend and softly said, "Thank you."

"No problem," Carrie – Anne said. Then, standing up, she left the room.

Angela shifted her gaze from the people outside to the Old Taylor whiskey bottle on her desk, and in her best John Wayne voice, she said, "Time to saddle up, Hombre!"

♦ ♦ ♦

"I need volunteers," Bethoon shouted over the den. "I need the bravest of you to join me in glorious battle." He was trying to work his minions into a frenzy. "I need vampires who are fearless of stakes, crosses, and wooden arrows. A demon who knows and understands that the path to success is lined by the corpses of the humans who wish to suppress us." He stared down at the hundreds, if not thousands, of vampires who were devoted to him and all he stood for. At this moment, he represented destruction.

"This Master Gardener, whom I know as Falstaff, he does not believe in me, or you! He has told me I will not survive this night, and that those who go with me will not return." Shouts of denial came from the group assembled below the rock upon which he stood. He continued, "These humans killed our beloved Queen, and the person I want to replace her with is in the compound where they are holding my beloved's ashes. Her name is Angela Harrison. She is the leader of the humans who are standing against us." Bethoon's creations were ready to fulfill their master's wishes. They were yelling, screaming, and pounding the earth with their excited frenzy. "Will you help me subdue and create a new queen for our family? For all of you?" He watched as the lowest of the low continued to shout and growl in support. The inter-sanctum of his closest disciples stood and waited as their fellow vampires were ready to mount an attack. Bethoon the Cannibal wanted to exact his pound of flesh. In fact, he wanted a million pounds of flesh, and his minions were primed and ready for the attack.

"We have only to wait until dark, my brothers and sisters. Come nightfall, we will go back to the building we left early this day and bring all of St. David to its knees. Then we will go to Falstaff and request, no, demand, that he allows us to harvest this town and make them in our image."

With his final statement, he turned to leave the rock he stood upon. Suddenly, Falstaff was standing in front of him in the form of Ethan Napier. "I have to hand it to you; you always could work up a crowd," he said.

"Did you come here to stop me?" Bethoon asked. The vampire knew he was the only one that could see the man for what he was, Falstaff the demon!

"No. I gave you my warning." He paused, gazed down at the vampire's minions, then said, "A vampire has to do what a vampire has to do. If you choose to come with me to the caves, I know, with my team and yours, there would be no opposition to what I have planned for this place."

"Just what are those plans?" the hulking vampire asked.

'He is curious,' the Master Gardener thought. 'This is very good.' He asked the Cannibal, "Why do you care?"

"You see, bone sucker, that's what makes my kind not trust you and yours." Bethoon spat his hateful words. "You have this massive plan in play, while me and mine worry about where our clan will be and how long we can survive. I have a responsibility to this clan, to my domain. I cannot trust in something I cannot see, cannot understand."

"I know that, my friend." Now he was setting the hook. "That's why, if you forego this fool's errand, I can guarantee your life until the end of time."

Bethoon said nothing, so Falstaff continued, "I promise you your life for as long as you want to live. As an extra bonus, I offer you a kingdom where you may live out your days, here, in the southwest corner of Arizona."

"What would I be expected to do?" the combative vampire asked.

"Nothing more than what you are planning to do in St. David this evening. However, if you're dead, you can't do anything but be fertilizer, just like your dead queen." The Master Gardener knew these words stung the vampire, but he also knew he had his attention. "I will still have my kingdom, but no one to keep it in line. I'll have to find someone. Maybe Tommy, I don't know. I do know that St. David is a great cover for what we are doing. If I'm to understand your plan correctly, the town is going to die tonight. I don't believe you can devour the entire town before they can call for reinforcements. They most likely have already done that."

"Something needs to be done. Those people killed my Queen!" Bethoon bellowed.

"How many queens have you had over the years, Bethoon?" Falstaff asked. "Just create a new one. But, not Harrison! She's all mine."

"So, that's why you are here, to protect the one they call the Angel?" Bethoon questioned.

Ethan Napier's body stood there, smiling with pride. As he did so, he changed into the familiar image Bethoon had always known him as, the one with the long black hair, the silver streaks, the Fu Manchu mustache. "Thank you, my friend," were the first words out of the Master Gardener's mouth.

"Falstaff, my ally, it is excellent to see you again."

"I want you to go tonight, but be selective in who you choose to go with you," Falstaff instructed. "Take those you don't mind losing, preferably members of Hoffenpiller's clan. Have them kill, maim, and destroy all the humans at the FBI encampment. Everyone except Angela Harrison. She is mine to torment until the end of time."

"Why so?" the vampire asked.

"That woman knows me better than she thinks she does. Harrison was in Hornersville. She and that simpleton, Stark Hansen, almost killed me. I can't let her give that information out. She tasks me Bethoon, she tasks me!"

"The others are to be disposed of?"

"Yes," Falstaff answered.

"There's a werewolf," Bethoon insisted.

"And a changeling," Falstaff added. "But the others are mere humans. Kill them and be done with it. Don't kill everyone from the town, however. Bring as many as you can to me, alive, to serve me as my mindless servants.

"Your will be done, Master!" Bethoon said obediently.

"Oh," Falstaff said as Bethoon turned toward the crowd to deliver his new orders. "Keep your best soldiers here. Have them prepare to allow the townspeople in, but with no possibility of escape. And, Bethoon, I cannot stress this strongly enough, don't die!"

As Bethoon turned toward his monstrous brood, he saw Falstaff evaporate. "Brothers and sisters," Bethoon boomed, "there has been a slight adjustment of plans..."

♦ ♦ ♦

"So, I guess I should explain," Jake said in a humbled voice.

"About what?" Angela asked.

"Stark. And the fact I let you tell me the story of how he died and never said anything about who I was," he said even more quietly than before.

"Did you know about my situation with him?" she asked.

"I was allowed to read the report you submitted eight years ago," he said in an official voice, "but I didn't realize anything for sure until you explained about 'the drop' when we were on the highway a couple of days ago."

He was quiet for several minutes and then asked, "Why do you think all these things with Missouri are coming forward now?"

"I don't know," she answered. "I do know Falstaff was there. Jake, if you could have seen those townspeople. Somehow, he turned them into zombie-like entities and was controlling them, forcing them into doing his bidding. I cannot allow that to happen to anyone in this town."

Professor Von Bruton was leaning on the door frame, listening to every word, when he interjected, "You didn't mention that before. The zombies, I mean. You didn't mention zombies to me. I have to work that into this situation." They both turned to look at Von Bruton,

"I'm sure we've all forgotten to mention things that could seemingly help with this situation. Suffice it to say, we should sit and have a roundtable discussion. Perhaps after we finish getting prepared for tonight's confrontation," Angela stated, after choosing her words carefully. Jake nodded his head in agreement.

"I believe," the professor said, "we are ready. Or, as ready as we can be, for an attack of this magnitude. Were you able to reach anyone in Tucson?"

"Yes," Angela insisted. "However, I was only able to reach a receptionist. I then contacted Washington, but I wasn't able to reach Cline, the man who assigned me to this case. I left a message, but I don't think he will be able to do anything to assist us here."

"Why do you say this?" the professor asked.

"This," she made a circling motion with her hand to signal everyone in St. David, "does not exist. It was just someone's idea of an afterthought. You see, the members of this task force all believe in what we are doing here. In Washington, they just want this fixed. No muss, no fuss. We are basically expendable."

Jake picked up on her theme, adding, "And screwed."

"I don't think so," the professor interjected once again. "I believe everyone is underestimating us." Jake and Angela both gave condescending smiles, to which the Professor reacted by saying, "See, neither of you believe we can do this. I do. We might not all make it out unscathed, but I'm sure Bethoon the Cannibal will not walk out of here alive."

"Sorry, professor," Jake said. "You've faced him before, what can you tell us about him?"

"The closest thing to pure evil I've ever encountered, except, perhaps, this Falstaff chap." He swallowed hard, as if he didn't like talking about Bethoon. "He will deliver vengeance tonight! But, I believe we will survive, because we have the right people for the job. That's all due to you, Ms. Harrison."

"So, it's agreed then," Angela said. "If we make it through tonight, we will then discuss what to do about the Master Gardener. Jake, I know you won't do it, but you and Kira need to try and get some rest. I will wake you if I need to."

"A little rest wouldn't hurt you either," the professor suggested to Angela.

"Everyone could do with some rest, including you, Professor," stated Angela

"I'll rest when I'm dead," he said, without hesitation.

"Professor?" shock was in her voice.

"It's just an expression," the professor insisted.

Jake, who was now standing, took a step forward, "I plan on taking on this Falstaff fella. I may not know what he is, or where he's from, but my plan is simple. Find him, destroy him, and take his people with me when I go."

Jake's aggressive move frightened the professor, but he did not surrender to his fear. "We will see, Mr. Taylor. We will see!"

Angela stood there and watched the two men go off in different directions. She knew they both were right. Tonight was going to be difficult. However, tomorrow, if they survive, it would be 100 times worse.

♦ ♦ ♦

Running his tongue over the outside texture of the bone he was manipulating in his hands, Falstaff was determined to get every succulent morsel of marrow from his meal. He extended his wiggling tongue, and it congratulated him by sending lightly charged energy throughout his body.

It was getting late, and while he was watching the FBI building, in his mind's eye, he was observing from the future. The first of the attacks on their enemy had started with no clear-cut winner. However, it would be a long, arduous night. While some lives from the FBI would be lost, hopefully, many, many more of Bethoon's minions would also be lost. It was the sudden sound from behind him that would catch his attention. "Yes, what do you want?" he said. He turned, but no one was there, or so it seemed.

He started toward the noise, but then he stopped. "What is it, Thomas? What do you want?"

"Why did you do it?" A hollow voice came from the shadows. "I've always known you've strived for world denomination and chaos, Father." He paused, and thought, dare he continue? "But, you've never turned against your kin. We are the same, you and I. We are of the same substances. We are assured of our survival. This is the only time I have asked for anything. I wanted the girl, and you threw her in the pit for Bel-Zog to devour."

"You are questioning me?" The Master's look was one of dismay. "I, who have given you everything. I, who have brought you back from the edge of non-existence more times than I care to remember. You are questioning my actions because of a girl? A dead girl at that! You have lost your perspective."

"Perspective?' Thomas shot back at his father. "The only thing I have lost is my respect for you!" he said, while finally stepping out from the shadows. "You would not be here if it wasn't for me and my actions in Missouri. I realize now that what I mistook as affection was merely you manipulating me into doing whatever you thought would benefit you!"

"Where is this coming from, Thomas? Who has gotten to you? Have you been listening to those fools from the FBI? Angela, perhaps?"

"No, Father." It was a different voice this time, a female's voice.

"Ah, Melissa. I should have known." The Master Gardener's face tightened with anger. "How long have you been trying to manipulate your kin?"

"Manipulate, no. Educate, very much so." Melissa stepped into the light to be recognized by her creator. "It was you who asked me to let the young woman, come out to play with you, to satisfy your desires. But, you needed to prove who was in charge. Her soul went into hiding, and I had to take control. I am just about finished nibbling around the edges of her consciousness. I will have full control of this form soon. I simply told Thomas what you did and why."

"I created you for comfort and support, not this, this treachery." Falstaff pitched the bone he was devouring at both his creations. "I can see I made a mistake."

"Master?" Melissa began to speak in her seductive voice while moving closer toward him.

"I will not hear you speak to me as if we are equals. I allowed you to enter that vessel because I wished it. Now, I'm..."

"You will do nothing, old man," Tommy interjected. "You have your battles to control. We are leaving. We will travel away from here, looking for our next sight to conquer. If, by some chance, you should conquer St. David, we will return and pledge our never-ending gratitude."

"Why this disrespect?" Falstaff asked. "Why this action? Neither of you has ever attempted to treat me this way before. Not since the beginning of your existence." As he shouted the words, spittle left his mouth, falling to the floor.

Both Tommy and Melissa smiled with satisfaction. Melissa began speaking, "You are going to lose here! You have made several wrong moves in the past few days. Climbing into the vessel of the vampire was not the first, but it was one of the worst."

"It was tactical. You both know that!" Falstaff, the King of all he surveyed, was on the defensive. Once he realized this, his body language shifted. His voice changed as his eyes narrowed. "I will not be questioned by the likes of you! Each step I have taken was sanctioned by those who are much more important than you."

"Father," Tommy asked, "why do you want this place so badly? We have seen nothing but pain, destruction, betrayal, and deceit here."

The Master turned on his son and screamed, "We ARE pain, destruction, betrayal, and deceit! All I ever wanted was to spawn a life that would be loyal and support this life, my life. This is the thanks I get? What is the real reason behind your questioning? It cannot just be about the female vampire, or my choices of vessels. What is causing this disrespect from both of you?"

"Vampires, oh great Master Gardener, our King. It's the use of Bethoon and his minions, my Lord. They are so unlike us. The zombies of Missouri were a good choice, but, vampires? They have plans of their own. They fight for their own causes, not ours."

Falstaff laughed loud, long, and hard. When he was done, he explained, "They are a tool, a weapon to bring all these people to their knees. I have known Bethoon since before you both were created. He is destruction incarnate. The devastation he brings with him is guaranteed. He cannot, and will not, be stopped. His drones are nothing more than worms that I use, much like darkness uses the night to hide the atrocities that are done to this earth. Bethoon does my bidding, as did you, until now. Nothing more, nothing less. Now, are we done with this questioning? I find it rude and distasteful."

Melissa made the first move as she slithered toward the Gardener and gently kissed his face. "We are so sorry, Master. We were confused and needed the guidance of your words." While she continued to caress Falstaff, her eyes gazed at Tommy, demanding that he do something to appease their master's anger.

"I, too, am sorry, Father. I was angered at your use of the girl vampire, but now I see the wisdom in your planning. It will not happen again, rest assured."

Falstaff turned away from the affections he was being given by Melissa and demanded, "Be good to me by fetching me something to eat." The Master Gardener was in control again, or so he thought.

As Tommy set to his task of getting the meal for the Bone Sucker, he reached into his pocket for the recording device he carried. Once Tommy was out of sight and hearing range of his father, he played the recording until he heard the words that were required. With some editing, Arthur Kensington had precisely what was needed to bring down Falstaff. Tommy slipped back into the time stream and moved into the space he needed. He then stepped forward to commit one of the last moves necessary in bringing about the downfall of Falstaff, the Master Gardener.

Chapter Seventeen

Damsel in Distress??

Slowly, one eye opened. Erin lay where she was and didn't move for several moments. Then, with all her might, she began opening her second eye. The first one tried to close, and she ordered it with her mind, "Not until we are out of wherever it is we are!" With both eyes opened, she realized she was on her belly, and her face was stuck to some kind of sticky surface.

She tried to raise her head. No deal. She closed her eyes and pulled herself upward with all the available strength she had. Her head raised about two inches, but then, as if a vacuum had formed between her head and the surface she was lying on, her head was sucked back down.

"Aaah," a voice greeted Erin. "Welcome Pretty, Pretty!" The voice sounded like someone with a mouth full of food. "You are in the kingdom of Bel-Zog. I am Bel-Zog." The creature's breathing was loud, wet, and erratic. "You rest, Pretty, Pretty. I will let you rest."

She wasn't awake enough to speak yet. For the moment, she was happy that she was no longer inhabited by the Gardener. She couldn't tell what kind of shape her body was in. Her next task was to try and roll over on her back. Erin suddenly had an uncontrollable urge to fall asleep in the kingdom of Bel-Zog, and she did!

A little while later, a surge of electricity shot through Erin. It felt like an insect bite that was stabbing the same area over and over. Eyes open, check. Lift head, check. Then she noticed little roots that were sprouting from the floor had attached to her cheek. Her thinking was becoming sharper with every moment she was awake. As she started to lift her head higher, Bel-Zog greeted her once more. "Hello, Pretty, Pretty!"

This time she knew she could talk, but didn't, because she needed to figure some things out first. With a sudden burst of energy, she raised her head fast enough to dislodge the vines boring into her face. While she did not feel any pain when removing the growth from her face, Bel-Zog did. He screamed in pain.

"Stop that, Pretty, Pretty!" The beast's breathing was heavy, and it sounded as if he was right next to her. "The Gardener said he was done with you. Said you were my gift. Why do you hurt Bel-Zog?"

She remained silent. Erin Hastings could feel the poison seeping out of her cheek, and her face healed over, immediately. The vampire's body was urgently reminding her that fighting was a bad idea. Erin concentrated and tried to roll onto her back. Bel-Zog shouted, "Stop hurting Bel-Zog! Lay there like a good Pretty, Pretty, and Bel-Zog will let you lie there for as long as you wish. Bel-Zog needs to feed to stay strong for Falstaff. Bel-Zog is Falstaff's favorite." He sounded proud of the words he spoke.

Even though vampires don't usually feel pain or emotion, Erin was a little frightened by Bel-Zog and decided to wait until she had more strength for her next move. Lying there, she realized she only had one garment on, her panties. If Bel-Zog had bored roots into the other exposed parts of her body, then Erin was in big trouble. It was at that point Erin made her most dramatic move. With groans of anger and rage, she fiercely flipped her body until she was finally on her back. Shouts of displeasure arose from inside the cavern Erin Hastings was in. She used her hands to cover her ears. As Erin stood, the first thing she looked for was something to cover her bare feet and skin.

The one thing Jacob Taylor had taught her in training was not to panic. She grasped for her wits while searching for answers. Two levels down, she saw a lump of clothing on a lifeless frame. It would have to do for now. She dangled her legs over the edge of the ledge. She dropped first, one level, and then to a second. Pulling herself up, she launched herself into the air, crossed the expanse, and fell hard on top of the dead corpse. She recognized it as the hollowed-out shell of Alden Napier. Bel-Zog was still screaming and shouting, but, for now, the young woman had a purpose. Bel-Zog would no longer feed off of her. She began removing the clothing from the body-sack of Napier. While dressing, Erin thought she needed to find out just how deep of a hole she was in, and if she could find her way out of this place. She decided to draw the creature's attention. "Um... Bel-Zog, is it?"

"Yesss, my Pretty, Pretty."

"Do you mind telling me where I am?" A loud, bellowing laugh roared from the beast. "What is so funny?" she asked.

"You are. You are Bel-Zog's pet, like Bel-Zog is Falstaff's pet. You can't leave, Pretty, Pretty."

"Respectfully, Bel-Zog, I need to leave this cave and help my friends," the vampire explained. "I will come back and visit you. We can be more than pets; we can be friends." Her voice was young and inviting to Falstaff's pet.

Bel-Zog answered once more with his booming laughter. Then, without warning, tons of garbage was dumped into the vast cave. As Erin watched the garbage fall to the bottom of the cavern, she heard a chewing sound. She quickly moved from the edge of the ledge she was on and asked more forcibly this time, "Bel-Zog, where am I?"

"Pretty, Pretty, you are inside of me. No cave, Me. You will get tired; you will wear down. There is no blood for you here, Pretty, Pretty. I will eventually devour your essence. Now, sit down and allow Bel-Zog to finish preparing you. I can make you sleep so the end will come quickly."

Erin Hastings realized she was in trouble. She couldn't see her way out of this situation. The vampire had not learned how to float or fly. If she had, she would already be out of this pit of despair. She had no answers. She was doomed to die.

♦ ♦ ♦

"Here you are, a vampire, stuck in the middle of this pit," Erin was thinking to herself. "It seems you weren't as strong as you thought you were," the voice in her head reminded her.

"How am I going to get out of here? Especially, if it's daylight out there?" she wondered. "Jake. He can figure this out. He'll be able to help me," Erin thought.

"Ok, princess, so how you gonna contact him?" her evil side asked. "Besides, that wolf-bitch Kira won't let go now that she's got her hooks into him."

Erin looked up and saw a glimmer of light at the top of the hole. "It must be daylight," she thought. "I have to save my strength. That will keep my mind clear. I need to climb as high as I can, in as short of a period of time as possible. Maybe once it gets dark, I can float up and out of this prison. If I can get close enough to the top, perhaps I can project a mental signal out for help. Now, raise your head, and get moving."

The negative voice returned, "Erin, you need to rest. Don't be in such a hurry."

"Shut up! Leave, if you don't want to help," Erin shouted to the voice in her head.

It was then she heard the noise from below. It sounded like a long, lowly scream. Erin thought, "I can't stay here anymore. I've got to move."

She forced herself up and started to claw at the sludge around her. She started with her right arm, then her right leg, then the left arm and leg. As she pushed her way up through the thick slime, she felt like it was sucking the energy from every inch of her being. Physically exhausted, she stopped moving. She realized she hadn't progressed that far. Then, concentrating all her mental strength, she shouted, "HELP! I am in a pit, behind a greenhouse." She repeated that brief statement over and over again in the hopes that someone, anyone, would hear her and come to rescue her from this mess.

"It's futile, don't you know?" a sickly sweet sounding voice echoed from around her. "Once you are thrown down here, you are mine to do with as I want, for all eternity."

Surprised by the voice, the only thing she could think to say was, "Who are you?"

"Pretty, Pretty, I have told you. I am Bel-Zog. I am the ruler of my kingdom," the voice answered.

"How long have you been here?" she asked, stalling for time. All the while, she was mentally sending her message for help.

"Erin, my dear," the voice seemed to wrap itself around its victim, "it will be over soon, if that's what you want. However, you are young, and beautiful, and I can make your stay quite pleasant for a while."

She started to push upward again, but each time she moved, the pit was drawing more and more energy from her. Once she stopped wiggling, she felt something quickly wrap itself around her ankle. "Please," she begged, "don't do this. Terrible things are going on in the world up there, and I need to stop them if I can."

"SSSweety," the voice sounded angry, "You can't ssstop anything. C'mon, let yourself go, and slide down here with me." Erin felt a sudden jerk on her ankle. As she grasped onto the oozing sludge for support, she discovered her ankle had been broken by the sudden snap. She realized now what the thing was doing. It was trying to disable her movement upward, so she would have no choice but to stay.

"You like doing this? Hurting innocent people?" she asked, stalling once again.

"You're not so innocccent, sssweety." The voice sounded like a never-ending jackhammer in her head.

"Maybe not, but no one deserves to come to an end like this, not even me." She sounded disgusted by her situation.

"You don't yet understand what you are doing down here, do you?" Bel-Zog asked. "I am a giant mulching machine. Once I devour you, I process your bones for the Master Gardner, and I get the rest. I will suck all the energy from you. I will devour the energy from your hair, skin, muscles, and everything in-between. You are going to be mine forever. Therefore, you have two choices: lay there and let the end come to you slowly and painlessly, or, struggle and fight me at every turn, which I will enjoy. I will get everything I want from you, either way."

Suddenly, the covering on the hole was thrown back, and the sun streaked through the pit. Erin's skin began burning and smoking. The yelping sound of pain from around her was unmistakable. Several things fell past her and traveled much further down into the pit as Erin continued to hang on to the side of her prison. Soon, the covering was replaced and the voice responded, "More sustenance. How good for me. As I grow stronger, you, my Pretty, Pretty, and all the other victims down here, become weak and unable to leave."

Erin said nothing. She was getting tired, but she continued to send her mental message for help. Bel-Zog realized she was trying to do something, so he wrapped another group of vines around her left ankle, and with a sudden snap, he exclaimed, "You are done now. All upward movement has been stopped. It's time to surrender yourself to Bel-Zog, my Pretty, Pretty!"

Erin was exhausted. As she closed her eyes to block out this world, she sadly told herself, "This is it. This is how I'm going to end my existence, in a slime-filled hole." She had stopped all movement. She had surrendered to Bel-Zog. It reminded her of the night when all her blood had been removed from her body. The hunger for sustenance roared inside her, but there was nothing she could do to appease it. Her last thought was, "I am finished!"

The beast known as Bel-Zog relaxed. He was satisfied with his role in this melodrama. Erin leaned up against the wall of her prison and watched as the nourishment vines began to bore new holes into her body. This would allow Bel-Zog to feed on his newest victim.

At the same moment Erin had given up all hope, Jake's upper torso sprang upright in his cot. "Erin!" he shouted. All eyes in the room turned to him. He immediately put his hands to his head, as if looking for an answer to why he had reacted the way he just did.

Once Jake realized where he was, and the fact that all eyes were on him, he bolted out of his cot and started gathering himself together. He looked as if he were getting ready to leave the broken down compound he was in. "Uh, Jake, what are you doing?" Angela asked.

"It's Erin." Jake sounded focused and ready for a fight. "She's in trouble. She needs me."

"Jake," this time it was Charles, "I hate to tell you this, but she's the bad guy in our little tale of woe."

"Not anymore." Jake was so focused on his preparation that he didn't notice everyone gravitating toward him. Once he did, he looked up and asked, "What? You don't believe me?"

Carrie-Anne cautiously approached Jake. "With everything that has happened in the last twenty-four hours, do you think it's wise to go off on a wild goose chase?"

"I'm not crazy!" he exclaimed. "You guys know that Erin and I have a link. Well, I think she just used it."

"You think," Angela interjected, "but you can't be sure?"

"Look," Jake directed, "if I'm wrong, you can chastise me later. Right now, I need..."

"There might not be a later, Jake, if we don't fortify ourselves now." It was the professor directing his words into the conversation.

"But, what if I'm right, and all of you are wrong? Then what?" He stopped gathering the tools he needed for the rescue mission and looked at them. "Angela, when have you ever known me to act on a whim? I just know this is the right thing to do. I will go it alone if I have to. If it's a trap, I will deal with it. But, if I can reach Erin, I've got to try! When Kira and I returned this morning, you gave us the intel we needed to mentally prepare for tonight. You ordered me to rest, so I'm rested. My friend, who is also a valuable member of this team, needs me. I am not going to let her die."

Three members started to say, "She's already..."

He snapped, "You know what I mean. She was the one who was tricked, manipulated, and deceived. She has more life in her than anyone in this room. Did you ever stop to think that's why Falstaff took her in the first place?"

Kira moved forward. "I'll go with you."

Jake ordered, "No, you stay here. We have got to be able to battle Bethoon for as long as we can." Then, moving his eyes from Kira to Angela, he insisted, "I have got to do this. Erin's counting on us to come and save her. I'll try to get back before dark."

"If you make it back at all." Angela had a distraught look on her face. Shrugging her shoulders, she added, "Watch your back! Do you know where you are going, Jake?"

"In my head, she was in some type of prison surrounded by sludge and filth. On the outside, there was a massive greenhouse. When I took Melissa home the other night, I noticed a huge building behind the Napier estate. That's where I'm headed." He paused and looked at his supervisor. "If I don't find anything, I will come back here straight away. However, I can't guarantee what form I'll be in."

He then turned to the professor and said, "Professor, I've got nylon rope, smoke grenades, and my pistols, but I need something with a little more kick to it."

"I've got just what you need." The professor smiled as the two men moved toward the room that held what was left of the professor's armory.

Angela turned to the others and said, "We need to get back to work if we expect to stop Bethoon."

♦ ♦ ♦

When Erin woke up from her brief nap, she found herself lying on the floor of the school cafeteria. She was dressed in a formal gown from "Nite on the Town" boutique, where she had purchased the gown for this year's homecoming dance. "Wait a minute," she thought. "Something's not right here." Suddenly, the music started to play, and people began to populate the dance floor. Quickly, Erin stood up and straightened her dress. No one had seemed to notice she had been lying on the floor. She looked all around the room for her date, but no one appeared. Finally, the sixteen-year-old girl heard her name. Erin turned and smiled as she saw Percy, in all his splendor. He walked up, took Erin into his arms, and the next thing she knew, they were floating around the dance floor. He leaned in for a kiss, which she gladly returned.

Erin leaned away from Percy because his breath gave off the scent of earth and moss, two things she had become very familiar with in the past several months. "Wait," she said, as she tried to push away from her beloved Percy. "Something's not right here." All eyes were on the couple now as she started to resist his advances. Within minutes, the scene had changed. Percy and Erin were now in the graveyard. She was lying on the cold ground, with Percy on top of her.

"God, I love kissing you, Ms. Hastings," Percy's light British voice insisted.

"I love kissing you as well," she sighed.

They kissed and touched one another, eagerly, hungrily, for several moments. The youthful Percy used his countless years of experience to arouse the woman he was with. Erin began to moan, "I want you, Percy. Make me a woman, right here, right now!"

Percy stopped caressing her and lifted his body. "Erin, I don't want your purity; not yet. You trust me, don't you?" Percy asked.

Erin realized, as she looked into the eyes of her man, that she had been here before. But, for some reason, she could not stop the event from happening again. "Percy, I'm willing to give you my most precious gift, isn't that enough?" Erin stuttered over the words, but couldn't stop herself from speaking them.

"I'm a vampire, and you know that! Your most precious gift to me, especially when your heart is beating so fast, is what flows inside you. I don't want it all, just a taste." Displaying his most precious, loving look, he added, "I have searched for you for hundreds of years; I'm not going to destroy the best thing that has ever happened to me."

As she continued to repeat the scene that destroyed her life, her eyes filled with tears. "I'm scared," she softly uttered.

"Erin, baby, I love you, and I don't want to scare you," he insisted. His face looked disappointed, hurt, and almost heartbroken.

Gazing up at her beloved Percy, her eyes screamed with fear. She softly asked, "You won't hurt me, will you, Percy?" She raised her wrist, thinking he would take her blood from there. When he frowned, she knew what he wanted. Slowly, she slanted her head to expose the jugular vein of her beautiful young neck.

Slowly, Percy gently moved his hands from the young woman's neck and slid them down to her shoulders. With a sudden jerk, the softness in Percy's touch was gone, replaced by a strength Erin had never felt before. Immediately, she realized she had made a mistake. The creature above her felt her fear. He stopped for a moment and scoffed, "I like it when my prey is afraid; it excites me." As he said the words, his voice changed. It was the voice of Bel-Zog. Something inside Erin's head snapped. She pushed back on Percy, and he could no longer pierce her neck with his fangs.

"This stops right now!" she exclaimed, as she threw whatever it was off of her body.

"That's not fair, Pretty, Pretty," Percy said with Bel-Zog's voice. "Master, she's not playing fair!"

Percy was gone, replaced by damp smelling air. But, the voice of the pit continued, "Lovely Erin, my Pretty, Pretty, relax, and enjoy the charade. It's for your benefit you know, to make you happy and allow you to enjoy your stay here."

"You pull up a memory from my past, the biggest mistake I made with my life, and you think it will relax me?" Her disgust could not be hidden from her voice.

The voice from the pit started to speak again when, suddenly, the lid from the top opened, and a voice shouted, "Erin, you down there?"

She tried to shout back, but the energy she needed to do so was gone. Instead, she thought the word, "Yes," and the lid went shut. When it opened again, there were three short puffs of smoke. Three more small canisters whizzed by her body, and once the cartridges were at what seemed to be the bottom of the pit, they exploded.

Billowing smoke clouds from the explosion along with projectile matter, including bone and tissue that had collected at the bottom of Bel-Zog, rose from the bottom of the pit and belched out of the now wide opening at the top. Erin tried to look up above her, but not only were her arms, legs, and torso rooted to the side walls of the pit, but now, her hair was densely matted with vines, which wouldn't allow her head to move. Just as she was about to give up, she felt something tickling her back, and then it was gone. Not knowing if whatever it was that brushed against her could bring her harm, Erin concentrated her thoughts for several moments, and with a mighty yell, she ripped her right arm away from the wall. She was exhausted, but she used the newly freed arm, and every ounce of reserve energy she had, and pushed against the mushy backdrop until she had flipped herself over, tearing all of Bel-Zog's nerve endings out of her body. While Erin continued to rip herself loose, the pit howled from both pain and anger. "He will not find you down here," Bel-Zog bellowed. "I will not let you go, Erin Hastings. You are mine! The Master Gardener has given you to me."

"Why don't you shut up?" came a voice from high above them, as three more concussive shells flew past Erin.

There it was again. Whatever had brushed up against Erin before, had done so yet again. This time she grabbed the thing and was surprised to see it was a rope. When the person from above pulled the line, she found herself so weak she couldn't control her grip. Then, the line was gone.

"Erin, it's Jake," the voice from above said. "I can't climb down. You'll see why once I get you up here. We can do this, Erin. I'm not going to tell you that everything is roses and rainbows up here, but it's better than where you are. Let's try this again. Only this time, you tell me when you are ready by jerking the rope."

The vines were starting to bore themselves into her legs again. Her left arm was dislocated and useless. Flexing her legs in and out like a snow angel to keep the vines from grabbing ahold of her again, Erin waited to feel the rope. Once the line hit her body, she wrapped it around her right arm and gripped it with both legs. In the time she had spent inside Bel-Zog, Erin's broken ankles had healed, so she now used her feet to clamp the rope and take some of the strain off her arms. With one last movement, Erin Hastings jerked downward on the line.

She felt a tug, but the vines that had intertwined around her waist weren't willing to let her go. When she heard Jake say, "My God, girl, what have you been eating?" she started to smile. Erin felt the jerk again and heard the sounds of screaming coming from all around her. He was doing it. Jake was getting her loose. After several strong tugs, her body was free from the walls inside Bel-Zog. As she hung there in mid-air, she realized there was another problem. The sunlight outside would burn her alive. It would just be another cross that she would have to endure. Up until now, she had thought she was doomed to the pit for eternity. Higher and higher she rose, until she felt the sting of the light on her face. "Faster," she thought. She was too drained to both hang on and talk at the same time. She kept her grip. Erin was not going back down in that hole. Her body started to smoke profusely as she felt herself being pulled over the lip of the pit. The pain was overwhelming. Suddenly, a blanket was placed over her to smother the flames. That's when she saw him. She welcomed Jacob Taylor's face. Erin smiled at her friend, and then closed her eyes to die.

♦ ♦ ♦

Jake picked Erin up and carried her to the back shadows of the greenhouse. He found a shed nearby. It was made of wood and provided excellent cover for shade. "You're not dying today, young lady. Not if I can help it." A loud roar came from behind Jake. As he turned to look, the thing that was Bel-Zog was trying to wriggle out of the ground.

The worm spoke, "I am Bel-Zog, and you can't have her. The Master gave her to me! Her body gives me energy and strength. She is my pet, my Pretty, Pretty. I will not let you have her!"

Jake was still bent over Erin. He covered her face and said, "You don't want to watch this." But she did. She pushed the blanket back enough to give her a peephole.

Jake stood, turned, and looked determined. "I don't have a problem with you," he said to the giant worm, who had stopped wriggling. "What I do have a problem with is the Master Gardener. Since you work for him, that means you have to die." Grabbing his assault rifle with its grenade launcher, he fired it three times at the large opening that Jake assumed was the worm's mouth. All three met their mark. He waited for the explosion of the grenades. Jake propped his rifle against the shed and pulled out a red colored pistol. "I have to be honest, I don't know how this is going to work, but Professor von Bruton is one of the smartest men I know. He thought I might run into something like you, all big, mean, and ugly. He explained to me how and when to use this, so I'll be saying goodbye to you now." He cocked the pistol, after putting round after round into the chamber, and then began running in a circle around the worm. He fired a shot every three feet or so, and stopped after encircling the beast. Bel-Zog tried to wriggle out of his demon hole in the ground, and was now about ten feet tall. It wasn't the height that was the issue. Bel-Zog was no less than twenty-four feet in diameter, which was why being inside of him made it feel so cave-like.

"It is you that will die!" The worm slammed to the ground, causing Jake to flip backward. Once he stood back up, the giant demon was erect once again.

Jake cocked his head. He didn't understand what was going on in front of him. Behind him, Erin found her voice. "Move, out of his way. It's me he wants!"

Jake glanced at her as if to tell her to shut up. When he turned around to face the ultimate evil, he had a look of determination. Jake lowered his sunglasses so that he could stare Bel-Zog down, and said, "She's mine, and you can't have her!" Then, he raised his left hand, which held a small activation device with a red button on it. While raising his thumb to activate the switch, he shouted, "Time for you to die!" He turned and began to walk away from the beast, and then pressed the button. The bullet-type object that was deeply embedded into the worm shot out a blast of electrical current from inside the creature. The electrical current acted like a buzz-saw and sliced through the circumference of the monstrous thing. The worm howled in pain as the electric current intensified in both diameter and strength. Jake then bent down to Erin. Giving her the remote, Jake said, "You had to put up with that," he nodded toward Bel-Zog, "for God knows how long. Would you like to do the honor of blowing that thing to hell?"

It hurt Erin to smile, but she did. She pushed the green button that was right next to the red one, and small eruptions from the explosives Jake placed into the beast were set off, one at a time, until all of them exploded. Ten feet of the worm's upper torso was blown to bits. Jake Taylor then looked into his friend's one bright eye and suggested, "Erin, honey, close your eyes. I don't want you to see this side of me." As he said the words, he pulled the blanket down to cover her face. Like a man on a mission, Jake loaded up his grenade launcher and pumped every shell into the belly of the beast. As the explosives were set off, the now angry Jacob Taylor reloaded his grenade launcher and emptied it as well. By the time the man had unloaded the weapon for the second time, he had walked back to Erin and picked her up. They turned to leave to the sounds of the beast being laid to waste. However, there was a new problem. In Jake's path stood Arthur "Tommy" Kensington.

"Jake, I have to admit, that was really cool. But, you should know that Bel-Zog didn't belong to Falstaff. By the way, that's the Master Gardener to you." Tommy pointed to the remains of the giant worm. "That was my pet."

Erin heard Tommy's voice and started to wriggle in the blanket. "It's still light out here," Jake said. She stopped moving.

"I can't believe you killed Bel-Zog all by yourself," Tommy insisted. "I always thought of you more like the eye candy of the group. You really are a natural born destroyer of monsters, aren't you?"

"Tommy, if you're going to kill me, then kill me. If not, Erin and I have somewhere to go," Jake insisted.

"I need a favor first," Tommy demanded.

Jake couldn't believe what he had just heard. "You want a favor from me? Aren't you the guy that set this whole thing in motion? Aren't you the one who kept Erin here as a prize for your pet? What favor could you possibly want from me?"

"I need you to kill my father," Tommy said. Then, he threw him a tape recorder.

"Your Father? I'm sorry, who is your father?"

"The Gardener. You know him as Alden Benjamin Franklin Napier. His real name is Falstaff. In truth, he has now taken another form, that of Ethan Napier."

"If this guy is who you say he is, why do you want him dead?" Jake asked.

"Jake," came a soft voice from inside the blanket, "I think we can kill him."

Jake paused for several moments, then asked, "What do you get out of this?"

"I am going to walk away, and I want to take Erin with me," he said without flinching.

"No," Jake said firmly.

From the blanket, Erin muttered, "We'll think about it."

"Listen, Tommy, I've got to get her out of the sun or else..."

"I understand," Tommy said. "I will contact you tomorrow, if you survive the night."

"No. You'll be with us tonight, or there will be no tomorrow," Jake insisted.

Tommy understood that Jake was enlisting his help. He realized that if he stood beside his ex-coworkers, he would have an excellent opportunity to save the girl and get out of town before their big clash with the Master Gardener. "Alright, I will join you later but I can't promise you, that you won't die just because I am there fighting alongside you. Also, there's a tape on that recorder of Falstaff. If you can get Bethoon the Cannibal to listen to what's on it, that would help your cause in stopping Napier."

"I don't understand, but I'll give it to Angela and let her decide what to do with it." Jake stared Tommy down and then said, "I will see you this evening." Then he added, "Be ready to help us, or not only will I figure a way to kill your father, but I'll also kill you."

"That will never happen, wolf-boy." You don't have what it takes to destroy me!"

Jake didn't say another word. Instead, he walked by Arthur Kensington and rushed Erin to his vehicle, which he had hidden in the woods just outside the Napier estate. Once he arrived at his car, he gently placed Erin in the back seat. That was when Jacob Taylor heard the snapping of a twig. Instead of turning to see what had made the noise, the FBI agent's instincts took over, and he buckled his knees. The ax handle barely grazed the hair on his head.

Jake turned to see a large man with an attitude. Martin Napier looked pissed. "My brother told me someone was nosing around and that I should come out here and put an end to you!"

Jake, who had already gotten more out of this trip than he bargained for, smiled and said, "You know, Cowboy, I've needed a good butt whooping from someone. I guess you'll do. But, I should warn you, I'm from Texas, and unless you've got four or five friends waiting in the trees, I think you're outmatched." To prove his point, Jake walked over to a large limb that had broken off in one of the recent storms. Picking it up as if it were a piece of Balsa Wood, he gripped it until the branch exploded in his hand. The shattered remains landed at the feet of Martin Napier.

Martin Napier turned pale. As he started to turn and run away, he shouted, "Who are you? Better yet, what are you?" Martin Napier tripped on some tree roots and fell to the ground. He stood back up and continued running, while looking back at the man who had just destroyed a large tree limb. He didn't stop running until he reached the sanctity of the Napier home.

Instead of driving back to headquarters right away, the half-man, half-wolf, climbed into the backseat. Politely placing the young woman's head on his lap, Jake rolled up his sleeve and uncovered the young woman's face. "Erin, I know you do not want to do this, but I need you to feed on me right now." She tried to resist, as he knew she would, but he slid his arm right under her nose and said, "I am not trying to be noble here. We are in trouble, and we need you. We need your strength, your abilities, to help us." He went silent.

"Do you need me, Jake? Will I be helping you?" she softly whispered.

"Yes," he said quietly. Once Erin started feeding, he said, "Oh, by the way, I hope by doing this, you don't get surly and crave raw meat."

She giggled like the sixteen-year-old girl she was at his suggestion. As she drank, she could feel his strength coursing through her body. His blood was delicious and had an extra kick to it. He softly placed his other hand on her shoulder and whispered, "Drink it slowly, and don't take too much. I will need my strength as well, or we won't be able to save the town."

When she was finished, she shyly said, "Jake, thank you for saving me." He said nothing, but gave her a considerable embrace of affection.

"How did you know you could use the mental link to reach me?" he asked.

"I didn't," the girl vampire replied. "Jake, can we just sit here for a bit, this is nice."

"I would love to, but..." he didn't want to finish his thought.

"But what?" she asked.

"You really need a bath before we go back to the office." She looked up at him. He looked embarrassed for having said the words. Then they both laughed for several minutes. The couple did sit in the car, holding one another, for a bit longer. Jake waited until she had settled into an uneasy sleep. Then, he wrapped her up in the blanket while she rested. He gently placed her head down on the seat and slid out of the back seat and into the front driver's side. With the evening sun baring down, he pressed on the accelerator pedal, hoping he would make it back to headquarters before "The Change."

Chapter Eighteen
Battle For St. David

Angela watched from the roof as the dying light from the sun descended in the far western sky and was finally snuffed out by the horizon. "Any sign of Taylor?" Kira asked, not hiding the anxiousness in her voice.

"Not since the last time you asked me," Angela Harrison snapped back at the woman below. She turned to climb down. The attack was swift and unexpected. Something grabbed her before she could descend down the ladder. Its talons dug deep into her skin, forcing her to scream from the pain. Instead of pulling her weapon, she withdrew a six-inch crucifix and placed it on the claw that was embedded into her right shoulder. The giant bat-like creature screeched in pain and let her go before it could gain any altitude. However, the ladder had been knocked away and was no longer in position to allow her to descend into the agent's makeshift fortress. Angela grappled for the edge of the roof and was seen hanging above everyone inside. By that time, Charles shouted for her to let go. Trusting him as she did, Angela Harrison released her grip. He caught her on the balcony and quickly ushered her inside the building.

"Did you think...," Charles didn't get his sentence out.

"Not this quick." She took an erratic breath. "I didn't think they would attack this soon after the sun went down." Angela's voice was resolute. "Get ready, everyone, because here they come."

At once, all the members of the team met in Angela's office and put on the specially made collars to protect their necks from slashing attacks. The Professor put his left hand on Angela's shoulder, which stopped her movement. The Professor sprayed disinfectant on her open wound. The sting of the medicine brought a stern look from the leader of their small band of heroes. Angela, in turn, placed her hand on Charles to calm him. Soon the room was quiet, and that's when the sound could be heard clearly. At first, it was a loud, booming noise. Ultimately, the noise turned out to be a chant. "Beth-Oon, Beth-Oon, Beth-Oon."

Instead of being frozen with fear, which was no doubt what the vampire leader was hoping for, Angela shouted, "Everyone to their post!" Then she roared, "Guys!" Everyone stopped and looked at their leader. "Take as many of those," swallowing hard, their commander finished with, "things with you that you can get before we give up on this building and this town. Do it for Erin."

Charles reached over and flipped a switch. The sound emitted from the stereo speakers, which drowned out the droning chants of "Bethoon," was the music of AC/DC and their anthem, "Thunderstruck." "If we're going down," Charles said, as he headed for his station, "we are going out in style."

Kira, with the beat of the song driving her, ran toward the front door. She was the one agent of the group who was trained in hand-to-hand combat and close quarters' fighting. While everyone knew she was no Jacob Taylor, she, in her own way, was a force to be reckoned with on this day.

Carrying double-pointed wooden stakes in both hands, the flaxen-haired beauty spin kicked the first monster through the door. The concussive force of the blow knocked the beast into the wall of chest-high stakes to her left. Steadying herself, Kira awaited the next two vampires, who felt the sudden strike of stakes in their abdomen and fell in battle. The next three demons were totally surprised as Kira ran straight toward them. They stepped to the side as she ran up the wall, kicked off, and landed on the shoulders of the middle beast. The monsters on either side of the middle one felt wooden stakes slam into their skulls. Finally, to finish the move, she flipped off the shoulders of the middle vampire. She brought both stakes to bear, and they were on target. One stake pierced the right side of the neck of the beast, while the other stake had found the heart of her enemy. She watched as all six monsters disintegrated in front of her, as she settled herself in the middle of the entranceway, waiting for the next group to plunge forth.

In the doorway stood Monti. He was one of Bethoon's newfound generals. He deployed several more vampires into the room. While Kira waited patiently for them to get in place, the head vampire of the group said, "Well, fellas, it looks like this is a whole new ball game, and this girl wants to play!"

♦ ♦ ♦

Four hours after Jake left the group, Angela's able group of FBI agents and scientists met for the last time before the battle. Angela laid out the plan for the upcoming fight. "We have to live with the fact that Jake most likely won't make it back in time to make a difference. Therefore, I believe our best chance of survival will be..."

The leader was interrupted by Carrie –Anne. "Angela, I don't mean to be the defeatist here, but do you realize what you are asking?" Her stare could have melted steel.

Charles broke in with, "Snooker, let the woman speak."

Angela started again, but stopped, looked at Carrie, then Charles, and asked, "Snooker?"

Neither of the Martins answered her, so she continued, "Yes, Carrie – Anne, I know what I am asking. We have to attempt to hold the Vampire King off for more than twelve hours before dawn, but I am hoping for help from," She paused, remembering that everyone she contacted had not been able to reach them.

"From where?" the Professor chimed in. "No, no, no, we can't rely on anyone right now, other than each other. They know that our strongest points of support are going to be both the front and the back of this building. Therefore, we need our best fighters at those two points."

"I'll take the front," Kira Knight quickly volunteered.

"I'll take back," Carrie – Anne added.

"You will not," Charles Martin quipped.

"Not now, honey," Carrie –Anne said, with her mouth tightly clinched.

"No, Charles is right," Angela said. "It should be me."

"Angela, you are the prize. You can't think you are going to protect either end of this building? I have a special area just for you. You are going to be right here." The Professor had pulled out a hand-drawn blueprint of the building. He had already penciled in Kira at the front and Carrie – Anne in the back. The drawing showed that Angela would be in the center of the building, which was so fortified that it would take a small army to make it to their fearless leader, Agent Harrison.

The Professor continued to explain where he and Charles would be stationed and why. Finally, he concluded with, "Should, by chance, Jake and Erin show up, I don't believe he will be in his human form. Remember, this is the last night of the full moon, and he will be on the prowl. That's why I think, Ms. Knight, you need to do whatever you can to keep him fighting with you in the front. That leaves a very weak Erin for you, Ms. Martin."

Everyone stood there and looked at one another for several moments, then at the Professor.

"This is an excellent plan," Charles said. "I am impressed."

The professor's skin started to turn a soft shade of pink, while Angela asked, "Are all the armament in place?"

Both Charles and Eric Von Bruton answered, "Yes, Sir."

Angela then tried her hand at motivation. "Seriously, I don't know what's going to happen in the next few hours, but I do know one thing, if it's a choice between you or them, it had better be you. Don't hesitate; take them down, then and there. Don't show remorse, even if you recognize one of them. They are dead, soulless creatures who are being controlled by an evil master. This Falstaff character is evil incarnate. Fall back to me if you come into contact with him.

On the other hand, if you face off with Bethoon, then use every weapon in your arsenal to bring him down. Professor," she stared into the eyes of the old gentleman, "this is not the time for revenge. If he gets by Kira, you may take him down, but you do not go toe to toe with this guy. He's got it in for you, and he is going to do anything and everything to bring you to your knees. So, you destroy him first, got it?"

"Yes," was the only word out of his mouth.

"Carrie – Anne, if you feel overwhelmed, you might want to fall back to Geek-Boy for support. If physical violence does not stop those wretched few who are dumb enough to try to come through the back door, then they have no idea what Charles has waiting for them. That room is rigged up every which way. They will be entering our form of hell!"

Carrie – Anne said nothing. Her eyes began to tear and she grasped for her husband's hand.

"Professor, Charles, all I have to say to both of you is, I hope your planning and gadgets work the way you say they will."

The Professor reminded her, "Angela, don't wait too long before you press the button on the console."

"I know. I'm to make sure the room is jam-packed before I press that damned button," she reiterated to Eric. "One last thing," she paused to make sure she had everyone's attention, "I believe this would be a good time to pray to the Lord, or whoever you pray to at times like this. I don't know how many of us will still be here in the morning, but I do know that my faith has got me to this...." She suddenly stopped in mid-sentence and exclaimed, "That's it! I know that is it!"

"What?" the group asked.

Angela answered, "I know how to beat that bastard, Falstaff!!"

She turned and started toward her office. The Professor and Kira followed. As Carrie turned to join them, Charles grabbed his wife's arm and asked, "Where are you going?"

"I want to find out what Angela is thinking," she said, sounding as if she were angry at her husband for not allowing her to follow the others.

"I thought this would be the perfect time for us to be alone, since we are facing death." Charles forcefully pulled his wife toward him and kissed her with all the affection he could pass from his lips to hers.

"You've got to be kidding me," she said, giving him a look of disbelief. However, when she looked into his eyes, all she saw was his love for the only woman he had ever wanted. His was a love that would be eternal, no matter what happened in the next few hours. At that moment, she saw her entire life reflected through her husband's eyes, and felt a love more powerful than could ever be explained. Carrie connected with her husband's lips and then mounted his slender body. He quickly carried her to the small room they used as a sleeping area.

Within moments, their passion was unbearable, uncontrollable. Carrie-Anne and Charles Martin knew that no matter what came next, they were going to express their love in the most desirable fashion. All too quickly, a moment that they both thought would last forever was over. They lay huddled with one another, and as their breathing slowed, the couple drank in a lifetime full of that beautiful, delicious warmth that a husband could share with his wife.

Once they finished expressing their passion for one another, Carrie-Anne softly spoke, "Charles, if I should not make it..." She wasn't able to finish her thought.

"You are not going to die. I won't allow it," Charles interjected.

"Face facts, Honey." She tried again to make a point.

"Carrie-Anne, you are a warrior. Are you on Jake's level? Heck, no one is on Jake's level. But, I saw you sparring earlier with Kira, and before that, with Angela. Trust me, you haven't lost your edge."

Carrie-Anne raised up and said, "It's not really myself I am worried about. I can't afford to lose you, lover."

"Hey, look, I may not be a trained warrior like the rest of you, but I believe I can take care of myself well enough. I have faith in each of you to do what needs to be done, and I believe that together, we can end what is happening here in this town."

As he went silent and she lowered her head to his chest and rested it there for several moments. While Mr. and Mrs. Martin embraced one another, there was a knock at the door. It was the Professor, suggesting that they rejoin the group for last-minute instructions before the night swallowed the day, and they had to fight for their lives.

♦ ♦ ♦

Thoughts of their last moments in the small room fired Carrie – Anne up enough to jump over the gate and run straight to the far end of the room. Several vampires had broken through the unlocked door, seeking destruction. What they received instead was one very inspired lawyer with an edge. Just before reaching her three victims, Carrie jumped high into the air and put both feet into the chest of the first monster through the door. That vampire was immediately thrown back into the two monsters behind it, knocking all three off balance. She had stakes sewn into her gloves, similar to the ones Kira was wearing while battling in the front of the building. Carrie - Anne plunged the stake from her right glove into the first vampire. As he turned to dust, she used enough force to plunge the same stake into the next vampire who was behind him. Carrie Martin saved her left glove for the third monster. Once she was finished with those three, she flipped backward and stood dead-center in the room. Carrie - Anne allowed as many of the monsters that wanted to, to enter the room. They stood three deep, surrounding the petite Carrie-Anne Martin. Suddenly, she shouted, "Now!" She ducked down on the wooden tiles beneath her as the room became filled with electrical current. It sliced through the back line of monsters and was working its way inward, toward the center of the room. As the current approached the next line of victims, the monsters tried to move backward, which put them in line with Carrie-Anne. The most inward line did not want to move any closer to the FBI agent. The vampires realized they had only one place left where they belonged and that place was in hell. As the swarm of vampires was eventually dispersed, either by electricity or by the beautiful warrior in the center of the room, more villains came streaming in. The system that Charles was using to help his wife, needed approximately 60 seconds to recharge itself before the next battle could begin.

Thinking quickly, Carrie-Anne shouted, "Charles, use the smoke. Now!" It was not a request. From the ceiling and the walls came billows of smoke that filled the room. As the monsters lost sight of their target, Carrie Martin knew precisely what to do. Four of her victims were destroyed before they could even see who their executioner was.

It was at this point, when Carrie-Anne seemed to have total control, that the monster known as Kip reached out and snapped her arm as if it were a dry twig. Instead of writhing in pain, Carrie-Anne showed her rage by grabbing Kip with her free hand and stepping upon his shoulders. Wrapping her legs around his shoulders, Carrie quickly stabbed the vampire with her good hand. As she regained her focus, she powered herself back to her feet and exclaimed, "Geek-Boy, give me more smoke!"

♦ ♦ ♦

At the opposite end of the building, Kira twisted her frame and round-house kicked the next oncoming vampire, knocking him back on his heels. She then locked her hands together and plunged both stakes into the torso of the enemy. He disintegrated underneath her. Suddenly, the vampire general, Monti, grabbed her by the scruff of the neck. He raised the agile woman high into the air and dangled her there, as if he were showing his prize catch. He tried to snap her neck, but her protective collar was in place, preventing him from doing so. Angered by this, Monti attempted to rip the collar from her throat. Kira turned herself around and brought her right leg up, wrapping it around the vampire hulk's head and pulling his face into her abdomen. Kira, using Monti's arm for leverage, leaned backward, causing him to lose his balance and fall forward. At the last second, she jumped upwards and landed on top of the vampire, smashing his face into the floor. Then, she pierced Monti's back with her stake. With Kira's problem now gone, she shouted, "Professor, more smoke!"

♦ ♦ ♦

In the center of the building, Angela's fight was beginning. The large hole in the middle of the roof, caused by last night's attack, had not been repaired in time. The team had covered it with a tarp, but that was the best they could do.

After hearing both women shouting for the smoke, was when the reign of terror from above began. One lone vampire launched himself into the middle of the tarp. Using his extra-long nails to cut through the canvas, he was victorious with tearing it open. As he landed on the floor, his victory was short-lived. Angela approached him from behind and shoved the stake into his abdomen. However, when she turned around, she saw four more beasts were ready to attack. Not being the physical warrior the other two women were, Angela drew her specially-made wooden bullet pistol. Pop, Pop, Pop. She had dropped three of the vamps, leaving one for Angela to battle. As the agent ran toward the disgusting looking vampire, it reached out to grasp her. She ducked and slid underneath its arms. Then, she quickly stood, and holding the stake she had retrieved from a nearby table, she drove it into the vampire's heart. Her challenger was finished. Feeling pretty good about herself, the lead FBI agent let out a long, cleansing breath. That was when she heard the large thump from behind her. As she raised her pistol and turned herself around, there stood the most malicious vampire known to the world, Bethoon the Cannibal!

♦ ♦ ♦

Jake had made a near-fatal mistake. One of the few he had fashioned while on this case. He was running out of time. He needed to take Erin somewhere safe to take a shower. Realizing what had to be done, Jake decided to kill two birds with one stone. The agent took the real Erin home to be with her parents. She could clean up there. It was late afternoon when he awkwardly stretched to ring the doorbell, while holding a smoking Erin inside the blanket. The door slowly opened, and Jake rushed inside. Erin's mother looked surprised by the FBI agent. "We had nowhere else to go," Jake told her. "I need you to let me take Erin to the bathroom to take a shower. I don't want you to see her yet. She has been through so much. But, trust me, she is fine. I need you to do this without asking me any questions. Can you handle that?"

From inside the blanket, a soft voice said, "Mom, it's alright, it's me. Jake saved me, but I've been lying in a pit, and I need to clean up. Please, can I use the bathroom?"

Shocked at hearing her daughter's sweet voice coming from the smoking blanket, her nervous response was, "Sure, honey." The covering rapidly sprouted feet and started moving toward the upstairs bathroom. Mrs. Hastings turned her attention toward Jake Taylor and asked, "What's going on?"

Jake took several minutes to explain the entire situation, and how Erin, himself, and the other members from the FBI were there to stop the spread of evil in the quiet little town of St. David.

"Mommy," came a shout from upstairs, "can you come and help me?"

Jake decided to sit down on the Hastings' couch and rest. He heard the women talking upstairs. The conversation was smooth and steady, which gave him a sense of security and safety. Jacob didn't realize how tired his body had become, and the next thing Agent Taylor knew, he was asleep. The agent began to waken when he felt something cold on his cheek, but he ignored it. Then, he felt a cold, metal object nudge him again, and opened his eyes to see. Mrs. Hastings was standing over him, holding the same shotgun she had used on the demons earlier in the week. "You need to leave!" the woman informed him, forcefully.

"Mrs. Hastings, what are you doing?"

"Saving my daughter from the likes of you and your friends." Her eyes teared up as she explained, "Erin told me what you did and how you have been taking care of her. I appreciate it, I really do. You have given us our daughter back. But we will take care of her from here on out."

"Mrs. Hastings, you don't understand," Jake began, and then he went silent. He turned his head toward the window just in time to see the last vestiges of sunlight sinking into the horizon. It was almost dark. Without thinking, he said the first thing that came into his head, "How long have I been sleeping?"

"An hour. Maybe a little more," Erin's mother answered. "Why?"

"We have got to go," Jake shouted loud enough for Erin to hear him.

"You can go anytime you want," Mrs. Hastings said, while pumping a shell into the chamber of the shotgun, "but, Erin is not going anywhere."

A voice came from the stairwell, "Mom," Erin shouted, "what are you doing?"

"You can't leave, my darling daughter. I can't handle losing you again." Erin's mother split stares, first looking at her daughter on the stairwell, and then at the FBI agent sitting on the couch. Unexpectedly, the front door burst open, and in walked the Mayor and what was left of their family.

This action distracted Mrs. Hastings just long enough for Erin to jump over the stair railing and land in front of Jake. "Mom, put the shotgun down. Jake and I really do have to go. My friends are being attacked by Bethoon the Cannibal, and we have to go and help them." Erin looked at both her parents and calmed her voice. "Even though this mess isn't my fault, I feel like it is. This whole thing came about because I believed what a demon told me instead of what you guys tried to teach me throughout my life. But, now, I have a chance to be a hero and to make things right. You guys need to understand, I am still your daughter, but I'm not your little girl anymore." She looked at her mother, who was slowly lowering the weapon in her hands. "You know, Mom, Jake has taught me how to take care of myself. If I wanted to, I could easily disarm you. Do you want to know why I don't? Because you are my mom, and I love you. Please, put the gun down and let Jake and me try to save my friends."

When Erin had finished, her mother fell to her knees and began to sob. Erin's father started to move toward his wife, but Erin grabbed his wrist and said, "No, Dad, if you don't mind, let me." The young vampire walked over and put her arms around her mother. She whispered something to her until she stopped crying.

Erin's brother asked, "When did you get to be so cool?"

"Christmas Eve, when I died," she answered. Erin walked over to the stairwell, grabbed her book bag, and said to Jake, "C'mon, let's go." Then, turning toward both her mother and father, she said, "I know it might be too late, but we are in real trouble at the office. If you could send some people to help, you know, you being the Mayor and all."

Her father smiled. "I'll see what I can do, baby girl."

As the werewolf and vampire turned to leave, Mrs. Hastings said, "Jake, take care of our little girl." In the blink of an eye, they were gone!

♦ ♦ ♦

Carrie-Anne was in pain. Her broken arm was taking its toll. Charles had joined the fray and stopped some hairy thing from ending her life. Seeing her husband fighting for their lives gave her new energy. She ran up a wall, backflipped onto the shoulders of a beast, and drove a stake into his brainpan. Carrie did another backflip in front of the door, just in time to welcome another vampire, whom she dusted, right then and there.

Charles was using his special made pistols to bring down the vampires as they entered the building until a new, hulking threat showed up at the door. Charles and Carrie-Ann knew this was going to be their defining moment. The beast broke through the doorway, head first, leaving a gap above the door that caused Charles to remark, "He's going to leave a mark."

The beast stepped closer to them, grunting and growling. A female voice came from behind him, "Hey, booger-man, leave my friends alone." Erin immediately ran up to the corpse before anyone else in the room could take a breath. She twisted the beast's head around like a Lazy Susan. As the monster crumpled to the floor, she ripped its head off its shoulders and threw it out the door. "God, I hate zombies," Erin said. Then, she gave her two colleagues her genuine smile, and they both knew they were going to be ok.

"Where's Jake?" they both asked at the same time.

She rolled her eyes in disgust and said, "I save the day and all you can ask..."

That was when they heard the loud thud coming from the center of the building. They all rushed toward the hastily constructed control room. Everyone in the back end of the building was halted by the booming voice of Bethoon. "Everyone will stop fighting this instant and join me in the center of this building, or Ms. Harrison will die! I have no problem with ending her life before Falstaff can have his way with her!"

♦ ♦ ♦

Before Kira could dislocate the jaw of the oncoming assailant, a giant ball of fur came crashing and slashing through the narrow entrance. Once it landed near the female FBI agent, Jake let out a wolf-like howl and flexed his arms to signal he was ready for a fight. "Way to go, Jake." Kira grinned and then asked, "What kept you? Traffic?" Letting go with another roar, the werewolf slashed his massive paw at three of the unsuspecting vampires. His razor sharp claws separated their heads from their bodies, and they all turned to dust before their bodies could hit the floor.

Everyone paused for a moment at the sight of the destruction. The attacks began once again once the dust had settled. Then, suddenly, everything stopped. Any momentum either side had was stifled.

Bethoon's booming voice announced that all fighting would cease, and everyone from the FBI should report to the center room. The vampires stood their ground, but they didn't try to stop Jake and Kira from leaving the room. When all the members of the FBI's team entered the center room, they couldn't help noticing that Bethoon was holding their leader, Angela Harrison, in the air by her throat.

Within a blink of an eye, Erin was in the face of the King of the Vampires. "You need to stop this! You don't have to do this!"

"Ahh, I finally get to meet the spitfire I sired," Bethoon said.

Suddenly feeling a strange pull toward the cannibal, Erin stepped backward and bowed, showing respect to the monster. "Sire, let her go, and I'll go with you."

The others in the room shouted their objections to her idea. Bethoon spoke up, "Little girl, you'll go with me regardless; I own you!"

Without hesitation, Erin stepped forward and plunged a stake into the middle of the monster's chest. Bethoon stood there and bellowed with laughter. He then swiped at Erin, knocking her into the opposite wall. "You expect to stop me with a puny stake in my chest? You have much to learn, young one," he said, as he pulled the stake out of where it was lodged and threw it to the ground.

"What do you want?" the Professor asked.

"I want my Queen back, old man!" Bethoon spat the words at his sworn enemy as if they were daggers.

"She was mine, long before she was yours," the Professor said, showing remarkable control in his voice. "You stole the only beautiful thing in my life, and I won't rest until you are turned to dust."

"Hah, and who's going to complete that task, old man? You?" Bethoon knew there was no way Eric Von Bruton could complete the task he suggested.

"Look, we are getting nowhere here, Sir," Charles stepped in, the one calming influence in the room. "What is it you want, Bethoon?"

"Funny thing you should be the one to ask that question. I want you, Charles Martin. I want you!"

"No, take me!" Carrie-Anne shouted, trying to protect her lover.

"It's not my choice to make," Bethoon said. Noticing her broken limb, the vampire then insulted the petite federal agent further by saying, "Besides, you are injured."

Two henchmen stepped forward to take Charles from the group, but Jake, still in his werewolf form, slashed at them, turning them to dust. Bethoon, in response, lifted Angela higher. As she struggled for both her breath and her freedom, Charles addressed Bethoon, "If I can prevent any more violence here, sir, I will go with you."

"That is very astute of you, Geek-Boy," Bethoon insisted. "The Master Gardener knows all about you. You have been one of his targets since you arrived here in this dead town."

"Does that mean if I go with you, everyone else here will be safe?" Charles asked.

"It means nothing of the kind," Bethoon said, callously. "My minions plan to harvest this entire town. We have already started moving some of our captives to the caves. Hoffenpiller's lackeys are going to stay here and finish you off."

"What?" the Professor demanded. "You are going to take Angela and Charles and then kill the rest of us anyway?"

"Well," Bethoon looked around the room as it filled with ghouls and demons, "actually, I have ordered them to kill you." As the monster grabbed onto Angela with both hands, he sprouted wings. With two powerful swipes of his extensions, he had hoisted himself and his prey out of the building. His two henchmen did the same, lifting Charles Martin out of the center of the room and off to his fate.

Every member of the team had a look of anger, betrayal, and utter disbelief. Suddenly, Erin grabbed Jake by the snout and said, "Wolf-Boy, time to show them what you're made of. Destroy anything that isn't us!"

Taking in as much air as his wolf-lungs would allow, Jake let out a howl that caused the walls to shudder. The real battle was about to begin!

♦ ♦ ♦

With a little help from the Professor and an injured Carrie-Anne, the warriors, Kira, Jake, and Erin, were able to withstand the first effort from the beasts. While both Erin and Jake mauled the oncoming vampires, Erin used her undeniable speed and agility to take down attackers to her right and left. Finally, it was the Professor who shouted to Erin, "Come with me, and we will bring this to an end quickly." Erin, along with Carrie-Anne, who was now using her wooden bullet gun, made a path for the Professor, who promptly shut and barred the door into the center of the room.

"Erin, dear sweet, Erin, I need you to go into the far left room. Not our control room, but the room next to it, and bar that door as well."

Carrie-Anne said, "I'll go with her."

"No, you won't. I don't know why Angela didn't use this weapon when she could. I would have preferred for Bethoon to be destroyed here. I suppose Angela has her reasons. I need Erin to go into the far room. It is furthest from the weapon I have in this room."

Almost at once, Erin went to the other doorway that was barred, and removed it, then looking at Carrie-Anne, she said, "Cover me, and drop anything that gets by me."

"You got it!" she replied, assuredly.

Erin removed the bar from the door, opened it, and threw herself into the room engorged with vampires and zombies.

Carrie-Anne fired three rounds into the crowd, and as the three vampires transformed into dust, she used her lame arm to slam the door and force one wooden bar into place. She wedged the second bar into place under the doorknob. Turning to Von Bruton, she commanded, "Do what you're gonna do, Professor! I'm not losing any more people today."

With that order, he pressed the small red button on the panel.

♦ ♦ ♦

Jake and Kira were getting saturated by the enemy. It reminded Kira of what she had read about the violence of the beaches of Normandy during World War II. They couldn't kill the enemy fast enough. Jake's werewolf form was surrounded by seven vampires that were biting and slashing him. For each beast he destroyed, it was replaced by two more. Kira, meanwhile, was starting to tire. Just as she was wondering how much longer she could withstand her attackers, the room was suddenly drenched with a brilliant glow from the floodlights mounted on the ceiling. It was so illuminating that it burned the vampires. The monsters began rushing toward all the exits. However, there was only one correct exit, and was blocked by two vicious FBI agents. The light came from every direction, and forced the monsters to flee any way they could. It was so bright, Jake howled in pain as his body started to change back into his human form. Looking around, he saw the vampire horde was gone. Nothing but ash and bone remained.

Kira could see in the light what she was not able to observe in the dark. The room was lined with mirrors, or some type of reflective device. The fifty or so vampires who had been in the center room no longer existed. The light was so intense, and reflected so well, it was strong enough to clear out the two rooms on either side of the center expanse that Carrie-Anne and the others fought to protect.

Quickly, Carrie-Anne ran into the room. She shut the door and jammed a wooden bar under the doorknob to keep all intruders out.

Then Carrie-Anne took inventory of everyone by asking, "You guys alright?" Kira answered for both of them by raising her arm in victory. The Professor finally shut off the blazingly bright lights from above. As the small group quickly reassembled in the Professor's lab, they knew they had at least one more fight ahead of them.

The Professor had moved to the back door and was unblocking it. Wolf-boy, Kira, and Carrie-Anne were locked and loaded, ready to dish out more punishment. "All set?" the professor asked.

All three of the warriors nodded. Then the Professor smashed the door open. What they beheld was beyond explanation. Erin was drinking what appeared to be blood out of a paper cup. Standing next to Erin were her parents. They were surrounded by no less than 100 civilians. When the young vampire saw her fellow teammates, she gave them a toothy grin and asked, “What took you guys so long?”

Chapter Nineteen

Caves

Angela, who now was in the clutches of Bethoon, was hovering about one hundred feet in the air with nowhere to turn. Therefore, she decided that while she was in the clawed feet of this madman, she might as well enjoy the ride and the view. The strange thing was, whatever awaited her at the end of this flight did not bother her at all. She looked to her left to see Charles being carried by two of Bethoon's slugs. He, too, looked unfettered, almost exhilarated, by the trip.

Not aware that the monster carrying her was paying her any mind, she let out a small sigh of relief. Bethoon countered with, "It is beautiful up here, isn't it?"

She shifted to look up at the clear night sky, and then at the mountains, which seemed close enough to touch. "I could get used to it."

"It is what stirs that empty space where my soul should be," he said.

"Bethoon, you're not showing me your softer side, are you?" In response to her question and while using the exposed talons of his right claw, he squeezed her right shoulder just enough to cause her delicious pain. "Ow, ow, ow," she said. "OK, I get it, humor isn't your strong suit. Sorry." Then, she went quiet.

After several moments in the night air, Bethoon said, "Angela, why don't you consent to come with me?"

"What?" she asked in disbelief.

"I would turn and head North right now if you would commit to come with me and be my Queen," he suggested.

"First, I don't want to be a Queen of anything. I'm from a small town in West Virginia, and I wasn't brought up to be royalty. Secondly, I'm not ready to die. I want to live for as long as I can. Don't get me wrong, if you had a better plan for saving St. David, its people, and my team, I would be more than happy to listen to it. However, I have never wanted to die, become undead, and then rule the world with an egotistical dictator." She felt a twinge in her right shoulder, meaning she had hit a nerve. She went quiet.

"You realize that once I deliver you, you are going to die, don't you?" Bethoon asked her.

"Well, that's the third thing," she said, hesitantly.

"Third thing?" Bethoon questioned.

"Yes, I plan on destroying him first."

Those words caused Bethoon to stop in mid-air. Pulling her up so they could talk face to face, he reminded her, "You cannot kill him. No one can! I have tried, time and time again, but he always seems to see right through me."

"I have help from places you can't go near," Angela responded.

"Angela Harrison," he paused, trying for the right words to say, "if you can do what you say you can do, it would free me from the devil's grasp.

"Just before you swept me away," Angela said, "Erin gave me this recording. She said that I, and especially you, needed to listen to it. She demanded it. Honestly, Bethoon, this is not a trick."

The King of Vampires looked down at the recording device. "I have no interest in modern tricks."

"Hey, she said, "suit yourself. I'm listening to the recording." She pressed play.

The voices on the recording were unmistakable. They belonged to Tommy, Melissa, and Falstaff. They were deep in discussion. "We don't understand you using vampires. Bethoon and his minions, my Lord, are so unlike us. The Zombies of Missouri were a good choice. But, vampires? They have plans of their own. They fight for their own causes, not ours."

Falstaff laughed loud and hard, and when he was done, he explained, "They are a tool, a weapon to bring all these people to their knees. I have known Bethoon since before you both were created. He is destruction incarnate. His devastation is guaranteed. Bethoon cannot, and will not, be stopped. His drones are nothing more than worms that I use as the dark has the night to hide the atrocities that are done to this earth. Bethoon does my bidding, as did you, until now. Nothing more, nothing less. Now, are we done with this questioning? I find it rude and distasteful." Angela stopped the recording and started to put the tape away.

Bethoon was surprised at what he had heard. So much so, that he gathered Angela Harrison up in his arms and carried her the rest of the way to the caves. "Play it again," the King of Vampires ordered.

Angela did play it again, while both of them listened intently. Once the tape was finished, Angela knew she needed to say something, but she didn't. She allowed Falstaff's words to fester.

"Angela Harrison," Bethoon's voice was dry and emotionless, "how did you come by this recording?"

"I told you, Erin gave it to me. I didn't know what was on it until now."

"And, do you have a plan to put that demon in his place, to free my people from his control?"

"Yes, but it's mostly theory. Things have to happen so precisely that it's not a foolproof plan, but, for the moment, it's all we have." She gave him just enough information to keep him interested, but nothing that would hinder her plan.

"You see that outcropping over there?" He nodded to the ground rising up to meet them about 400 hundred yards away. As she nodded yes, he continued, "We will stop, and I will listen to your plan. But, no tricks, or you will die, and then I will be done with this."

Angela agreed. As he unexpectedly started his descent, she became nervous. While they were falling, she reached for his massive arm for support. This startled the King. There was something in her touch that brought his senses to the forefront. He stared down at the woman and stated, "This would be so much more desirable if you would just agree to come north with me." The Vampire King altered his wingspan and prepared to land, a mere five miles from the caves, which lay in the Arizona desert. Angela could see the glow of lights coming from that direction. In the distance, Charles watched the entire scene unfold in front of him, and he couldn't believe what he saw. Commenting into the night air, he said, "Here we are, being taken to our enemy, for who knows what reason, while she's getting cozy with the guy that's trying to kill our entire team! What else could possibly go wrong?"

One of the henchmen replied, "We could drop you!" Charles was not amused. As the two subordinates angled their wings to land, Charles Martin couldn't help but ask himself, "What now?"

♦ ♦ ♦

With the townspeople involved in the situation at hand, the members of Angela Harrison's crew, slowly and steadily, began to pick up the pieces. The vampires had been chased out of the center of town by the good citizens of St. David, with assistance from Erin Hastings. The doctor volunteered his services to patch up members of the warriors, including Carrie-Anne. No one, no matter how they tried, could explain the actions of Jacob Taylor, a.k.a. The Werewolf. Basically, Kira told him to sit in a corner and behave himself, and to everyone's surprise, he did. Before Erin left with some of the more brave members of the townsfolk, she whispered something in his large wolf-ears. Whatever she said to him, it must have worked, because there he sat, making everyone in the FBI building uncomfortable.

After several moments of explanation from both sides, it was Erin's father who continued his report. "When we saw our townspeople being herded into covered transport vehicles, my wife and I decided that none of this would have happened if I hadn't been so worried about politics instead of the people. Thus, she made some calls, and I went door to door to help our little girl."

"Well, Mr. Mayor," said Carrie-Anne, who was now firmly in charge, "it may be a situation of too little too late." The effect of the moon must have been waning, because, after several moments, Jake had transformed back into himself, a fact lost to everyone except the professor.

Carrie-Anne was explaining the situation to onlookers when the Professor interrupted her. "Wait a minute," Eric von Bruton said. "You say you don't know where they are going, right?"

"Right," Carrie-Anne said.

"But, we do know!" The Professor answered back. "Bethoon told us!" he exclaimed. "They're in the caves!"

"But, we don't know which caves," Jake interjected.

"Excuse me," Erin's father said. "The only caves that anyone has talked about for the last few years are the caves at Vista Verdi. I can take you there if you would like?"

All eyebrows, including Erin's, who had returned from the hunt, raised at this surprising news, "Give me a few minutes to prepare," the Professor said.

"There's no time to prepare," Carrie-Anne insisted.

It was Kira who spoke up, "Carrie, you've got to get your arm set and put in a cast. We need the Professor's brain, because, in truth, none of us would be here if it weren't for him. Let's all take a breath. The Mayor will get us vehicles to make the trip, and then we will go get Charles and Angela."

Carrie-Anne looked at everyone in their small group and asked, "Are you sure we will find Charles alive?"

"No. We're not sure of anything." Jake stepped forward to take up the helm for the first time. "But, Angela knows something the others are not privy to. Why else wouldn't she use the Professor's weapon, or fight harder to get free from Bethoon in the first place?" Stopping long enough to take a long look at everyone, and grasping Carrie-Anne by her one suitable hand, Jake continued, "I promise you this, I am going to that cave, and one way or another, I will not rest until you are in the arms of our favorite techno-geek." Everyone smiled at his comment, except the Professor. Then, Jake ordered Carrie-Anne, "Go get that arm set, 'cause I'm not leaving here without you!"

Once she walked over to the emergency vehicle where the paramedics waiting for her, the Professor and Kira walked back into what was left of their building. The Mayor and his wife went to coordinate the transportation, leaving Jake alone with Erin. She asked him, "Do you really think we can save Angela, Charlie, and this town?"

He looked into her incredibly blue eyes and said, "Hell, no. But I had to say something to get her to at least fix her arm."

"In that case," she leaned into Jake and kissed him for the very first time.

"Hey," he said suddenly, "we have boundaries, or so I thought." He was smiling, however.

Erin responded with, "Those of us who are about to die, salute you!" And she kissed him again.

From out of nowhere, Jacob and Erin heard, "Well, isn't that touching?" followed by the sound of a single person's applause. Then, Tommy walked into the center of the room.

"You never showed," Jacob announced as he walked over and punched Tommy in the stomach. As the entity doubled over, the werewolf exposed his hairy arm, and using that same arm, delivered an uppercut. As Arthur Kensington stood with blood streaking his face, Jake and Erin smiled, pleased with the results.

Tommy spoke, his face magically healed, "You two shouldn't be so pleased with yourselves. You may be able to disfigure me, but you can't kill me. That means I'll be around for a long time to come."

"I don't want to kill you, Tommy, but if it weren't for you, all this, most likely, would have never happened." Jake took several steps toward the demon and continued, "Your friends, Bethoon and Falstaff, have taken two people from our team, and you are going to tell the rest of us how to get them back."

Erin stepped up to Tommy and slapped him across his smug face. "You allowed those things to kill me. I can never forgive you for that." Another Slap. "Falstaff put himself inside my body, which is another insult I can't deal with right now." Slap. "But, worst of all, Tommy, I liked you, at one time. Now, there is no way I will go with you, anywhere." Slap. Slap. "And what about Melissa? Maybe she wasn't the best friend I could have chosen, but there is no way the Melissa Napier I know would have ever thrown me into Bel-Zog, or given me to Percy." This time when she went to slap Tommy, he caught her by the arm.

As Jacob rounded on the traitor of the group, Tommy quickly released Erin's arm and explained, "This has all gotten out of hand." Looking into Erin's eyes, Tommy said, "One of my weaknesses has always been you, Erin. We needed someone to introduce us to you and your family. That was Melissa's job. Something you should know Melissa is, well, Melissa's soul has been devoured by my sister. The Melissa you know is no longer of this earth. I'm sorry, but the truth is, we, the children of Falstaff, are ruthless creatures. We devour souls like you consume chocolate. I came here tonight to ask you, Erin, to come with us. Because if Angela does succeed, you could die this night."

The room became deathly quiet. Erin's parents turned in the direction of their daughter and moved to be near her. Suddenly, Melissa Napier arrived. "Tommy, let me take over here. What my brother is trying to say is, if Falstaff dies, you could cease to exist as well."

"I thought Bethoon sired me. I felt the pull." The look of devastation was mirrored on the faces of Erin and her parents.

"We are not totally sure of anything at this point," Tommy interrupted. "You see, Bethoon wouldn't be here if it weren't for Father. Falstaff only fostered one vampire, and that was the Cannibal."

"So, either way," Erin considered, "I'm screwed. If we kill Falstaff, I could die. If we take out Bethoon, I could die. I can't believe this. All because I wanted to believe in romance, in love. God above, how stupid could one teenager be?" She whimpered, but no tears came.

While Erin turned to her parents for support, and Jacob was getting prepared to open a can of "Whoop-Ass," there was a surprising turn of events. A bright light appeared from out of nowhere, and into the room stepped the Indian Goddess, Aqualax. Jacob Taylor immediately bent a knee out of respect. Tommy and Melissa tried to turn away to flee, but the Indian maiden wasn't having it. "You two need to stay where you are until I am finished with you." Her voice was not angry, but piercing.

Jacob raised his head long enough to say, "I really wish I could do that with them."

Ignoring the agent's words, Aqualax focused her vision on Erin and her family. "I am sorry for your plight, young woman. You should not be so hard on yourself. If it weren't for the mistakes made in this situation, my friends and I would not be here this day. Mr. and Mrs. Napier, your daughter is in a good place here. While we cannot revert what has happened to her, we can tell you that her love for you is real. Her soul is intact. That is our gift to her. However, she will have to continue her service with Angela Harrison for as long as necessary." Turning to Jacob Taylor, the maiden continued, "Jake, that was a brave thing you did when you set out to free Erin from the claws of Bel-Zog. We've needed someone to put an end to him for a millennium. But, you and your small band are not quite finished. You must get to the caves. Angela needs you."

By this time, Carrie - Anne returned from the emergency vehicle. She walked right into the middle of the room and Aqualax immediately called to her, "Carrie - Anne, please come closer." The petite warrior cautiously stepped forward, and the maiden pointed to her wrapped arm. As Carrie-Anne raised her hand to the woman, and the bandages floated away, just as Aqualax touched her arm, and she was healed. "Your love of family and this group has not gone unnoticed. Thank you. Charles is in good health and will continue to be so, but you must make it to the caves."

Eric von Bruton tried to shy away from the maiden in front of him, but she held his attention when she said, "Mr. von Bruton, I know you are science through and through. However, you are the Father of this group, to Angela's mother. You must assist her in raising and educating this family. Also, with Ms. Knight's help, your wife's soul has finally found peace. You need to find some peace for yourself."

"One last thing. Erin, you cannot go to the caves. You cannot align yourself with Tommy. You must allow yourself to go with the Vampire King when he leaves, and he will be exiting very soon. You must let Bethoon find you. He will guide you to safety. Don't worry. Go home with your parents, and Bethoon will find you."

"I'm sorry," Jake interrupted. "We appreciate all that you are doing here, but we have already fought the fight. Now you're telling us we have to make a break for the caves and we can't take our best weapon with us? I'm afraid I don't understand any of this."

"Jacob," the maiden's calming influence was working on everyone in the room except for the werewolf. "We know it does not seem fair, but everything is going according to plan. Now, all you have to do, is be there to execute it."

It was at this point both Tommy and Melissa were drawn into this discussion. They wanted to know the plan. Aqualax recognized their interest. With a flick of her right hand, Melissa was gone without so much as a sound.

Tommy became brave. "What have you done? You cannot interfere with the minions of Falstaff on this plain."

"You would be wise to hold your tongue, Demon!" Aqualax commanded. "All you spawn of Falstaff's have been playing on an uneven field for far too long. I am trying to bring balance to this situation. You should understand that I am here to correct many of the mistakes you and your Master Gardener have made, without being brought to bear the cost."

"You can't do..." Tommy started.

With a subtle movement, Tommy was thrown into some type of vortex and catapulted not only out of the room, but to another part of the country. The maiden's face looked content. She continued to address Jacob. "Mr. Taylor, you need to go do what you do best. I have finally brought some balance to the situation by dispersing two demons on this day. You need to go do the same. Everyone but Erin may go. I am sorry, but that's the way it needs to be. In the end, all that is unbalanced will be balanced."

"Will we all make it back from the caves?" someone asked.

"Only time will tell. But, the balance must be kept."

As sudden as the light came, it was gone, and everyone began moving again. Jacob walked toward Erin and her family. "We've got to go. I am sorry, Erin." He spoke the words with a heavy heart.

Erin and her family were in tears. Jake tried to console them when he felt someone pulling on him. He turned to confront the faces of Carrie – Anne and Kira. "We need to leave now," they said.

He raised a finger, telling them to give him a minute. He subtly pulled Erin to the side. "Don't try to be brave, Erin. If going with Bethoon keeps you safe, you do that. I give you my solemn oath, no matter how far you go, I will make it my life's mission to find you."

He was half-man, half-wolf. Erin was one hundred percent vampire, but with a soul. Somehow their connection worked. As everyone watched Jake and Erin embrace, no one said a word. Everyone looked away to give them some privacy. They hugged one another as if they would never be able to do so again. Once they pulled apart, Jake noticed something he had never seen before on Erin - tears. He put one of his finger-tips to her youthful face and let a tear fall onto his finger. Without

Erin saying anything, Jake pulled away, grabbed his equipment bag, and headed for the vehicle that was going to take them to Vista Verdi.

"Daddy," Erin spoke, as she turned to her father, "I won't be here when you get back. Don't get dead, OK? And if you get a chance, please bring Jake back with you."

Bruce Hastings embraced his wife and then Erin. "Take care of your mother, until you can't." He kissed his wife again and then was off to the Humvee that would carry the team to their destiny.

♦ ♦ ♦

Bethoon saw the headlights of the vehicles bringing the townspeople to the caves. and said, "Angela, I have to put you back into the position."

"You don't have to explain." She allowed him to lower her down so he could grasp her by his talons, and then they were in the air again. The closer they came to the caves, the more vehicles Angela and Charles could distinguish. Bethoon began to rise higher in the air to surpass the first buttes in the South-Western Arizona terrain. Once past the first one, the King of the Vampires made a sudden one hundred and eighty degree turn to reveal a view that took Angela's breath away. Bethoon began to lower himself to an area filled with people, and vehicles, and high-walled animal pens. She noticed lines of people milling about. They looked healthy at the moment, but there was a turnstile that people were passing through. Once through the turnstile, they would transform into zombies and huddled together in a corner. She could see the mindless, directionless people standing expressionless and emotionless.

"Bethoon?" She needed the monster's attention. "I think he's getting ready to dust you and your kind. Don't trust Falstaff. You can drop me from about six feet, and I'll be fine. You need to get out of here. Save Erin and anyone else you deem worthy. Find a place to hide until the outcome here. I suggest the Grand Canyon. There are plenty of places to hide there."

"This is a waste of time, but I will do as you ask. If you should survive this, you might consider what I have asked of you earlier." The vampire then observed his target, Martin Napier, who was carrying an assault rifle. Once he knew he was close enough, he dropped Agent Harrison to the ground. Actually, he targeted Martin, and the woman landed on top of him, taking him to the ground. The man stumbled to his feet as Angela quickly recovered from the planned drop. Bethoon dropped backward about 200 yards from the cavern and watched as his two henchmen dropped Charles Martin to the deck. As they turned to leave, there were about ten bowmen who appeared out of thin air. They hit the first vampire in the heart and he disintegrated into the air. The second henchman immediately headed for higher ground, but didn't back away from the buttes. Bethoon the Cannibal watched as three warriors appeared at eye level and shot the second vampire several times, but nothing pierced the heart. As quickly as he could, the vampire known as Lowjack climbed above the buttes and waited for his Master to fly to him.

Bethoon pulled several arrows out of the fellow vampire, and once he was finished, said, "Lowjack, I made a promise to that woman. We need to collect the girl vampire and get out of this cesspool." The second vampire nodded, and within seconds they were on their way to pick up Erin and head for the caves in the Grand Canyon. There, they would wait for the outcome of what would happen in Vista Verdi.

♦ ♦ ♦

Three black Cadillac sports utility vehicles were speeding toward the Vista Verdi Valley. Inside the front car, Jacob Taylor, Carrie Martin, Dr. von Bruton, and Kira Knight were going over their plan for infiltrating the camp once they arrived. Bruce Hastings was driving them and didn't say much. He slowed the vehicle as the road changed from blacktop to dirt, and spoke for the first time, "Professor, was my daughter really an integral part of your team?"

"Yes," Jake answered from the front passenger seat.

"I didn't work with her all that much, Mr. Hastings," the Professor answered. "But, Jacob there, well, he trained her. She has unbelievable strength and agility." He nervously stopped talking. Von Bruton already thought he had said too much.

"Sir, your daughter is a fighter. Best non-agent I've ever trained," Jake added.

"We saw that, her mother and I, when we watched her battle." Bruce paused and wiped his eyes. "She was so fierce, it was scary."

"Mr. Hastings," Jacob let out a soft breath. He needed to get the words right. "Erin can take care of herself now. When we first met, she was weak in spirit. Your daughter had given up. Erin thought her world was over, and she lashed out at everyone. But now, well, you've seen her in action. Not only has she broadened herself, but Erin has also saved my life too many times to count." He lied. "I meant what I said. I will find her after this is over." There was a long, thoughtful pause. "If we live through this."

Bruce Hastings brought the car to a slow roll and, eventually, it stopped. He turned the headlights off, which allowed everyone to see the glow of the cave lights in the distance. Jake turned around to look into the back seat of the car. He stared at Carrie -Anne and waited for her to give the orders. She stared back at Jake, but no words came from her mouth. It was the professor who started the uncomfortable conversation. "Jake, why don't you give us the rundown?"

"The way I see it, they don't know we are coming," Jake responded to the professor's suggestion. "The vampires that have made it here don't want anyone to know they had their asses handed to them by the FBI and some civilians. We have surprise on our side. No provoking here, unless we have to. Is that clear?

Kira, you take point, in wolf form. I'll bring up the rear. Carrie – Anne, I want you right next to me. We don't know what they've done with Charles; therefore, I need you controlled." Jake stared into her eyes to make sure she understood the rules. She did. "Finally, we do our best to protect the locals, including the sheriff's department, and the citizens of this county." He was done talking.

He moved to get out of the vehicle when Bruce's hand landed on his shoulder. As he turned back to look, he saw Erin's face say, "Don't get killed."

Not making any reference to the girl, he led the group by saying, "C'mon, Mr. Mayor, let's go get your town back."

After twenty minutes of cautious movement, the small group of twenty members and a wolf came to a halt once they saw the compound. It looked as if a portion of the cave had been hollowed out. Using his binoculars, Jake found all the main players. He saw the zombie servants pampering their master, the Gardener. In the center of the staging area, he saw both Charles and Angela. They looked unharmed. He moved from the rear to the front, where Kira had reverted back to herself. They were discussing the situation when a voice came over the loudspeakers. "Jacob and friends, welcome to my new home. I am impressed. I didn't think anyone could withstand one of Bethoon's attacks, and yet, here you are!" While he could barely see his host, everyone knew that Falstaff was doing the speaking. "Come forward, and I give you my word, not one person will be harmed. Make me work to find you, and some will die. Others will become my lifelong slaves." His voice changed as he added, "Mrs. Charles Martin, do come to be with your husband. He is refusing to help me. Maybe you can change his mind."

Carrie – Anne immediately moved forward, without hesitation. The rest of the group followed suit. She was stopped at the gate and disarmed. It seemed that not only did Falstaff have zombie servants, but he had brought most of his staff from his home. He had also brought an army for his protection, most likely mercenaries. As Jake and the rest of the group walked through the gates, they were disarmed as well. They were now foxes in the henhouse. Therefore, they analyzed everything they could, for future reference.

It took the group several minutes to go through the gate. Once the main people were through, the rest of the sheriff's deputies and townspeople were shuttled toward the pen. Jacob and Dr. von Bruton tried to protest, but nothing could be done. There were too many of the enemy and not enough of them.

Eventually, they made it up the four levels of caves until they were eye level with the rest of their crew. Immediately, Carrie – Anne sprinted toward her husband. But before she could feel his touch, she was snatched out of the air and forced to her knees.

Jacob Taylor and Kira Knight, who was once again in her human form, were restrained from behind and also brought to their knees. Sunrise was two or three hours away, but, on the horizon, the morning glow was beginning. Jake had already decided that the wolf inside him was going to make a sudden appearance. "I wouldn't do that, Mr. Taylor," Falstaff ordered. "If you continue to be a problem, you could cost everyone here something important, such as their life." A sudden blow to his midsection was distraction enough to keep him from executing "the change."

"So, this is the great team the FBI sent to deal with me?" Falstaff glared at them. "But where is Erin Hastings? Surely she wanted to be here. It matters not. I will seek the girl out after I am finished."

Professor von Bruton stepped forward and demanded, "Who do you think you are to desecrate these tombs of the ancient noble tribe of long ago?"

"I am Falstaff!" He motioned with his hand and von Bruton's body was slammed into the cave wall. "You are a guest in my home. You will not question me here."

To everyone's surprise, the good doctor seemed unfazed by the violence his body was subjected to. "You are such a fool, Falstaff," the Professor said. He appeared to be getting stronger. His voice had changed, and it was a voice that all the leading players in the room recognized. "You are a liar, a cheat, and a scoundrel," the sound coming out of Eric von Bruton commanded. "And, in truth, those are your better qualities. Your time on this planet has come to an end."

The people standing closest to Dr. von Bruton and Falstaff withdrew from the area. They could sense something was about to occur, and no one knew from which direction it would come. A dark hue came over Falstaff. His eyes became bloodshot, as if embers were smoldering in his head. Eric von Bruton's body began to glow. In the blink of an eye, appearing next to him, was Aqualax. From the glare on her face, Aqualax was not pleased with Falstaff, nor with standing in his presence!

♦ ♦ ♦

Bethoon landed softly outside the domicile of Bruce Hastings. The vampire considered bashing the door down, but thought of the promise he made Angela Harrison. Ignoring the moves of his brethren beside him, his thoughts turned to the clandestine meeting on the hills just before the caves.

They had landed on the crest of the chosen hill. As soon as he released Angela, she turned on the vampire, but instead of attacking him, she made plans with the Cannibal. Midway through their discussion, Angela took the lead. "Once you drop me off, you get away and into hiding. I can all but guarantee you that Falstaff is willing to sacrifice you and your brothers and sisters. Your part in this is over. No offense, Bethoon, but you were nothing more than a distraction. What I really need you to do is get Erin out of here. She may fight you, and you will get resistance from her mother, but do not hurt any of that family. They have lost enough in this case."

"Why do you care about this Erin so much?" he asked.

"I don't know," she replied. "There's something about her. She wasn't supposed to be a vampire. She was supposed to be dead, but Falstaff convinced you to give some of your blood to bring Erin back from the dead. Did you know about this when you gave your blood?"

Bethoon stared down at Angela and stated, "It was actually Tommy who tricked me. It was back when I was battling von Bruton. He showed up out of nowhere. I was allowing Agnes to feed, and he stole it then. Tommy recently explained that the girl had been given my blood, but I do not feel the pull, no strong attachment to her."

"I have to ask, Bethoon," Angela was respectful in this situation. This vampire was like a powder keg. He could go off at any moment. "Do you think you will be safe if I can destroy Falstaff?"

"What makes you think you can accomplish something that no one has been able to do before you?" the vampire asked.

"Just do me this one favor and get Erin to safety before dawn. After that, there are no guarantees." She stood beneath the monster, looking confident.

Suddenly, Charles Martin landed next to her. While he fearlessly walked toward Angela and the Cannibal, he asked, "What's going on? Why did we stop?"

"Better yet," Angela interrupted him, "why does Falstaff want you? Have you done something I'm going to regret?"

"I have no clue," Charles commented. Then, slowly, both humans looked at the three vampires for answers. They had nothing to offer.

Angela went on to explain "the plan," and their group's part in it.

Bethoon the Cannibal's vision was now back to the present. As he dropped down to the porch of Bruce Hastings' home. He didn't understand what he did next. Instead of standing in front of the door as Bethoon the Cannibal, or even King of the North, he had taken the form of days long past. He was the young shepherd boy of over 3,000 years ago. He knocked on the door.

As the door slowly opened, Erin's mother was standing there, holding her shotgun in front of her. "Ms. Hastings, Angela Harrison has asked me to collect Erin and take her North for her safety."

Erin, who was standing next to her mother, exclaimed, "Bethoon? Oh my God, look at you!"

"Agent Harrison has asked me to collect you and take you North. It is for your protection. She thought this form would be best. She said it would make your mother more comfortable."

"Thank you, young man," Marilyn Hastings interjected, as she opened the door to invite him in.

"Mom!" Erin grabbed the screen door and pulled it shut. She paused, as if the words she was saying were very hard for her, "I have to go with this man. Angela's afraid something bad is going to happen to me." Erin looked at the new and improved Bethoon and added, "She's afraid for all of us. If we live through tonight, I promise you, someday soon I will come back. If I can." Then, from somewhere inside her, Erin's dam broke, and a flood of tears flowed from her.

Bethoon stepped forward and offered words of encouragement. "Mrs. Hastings, Angela Harrison has promised me that if I don't get your daughter to safety, she will hunt me down like a dog. You have my word I will protect her at the cost of my life." He slowly opened the screen door and stated, "But, we have to go now."

Marilyn Hastings let loose of the grip she had on her beautiful daughter and slowly allowed her to slip through the opening. "I love you, baby girl," were the last words her mother said to Erin.

The young girl didn't want to go, but knew she had to. "Bye, Mommy," she said without looking back, and suddenly the vampires vanished into the night.

♦ ♦ ♦

Falstaff stood in front of Dr. von Bruton and Aqualax. They were encircled by a demon horde of his choosing. He did not cower in front of the heavenly vision. His minions, however, started to back away, but he ordered them back.

"You cowardly devil from Hell. How dare you come here and attempt to spoil this land!" Anger was written on the face of the angelic Aqualax. Dr. von Bruton's body took a kneeling posture as Stark Hansen stepped out of the form and stood next to Aqualax.

"You!" Falstaff shouted. "It's you who have caused all this. How dare you come to this plain and try to stop me! It is you and your Master who have brought villainy to this place, not I!"

"Shut up, Ghoul!" Aqualax ordered.

Instead of Stark Hansen saying something to the demon Falstaff, he walked over to Angela Harrison. Once their hands touched, the room went still. She said to her long-lost friend, "You've got to stop hitching a ride with him," and nodded toward Eric.

"He handles himself pretty well, if you ask me." The glowing warrior leaned over and kissed the woman of his dreams. Once finished, he leaned away from her and noticed her eyes were still closed. "Angel, if you haven't noticed, everything has all been leading up to this moment. Do you think you are ready for this?"

After reopening her eyes and adjusting her focus to the room, Angela said, "I have to ask, Stark," she swallowed with difficulty, "why me?"

"I can't tell you that, Angela, because I really don't know. I can't tell you why you were in Missouri either. I don't even know why I was there. What I can tell you is that you have everything you need to take this guy down."

"I'm not so sure," she answered him back. "It's just a theory. I've run it over with Dr. von Bruton. He said it's highly plausible."

"Would it help if I told you that you were correct?"

"It would help if I knew I couldn't fail."

"You know, Angel," he squinted his eyes, "you are going to hate me telling you this, but this is another test for you, like Missouri. You have to forget about everything and rely on the one thing you have more of than anyone else in this room, faith. I slipped in the end, you know?"

"What do you mean?" Angela asked.

I asked you to take the shot because I didn't think I could handle doing it myself. I didn't know if I was doing the right thing. I made a snap decision, and it just happened that I was right. You are strong, and if I do say so myself, a beautiful woman. I hate that the burden of dealing with this demon has fallen to you and your people, but you are the right person for the job!" He leaned into her and gave her a long, sensual kiss that allowed her to wrap her arms around her Stark Hansen. As she held him, he whispered, "You can do this." She opened her eyes, and Stark was gone.

In the room, all eyes were on her. The members of her crew were flabbergasted at her appearance. She turned to Jacob Taylor and asked, "What are you staring at?"

"You're glowing, Angela," he replied.

"Enough of this!" Falstaff shouted. "This is my show, and you, woman, aren't going to stop anything. Get back down on your knees and pay homage to me!"

Angela walked over and took her place between Jacob and Carrie-Anne. She quietly asked them, "What did you see?"

Jacob replied, "You started glowing. In fact, you still are."

Suddenly, she stood back up, and with both eyes focused on the Falstaff, who seemed to be busy flowering himself with accolades and compliments, Angela shouted, "This charade has gone on long enough. It's time to end this. And, Falstaff, it's time to end you!"

Chapter Twenty
Confrontation

Angela glared at Falstaff. When she started to stand, she was shoved back down to her knees. Angela tried to rise up three more times, and after each attempt to rise up, she was pushed back down. She finally gave up. A grueling smile creased the demon's lips. Agent Harrison tried a different tactic. She opened her mouth to speak, but was met by a scolding voice, "Tut, tut, little one. You are not in charge here."

The anger started to boil inside her. Falstaff could tell she was ready to burst when he stated, "You have no power here, Angela. The glow you seemed to have developed will not work on me. I am too powerful for you, or that bimbo, Aqualax. I have destroyed the balance of this plain, and there is nothing anyone can do about it."

Turning his attention toward Charles Martin, the demon suggested, "You see Agent Martin there?" Charles and Falstaff both looked at Carrie – Anne as the monster continued, "If he doesn't connect me into the world wide web, that good looking lad over there is going to gobble his lovely wife up." A vision flashed in Charles' mind of "the lad" swooping down on his wife and swallowing her whole.

"Don't you give in to him, Charles Lee Martin. I will never forgive you if you do what that thing is asking of you!" Carrie shouted the words at her husband.

"No," Angela Harrison spoke up. "Go ahead and make his connection to the web. It's not going to matter. Besides, you can always remove it later." She shifted her attention to the monster of a man standing before her and asked, "Why do you want the web so badly, anyway?"

"Simple. Expansion!" Falstaff bragged. "Mr. Martin here is going to design a program that will entice more and more people to this region of the United States. We will lure the young, unsuspecting teenager who is angry with his or her parents. The girlfriend and boyfriend who were torn to shreds by the heartache of a bad relationship. Middle-aged people who are tired of fighting the machine, built by man and run by men. And the elderly and the old, who are the most consistently and constantly ignored.

I will invite them all to the confines of my humble abode. How about the drug addicts, the alcoholics, the homeless who need someone to care for them? I will offer them safety, security, and anything else their hearts desire. Then, once they are here, in my grasp, I will pull the rug out from under them. The information I will be sending out will be directed at all people between the ages of 10 through 80. I have figured out how to drive my spigot deep into the heart of both the young and the old, and drain every drop of life from them as my own reward."

Charles Martin walked over to the computer and started to work. Almost immediately, the screen exploded with characters and lines of data, moving so quickly that everyone's eyes could not keep up with the action.

Falstaff turned to Angela, and in a conciliatory tone, said, "Thank you, Ms. Harrison. Who would have thought you'd be so helpful?"

This time when Angela attempted to stand, she had help. Jake Taylor bounded in behind Agent Harrison, knocking into two of Falstaff's servants and causing them to fall to the floor like bowling pins. Raising his hand up to stop everyone from moving, Falstaff flinched a bit when he saw that everyone had stopped except for one very pissed off FBI agent, Angela Harrison.

She rushed toward Falstaff and knocked him over, and the commotion around them began again. However, this time, it was Angela who looked around the room and uttered the word, "Stop!" Everything came to a stand-still.

"You can't do that!" Falstaff screamed.

"I just did!" she fired back at him. She now held the upper hand, and Angela wasn't going to waste time. The glow around her never wavered. "You know, the first time I met Stark Hansen, he called me Angel. Not Angela, but Angel. I didn't understand until just a few hours ago. When I began to glow, I realized that I apparently am an angel, sent here to deal with the likes of you. And while I may not be as powerful as you, Mr. Falstaff, I know your secret. I'd say that gives me an edge."

♦ ♦ ♦

Because she was a vampire, Erin Hastings was light. Therefore, Bethoon didn't mind carrying her through the blackened nighttime sky. They wasted no time heading North, away from the south-west corner of Arizona. Along the way, other vampires joined the King of the North on his quest to find shelter before first light.

"Why can't I fly?" Erin asked the King.

"You are too young, too new," was his curt response. He noticed Erin put her face into her abdomen as if she were embarrassed. "What is bothering you, Erin Hastings?"

"Are you ever worried about dying?" she inquired.

He answered her question with one of his own. "Do you ever wonder why they call our kind monsters?" She was silent. Therefore, he explained, "A normal lifespan today is said to last 70 years; yet, I am over three thousand years old. People have to have labels for things they don't understand, so we have been labeled vampires, or monsters, because they can't explain our life spans. Oh, make no mistake, I have done things in my lifespan that are barbaric, but only to survive. Professor von Bruton understands this. Still, Eric hunts our kind, and he was very successful at it until I altered his world. Now, he will not rest until he sees me dead. I ask you, Erin Hastings, who is the real monster?"

"Hey, the whole reason I'm in this mess in the first place is because of our kind. But, what will happen when I have to feed to assure my survival?" Erin continued to gaze into the night when she noticed the crater in front of them. As the opening started to expand wider, she said, "That's the canyon. Isn't that what you are looking for?"

Bethoon lowered himself down into the Grand Canyon. This move would allow the vampires to work long into the morning. It would be hours before the sun would be high enough to pierce the shadowy veil deep inside the Canyon.

As the vampires found a safe and secure cave to land in, they started to settle into their temporary domicile. Some of the dim-witted monsters had no fear of Bethoon or his charge. When three of them made their move to dislodge Erin from the Vampire King's protection, he proved his worth by throwing one onto a spiked stone that pierced the monster's chest and turned him to dust.

Unfazed, the other two vampires continued their attack and soon found Erin's Nike running shoes buried in their mid-sections. As they were doubled over, she knocked them to the cave floor. Before she could drive her death blow into them, her arm was stopped in mid-air by the Vampire King. "They've learned their lesson. Besides, we also have allies in this cave." Two of Bethoon's henchman jerked the two newcomer vampires up to their feet and then lead them toward the mouth of the cave. No more actions were required. "You fight well, young one," Bethoon said, then turned and walked away.

For the rest of the time in the cave, the vampires waited for either their eventual destruction, or redemption. Whatever happened next, those who were left alive would be flying to the northern reaches of Canada.

♦ ♦ ♦

"I have no secrets, hag!" Falstaff blurted.

"You have plenty of secrets that I don't know about. However, there is one secret I am sure of," Angela stated confidently as she watched the evil man's eyes. His evil glare could not stop the words she delivered next. "Where do you come from, Falstaff?"

"I was formed in the consciousness of man," he stated proudly. "First, I was a single thought; then I became several thoughts. I took physical form once man realized their emotions such as rage, hate, envy, pride. I am most like fear and loathing. I am that thing that goes bump in the night. I am the monster under the bed. I am your worst nightmare."

Angela knew it wasn't time yet for her to make her move. Something wasn't quite right. Therefore, she changed the subject. "Why do you hide in other people, Falstaff? Why is it you feel the need to invade someone else's space? It can't be just because you need their soul to survive. It has to be something more."

Suddenly, the shape in front of her changed. Standing before the FBI agent was the only other form she had ever seen, the man with the coal-black hair with the white streaks. She had done it. Angela had made the monster more vulnerable. She couldn't stop now. "It's not that form I am referring to, you worm. What are you so afraid of? You are in your home. If you are this all-powerful being, let Napier go. Let this form go as well. I want to see the true form of evil that you are."

Falstaff began to smile. He understood what she was trying to do. She was trying to get him to reveal the darkest part of himself and leave himself open for attack. He wasn't about to let that happen. "You do know my secret, don't you, little one? I understand what you are trying to do. You cannot win this fight, Angela Harrison."

As he started to move toward her, the body of Ethan Napier fell to the cave floor. It appeared to be a painful process for the demon to separate from his human host. At the same time, Falstaff made a slight motion with his neck and an opening was made. Angela ordered, "Jake, get this man out of here!"

Jake was on his feet in seconds and entered the protective dome to retrieve the spasming mess that was Ethan Napier.

This was when Angela made her only mistake inside the dome. She looked at Jake and said, "My friend, it's up to you to lead everyone out of here. I've got to finish this."

Outside, a storm was gathering above the catacomb. Jake grabbed the body and slid it through the small opening. As the dome closed up behind him, he looked at the remains of his team and said, "It's time to go!"

As Angela turned her head back toward the demon, a hand shot out of Falstaff's skin and grasped the FBI agent by the throat. She felt her air being cut off. She could see that the monster had granted her wish. He stepped through the skin of the dark-haired man's form to reveal a new form of Falstaff. Standing before her was a demon form whose skin was ashen red. The deep-set eyes were the same as the dark-headed man that had stood before her just moments before. His ears were large, and his head had one spike coming out of the top. "Do you like what you see, Angela Harrison?"

♦ ♦ ♦

"It's time to go!" As Jake said the words, it seemed to spring everyone into action. Kira quickly dispatched with the two zombie-like monsters watching her. The Mayor reached through his legs and grabbed the leg of his unsuspecting guard. With a sudden jerk, the monster was on his back and knocked unconscious.

Carrie-Anne didn't have to worry about her guard. He was taken care of by Kira. Carrie ran toward Charles, but he was frantically working on the computer. "C'mon, we've got to go," she said. Her husband ignored her. "Charles Lee Martin, you need to stop that right now and come with me! I am taking you home to our children." When Charles didn't make a move to leave, Carrie-Anne began to panic. She couldn't break her husband away from the computer. It was as if he were in a trance as he worked at that computer station.

Professor von Bruton recognized the panic in Carrie-Anne's eyes and moved to analyze the situation. Before doing so, the older man disposed of with his adversary with little difficulty by shooting a bullet into the zombie's brainpan. He then stepped forward and noticed that Charles was writing code at a phenomenal rate. "Cut the power," he shouted to Carrie – Anne, but she didn't move. The professor explained as he searched for the power cord of the computer, "While Falstaff is busy with Agent Harrison, he cannot control all of the aspects of this operation. However, through the use of electricity, he seems to have locked Charles into a sort of loop. He hears nothing, sees no one, and will continue working at the computer until we break the loop he is in."

The professor found the power cord and disconnected it. Charles continued to work, seeing only the computer. As the other people in the group raced to follow Jake out of the caves, Eric took the laptop computer and raised it as high as he could. He slammed it to the stone floor, where it broke into small pieces. Still nothing. There was a perplexed look on the professor's face. He thought that his actions would snap Charles Martin out of the state he was in.

Carrie – Anne gazed at her husband and then at the professor. "We are overthinking this." She reached down and kissed the man she loved. His hands stopped moving. As Carrie continued to kiss her husband, he wrapped his arms around his wife and began leaning in for the embrace.

Carrie-Anne Martin quickly withdrew from his mouth and said, "Both electrical and chemical, Doc!"

All members were present and accounted for, including the Mayor and the County Sheriff. They all stood there looking at the dome and wondering what was going to happen to their leader. Angela was trapped inside the dome, and not one of them could think of a way to help her. Finally, Jake said, "She'll be fine. She's been in this situation before." Everyone watched the second in command as he bent down and threw Ethan Napier over his shoulder. "She faced him at a place called Hornersville, Missouri, eight years ago. Now, we need to go." Jake then pointed himself toward the exit. Kira, the Mayor, and the others followed him. No one looked back.

♦ ♦ ♦

Gasping for breath while trying to consider his question, "Do you like what you see?" Angela grabbed the behemoth's arm. Then, raising her legs, she placed them in his chest and pushed backward. She had broken herself from his grasp and slid back toward the edge of the protective dome.

Lying there for a few seconds, she had the chance to get a full-sized view of her adversary, and she suddenly convulsed. Falstaff stood watching her, not realizing he was the reason for her choking up. The thing before her was no less than seven feet tall with layers upon layers of pouches all over his body. The bloated overlapping flaps were covered with puss, sweat, and dirt, and seemed to be full of something. What Angela finally rationalized was that he was filled with all the sins he had brought forth and exposed the human race to. It sickened her. She could not bear to look at this glutenous thing that had brought so much hurt, pain, and anguish to the world. "I see why you disguised yourself," she said, finally.

"All you spiritual people are alike," Falstaff blustered. "You think you can save the world. Well, Angel, you are going to die here."

Once she brought herself under control, she said, "No, I am not going to die here, and neither are you." The words were literally being choked out of her by the demon. "You don't belong here in the first place."

He froze. His eyes flickered just for a moment, and then he saw it out of the corner of his eyes. An opening, a vortex, was forming further inside the cavern. For the first time in the millions of years he had inhabited this planet, he felt a twinge of fear.

"I couldn't figure out how you were able to do all the things you do," Angela commented. His confidence was starting to slip, and his grip on her throat loosened. "If you are what you say you are, especially regarding your abilities, then you cannot be of this world."

The look in his eyes indicated she was correct, so she continued, "You didn't just suddenly appear here. Somehow, someway, you sneaked your way to our plane of existence. But, like most living things, you became lonely. So, you created the figment of having children. You chose a boy at first, and that boy would be just like his father. You lacked companionship; then, suddenly, you had that with your son. At least until he got bored with his life and wanted yours. Where is Tommy, by the way?" Falstaff started to grow and then roar, as if he were in pain. His body seemed to be spasming.

Angela Harrison's confidence in what she was saying was steadfast. "You have upset the delicate spiritual balance here long enough. It's time for you to leave!" As she said the words, the protective dome surrounding them shattered to the floor of the cave.

Suddenly, in their presence, stood the spiritual entity, Aqualax.

"I am too powerful for you, Witch." His words were aimed at the Goddess of Light.

As he was shouting expletives and curses, Aqualax glided forward and wrapped herself around Angela. It was as if the FBI agent absorbed Aqualax into every pore of her body. The voice that came from the Aqualax/Harrison combination was both spiritual and human. "The balance has been achieved."

Angela felt empowered as she stood looking at the satanic villain in front of her. She stepped forward, and grabbing the monster by his arm, Angela felt a surge of adrenaline flow through her as she held his wrist and started walking toward the vortex. "I will not go with you!" Falstaff shouted. As she lost her grip, he began to move away from Harrison.

Something urged the agent to grab the monster by his most vulnerable point, his large, gangling ears. However, they were slick with slime, and she couldn't keep her grip. Angela stepped forward again, causing the beast to flinch. He seemed off his game. She reached up and grabbed one large ear and joined it with the earlobe on the other side of his head. He shouted his anger and contempt, but he could not remove himself from the agent's hand. Whatever was guiding Angela had helped her to make the proper choice.

Agent Harrison was being pulled toward the vortex. It was as if the gravitational pull from the whirlpool was a magnet, drawing her and Falstaff closer to his destiny.

He tried to pull away from the agent, but her grip did not loosen. "You will die if you get pulled into the vortex with me, little one." Fear was now his enemy, and he was losing control of his reality. He screamed, "There will be no hope for you, Angela Harrison!" Suddenly, his left hand came at her and swatted at her, knocking her backward. The cave floor, however, seemed to clamp the monster in place. "This cannot be!" he shouted. "There is some type of magic at work here, upsetting the balance."

"Your mere presence on this plain has upset the balance, Demon. Now, close your lying mouth before I seal it shut," Angela responded. Suddenly, Angela moved toward the monster once again, grabbing it more firmly this time. She made sure she had the villain's attention. "Your time is ending here. Your punishment will be to return to your dimension and suffer through just being an average, every day, run of the mill demon. You will never again be devouring human remains. Never taking over bodies that are not your own. It is time to end your existence here, Falstaff." The monster's feet were released from the floor, and Angela Harrison was, once again, sliding toward the vortex. She was at the entrance when she paused.

Aqualax spoke into the air, aiming her words for the woman who had been chosen for this mission. "Angela, you can do this. You must drag him into the vortex. It has to be you who rids the world of this evil. Have faith, Angela, that you are doing what's best for mankind."

While Falstaff continued to struggle for his freedom, Angela closed her eyes and stepped into the void, dragging the unwanted and unwilling demon with her.

Both entities were surrounded by the whirling sounds of the void. Angela's eyes remained closed. Therefore, she did not see what happened next. Aqualax's form pulled itself from inside the woman known as Angela Harrison. Aqualax still held on to Falstaff's ear like a mother who was punishing her son. Angela opened her eyes just in time to see Falstaff and Aqualax be pulled into a dimension unbeknownst to her. Then she began to fall as well. The FBI agent closed her eyes once again because she didn't want to see her end coming. There was a slight shockwave that started at the point where the demon, Falstaff, and the agent of good, Aqualax, had found the demon's dimension and moved into it. She knew the end was near and did the only thing she could think to do. She thanked the Lord for allowing her to experience the life she had. Her only regret was not getting to spend more time with her one true love, Stark Hansen.

♦ ♦ ♦

The vampires were deep inside the cave at the Grand Canyon when they felt the shockwave that was created by Falstaff and Aqualax crossing into a different dimension. As the wave spread across the entire earth, vampire after vampire began to turn to dust. However, Erin Hastings did not. She stood steadfastly and watched as members of the group turned to dust and disappeared.

Suddenly, the beautiful vampire heard a guttural growl from Bethoon the Cannibal. "I knew it was too good to be true," he stated, as he, too, began to disintegrate in front of her.

"What can I do to help you, Bethoon?" Erin Hastings asked.

"Nothing," he returned. Something was different in the slowness of the disintegration of the Northern King. This was a signal to Erin that maybe the powers that be had a different plan for him. With each piece that turned to dust, the monster gasped in pain. It was intense, unlike anything the vampire had felt in decades.

Erin looked around and noticed that a few others were slowly turning to ash, like the King of the North. The young vampire saw one couple in the same predicament as Bethoon. She watched as the male stuck out his wrist to his mate and ordered, "Drink." As the second vampire fed on the first, the female shape solidified.

Rolling up her sleeve, Erin directed the male vampire next to her, "Drink."

"I will not!" Bethoon snapped back.

Even though she didn't know what to expect by helping Bethoon, she did feel the pang of hesitation as she presented her arm to him. "It's not like we're going steady. But, you do want to live, don't you?" As he grabbed her wrist, she said sarcastically, "Be gentle, it's my first time."

Surprisingly, Bethoon gently caressed her arm as he slid his teeth into the vein and started to draw just enough blood to ease his pain. Erin's blood was like the sweet nectar he had always searched for. The more he tasted, the more he wanted. After a few moments, Bethoon pulled away. He was feeling better. His self-destruction had stopped. But, after sitting for mere moments, his body was jerked upward as he convulsed. His body rose up high into the roof of the cave. Suddenly, it slammed to the floor. Within a few moments, he rose again, but was slammed to the ground once more.

As Erin watched what was happening, she became unsure of herself. All she had wanted to do was save the man who had saved her. As sudden as he had started jerking, he stopped. Lying on the cavern floor, even though he looked banged up, he was still alive.

Bethoon the Cannibal slowly stood. "What have you done to me, Erin Hastings?"

"I don't know," she answered in a confusing tone.

He was on his feet and started to stagger a bit. His skin was tingling, and he could feel things he hadn't felt for thousands of years. Tears formed in his eyes. Suddenly, he turned toward the young vampire girl and said, "I don't know how this has happened, but you've cursed me with a soul. I can now feel all the things I chose not to feel in my lifetime.

Young woman, I have done despicable things that I have not wanted to be held accountable for, but now I will be. Why have you cursed me like this, Ms. Hastings?"

The Cannibal did not appear to be angry. Instead, he was dumbfounded by his predicament. Erin stared at him. Her only thought was something Aqualax had said to her. "The angel told me my soul had been restored. When I tried to help you just now, maybe, somehow, you've been blessed."

"Blessed?" Bethoon questioned. "It's more like I've been damned for all eternity. With this soul, I will have guilt and remorse. I will go mad before I can return to the North." He started to stomp around and slam his fists into the cave walls. Once he finished abusing himself, he found a quiet hole and sat down, away from everyone else.

"Maybe this is a good thing," Erin stated, while receiving a look of disdain from the Vampire King. "You have been around for a long time. Possibly, because of the kindness you have shown me, my parents, and Angela, you are being rewarded." She was searching her thoughts for a better explanation of his situation, but she had none.

"You must come with me to the North, Ms. Hastings. There are people there who will try to bring harm to me in my present state. You must return with me and help me navigate these new circumstances. I will not take no for an answer."

Erin Hastings understood what he was asking. While pondering the Vampire King's request, her eyes became wide, and she demanded, "I will not be your Queen! Ever since your previous Queen was destroyed, you have been searching for a mate to replace the woman you lost. I will not fill that void. However, I will go with you. I will do my best to support you, since I may have caused your situation. However, I have plans, Bethoon. I plan to return to the others, if they will have me. I have plans to see my parents and try to live as normal a life as possible. Do you understand?"

"That is something you will never be able to do as long as you are what you are." He spat the words at her because he was jealous of the possible future she yearned for. "For now, let's put this bickering aside and head North. We can sort all these other things out later. After all, we are still alive, and if that shockwave was an indication of anything, Falstaff is dead."

The other vampires started to herd toward them, looking for direction. Bethoon the Cannibal stood to face them. Being aware that, at this moment, appearance was everything, Erin Hastings took her place behind him, as if she were his mate. The closer the other monsters came, the closer she moved to Bethoon. "What do you want?" Bethoon commanded.

"Direction, My Lord," someone from the newly formed crowd insisted.

"Come nightfall, we head North to my Kingdom." This comment seemed to appease them. He added, "I suggest we all rest until the time comes that we can leave." They began to disperse to find places to sleep until nightfall. To keep up appearances, Erin followed the King to his spot and used him as her pillow.

"If you try anything, my King, this will not end well for you," she told him.

"Young woman, I may be a vampire," he started, but then stopped. "Sleep," he said instead, "It will do us all some good. Nightfall will take care of itself."

Erin was asleep in mere moments. The Vampire King followed a short time after that. For Bethoon, it was sleep he had not had in a millennium. Bethoon began reminiscing about the times he spent tending his flock of sheep. Bethoon was sitting in a beautiful green meadow, and he could hear the sheep bleating everywhere. Smiling, he stood to view his flock. The smile on his face soon disappeared, however, when he noticed all the dead bodies. Bethoon did not sleep again for several weeks.

♦ ♦ ♦

Once the shockwave knocked the remnants of the FBI crew to the ground, everyone stood up and noticed they did not have to fight their way through any more zombies or henchmen. They headed directly to the corral to release the rest of the Sheriff's deputies who were being held. As the group started to move to where they had parked their vehicles, Jake stopped and turned to gaze at the caves, looking for proof of life of his partner and friend, Angela Harrison. He felt a hand on his arm. He turned to see the Mayor.

"Jake, I don't know if you've noticed, but the ground is trembling, which means something bad is about to happen."

"I understand, Sir, but my friend is up there. I have to go find her and bring her to safety." The look on his face was resolute.

The two men were joined by the others when Mayor Hastings said, "We both know she is gone, Jacob. There is nothing we can do but get everyone here to safety, to their family and friends."

The ground below them began to tremble more intensely than before. The group of survivors was more than a hundred yards from the catacombs when they started to crumble. Carrie-Anne grabbed Jake Taylor by the collar and commanded, "We've got to get these people to safety. There is nothing else we can do for Angela, or for the others trapped up there. We have got to get to the cars and get out of here, right now!"

There was a sudden blast of white light, and everyone was caught up in it. The entire group was lifted up and tossed another two hundred yards, away from the collapse of the caves. Once the smoke cleared, everyone who had been former zombies and servants of the demon Falstaff was with them as well. The monsters and servants were human once again, and therefore, needed to be taken away from this place. The members of the FBI task force went around gathering the unfortunate people who had been brought into Falstaff's reign of terror. They were safe now.

Once Jacob Taylor finished helping the people to their feet, he turned back to look at the rubble. He was speechless. Eventually, he was joined by Carrie-Anne and Charles Martin, Professor von Bruton, and Kira Knight. Their task force had been broken with the loss of Angela and Erin. "Jake," said the Professor, "I know it sounds cliché, but you and I both know she's in a much better place now."

"Yeah, I know," Jake commented, "but, it doesn't mean I have to like it."

"I hate to be a stickler here, but what do we do next?" Charles Martin asked.

"We get all these people to St. David, and to their families," Kira answered. "But, we also have to get statements from each one of them."

Everyone in the group looked at her, but said nothing. She cleared her throat out of embarrassment and added, "But, first, let's shower and rest. The reports can wait."

A small smile appeared on Jake's face as he moved toward her and put his arm around her. They all started the mile walk to the cars. Along the way, they were still picking up survivors. When they finally reached their vehicles, the Professor noticed a small group of deputies had surrounded a body that was lying on the ground. As the FBI team arrived and looked down, they recognized the person immediately. It was FBI agent, and their leader, Ms. Angela Harrison. She was curled up into the fetal position and looked as if she were "Sleeping Beauty."

Jake stepped forward and checked for any signs of life by placing his fingers on her throat. His eyes were wide when he said, "She's alive!"

♦ ♦ ♦

Angela could feel herself falling into the abyss, and there was nothing she could do. Falstaff was gone. Aqualax was gone. She was all alone to face her own demise, which is what she had always thought would happen. Over the years, she had learned that death was something that the FBI agent would have to face by herself, and there would be nothing she could do about it. She felt that once her judgment was held, she would be allowed to go on with the next level of her life. She was not perfect; she had made mistakes. But, overall, she was ready to take the next step in her existence.

It was at that point she felt a pair of arms wrap around her waist. Angela's eyes snapped open. When she looked up into the eyes of the only man she truly loved, she relaxed. She understood her soul was safe with this man. "Hello, Stark," she said softly

"Hello, Ms. Harrison," he answered.

She tried to shift into his embrace, but there wasn't much room to maneuver. "Angel, you're not going to die this day. You have done the one thing none of the rest of us could do. You have brought a somewhat fragile balance to the war between good and evil. You should be proud."

"But, why am I here?" she asked.

"We needed your physical form to drag Falstaff into the threshold of the abyss, where he is absolutely powerless. Once you did that, Aqualax was able to transfer him to his plane of existence. He will not return."

"So what about you, Mr. Hansen. Where do you belong?"

He smiled and softly said, "With you!"

As he said the words, Angela closed her eyes in satisfaction. She was finally going to get what she wanted, the man of her dreams. God was going to reward her for a job well done by giving her this gift. She leaned in for a kiss that did not come. She opened her eyes to Stark's handsome gaze. Once the word, "However," escaped from his mouth, Angela's shoulders slumped. "There is still much work to be done in your dimension. Even though you were able to stop a single source of evil in the world, there is still much more evil for you to ferret out and put a stop to."

"So, basically, you are saying that I have to do God's work? I suppose you can't be there?"

"No, but Jacob can be. He is a direct link to me. Also, while you may not see me every day, I will be there to help and protect you, when and where I can. If you walk into another vortex, I will be there to pull you out."

She continued to gaze at him for several moments, running her fingers through his silken hair. Then she asked, "So, Angel man, what's next?"

"You will need to help your colleagues finish up in St. David and then work to keep your team together. A few of them are wavering, but that's because they think you are dead."

"I am dead, aren't I?"

"Far from it," Stark stated, and then explained, "You have done wonderful work here, and you need to present your findings to Washington ASAP. The rest you will have to figure out on your own."

"Stark," she had a shy look on her face, "thank you for saving me."

Stark said nothing as he stared into her stunningly beautiful brown eyes. Then, she asked, "Since I have to go back to the land of the living, can I ask one more favor?"

"Anything." He replied.

"Will you give me a kiss? Not just an ordinary kiss, but one that will have to last a lifetime."

Stark covered her mouth with his own. It aroused her. She opened her eyes and saw the light as it exploded into the area around her, and she had to close them again. He tried to release her, but she would not let him go. Her arms clamped down on his. She was not giving up the ghost. Finally, she felt a difference in his embrace, and she decided to open her eyes. When she did, she was no longer with Stark Hansen. She was in a hospital room, surrounded by her team and her friends.

Chapter Twenty-One

E.C.H.O.

Six months after the final cleanup of the case in St. David, Arizona, Special Agent Angela Harrison was still being questioned by the Bureau about her team's involvement in the case. Three months before the current questioning, Angela had submitted her report as to what happened in that sleepy little town. While accepting the story that was laid out in the report, the Federal Bureau of Investigation didn't, for a minute, take Angela's account of the situation as factual and accurate.

After the agent in charge disbanded her group of participants, they scattered to the four winds. However, being a federal agency, the FBI started investigating its own people for improprieties. Although he was a bit different than the other members of the team, the investigative committee planned to begin by interviewing Jacob, "Jake" Taylor. But, he couldn't be found, anywhere. Angela, who had been in charge of the St. David case, had ordered him to search for one of their valuable assets, one Ms. Erin Hastings, a reported vampire, who went missing after Ms. Harrison had her clandestine meeting with Mr. Ethan Napier, a.k.a. Falstaff.

Agent Taylor was following the trail of Bethoon the Cannibal, said to have lodgings somewhere in Northern Canada. Jacob does check in weekly to give a report of his findings. Apparently, Ms. Harrison believes it is more important to find this vampire than to help the committee get to the truth of the situation in St. David.

Once the investigative team ruled that this avenue of investigation was fruitless, the agency turned to the other two agents on the case, Ms. Kira Knight and Carrie - Anne Martin, the fired agent who was reinstated for this case. Kira is refusing to add any information to the report she has already submitted. It should be noted that Ms. Knight is exceptionally loyal to Angela Harrison and other members of her team. Whatever happened in St. David has built an unbreakable bond between the them. She did say that she is more than willing to answer more questions, but only if the entire team is assembled. According to Ms. Knight, "I am not trying to cover anything up. I just think if you don't have all the answers you want, then assemble the team and allow us to answer in unison."

Carrie – Anne and Charles Martin are back home in Seattle and reunited with their children. Charles, or "Geek Boy" as he is known to the other member of their group, refuses to answer anything until he is in the same room with Angela Harrison. Carrie – Anne is following her husband's lead.

Professor Eric von Bruton has been the most cooperative. He is back in Michigan, working at Adrien College. The Professor has buried himself in his work. He seems to be energized by his involvement in St. David. Yet, if the agency were to believe the professor, who has given practically the same information that was provided by the others, then the committee would have to find this report plausible, and we would all be considered certifiable.

Angela finished reading the brief summary she was given and placed it on the table. She faced the sub-committee and waited for questions to be fired at her. She folded her hands together, and as she did, the agent received her first question. "You expect us to believe any of this?"

"Senator, I cannot help you accept what happened. Every time I read the reports our team has submitted, I can't believe them myself." Angela took a deep breath, relaxed, and then continued, "When the assistant director asked me to take this case, he reminded me of the case in Hornersville, Missouri. We were able to save the townspeople there, just as we did in St. David. However, some situations happen that no one wants to report. Do I want to sit here and tell you we lost personnel that I wish had not died? No. But it's a fact. We did lose people. Monsters are real. No matter what shape they come in, they are real. There are wolves out there in sheep's clothing. It doesn't matter if you can see them or believe in them, they do exist. If you allow me and my team to continue our work, we will do our best to stop what we can. Thank you!"

Angela started to stand. "Agent Harrison, you haven't been excused yet," a voice from the sub-committee panel commented.

The FBI agent sat back down, leaned into the microphone, and said, "Unless you have new information to discuss, I have nothing further to say.

I have a town that is slowly trying to pull itself together, run by a Mayor who only stayed in place because I asked him to. In that town, we faced both angels and demons. I understand you don't want to face these issues, because if you accept my team's reports, then you would have to admit these things do exist. So, fire me, don't fire me; suspend me, or don't suspend me; I am done with this. I have got to get back to work." She paused and gazed at the panel until she found Michael Cline, her mentor, friend, and her boss. "I'm sorry, Michael, but that's the best I can do."

Angela stood up and walked out of the meeting. After she left, all eyes turned to Michael Cline.

"Well, Michael, what do you have to say about your subordinate?" the senator from Arizona asked.

"Personally, Senator, I believe she spoke eloquently. Ms. Harrison has been to hell and back on this case, while we sit here and judge her and the members of her team on a situation none of us can comprehend. The mere fact that she is still on the job after such an ordeal completely amazes me. Why don't you just label this as an anomaly and move on? Quite frankly, I have an entire filing cabinet drawer full of instances that are unexplained. We need someone with the focus, knowledge, and understanding of issues such as these, to deal with such situations. We need the members of her team as well. We can't be expected to go it alone. I'm not sure if they will all want to return to the team after what they went through, but we do need to consider them for the job, if for no other reason than they are the only ones willing to do the job."

"But, what about Agent James Stasher? His death is unsolved. And this Agent, Arthur "Tommy" Kensington, there is no record of this man at all," the Senator insisted.

"James Stasher was, by all accounts, a good agent who was caught up in a bad situation. The agency is very sorry for his death. However, Tommy Kensington is a whole different kettle of fish. According to the reports you have been given, Tommy is a descendant of this Falstaff character, and his whereabouts are unknown at this time. But, rest assured, he is number one on our priority list. The only problem is," Michael paused. His face had an astounded look on it. "It took us several lifetimes to even find out about the likes of one evil villain that went by the name of Falstaff. How long do you think it will take us to find this "Tommy Kensington?"

The room was quiet. After several moments, Michael Cline spoke one last time before he exited the room. "Look, I don't mean to be flippant about the situation. However, we need these people to help protect us all from things that go bump in the night." Then the assistant director of the FBI scratched his head and added, "I can't help thinking about something Professor von Bruton suggested in his report. 'If Ms. Harrison,' the Professor says, 'is correct, and all these things, these anomalies, should not be here in the first place, then how are we, the common man and woman, going to combat them without someone like Angela and her team?'" Michael threw the paper down he was reading. "Ladies and gentlemen of this committee, we need Agent Angela Harrison and her people, if, and when, these bad guys return." He cleared his throat. "I hope you will allow me to continue to work with them. Thank you!" He turned and left the committee to themselves to review the reports and make the decisions they had to make.

Three days later, Michael Cline received the clearance he needed to put Angela back to work. She was to her bring her team to Washington and get started on the mountain of cases stacked on the director's desk.

♦ ♦ ♦

The eastern side of the Rocky Mountains was bitter cold this time of year. However, this did not bother Jake Taylor. He had left the Canadian town of Blasterville, population 757, on his quest to find Ms. Erin Lee Hastings.

Jake had found the cave in the Grand Canyon, which was not an easy task. He climbed down into the cavern about a month after Erin and Bethoon the Cannibal had fled the great Southwest of Arizona. Finding that cave was the hardest part of picking up the trail, because once they left the cave, the vampire horde had left a trail of dead that was very easy to follow.

The trail was, indeed, filled with dead bodies of animals and few unsuspecting humans. Jake could not allow any of the unfortunate victims to turn into the demonic creatures that he had faced while in St. David. Therefore, he would wait for the human being to turn into a monster and then give it a very deserving peace by removing it from this earth. To allow even one of those things to live was inhumane. The agent tracked them from Arizona through Utah, Idaho, and finally, Montana. He had hoped to reach them before they crossed into Canada, but a strange occurrence in the border town of Mitchell, in Montana, had required that he stay long enough to take care of the vampire issues. He crossed the border in early November, but the foul weather was kicking his ass all over the road. He often had to stop his Jeep Cherokee to allow the weather to pass, and then shovel himself out before moving on to the next town.

The other issue Agent Taylor had to deal with was "the Change," though he only had to deal with this problem two or three days a month. The professor had given him some concoction of garlic and silver nitrate to inject on the worst days. He would find a secluded piece of land with lots of trees and run wild for as long as he had to. One day he woke up to find himself with a she-wolf draped across his torso. She stayed with him, even when he returned to the human race.

Jake had arrived at the town of Blasterville in early December, just in time to prevent the newly ordained vampire from taking out the town's mayor. Fortunately for the FBI agent, because of his heroic deed, the townsfolk gave him all the information he needed to follow the pack into the mountains and find what he was looking for.

It appeared that there had been several attacks on the townspeople by this beast. While folks in Blasterville were known for their hunting experiences, it seemed that they had found several elk with their throats cut, and, occasionally, a human would be drained of their lifeblood as well. It was sporadic when one of the tribesmen from that area returned in the form of a monster. If anything, they didn't return at all.

A hunter's guide gave Jake directions for where he might find the group of people he was looking for. He thanked them for the warm bed and the fantastic food, including the elk jerky he took with him. Then, Jacob Taylor headed off to find his friend and Bethoon the Cannibal.

On the third day out, he parked his jeep and walked toward where he thought Erin and the others would be. The skies were clear on this day, and he could see for miles. It was almost dark, but Jake knew he was close, and with his female wolf with him, he felt no fear. Then, just as the sun started to set, he spied an opening in the rock face and headed straight toward it. He knew that he had found what he was looking for when his wolf-friend refused to go any further. He calmed his female companion, then pulled out his FBI jacket and put it on. Jake ordered his new friend to stay put. The wolf whined, but didn't move from her spot.

Once he reached the mouth of the cave, he loudly entered. While stomping the snow off his feet and brushing his jacket to remove any residual snow, he shouted, "My name is Jake Taylor, and I am looking for my friend Erin Lee Hastings." He suddenly realized he was standing in the early evening light. Therefore, he took several steps further into the cave until there was no more light. He repeated the same words adding, "Look, I don't want any trouble. I don't have any wooden weapons on me. Please, if Erin isn't here, let me know. I'll leave quietly, and you'll never hear from me again. Although, I have to give you guys a little advice. Someone in your group isn't doing a thorough job of hiding your trail. In my quest to find Ms. Hastings, someone in your group is leaving reminders of who and what you are, along the way. That is why it has taken me so long. I was busy cleaning up after you."

There was a sudden noise from deep in the cave. Someone was sprinting toward the FBI agent at full speed. The sound caused him to pause, and he took a few steps back into the light. Erin was upon him in moments, shouting his name, and planting a huge kiss on his lips. "You've found me! You actually found me!" She slid off his body and noticed she had bitten him, and there was blood. She wiped a little with her thumb and put it in her mouth. Then, without warning, she punched him in the arm and asked, "What took you so long?"

Jake explained the particulars of his quest to find her. Finishing, he said, "You look fantastic." She glowed with pride at his words.

"Bethoon, come and meet Jake," she yelled.

Both Jacob Taylor and Erin looked into the dark and listened and waited. Eventually, the monster known as Bethoon the Cannibal appeared in front of him. Jake thought Bethoon looked different, but never mentioned it. "I take it Angela Harrison was able to rid the earth of Falstaff?" Bethoon asked.

"Yes, she did. And she survived." Jacob spoke with an enthusiastic tone.

"You said we're leaving evidence. Are we okay here?" Bethoon questioned.

"Yes," Jake said, while keeping his eyes on the Vampire King. "Every so often, someone in your group apparently turned someone. They would then attack the townspeople and leave the bodies lying everywhere. That's how I tracked you. You need to police yourselves better so that no one else can find you here."

The smoldering eyes returned. Bethoon's anger was starting to boil. Erin placed her hand on his arm, and he calmed down. Jake gave them both a look of disbelief. Then he asked, "What's going on here? You're not his Queen are you?" he asked Erin.

Erin released the Cannibal's arm and moved to Jake. "Bethoon saved me by getting me to safety. However, he started to turn to dust, so I let him feed on me. I didn't think anything would happen, but now, I think he has a soul."

Jake was dumbfounded. He walked over and urged Bethoon, "Hit me!" Bethoon started to walk away. "Wait, Bethoon, there's got to be something we can do to help you."

"Nothing will help me," the Vampire King lamented. Then, he began walking back into the darkness and was gone from their sight.

"Maybe the Professor can help," Erin innocently suggested.

The Cannibal turned back at once, and seething with anger, he shouted, "If you tell that man anything about this, I will find you, little girl, and I will kill you myself! That man would rejoice in the fact that I can feel emotions. Just go, Erin Hastings. You are no longer wanted in our clan. You have done quite enough."

Erin was cut to the quick. Throughout the past months, she had put herself on the line to protect him from the other vampires of the clan. "So, that's how you want to be, old man?" She started to tear up as she spoke, "After all we have been through, you just toss me aside? I should have never saved you!" Her anger was starting to make her blood boil, and Jake knew that was not a good thing.

"Erin, why don't we just do as he said? Get your things, and we'll leave," Jake suggested. She didn't hesitate for a second. She left the two men to gather her belongings. While she was gone, Jake addressed to the Cannibal, "She never meant you any harm."

"What's it to you, Jacob Taylor? I see the spark between the two of you, but anything more will never work. So, if that's why you came here, you should just leave her be," Bethoon spat.

"I came up here to retrieve her because I told her I would. You may be house-broken for now, but we both know you will one day return to your old ways. When you do, I promise I'll come back, and we will settle things then," Jake replied, angrily.

The words of violence brought a smile to the monster's face. About that time, Erin returned. She was all bundled up in an insulated parka, and they could barely see her face.

As she and Agent Taylor moved toward the cave opening, when they both heard Bethoon say, "Werewolf! She cries, you'll cry!" It was something a father might say to protect his daughter.

"I'll do my best to see that she's always safe," Jake responded. With that, he and Erin stepped outside and left Bethoon to his misery.

On the way down the hill, Jake introduced Erin to Belle. The wolf wasn't sure if she was going to like having another female around. However, after a few moments, things fell in line, as they all walked the two-mile downhill trek together to his vehicle. Once they were close to the car, Erin asked, "What month is it, Jake?"

"December," he said. "December 10th, to be exact." He opened the door to let her inside the Cherokee. "I promised your mom I'd have you back by Christmas."

"Really?" she questioned. "You're pretty sure of yourself, Wolf-boy."

At the mention of the term "Wolf-boy," Belle turned and growled at Erin. She was startled, but Jacob soothed Belle. "It's ok, girl. She's just joking." The animal took her place on the blanket in the back seat. "She's a little protective of me. I can't really say what happened, but after one of my wild nights, I woke up, and she was right there. She hasn't left my side since. I tried to make her leave, but she wouldn't go."

"I'm gone six months, and you have another woman," Erin scolded.

"That's not even funny," he replied.

He put the Jeep in gear and they started the long drive back to St. David.

"Listen, Erin, I told Angela I was going to get you home to St. David. While you're there, I'm going to Tucson and work with Kira for a couple weeks. Then, after Christmas, all three of us are going to fly back to D.C. Angela needs us back in Washington to clear up the Falstaff situation."

He looked to see how Erin would respond. She smiled and said, "I can't wait. But you should know, I can fly now!"

♦ ♦ ♦

It was less than a week before Christmas, and the Martins were out shopping for their children. Carrie – Ann looked exhausted. She had every right to look tired; she was carrying their third child. She had told Charles, "Accidents happen." She reminded him of their passionate night just before the Battle for St. David. The results of that night were before them, but neither one seemed to mind.

Entangled arm in arm, the young couple approached the car with their packages. They had told no one at the agency about the child. When they had left St. David, they were informed by Angela Harrison to take as much time as they needed to rest, recover, and decide what their next steps would be.

Their first priority was the children. When they first got back, they had spent several days just watching their children grow. The proud parents took their children to the Seattle Zoo and realized how much they had missed them while they were away fighting demons.

Everyone was having so much fun that the first two months of their return passed in a blink of an eye. It was on a Sunday outing at a local park that Carrie – Anne hinted there might be a third Martin coming into the family. A week later, the doctor confirmed it. Charles was pleasantly surprised by the news. "Who would have believed anything good could come out of the St. David incident," he said. Carrie – Anne agreed.

Charles, begrudgingly, dove right back into his work. He assessed his businesses' performance up to that point and was pleased. The man acted as if there was nothing out of the ordinary in his life. However, the arrival of a third Martin did force him to take stock in his most recent escapade. "Should I be risking my life anymore? What about Carrie – Anne and the children?" he thought to himself. He began looking back on everything that happened, on missions that nobody even noticed. It seemed that the way the world was when he departed for Arizona was no different than it is now. So, why should they waste their time and energy battling things they don't fully understand when it keeps them away from their children?" His mind was made up; he wasn't going back to work with the FBI. Angela Harrison and the others would understand. He was sure of it.

Carrie – Anne didn't understand, however. She was adamant about getting Charles to change his mind. For her, it was the wrong choice. "I feel we have a lot more work to do, Charles, and I, and the rest of the team, need you with us."

He tried to reason with her. "When I was taken by Bethoon's goons, you came unraveled. I read your report. You didn't know where to turn, what to do. What if that were to happen again? This time our kids could be the target. How can you ask us to risk everything again?"

"You know, Geek-Boy, I'm surprised at you. You were in your element in St. David. You and the Professor clicked. You two worked great together." She smiled at her husband, knowing she made sense. "Besides, we saved the world from that evil down there, though nobody's the wiser. Wait," she paused for a second, "unless you're disappointed that no one noticed. Did you want vindication?"

"It's not that," he replied, "At the office, when we fought, you were everything I wasn't, a fierce warrior and defender of St. David. All I could do was stand back and watch." He looked into her deep blue eyes and said, "I must admit, I was jealous."

"From what I saw, handsome, you had some pretty good moves with those special weapons." She moved in closer to her husband. "Besides, I had a butt load of training to prepare for that battle stuff. I tell you what, if you change your mind, I'll talk to Angela and the others and see if we can get you trained so you can stand up to a gorilla if you have to. What do you think about that?" She then pounced on his thin form and was on top of him in moments. She then leaned down and kissed him with a long, sweet kiss, then leaned back up and awaited his answer.

He was pondering everything his wife had said. Finally, as a smile came to his face, he agreed to stay with the group. Carrie – Anne was relieved she had changed his mind. She kissed him on the cheek and said, "C'mon, Geek Boy, you can show me the moves that got me in this condition in the first place." She tugged on her shirt, which read, "Baby on Board." It pictured a small child on a surfboard, riding the waves.

They both snapped back to the present and were walking toward their Mercedes – Benz automobile when they noticed two figures standing in front of their car. "Hey, you two, aren't you a long way from home?" Carrie – Anne asked.

Kira Knight smiled. When she noticed the baby bump, she grinned while saying, "You two have been busy."

Suddenly, from the heavens, a third party dropped in. "She can fly now," Jacob Taylor announced as Erin quickly retracted her wings and stood next to the two FBI agents. All three were surprised at Carrie's condition. However, they were too busy welcoming each other with hugs and smiles to talk about it.

Charles spoke up, "Not trying to be rude, but why are you here?"

"Angela wanted us to check up on you two and make sure you hadn't changed your mind about joining us in DC," Kira stated.

"Well," Charles started, "I had my doubts, with the baby and all, but..."

"I straightened him out!" Carrie finished. "What about you and Erin? When did you guys get back?"

Erin's youthful exuberance could not be contained. "Jake came to get me, like he said he would. We got back home about a week ago. He's been working in Tucson while I have been getting reacclimated with home life. Everything's fine, except my mom's driving us crazy."

It was dark outside, so no one noticed the three large forms coming toward the group until one of them jumped high in the air and landed among all five members of the St. David team. "What in the hell are you doing in our city?" the vampire asked, while reaching for the throat of Erin Hastings.

Without hesitation, Erin staked the vampire. Jake and Kira used the professor's wooden stake guns and put the other two down as well.

"That's the other reason we're here," Jake said. "It seems there's a nest of these things somewhere in Seattle, or possibly in Bremerton, and Angela thought you could give us a hand."

Once finished with her target, and without missing a beat, Erin asked, "So, Carrie-Anne, is it a boy or girl?"

♦ ♦ ♦

Professor Eric von Bruton was now popular. He hated being popular. However, he did like the perks that came with it. His fictional book, entitled, "The Battle for Tombstone," was a hit. It was actually an account of what happened in St. David. While no one believed the premise, Eric's books were exploding off the shelves. The professor had just finished another term at his beloved Adrian College, and all of his classes for the next term were full. People seemed to love talking about the occult. The college appreciated the increased enrollment due to his success.

He was returning home from the faculty Christmas party on campus and entered his home. The good professor turned on the lights and then walked over and kissed the picture of his lovely deceased wife. He put his things down on the table he used to hold his car keys, hat, and briefcase, when he suddenly saw movement out of the corner of his eye. He reacted by grabbing his umbrella from its stand. "Good evening, Professor von Bruton." To his surprise, it was Bethoon the Cannibal. However, it was a younger form of the monster. The professor recognized the lad, Azahd.

"To what do I owe the pleasure?" the Professor asked, moving over to a chair opposite the one Bethoon occupied. "Surely, you haven't come all this way just to kill me?"

"It is I," Azahd answered, " who's come here hoping to have you kill me." He looked serious. "I could have tried to cause an attack or something, I suppose, to get you riled up so you would do the deed. But, I chose instead to meet you, face to face."

"I'm afraid I don't understand," the Professor responded. "You want me to kill you? What's the point? What am I missing?" Eric stared at the vampire. There were several long moments where nothing was said. Finally, the Professor said, "Wait a minute, something's different about you." Eric had gotten out of his chair and moved closer, to view his arch-enemy. "Oh my stars, you've been reborn. You have your soul!" Eric started to laugh so hard he began coughing. His eyes were watering as he returned to his chair. Surprisingly, the professor said, "I've got a bottle of 150 year-old scotch, old man. May I offer you a taste?"

This turn of events startled Bethoon. "Why, yes, I would like that." Eric poured the whiskey and handed it to the obviously uncomfortable vampire. Bethoon took a drink, and it was like reliving the best parts of his life. He closed his eyes and enjoyed the flavor of the moment.

When he opened his eyes, Eric von Bruton was holding a gun in his hand. He spat his words, "You come into my house and ask me to end you so that you don't have to feel the pain of carrying a soul? I'll bet you have been suffering like no one before you with all the deaths you've caused, the lives you have taken. Why would I do you any favors when it was my wife whom you used for your pleasure? I'm not going to help you in the least. In fact, I want to help you live longer, in any way possible. I want to watch you suffer as you made others suffer, as you made me suffer. It will be good for you."

To the professor's surprise, Bethoon finished his drink, politely placed the glass on the table, and stood to leave. Under his breath, he said, "I told her this wouldn't work." He put his coat on to head out into the cold Michigan winter.

"Who did you tell it wouldn't work?" the Professor asked.

"Why, Erin Hastings, who else? She told me that you might be willing to help me. I told her you wouldn't dare. I have to admit though, I would have thought you would be happy to kill me and be rid of me."

"Sit down, Azahd, or Bethoon, or whatever name you are going by these days. Would you like another sample? Remove your coat, and we will discuss this matter as friends, not as enemies."

The vampire followed his request and handed his glass to the Professor, who promptly filled it up. "Erin's a special lady, you know. She didn't ask to be what she is," the Professor stated.

"Frankly, neither did I," Bethoon said. "In my time, you did what you did to survive. I never expected to be around this long. I really need to die."

"Yes, yes, you do. But, to ask me to end you, well, I just can't do it. Not only because watching you squirm brings me great pleasure, but because killing you now that you have a soul truly would be criminal."

"I never knew you had this side to you, Eric. You've always hunted me and my kind for the death and destruction we caused. Now, when faced with this, you're different."

The doorbell rang. The Professor looked surprised as he rose to answer the door. "That's because you're different, my friend." He paused and thought about what he said, and added, "I didn't mean that 'my friend' part."

"I know," Azad said, smiling and taking another delicious drink from his glass.

In the other room, the door opened and then closed. Bethoon stood, while changing into his more dangerous form, preparing to greet whoever had arrived. To his amazement, standing next to the Professor was Angela Harrison. She was holding another bottle of 150-year-old scotch, with a red bow on it.

♦ ♦ ♦

Erin lay back on the blanket that had been put down in the exact same spot one year ago on the night she died. Ms. Hastings was looking up at the stars this particular December 23rd, grateful to have her friend beside her. She turned to face Jacob Taylor, thanking him for bringing her out to this spot one last time before they had to pack for Washington, D.C.

Kira, Jake, and Erin spent two days in the Bremerton/Seattle area, preventing a new clan of vampires from settling in. Charles Martin helped them by using various thermal scanners to go over the city, looking for a vampiric signature. Within 24 hours, they confronted the leader and told him he had two choices, leave or die. He chose to leave. Erin reminded them to head north to the mountains where the King of the North lived.

Leaving the Martins in peace, the two FBI agents and the vampire returned to Tucson. They checked in; then Erin flew home to St. David. Before Jake went back home to Texas to visit his family, he made one last stop on his trip to St. David. While there, the gallant gentleman asked Erin what he could give her for Christmas. She chose to visit the graveyard one last time because she would never go back there by herself.

The two, at present, were staring up at the stars when Jake asked, "What's it like when you fly?"

"I could show you," she suggested.

"No, I'm quite safe on the ground, thank you very much!" They both started to laugh, and their chuckles ending with a sigh.

"Jake, could I ask a favor of you?"

"Anything," he replied, propping his head up with his elbow.

"Kiss me! Please, Jake," she pleaded. "Just once? I promise not to tell anyone."

"You're sixteen, Erin. In Texas, we string people up for taking advantage of young girls."

"Actually, since we've been working together, I've turned seventeen. Ten years from now, it wouldn't matter. You'd be thirty-seven, and I'd be twenty-seven. It wouldn't matter."

"Darlin', it would matter. You would still look the way you do now, and, well, as a Werewolf, while I will age, it will be gradual."

"Please? Even my mother likes you, and she doesn't like any of the boys I date," she said, realizing she just called him a boy, and he was anything but that! "I'm so sorry," she sputtered, understanding the mistake she had made.

He started to laugh. Then, he took her hands in his and said, "Erin Lee Hastings, you are the bravest woman I know, except for Angela. I would be honored to kiss you."

He positioned himself as close to her as he could and covered his lips over hers. They continued with their embrace for several minutes, as though they could not quench their thirst for one another. Suddenly, they heard the sound of crunching twigs coming from the grove of trees behind them. They flew apart, and sprang into action. Jake pulled his 9mm Glock pistol from its holster, while Erin withdrew two stakes from the cowboy boots she was wearing.

Even though it was night time, both the vampire and the werewolf had outstanding night vision. They focused their attention on a bush, barely 15 yards away, when out stumbled a young woman who appeared exhausted and out of breath. She spoke, "I'm looking for a Jake Taylor or Erin Hastings."

Her voice sounded very familiar to Erin. Then, she noticed the friendship bracelet she had given the girl back when they were in elementary school together. It was Melissa Napier. "Melissa, what are you doing out here?" Erin asked.

"I wish I could tell you," the frustrated woman replied. "The people who took care of me instructed me to tell you that I'm a gift from Aqualax, and some hot guy. I can't remember his name. It was something like Stan, Star, or Star Handsome. I'm not sure. Anyway, you're supposed to take me back home. By the time you get me there, my head should clear up."

"The man's name," Jacob Taylor responded, "is Stark Hansen. He was a former Navy Seal and my half-brother. I'm sorry to tell you, he's dead."

"Well, he looked pretty alive to me." She started to move forward, toward the small road that ran the circumference of the graveyard. "Listen," she began again, "they told me to tell you guys to stop fooling around and get your business tied up and get to DC, no later than January 31st. Also, somebody called Bethoon is on his way to Nova Scotia, and Erin needs to get there as soon as possible and find this guy. That's all I got!" She passed out and fell into Erin's arms. Erin carried the young woman the rest of the way to the car while Jake gathered their belongings and headed to their automobile as well.

Eventually, they escorted the Melissa Napier home and handed her off to her father, Ethan. The two FBI employees were happy to discover he was back to normal now and getting the Napier estate back on the road to legitimacy. Melissa recovered her senses once she was back home, and the story she had to tell was nothing short of unbelievable.

"Grandpa wasn't Grandpa. He was this guy by the name of Falstaff, and he was running the family business into the ground." She paused a moment and asked her father, "Did you clear out the greenhouse? I was told you must burn everything in there, something about how the fire is the best thing to use to cleanse the earth." She then turned back to Erin, her best friend, and said, "He put this thing inside me. It was him, but not him. It devoured my soul until there was nothing left. That's why I've been missing. Aqualax said they were 'restoring the balance' in this area, and I was the last piece to the puzzle."

Erin sat near her friend and told her the story about Percy, the graveyard, the FBI, and finally, Jake. She also explained who, or what, Falstaff was.

"So, when do you have to leave, Erin?" her best friend questioned.

"Not until January 30th. Can we get some time together? Go clubbin' or something?"

"I don't see why not," Jake said. "I think the FBI can get along without you for a while." There were smiles all around the table after that. For now, all was right with the world.

♦ ♦ ♦

All the members of the task force had checked into the FBI training facility at Quantico, Virginia, by January 31st, except for the Martins. That was because on February second, one Loretta May Martin was brought into the world. She had all ten fingers and toes, and her APGAR score was a five, which, by all indications, was the best score the baby could earn. Loretta's parents, Charles and Carrie-Anne, thought she was perfect.

While the team waited for all their members to arrive, they trained. Angela had regular meetings with Michael Cline three times a day. Some sessions were very productive; some were not. A few were loud and combative. By the 15th, all the FBI Agents, Vampires, Changelings, Werewolves, Professors, and computer experts were present and accounted for. They were placed in a secluded room. All blinds were pulled shut to keep out the light, and the room was a quiet room, which meant no listening devices of any kind.

Michael Cline spoke to the group first. "Ladies and Gentlemen, you all did a marvelous job in St. David. My brother-in-law, Bruce Hastings, is still trying to get someone higher up on the ladder to listen to him sing his praises about this group. Congress is another kettle of fish."

At this statement, the other members of the team started looking at one another. Looks of uncertainty began to pop up. "They have sent us to committee after committee to try and poke holes in your story." He sighed, adjusted the waistband on his trousers, and continued. "I never said I understood how this team worked, but I do know you were successful under some pretty undesirable circumstances. You are to be congratulated."

He cleared his throat, and someone said, "Here comes the other shoe."

"While Congress isn't convinced your story is true, based on the information that everyone has presented, they can't disprove it either. As of February 1, you all have been cleared to work on the cases that I have stacked up in my office. Well, actually, they are in Angela's office. I wish you all luck, because from what I have seen, you're going to need it. I now turn over the reins to Ms. Angela Marie Harrison."

As Michael Cline quietly sat down, Angela stood. She tried twice to speak, but couldn't. On the third attempt, she found her voice. "First and foremost, you all need to thank this man." She placed her hand on Michael's shoulder and continued, "We are going to be a special task force for investigating the paranormal, and any other types of strangeness that are out there. Michael and I have agreed on the acronym E.C.H.O. It stands for Elite Counter-Horror Organization. I know it sounds elementary, but I think it works." Heads were nodding in approval.

"I am going to be in command; however, each of you will have an essential position on our team. Jacob Taylor, you are our tactical expert. Even though you are different, your performance in the field has been nothing short of spectacular.

Agent Kira Knight, also tactical, you're a real badass. I don't usually have a whole lot of good to say about Agent James Stasher, but when he brought you on board, it was one of the smartest things he could have done. I am sorry for your loss, by the way. He didn't deserve to die the way he did. We have Tommy to thank for that, and, believe me, someday soon we will. Also, you should know that while Aqualax inhabited my body, I was able to ascertain that your condition was a manipulation from a higher authority. You are a rare concoction of inspiration and dedication, and you are very good at your job. Your gift of molecular manipulation is a gift that I plan on using to assist us in our quest for the safety and sanctity of human life.

Carrie - Anne Martin, you saved our butts so many times in Arizona. Your ability is unquestionable. However, it's your legal skills we will need. I will depend on you to give me what I need when I need it, like you did in St. David. You set me straight on several occasions. Plus, you have a thumb on the pulse of your husband, who could single-handedly bring a third world nation to its knees with his laptop.

Charles Martin, you are calm under pressure, and an absolute wizard at gathering and sifting through the information superhighway. Your computer skills will be needed by every member of this squad.

Professor Eric von Bruton, you are a scientific marvel. With your knowledge and expertise in the paranormal field, and the world of vampires, werewolves, and changelings, you can give us insight and direction that nobody else can.

Last, but not least, Erin Lee Hastings, you serve a purpose in our world of crime detection, even though you are no longer a part of the real world. While I didn't think you and I would ever be able to work together at first, you were an asset in the St. David situation. You're young, undisciplined, and often have no idea what you're doing, but, truth be told, none of us do. Everyone wants you on this team because of the courage you showed throughout this case, especially during the Bel-Zog incident. You have unique needs, like no sunlight, and feeding on human blood and so forth, but as I've said before, your situation is not your fault.

In truth, Jacob, Kira, and Erin, none of you should be here. Falstaff opened that door, and even though we sent him packing, he's left enough baggage behind that we have several lifetimes worth of work to complete. I need you all, and I hope you will continue your association with us for as long as you're needed. Thank you." When Angela was finished, there were tears in her eyes.

"I don't know about the others Angela, but I'm in," Jake Taylor announced.

Then Kira, the Martins, and the Professor vowed to join the crew. Finally, Erin Hastings spoke up, "I thought you were going to dust me right here. I definitely want to join this dance."

After a short pause, Angela smiled and said, "Good, because we've got a case lined up already." The lead agent glanced around the room and saw the team hungered for another investigation. "Two months ago I went to see Professor von Bruton for the holidays, and he had a special guest in his drawing-room, Bethoon the Cannibal. It seems the Cannibal is in dire straits because he now has a soul, thanks to the quick thinking of Ms. Hastings."

Angela was interrupted by Erin. "Hey, he was nice to me, and I didn't want to see him die."

"We know you didn't," the Professor said. "Personally, I would much rather have the Vampire King working with us than against us."

There were murmurs of agreement throughout the room. Angela continued, "In exchange for the Professor's help in either killing Bethoon, or making him soulless again, the Vampire King has agreed to go undercover for us."

"What?" There were startled looks from everyone in the room.

"A week before Christmas, Michael and I took a meeting with the Canadian Ministry, and they need our help," Angela explained. "There is a sinister cult working there in the business industry. We need you, Erin, to go deep undercover with Bethoon."

There were looks of shock and dismay from every member at the table. Angela countered with, "Hey, are we an Elite Counter-Horror Organization or not?"

That is when the group all started talking at the same time. Angela Harrison sat down and let them go at each other. "This is good. They are eager to begin," she thought.

Chapter Twenty-Two

The Master Gardener

The new E.C.H.O. team was just finishing up arguing about the next case on their docket when Carrie – Anne cleared her throat, and everything came to a screeching halt. A hush came over the room. Angela looked in her direction. "Yes, Carrie-Anne?"

"Well, Ma'am, I appreciate all that you've done to allow us extra time for our next project and everything." She stopped talking, trying to approach her question with the right finesse, but she couldn't find the words.

"Carrie-Anne," Angela placed her hand on her hips, "we've been through life and death together. Just spit it out."

As Michael Cline reentered the room and walked toward Angela to take his seat next to her, Carrie-Anne asked, "Well, Angela, you've named our next case Dark E.C.H.O. a.k.a. The Devil's Hoard and the last case was False E.C.H.O, a.k.a. The Master Gardener. I was just wondering, where do the titles come from?

"Yeah, you know, Angela, I was wondering that myself," the Assistant Director said.

Angela smiled and said, "Well, the simple answer is-my father. My daddy was from Beaumont, Texas. However, the day he joined the Navy, he left Beaumont and never looked back. He was one of a handful of black sailors who were assigned to submarines. In his case, he went to college earned an associate degree and was a part of the Navy's ROTC program. He was assigned to diesel boats, first, the USS Sailfish and the USS Tang, at a time when the Navy was phasing out their diesel boat program. My daddy finished up his submarine tour on the Tang once the Sailfish was decommissioned. He was the sonar officer and from what I understand, a damned good one.

Anyway, he used to tell me that they would get these things called False Echoes out in the water. That meant, for a brief moment, the sonar officer believed there was something substantial out there in the water, and they would have to prove whether it was real or not. He loved his job, and learned to love the sounds of the sea.

That concept of thinking something is real, but eventually having to disprove it, became stuck in my head. For all intents and purposes, The Master Gardner, and all he had created or destroyed, appeared to be real. We, the people living in this reality, don't usually believe in demons, vampires, werewolves, or even changelings. Yet, here I am, sitting in a room with real examples. So, how can that be?" She stared at each member of her team.

Jake came to Angela's aid, "If we believe in something strongly enough, it becomes real."

She slapped the table, "That's right! It's what we choose to believe! If it's true that the Gardener has been here since the beginning of time, and he was able to sow his seeds of evil and disbelief undetected, then, isn't it a fact that there must be something good we can to use to fight back with? Every mystical entity that I met kept hammering home, 'keep the balance.' Stark told me that, as did Aqualax. We needed to have faith, but they also kept insisting that balance was an essential key to our situation. All anyone has to do is sit in on one congressional meeting to understand that they don't want to believe in angels and demons, because if they did, that would mean there are alternate dimensions, and they can't accept that. Well, there are demons, and there are definitely angels. My boyfriend is one.

So, based on all the facts that I know about this case, I believe that the Master Gardener a.k.a. Falstaff was the 'False Echo.' Once people started believing in him, or better yet, fear him, his power grew. Eventually, he was able to create all the evil that spewed from him. Falstaff urged man to create the sins of hate, lust, gluttony, and so many more. It was his pleasure to leave it all behind for us when I, or rather Aqualax, sent him back to his dimension.

You need to be warned, Falstaff left behind some nasty stuff. We must battle this evil without any interference from either side. I believe a higher power is guiding us. I'm not sure if I understand it all, but I think Falstaff, and Tommy, who, if you really examine that dynamic closely, is also Falstaff, and still exist somewhere on this plane. Eventually, we will have to deal with his 'False Echo' once more."

Angela was finished. She leaned back in her chair and settled in for questions or comments.

"So, what you're saying is, Falstaff couldn't do anything to us if we didn't believe he was what he was?" The question came from Charles Martin.

The Professor answered, "Yes, yes, I see now! The stories of vampires, zombies, werewolves, and everything else through the years that people have read or seen movies about have helped to cause the problem. People make assumptions and presume the stories and creatures are real, when it's all basically false."

"So, why are we here?" asked Erin

"I would say it's because society, as a whole, believes in those demons." Michael Cline interjected. "Society accepts the concept that any evil entity can be saved. Kind of like the young woman who dates the bad boy just to piss off her parents." All eyes turned to Erin Hastings. She looked down, embarrassed. But, now, she understood why she was with this group.

Charles Martin wanted to research this more. "Let's say I accept your premise, Angela. What about this fragile balance you've been talking about? How do we keep a balance between good and evil?"

"We do our jobs," Angela said. "We stay focused and stalwart, but we also choose our battles wisely. Most of all, we have to have faith that we are doing the right thing. So, my friends, that is why you are here. Wherever evil attempts to overshadow good, that's where we must go."

The professor cleared his throat, and not waiting for permission to speak, he asked, "What about Arthur "Tommy" Kensington?"

Snow was one enemy that Arthur "Tommy" Kensington hated. When he was shoved, pushed, thrown, or jettisoned to Caribou, Maine, he was forced to leave his nice warm body behind and endure this frozen tundra. The cold made him feel even weaker than he was. Tommy was merely a wisp of his former self.

He had found refuge in a small church basement. He didn't take up much space, so he stayed underneath the steps and waited for his strength to return. That's what smart demons do, they bide their time and wait for the opportunity to strike. And, that is precisely what Tommy did.

One Sunday, after church services, the congregation was having a potluck dinner. Unbeknownst to anyone, Tommy's essence snuck up to the dessert table and watched as person after person walked by and put dessert on their plate. Suddenly, there she was, an 82 year old retired school teacher turned librarian, who was going to take a piece of the apple crumb pie he was hiding under. He made a leap of faith and jumped onto the fork she lifted her slice of pie with. He quickly slid onto her hand, then her wrist. He finally came to rest near the nape of her neck, under her hair. There, he watched and waited. As Gracie Park lifted the eating utensil with the piece of pie on it, Tommy, a.k.a. Falstaff, waited until she had made just the right move, and then he jumped into her nostril. He slipped back out of her nose and over to her ear canal. He would rest here until nighttime, and then he would make his move into this lovely lady's abdomen.

He wouldn't rush Gracie's demise because she seemed nice. Besides, he had to be careful. Angela and her goons would be on the lookout for him. He had felt the shockwave when the original Falstaff was taken to his own dimension. Now, Tommy was the new and improved version. He was bound and determined to do much better than his predecessor. He should thank Angela Harrison for making him a new Master Chef of Evil on this plane of existence.

While he waited, he started to think about the love of his life, Erin Lee Hastings. He wondered if she was still alive, if she had escaped with Bethoon the Cannibal, or if that idiot Jake Taylor had wormed his way into her soulless heart?

All answers would have to wait until he could eventually take over this body and regain his strength. Maybe he would grow a Fu Manchu mustache. He would inherit the white streaks in his hair from his father. "Behold," he thought to himself, "In a few months I can once again resurface as Falstaff, and no one would be the wiser!"

Acknowledgments

When my daughter was eight years old, a new show came on television. It was called "Buffy the Vampire Slayer." While my little girl had a bedtime of 8:00 p.m., she demanded that I tape that show on our Video Cassette Recorder (VCR). Then, the next day, with the lights on everywhere, we would watch it together. When she would get scared, she would sit on my lap, and I would always tell her that it was make-believe. She didn't care that it scared her, she had to watch that show. She and I were both hooked, and we eventually watched the entire series together.

In 2011, she passed away in a car accident, and until 2014, I only wrote one thing, a short story called "How, How!!" I wasn't blocked, I just didn't have anything I really wanted to write about. I started three or four stories but would eventually quit after the first couple of pages. Then, in the summer of 2014, I wrote a short story called "The Drop." That same story has flourished into Chapter 11 of this book, and the rest, as they say, is history. Over Christmas vacation, I started writing E.C.H.O. And finished it one year and one week later.

The funny thing about this book, when I took it out of mothballs, I found it was missing the last three chapters. So, I rewrote them and decided to add a fourth chapter. I think it's better now than the original story was. However, you will have to be the judge. Now it's late September, and I am almost ready to publish E.C.H.O. for public consumption. I am nervous; however, I have two things going for me. First, my wife told me that while it wasn't her cup of tea, she thought it was good. As long as I have her approval, I can do anything. Secondly, my daughter (Alison) inspired every single word.

I would like to thank my family and friends for standing by me while I worked on this novel. If you find yourself asking, "How in the world did you come up with this?" I should explain that I grew up on the old Hammer Films of Dracula, with Christopher Lee playing the Count and Peter Cushing playing Dr. Van Helsing. I also had a cousin who took me to see Zombie movies in the late '60s and early '70s. Do you remember "Night of the Living Dead" (1968) by George A. Romero and how that movie blew everyone away? Those movies shaped the horror vision in my brain, which I used them to complete E.C.H.O. The horror genre is alive and well in films and on television. So, I came upon a concept where I asked myself, "What if there were a group of people who were trying to explain the unexplainable and just couldn't do it?" I had to come up with an acronym that could sustain this concept; thus, E.C.H.O., the Elite Counter-Horror Organization, was born. Also, echoes are reflective, hollow sounds that we can't really touch or feel. They are there, but are they really there? Believe it or not, the book just fell into place. I cannot explain it any better than that.

I want to take this opportunity to thank all the people who read my material, whether it be my books, my Facebook author's page, my Amazon author's page, or my blog, crosbyscorner.net. I am truly humbled by your support. It is my hope that if you read this book and like it, you will spread the word so that I will be able to continue doing what I love doing, which is writing.

Praise for "*Fauntleroy*"

Fauntleroy is a refreshing twist on the classic boy meets girl story. This tale has everything from the charming boy next door to the stiff and formal upper crust English nobles and everything in between. The characters are relatable and pull you into their world, cheering for them to succeed. This story made me laugh, cry, and keep turning the pages to find out what happens next. --***HB***

I thoroughly enjoyed reading Fauntleroy! The story centered on young romance blossoming - as well as growing up and the lessons learned. I want to be friends with Laci. I want my daughters to fall for a boy like Connor.

I was completely immersed in the storyline from the beginning! Just like a "Hallmark Movie," I was "watching" a fairytale come true. I highly recommend this book! It was easy to read, entertaining, funny, and left me longing for a sequel. --***MS***

Praise for "Cratchit" Formerly Known as, "*The Gift: Judgement Day for Tim Cratchit*"

"The Gift: Judgement Day for Tim Cratchit," by J. D. Crosby, is a creative and unique story involving a beloved Dickens' character. Crosby chose a wonderful Dickens' story to write about, since everyone is familiar with The Christmas Carol, or, at least, the concept and key characters. The author lets the reader know right away his intent by mentioning Ebenezer Scrooge, so the reader grasps the concept of the novel. The writing is interesting, and the story grabbed me from the get-go. Overall, a great concept that will intrigue and delight readers."

"Judge, 25th Annual Writer's Digest Self-Published Book Awards"

From Amazon Books:

5.0 out of 5 stars "A Gift to read"

A tale involving several intriguing characters and how their lives intertwine with a beloved character we all know. Very well written and easy to read.

5.0 out of 5 stars

Great read, it will take you on a great journey with an interesting ending.

5.0 out of 5 stars "A good read"

An interesting tale about the beloved Dickens' character, Tim Cratchit, and how he grew to help and touch the lives of those around him. So nice of the author to take us on the journey from the small, crippled boy we all know and love to the kind adult man he grew to be. I enjoyed reading the tales of each person at the estate, but the best part comes at the end when the author ties the tales and the lives of present and past together. If you enjoyed the original Christmas tale, you should appreciate reading this book.

Amazon Reviews for "The Jefferson Chronicles"

5 out of 5 stars "Loved This!"

I truly admire the work of this book. It was well thought out and on point of modern, everyday high school life. I believe I could've actually been standing in each setting, especially "The Patch," which in all honesty I'm jealous it's not a real place. I also love the added elements and the small details. They make you think a bit. Great story. I would definitely recommend to others for a good read!

5 out of 5 stars

I truly enjoyed reading this book. It is full of your typical high school drama. You get invested in the characters so much so that I find myself wondering what happened to them after graduation. Great job!

4 out of 5 stars

James, I finished reading your book on May 4 so I probably didn't have the latest revision. However, I did find the story hard to put down. Completed in four days and found it well written but probably more suited for a younger audience than me. I intend to pass the book on to my grandson who just turned 15. Good luck with your book.

Amazon Reviews for "My Shorts"

4 out of 5 stars **"Love, Friendship, and 4-H"**

An enjoyable collection of short stories covering a wide variety of topics. The author shares his personal experience with cancer, abuse, and grief, but also provides more whimsical tales such as "Thomas the Teddy Bear", which invokes memories of the wonder and imagination of childhood.

Particularly well written is the inspiring tale, "How-How". What begins as an attempt for the author to memorialize his late daughter and express his grief, becomes a heart-felt tribute to an organization that has been touching and molding young lives for generations. Anyone who has ever been associated with 4-H in any way, should DEFINITELY read this story. The role that 4-H, its members, and all it stands for played in the life of this author, his daughter, and his family is proof of the healing powers of love, friendship, and compassion. We all could learn from this. "How-How" will move you and stay with you long after the story ends.

5 out of 5 stars Heartfelt book

Absolutely wonderful... the stories are very well written and easily relatable. I would totally recommend this book for anyone looking for a good read.

Also written by David C. James/J.D. Crosby

"My Shorts,
A Short Story Anthology"

"Cratchit" Formerly
"The Gift: Judgement Day For Tim Cratchit"

"E.C.H.O."
(Elite Counter Horror Organization)

"The Other Day... Volume One"
Non-Fiction

"Fauntleroy"

"The Jefferson Chronicles
Untouchable"

Made in the USA
Middletown, DE
04 September 2024

59757829R00166